BEYOND JUDGMENT

BEYOND JUDGMENT

BRAINRUSH 3

RICHARD BARD

The characters and events portrayed in this book are fictitious. Any similarity to real persons, living or dead, is coincidental and not intended by the author.

Printed in the United States of America.

Published by Thomas & Mercer
PO Box 400818
Las Vegas, NV 89140

ISBN-13: 9781611099768
ISBN-10: 1611099765
Library of Congress Control Number: 2012922580

Dedication

For my wife, whose unconditional support frees my time and fuels my imagination.

Part I

Humanity is in "final exam" as to whether or not it qualifies for continuance in the universe.

—R. Buckminster Fuller

Chapter 1

Le Focette, Marina di Pietrasanta, Italy

HE HAD NO PAST. BUT THE FUTURE HELD PROMISE.

The woman seated across from him was in her late twenties. An American tourist who'd blushed when they'd met. Her Italian was broken. Her alluring curves and inviting smile had inspired him. A sip from her cappuccino left a thin line of foam on her upper lip. It disappeared behind a slow lick of her tongue. Her eyes never left his.

He wore an open linen shirt, casual slacks, and three-day stubble. His skin was tan. They sat at an outdoor café and *ristorante* in Le Focette, a quiet Tuscan enclave situated a block from the beach resorts of the Mediterranean Sea. It was a warm and sunny afternoon. A salty breeze stirred the thick canopy of trees overhead, dislodging a pine nut that bounced off a nearby Cinzano umbrella and skittered to the ground. He leaned over and picked it up.

"They used to serve these at the outdoor cinema down the street," he said in Italian. Her expression told him she hadn't understood, so he brushed off the nut and popped it in his mouth. "Mmmm…*buono*!" he said.

Her eyes widened. He winked. She smiled.

"*Bella*," he said. His hand patted the air as a signal to hold the pose. The pastel stick in his other hand moved swiftly across the canvas. She blushed and it was his turn to smile. He wondered if she would be the one.

The café was filling up for lunch. A group of local teens crowded around their customary tables not far from his corner. Two of the boys strummed guitars while the rest chatted with an infectious effervescence. A middle-aged couple sat nearby. German, he thought, judging from their stiff demeanor. That would change after they'd been in the area a few more days. The magic would set in: the easy pace, the food, the friendly smiles—impossible to resist.

He switched sticks, working a blend of colors into her luminescent eyes. There was eagerness in her stare that stirred him. His movements were automatic. His brain orchestrated a talent that he'd discovered when he'd awakened four months ago. When he had asked how long he had been in a coma, no one had any answers. The doctor who cared for him told him his name was Lorenzo Ferrari. Everyone called him Renzo.

His mind wandered, but his strokes didn't falter. The closer the portrait was to completion, the faster the pastel stick moved—as if it had a life of its own. The doctor had told him what little he knew. Renzo had been wheeled in by an anxious young American man. Renzo had been unconscious. His skin hung loose on his 180-centimeter frame. His muscles had atrophied. Money had changed hands, a room in a local *pensione* had been leased, and the doctor had accepted the assignment of restoring the patient's health. The American had left in a rush, leaving final instructions for Renzo in a sealed envelope.

The hiss of the latte steamer brought his attention back to the sketch. When he took in the final image, his shoulders slumped. The portrait was perfect in every detail—except for the eyes. They belonged to someone else. Instead of sky blue like those of the girl seated across from him, they were liquid chocolate, filigreed with rings of gold dust. They were penetrating.

The girl sat forward. "Is it ready?" she asked in broken Italian.

"No," he said, flipping closed his art tablet.

She frowned.

"I must apologize," he said. "I'm having an off day." He pushed back his chair as if to leave.

"Wait," she said softly. Her hands reached out and cupped one of his. Her touch was tender. Her gaze was an invitation. "I go with you?"

Renzo faltered. How long had it been? Longer than he could remember—like everything else. She was beautiful. And his *pensione* was only a block away. All he had to do was ignore the feelings of guilt. His free hand absently patted the pocket of his slacks. The wrinkled envelope from the American was there—his only link to the past. The hastily scrolled message had been brief:

Trust no one. Lives hinge on your ability to remain anonymous.

Surely, this young woman posed no risk, he thought. He was torn.

The decision was made for him when he noticed two men stop short on the opposite side of the street. One of them stared his way. The other had a hand to his ear. He seemed to be speaking to himself. They were dressed in casual clothes. But Renzo's artist's gaze narrowed at the incongruence of the matching pair of rubber-soled shoes and dark glasses. The hand dropped from the man's ear, and a whisper was exchanged. They started toward him.

A buried instinct set off alarms in Renzo's head. He rose. His chair toppled, the girl yelped, and the tablet fell from his lap. The pages fanned on the way down, and a corner of his mind saw the same pair of brown eyes staring back at him from each portrait.

They all shouted the same command in his mind:

Run!

He shouldered through the woody hedge beside the table. Brambles caught on his shirt. He pushed through, shredding his skin. Angry shouts behind him. A girl's scream. Rapid footfalls. He raced down the tree-studded lane, thankful for the snug fit of his running shoes. He headed inland. Past villas, the old church, and the rows of stone counters that had supported the fish market for a hundred years. The *pineta* was four blocks ahead. They'd never track him through the myriad paths in the forty-acre forest. He filled his lungs with the pine-scented air and dashed toward it. He knew the men behind him wouldn't be able to keep up. He'd yet to meet anyone who could. Sure, Renzo had memory issues, but his physical rehabilitation had revealed that he had remarkable endurance—thanks to a heart that the doctor had proclaimed a miracle of science. According to him, it had been formerly owned by a seventeen-year-old female athlete.

He wondered at his instinctual decision to flee the café. He didn't doubt the validity of the command his subconscious had generated. But he wished he could pull up the memories that prompted it. Perhaps it was the assuredness of the movements from the two men. He'd sensed the spark of recognition in their expressions even behind their dark glasses.

Lives hinge on your ability to remain anonymous.

He hungered for answers, but only questions were served: Who were they? What did they want with him? Did they know where he lived?

Renzo was a block from the pineta when a car careened from a side street to block his path. Doors opened. Three men exited. They had the same feel as the two behind him. They held silenced weapons. The flush of adrenaline triggered a doubling of his heart rate, fueling his muscles. He jinked to the right between two villas. Bullets hammered into the limestone walls behind him—and the question of what they wanted was answered.

Chips pelted his trousers. A ricocheted round spun past his ear with a hornet's buzz. Terror filled his gut. He leaped a stone wall and wound a serpentine trail through gates and yards and streets. The solitude of the woodland was no longer an option. But maybe the anonymity of a crowd would provide an escape. The beach was dead ahead.

He twisted through traffic across the four-lane coastal road. Cars skidded, scooters dodged, and motorists shouted. Renzo ignored them. He sped across a gravel parking lot, through a busy open-air trattoria, past a row of private cabanas and showers, and onto the sand. There was no sign of his pursuers.

Each section of white-sand beach was privately owned, passed down one generation to the next, demarked by the color and style of the umbrellas and lounge chairs that extended in neat rows to the water. It was packed with tourists, in large part because of the influx of college students visiting during spring break. Renzo kicked off his shoes, removed his torn shirt, and plopped himself in their midst. He was shaken. He dug his hands and feet into the warm sand, searching in vain for the familiar calm that the act usually brought. Two bikini-clad girls offered an approving stare. He was accustomed to the attention, more for his tan physique than for his crooked smile. He forced a wink. They giggled. He blew out a breath and sank deeper into the sand. He needed time to think.

"Ciao, Renzo!" a man shouted.

He recognized the voice before he turned around. It was the *bagnino*, Paolo, responsible for this stretch of beach. The fifty-year-old, potbellied lifeguard was a bronze fixture who always had a kind word. Unfortunately, he also loved to hear the sound of his own voice. Once he started talking, it was impossible to get him to stop. He waved as he approached.

"Another run today?" the man asked in his booming voice.

Tourists turned their way. Paolo appreciated an audience.

"It's a wonderful day!" the lifeguard proclaimed, his arms outstretched as if to soak in the sun.

So much for blending in, Renzo thought. He rose and glanced nervously about. A man with dark glasses and familiar rubber-soled shoes stared back at him from the trattoria. His hand was to an ear. His lips moved urgently.

Renzo took off. The *bagnino* shouted behind him, "Renzo, you forgot your shoes, your shirt!"

He hit the wet sand that was his daily running track and poured on speed. One familiar resort after another passed in a blur. His plan was simple. He wouldn't stop running until he came abreast of the police station in Forte dei Marmi. Renzo needed help. After four months in hiding, remaining anonymous was no longer an option.

He was nearly there when he saw the girl from the café. She blocked his path. So did the two men who gripped each of her arms. The girl tried to act natural, but her fear was palpable. She was a hostage, not an accomplice. The men's deportment left no doubt of the deadly consequences of noncooperation. A big part of him screamed to keep running, to put behind him the two men and the girl whom he had only just met. But he could not. Amnesia or not, a man's character doesn't change. He stopped.

The men were all business. They had crew cuts and chiseled features. The taller one removed his glasses. He had angry dark eyes and a boxer's crooked nose. Through tight lips he said, "You for the girl." The words were English. Renzo didn't understand.

"*Cosa?*" he asked.

The man's eyes narrowed. He seemed surprised. He switched to Italian. "We trade you for the girl," he said. His Italian was good, but Renzo caught the trace of a German accent.

The girl's expression pleaded.

"Let her go first," Renzo said.

The man stiffened, as if unaccustomed to conditional surrenders. Renzo figured he was in charge. He scanned his surroundings with military precision. "We make the exchange in the parking lot."

Where it will be easy to stuff us into a car and kill us later with no fanfare, Renzo thought. No thanks. He considered his options, grateful that the physical trainer hired by the doctor had included martial arts in his regimen. The movements had seemed natural to him. He remembered wondering if his muscles held memories that his brain could not.

Renzo pointed to a Ping-Pong table by the showers. It was still in view of the crowded beach but only a step or two from the walkway leading to the parking area. "We walk together to that point," he said. "Then she goes free."

The second man nodded to the first, and they escorted the girl up the beach. Renzo followed, recalling the key weakness that his trainer had identified in his fighting skills. *No killer instinct*, he'd said. *Stick to running.*

That was his plan.

The walkway between the beach and the parking lot was lined on either side by rows of cabanas. The men turned to face him, stopping beside a bathroom stall. Their grip tightened on the girl's arms. She winced. The leader inched up the hem of his polo shirt to reveal the pistol tucked at his waist. "Any tricks and she dies," he said.

The girl's breathing quickened. Renzo nodded. He readied himself. The leader motioned to his subordinate.

The man shoved the girl into the stall. "Not a sound," he growled as he closed the door behind her. Her soft whimper was filled with relief. Renzo could imagine her huddled in a ball beside the toilet, watching their shadows through the slats in the door. Both men turned to face him.

"Let's go," the leader said. The girl was safe for the moment, Renzo thought. The sooner he and the two men turned the corner into the parking lot, the sooner she could slip away. He allowed himself to be taken. Each man grabbed an arm.

They stopped when they reached the graveled lot. The leader's gaze panned the area. The black BMW that had blocked Renzo's path earlier was parked by the entrance. Its motor idled. The driver nodded. His hand went to the dash, and the sedan's trunk popped open.

My coffin, Renzo realized with a start. There was no one else around. They would kill him here and dump him later. The men tightened their grip and walked him forward. But instead of responding with tension, Renzo relaxed his muscles—as he'd been taught. The subconscious reaction of the men holding him was instinctual. They relaxed as well.

He sagged, allowing his dead weight to pull at the men's grip. They held on with angry grunts and yanked upward. In the same instant, Renzo combined his force with theirs by springing into a backflip. Grips gave way. Renzo turned to run. But instead of freedom, he found himself staring down the barrel of a silenced weapon. It was wielded by a third man, who had followed them down the walkway. A wisp of smoke leaked from the muzzle—and Renzo knew that the girl was dead.

"*Bastardo*," he gasped. The other two spun him around.

"You're fast," the leader said. He pressed his own pistol against Renzo's chest. "But experience trumps speed every t—"

He cut off when the horn sounded from the waiting sedan. A van filled with bobbing heads drove into the lot. It was followed by a man on a scooter. Guns disappeared. A door slid open on the van, and a family of six piled out. Two of the youngest children jumped up and down with enthusiasm. The leader patted Jake on the back as if they were old pals. He whispered, "They will die unless you get in the car." Renzo could barely breathe past the rage he felt over the death of the girl. But he didn't doubt the truth of the man's words. He allowed himself to be ushered toward the sedan.

The scooter idled under the shadows of a tree. The rider wore an oversize helmet that looked odd above the shorts and baggy shirt that revealed thin arms and bony knees. The tinted helmet visor hid his face. His head tilted to one side as if he were taking in the scene. Renzo willed him to leave for his own safety. The man didn't budge.

The two thugs walked on either side of Renzo. The one who had killed the girl moved ahead of them. He opened the rear passenger door, motioning for Renzo to get in. But Renzo's attention was still on the scooter driver. It appeared as though the man stared directly at him from behind his visor. His helmeted head shook slowly from side to side as if he were warning Renzo not to enter the car. But a firm hand on Renzo's lower back reminded him that he had little choice. He glanced over his shoulder. The family had gathered their beach bags. They were walking toward the sand. The kids ran ahead.

The sudden whine of the scooter sent a shock of tension through the men surrounding him. The bike raced toward them. The rider had flipped up his visor. His teeth were bared, his eyes narrowed, and he held a dark object in an outstretched hand. The Germans reached for their guns.

Renzo cried out, "Nooo!" The young rescuer didn't stand a chance. Renzo stomped the instep of the man to his left. The German folded to one knee with a surprised grunt. Ducking to avoid the leader's fist, Renzo countered with an uppercut that smashed his nose. Cartilage cracked. Blood flowed. He turned to face the third man, when out of the corner of his eye he saw his would-be rescuer fling the object. In the same instant, there were muffled gunshots from within the car and the helmeted scooter rider was thrown backward onto the gravel. But the object he'd hurled continued its arc toward Renzo in a wobbling spiral.

It looked like a small pyramid.

Renzo felt a tingling sensation in his forehead.

Chapter 2

Le Focette, Marina di Pietrasanta, Italy

SOUND MUTED. THE WORLD AROUND RENZO SLOWED AS THE miniature pyramid tumbled through its arc. The closer it got, the stronger the tingling in his head and limbs. Gulls hung as if suspended midflight. The driverless scooter skidded on its side in frame-by-frame motion, furrowing a bow wave of gravel before it. The silenced barrel of a pistol rose toward Renzo's face. His gut tightened. Fear fueled his supercharged reflexes.

His hand chopped at the nerve bundle in the man's forearm. The move must have appeared impossibly fast to his assailant. Fingers numbed, grip loosened, and the weapon dropped to the ground. Doors unlocked in Renzo's brain, and he recognized the gun as the tactical version of a Sphinx AT380, with 9mm slugs, a sixteen-round magazine, and manufacturing tolerances that rivaled that of a Swiss watchmaker. Details of the weapon flashed through his mind like he was reading a Wikipedia page.

The pistol settled in the gravel. The black pyramid dropped beside it, and an explosion of memories expanded in his mind. The force of it nearly knocked him off his feet. But instinct held him steady. Arms grappled from behind. His body responded in a blur of action. He grabbed a wrist, spun, and flipped the leader onto his back. A heel to the temple and he was out cold. A stiff-fingered gouge to the throat of another. A vicious side kick to the chest of the third man. The BMW driver moved around the front of the car, a compact assault rifle pressed to one shoulder. Renzo somersaulted toward him. In a single fluid motion, he grabbed the Sphinx and double-tapped the trigger. Twin holes blossomed in the driver's chest, lifting him from his feet. A shuffle at Renzo's back set off alarms. He tumbled to one side as spits from a silenced weapon left a trail of slugs puckering the gravel beside his head. He rolled to his back, extended his pistol, and squeezed the trigger three times. The killer's body jerked with the impact of each slug. He folded to the ground and lay still.

Time settled.

Renzo felt the throb of his heart at his temples. The high-speed effort had taken a toll. He staggered to his feet. The scene shocked him. He fought a sudden urge to vomit. The scooter driver was surely dead, as were two of the gunmen. A third gasped a final, rasping breath through a crushed larynx. The fourth—their leader—lay unconscious. There was a seesaw of sirens in the distance. The family must have called the authorities, Renzo thought. He needed to leave. He gathered the weapons, tossed them into the sedan's trunk, and slammed the lid.

On his way around the car, he retrieved the miniature pyramid. It was the size of an apple. When his fingers closed around its smooth surface, his body seized. His mind reeled with a rush of images. Like flipping channels on a TV, each scene was replaced by another before his consciousness could cling to its details. Faces, bodies, and explosions swirled amid a tornado of emotions that brought forth an overwhelming sense of hopelessness. Each image kindled a memory more painful than the last. Rather than embracing them, he pushed them away, corralling them into a closet deep in his brain. His body shook with the effort.

It was the groan of the man from the scooter that broke the spell. Renzo's wits returned. He rushed forward and knelt beside the fallen man, setting the miniature pyramid on the gravel.

The man still wore his helmet. His eyes fluttered open. Renzo pushed aside a sense of familiarity as he dealt with locating any injuries. His movements were swift and sure, drawing on knowledge that he hadn't known he possessed. The man bled from a shoulder wound. An exam confirmed that the bullet had been a deep graze. It bled freely, but it was noncritical.

"M-my fault," he said. His words were slurred. Shock was setting in.

"Quiet," Renzo said, ripping off the man's rolled-up sleeve.

"They followed m—" He grimaced as Renzo wadded up the sleeve and pressed it against the wound.

"Keep pressure on this," Renzo said. The kid gripped the bandage with his good hand. Bleeding slowed to a trickle. Renzo unhooked the chin strap and removed the man's helmet. He was in his twenties, with scruffy dark hair, pale skin, and a number of tiny holes on his brow and ears—evidence of previous piercings. Renzo gasped when he recognized him. Memories dropped into place: an underground bunker, assassins, death, an alien pyramid…

"Timmy?" Renzo asked.

The kid's eyes widened. "You recognize me!"

Renzo retrieved the mini. It felt warm in his grasp. Images clarified. "Yeah," Renzo said, pushing through the cobwebs. "Area 52. There was you, and Doc, and—"

"Right on! Six years ago…" Timmy said. He hesitated a moment before continuing. "Hey, wait a minute. You're speaking English!"

Renzo shook his head. *Six years?* It couldn't be. He tried to superimpose a timeline onto the jumble of memories, searching for the code that would unlock the encryption in his brain. But before the last tumbler clicked into place, the kid's gaze snapped to a point beyond Renzo's shoulder. His eyes widened.

The leader tackled Renzo from behind. The air was blown from his lungs, and the mini flew from his grasp. It skittered into a drainage culvert.

So did his past.

They rolled past Timmy. The German assassin ended up on top. He straddled Renzo, fists pummeling. Blood from the man's broken nose drooled onto Renzo's face. He defended the first three blows, but the fourth hammered into his jaw. The fifth impacted his temple, stunning him. Thick hands wrapped around his throat. Fingers dug. Renzo arched his back and flailed at the bigger man. But the vise grip around his neck tightened. Renzo clawed and came away with a torn shirtsleeve, exposing rippling muscles and a stylized tattoo of the phrase *Cæli Regere*. Renzo's throat burned and his vision blurred. He reached desperately for the man's face, groping for eyes. But the experienced fighter twisted from his reach. He continued to squeeze.

A shadow passed behind the German. There was a hollow thunk as something cracked against his skull. The man groaned; his eyes lost focus, his grip released, and he toppled to one side. He lay still. Renzo sucked air through his tortured windpipe, wriggling from beneath the man's bulk.

Timmy stood above him, wobbling back and forth like a drunk. The motorcycle helmet dangled from the chin strap he gripped in his good hand. He'd used it as a mace. Suddenly, the kid's eyes rolled and the color drained from his face. He had a dull grin as he collapsed into Renzo's arms.

"Bravo," Renzo rasped, lowering him to the ground. The sirens were a few blocks away. The kid was woozy, but still conscious. Renzo would stay with him until help arrived. He owed his life to...

He'd forgotten the kid's name. He'd known it just a moment ago. "*Come ti chiami?*" Renzo asked.

The kid's eyes narrowed. "In English?"

Renzo shook his head. "*Non parlo inglese*," he said. He'd never had a knack for languages.

"But you were just speaking Eng-wisssh!" the kid slurred.

There was a blare of horns. Renzo turned from the meaningless words. Cars were backed up at a traffic light. Another black BMW jerked and twisted as it attempted to nose past the cars ahead of it. Angry fists and more horns, and Renzo realized that the rest of the hit squad had found him. The sirens coming from the other direction wouldn't be here in time. He moved even before the decision had fully formed in his mind.

The kid yelped as Renzo dropped him to the ground and ran toward the parked sedan.

"Wait...*Alto*!" the kid shouted.

But Renzo couldn't stop. Seconds counted if he was to draw the threat away. He jumped in the car and floored it. The vehicle fishtailed in the gravel, and Renzo had to slow to avoid hitting his new friend. As he drove past, the kid yelled, "Piazza San Marco, *domani, mezzogiorno*, Danielle!"

Renzo didn't have time to wonder at the kid's words. He skidded onto the road and sped toward the sirens. The other BMW broke through traffic and shot after him. A man leaned out the passenger window. There were muzzle flashes, and the rear window exploded. Renzo jerked the wheel from side to side to throw off the man's aim. Hammer blows impacted the rear trunk. He jinked too hard, and the passenger side—starting with the fender—swiped a traffic pole. A gut-wrenching screech of metal against metal. Sparks flew and the side mirror went airborne. He centered the steering wheel, stomped on the accelerator, and let out a long growl through his burning throat.

A string of flashing emergency lights appeared ahead. Two police vehicles wound through the oncoming traffic. The car in the rearview mirror suddenly slowed. It turned east and disappeared toward the hills.

Chapter 3

Swiss Alps

JAKE BRONSON WAS ALIVE AFTER ALL, VICTOR BRUN THOUGHT. He'd suspected as much. The American had been reported dead four months ago—his comatose body consumed in a fire. But Victor's assassin who'd sparked the blaze at the secret US facility that housed the American had never seen the body. That wouldn't be the case in this instance. The team in Italy should report soon with confirmation.

He propped his feet on the ottoman and allowed himself a rare opportunity to enjoy the comfort of the castle's great room. A white Persian cat jumped up and curled on his lap. He stroked its fur. The pet was his constant companion.

The crackle of burning logs from the grand fireplace, the plush furnishings and ancient tapestries, the dim lighting, and even the dampness that spilled from the stone walls combined to embrace him in a cocoon of harsh memories that would chill the bones of most men. He drew strength from them.

Château Brun had been built in the tenth century. But it was relatively new compared to the ancient maze of tunnels and caverns that burrowed beneath the mountain that supported it. The mansion was hidden among the alpine peaks of Switzerland. Thanks to its obscure location and crenellated battlements, it had never been breached.

Feathers of snow drifted across the French panes of the picture window across the room. Another late-season storm grayed the sky, obscuring the view of Mont Blanc. Victor swirled cognac in a snifter. His other hand stroked the cat. The pet purred under the attention.

Victor's gaze drifted to the tall man standing across from him. "Two more days, Hans," Victor said in English. His Swiss-German accent was refined. He spoke seven languages. But of late he'd preferred to practice English. It would become the language of choice.

"*Jawohl, Mein Herr,*" his confidant said with a slight nod. Hans had a military bearing—solidly built with a protruding jaw, a blond flattop, and an ice-blue stare. The knots and calluses of his hands testified to his daily training regimen. "All is ready."

A hammering from a nearby room quieted, and a pair of white-gloved workers entered the room. They offered a deferential bow to the lord of the château.

Victor acknowledged them with a smile. By all public accounts he was a gentle man. Like his father before him, he was renowned for his generosity and old-world charm, garnering standing invitations to the elite circles of European upper-crust society. His Swiss heritage shone through his broad forehead, high cheekbones, and slanted green eyes. Though he'd never married, his warm smile and attentive manner provided him with ample companionship. His sharp, analytical mind made him a trusted advisor to corporations and governments alike—where he exhibited a unique ability to guide opposing factions to a common view. While he preferred to avoid the direct spotlight, he would be center stage at the upcoming summit in Geneva. The public had been told that the unprecedented event was to be the first of a series of conferences to discuss the issue of world hunger. Leaders of every major nation would attend.

Carefully, the two workers removed a painting from the far wall. They exited the room. The priceless piece of art would be crated along with the others, Victor thought, bound for humanity's new birthplace. Soon the castle walls would be bare, save for his favorite piece. He glanced up at the fresco that stretched above the mantel. It filled most of the thirty-foot-high plastered wall that had been the artist's canvas. The ornate swirls and colors depicted a family tree that reached back a thousand years. He'd memorized every branch, leaf, and curl. The names, dates, and images would be forever ingrained in his mind. He regretted that he had to leave it behind.

He would also abandon the strategically placed mirrors throughout the mansion. Soon, they would no longer be necessary.

It was hard to believe that the end was finally here, he thought. Centuries of planning coming to a head during his reign as head of the Order: nurturing allies, positioning spies, preparing for the final conflagration—all while guarding the greatest secret the world had ever known. It was appropriate that it should happen during his reign. It had been predicted by his grandfather at his christening sixty years ago. His father's eyes had glazed each time he recounted the event to young Victor. *The age of technology is upon us*, his grandfather had said as the priest anointed Victor. *With this child our line will reign over a new world order, an order of peace, prosperity, and freedom from the risk of violence.*

Victor tapped a computer tablet resting on the end table beside his chair. The blank screen lit up. He stared at the live images of the twin pyramids orbiting above the planet. "*Cæli Regere*," he said softly, reciting the Order's Latin credo.

Hans raised a hand to one ear. The team was reporting in. "*Ja*?" Hans said. His voice was transmitted through a miniature jawbone implant. A beat later, the former soldier stiffened. His face reddened. "Bronson escaped," he reported to Victor. "Three of our men were killed. One was arrested."

Victor removed his hand from the cat's dense fur. The purring stopped. He studied his reflection in the decorative mirror on the coffee table, running his fingers through his wavy coiffure of silvered hair. His expression remained casual. There was no hint of the sudden anger that boiled within.

"He will not be easily found now that he's been alerted," Victor considered aloud. His voice was pleasant. "What of the young American scientist?"

After a quick interchange with the man in the field, Hans said, "Wounded, but alive. He's in the hospital."

Victor nodded. His mind cataloged options. "Put a man on the scientist," he said. "But focus the teams on Mr. Bronson's friends and family. Now that he's broken cover, he'll undoubtedly seek them out."

"*Jawohl, Mein Herr*," Hans said. He turned sharply and left the room.

Victor steadied himself. Jake Bronson was the lone obstacle to their mission's success. He could not be allowed to live. The table mirror beckoned, and he noticed a brief microexpression around his eyes. It was a tell. It revealed anxiety. He felt a jolt of disgust at the weakness. It opened cold closets in his mind.

Letting out a slow breath, he lifted the cat to his chest, rose, and left the room.

He needed a moment alone.

His brain required another lesson.

Chapter 4

Venice, Italy

FRANCESCA FELLINI NEVER TIRED OF RIDING IN HER FATHER'S gondola. Standing behind her, the proud gondolier moved with a rhythm that had been anchored in his bones since childhood. She was lulled by the gentle sway of the boat as he swept the oar back and forth. He hummed a familiar tune.

Seated beside her on the red-velvet love seat, Francesca's twelve-year-old daughter, Sarafina, hummed in harmony with her adopted grandfather. Music was her anchor. Her fingers tapped absently in the folds of the white dress that spread about her lap. She'd be a woman soon, Francesca thought. Too soon. Her sparkling brown eyes and pouty lips had already turned a few of the older boys' heads. That is, until *Nonno* Mario's glare set them running.

It was a beautiful day for a wedding. The sky was clear, the breeze gentle, and sunlight sparkled on the water. The small procession of gondolas was adorned with colorful regalia. The hulls shimmered and the brass ornamentals were polished to perfection. What had been intended as an intimate affair had grown to something more. Ahead, crowds lined the dock fronting the Palazzo Dandolo. Tourists spilled from the nearby Doge's Palace and Piazza San Marco. Paparazzi jostled for position. Every one was anxious for a glimpse of the actress whose debut role as a modern-day Mata Hari had captured the box office.

In the boat ahead, the bride turned to Francesca. Her turquoise eyes sparkled. Her smile beamed with excitement.

Lacey and Marshall had been a couple for over six years. The actress had wanted to marry Jake's best friend after the first few months. But one thing after another had stood in their way: Battista, their mourning after Jake's death, her film career…

But all that was behind them now.

Lacey offered a subtle thumbs-up in their direction. Sarafina bounced in her seat and waved in return. Francesca's daughter idolized the actress. They'd been famous friends ever since their shared brush with death on the underground river in Mexico. Lacey looked beautiful in her strapless wedding gown. Her hair was up, and she wore a pearl necklace that reminded Francesca of the night she and Jake had attended the masquerade ball. Her eyes moistened at the memory. She used a white-gloved finger to absorb a tear before it fell.

Francesca's five-year-old son sat on her other side. Sensing her sadness, he squeezed her hand. Alex had been in tune with her feelings since the day he was born, smiling or frowning in concert with her emotions.

"I'm fine, *caro*," she said in Italian. She straightened his bow tie, brushed lint from the satin lapel of his jacket, and added, "Women are supposed to cry at weddings, *sì*?"

Another squeeze and a look that told her he knew better. Her young son was good at that. Though he rarely made eye contact, he could communicate with no more than a facial expression, a turn of the head, a shrug. Sometimes it seemed as though his very thoughts coiled outward to embrace her. Francesca was thankful for that, because her precious son—the miracle who had held her life together when the man she loved had died—couldn't speak. Doctors credited it to a spectrum disorder. Alex was autistic.

He was also a genius.

A five-by-seven computer tablet rested on his lap. It was his constant companion—his link to the world around him. When he wasn't using it, he tucked it in a side holster clipped to his belt. But for now he stared at it. An ever-changing swirl of fractal patterns filled the screen.

The first boat arrived at the dock, and onlookers made way as Tony and Ahmed stepped out. They looked splendid in their black tuxedos. A string quartet struck up a traditional Italian wedding song, and the crowd stirred in anticipation. A group of teens added their voices to the popular music. Others joined in, and soon the swelling chorus drew eyes from up and down the walkway that skirted the lagoon.

Lacey lowered her veil. Marshall sat beside her, handsome as ever, even beneath the red blindfold he wore. He'd been honored to oblige Lacey with the unusual ritual. It symbolized trust and mutual respect. The blindfold would remain in place until they reached the altar, the groom guided there by the woman who would then follow his lead until death. Francesca was touched by the gesture. Lacey danced to her own tune. This was her way of embracing her unique spirit while professing faith in her man.

Once the party was gathered on the dock, a score of striped-shirted gondoliers cleared a path leading to the entrance of the Hotel Danieli. As they set off, Alex hesitated. He let go of Francesca's hand and stared through a break in the crowd. She followed his gaze and noticed a commotion atop the arched walkway in front of the Bridge of Sighs. There were shouts. A man sprinted down the opposite side toward San Marco. Two men pushed through the crowd and sped after him. The ruckus startled her. She pulled Alex into the folds of her dress.

It was over before it began. The three men disappeared around the corner. Tourists filled in the gaps left in their wake. But Francesca's racing heart wasn't so quick to settle. Even after years of peace, her nightmares surfaced easily. She blew out a breath to calm herself, releasing her protective grip on Alex.

"It's nothing, my son," she said. "Crazy tourists, that's all."

Chapter 5

Venice, Italy

THE WEAPON FELT ODD UNDER HIS CLOTHING. RENZO HAD taken it from the car before he had ditched it. The need for it angered him. He wore a linen sport coat over a polo shirt, pleated trousers, and runners—paid for with cash from a rushed closure of his bank account.

He grabbed another handful of seeds and held out his palm. A frenzy of wings flapped around him. Two pigeons alighted on his hand and pecked at the morsels. More birds hovered nearby, their heads twisting and turning as they searched for an opening to the easy feast. Dozens more surrounded his feet, grabbing at leftover scraps. Other tourists joined in the fun, tentative arms outstretched. Cameras clicked, vendors smiled, and children ran in circles.

Piazza San Marco was famous for many things. Pigeons were the least of them. But they provided the perfect blind as Renzo studied his surroundings. The expansive piazza was framed on three sides by the former state offices of the Venetian Republic—now an arcade of shops and restaurants. Regimented rows of small tables spilled into the square—where white-gloved servers attended a buzz of diners. The eastern length of the piazza was commanded by the great arches, domed rooftops, and Romanesque carvings of Basilica di San Marco. Tourists waited in roped-off lines to catch a glimpse of its ornate interior. The towering orange-brick campanile, or bell tower, presided over the scene.

Renzo was nervous about his next move. The kid's parting words the day before had been in Italian, signaling their importance. He'd said, *Piazza San Marco, tomorrow, noon, Danielle.* Renzo checked his watch. It was ten past noon. But now what?

Instinct told him to hide. Instead, he brushed off his hands, removed his dark glasses, and stepped beyond the swirl of birds. If Danielle was to find him, he needed to present a tall target. He strode toward the basilica.

He noticed a group of tourists abandoning their positions in line at the church entrance. They'd been drawn by music around the corner. Renzo followed, capturing gazes along the way, searching for signs of recognition. Walking along the waterway, he saw a wedding party disembark a gondola among a throng of spectators. He strode across an archway to get a better look.

The music was cheerful. The bride was stunning. She twirled to the applause of the crowd. But it was the young boy behind her who captured Renzo's attention. The child stood frozen in place. His head tilted. Eyes narrowed. It felt as if the boy stared into his soul.

A disturbance behind Renzo broke the spell. Two men shoved their way through the crowd. Dark glasses. Rubber-soled shoes. Their eyes fixed on his position. One had a hand to his ear. They ran toward him.

A familiar panic swept through him, and Renzo raced back over the arched walkway. He pushed through the crowd and ducked into the south entrance of the Palazzo Ducale—the Doge's Palace.

"*Alto*!" the entrance guard ordered.

"*Emergencia*!" Renzo said, as he rushed past the guard and into an open-air courtyard. He kept moving, ignoring the shrill of the guard's whistle. He ran past a grand staircase guarded by two colossal statues, skirting a richly decorated arch and ducking through the southeast portico. Angry shouts confirmed that the men were close behind. In the next salon, tourists milled at the foot of a roped-off golden staircase that led to the upper floors. Beyond the ropes, at the first landing, a tour guide had opened a hidden panel. She was ushering the last of her guests through a narrow passageway. Renzo leaped the rope and took the steps two at a time. He caught the door just before it closed, slipping in with the group.

"*Scusi*," the attractive and petite guide said with a stern edge. "This is a private tour."

"Yes, I know," Renzo replied casually. The run had tousled his hair, but he was barely out of breath. He offered her his best smile and peeled a hundred-euro note from his money clip. "The gentleman below said I might join you."

She appraised him, shrugged, and took the money. The sounds from downstairs muted as the panel clicked shut. The woman brushed past him toward the head of the line. She left a pleasant hint of jasmine in her wake. "*Signori e signore*," she whispered conspiratorially to the group in Italian, "the Doge's Palace is layered in secrets." She winked at Renzo. "Let us explore the fate of the man who stole a kiss from one too many wives. Follow now in the footsteps of Giacomo Girolamo Casanova!"

She ushered the group up a dark staircase. The wooden planks creaked with each step. The narrow corridor smelled of moist wood and decay. "Casanova was thirty years old when he was arrested," the guide said. "The charge was irreligious behavior…"

They continued forward, and Renzo tuned her out. He tightened his belt around the pistol at his back and wondered if he could actually use it. He was an artist, not a killer. At least that's what he believed. The men following him had known he would be in Venice, he thought. But how? And why did they so desperately want him dead? His past haunted him, and the only person with answers was the wounded kid on the scooter.

Renzo recalled the vague sense of familiarity he'd felt when they'd met. There had been a flash of memories. But they had faded when the small pyramid had been flung into the gutter. His consciousness had been unable to recapture it. He'd hoped that Danielle—whoever she was—would provide him with answers.

But it was too late for that now. If he didn't get off the grid soon, he'd be dead.

There was a sudden rumble of footsteps behind him. Renzo shouldered past the other guests. But when he tried to slide by the guide, she placed her hands on her hips and blocked his path. "You really must stay with—"

She cut off when Renzo picked her up by the waist and spun her around behind him. He kissed her, winked, and dashed off. A brief round of applause from his tour partners was quickly replaced by angry shouts.

The first exit door was around the next corner. He barged through and kept running. His route took him through the State Inquisitors' Office and the Torture Room. Then up a staircase to *I Piombi*—the Leads—so named because the attic prison cells had a lead roof that created an oven in summer and a freezer in winter. The cells were tiny, and Renzo shuddered as he ran past. He hated small spaces.

He darted down one corridor, then another, down service stairs, always moving north. He made the ground floor, spotted the exit, and skidded to a stop. The palazzo guard at the door had spotted him. He'd been alerted to the chase. One hand unstrapped a baton. The other brought a whistle to his lips.

Renzo was about to double back when the plastered wall beside his head exploded. A spray of debris stung his cheek. He bolted forward like a racehorse out the starting gate. One of his pursuers was at the far end of the corridor, his silenced pistol extended. Two more rounds ricocheted off the marble floor at his heels. A woman screamed, tourists scattered, and Renzo barreled into the exit guard. Both men went down in a heap. Renzo's pistol slipped from his waistband. It skittered across the marble floor. The startled guard kicked it out of reach. He latched onto Renzo's leg, and the shrill whistle sounded between his lips. Renzo tried to twist free, but the man hung on like a mastiff to an extended towel. It took a kick to the man's temple to loosen the grip. Renzo wrenched free and rushed out the exit.

The sudden brightness narrowed his vision, but he didn't stop running. He weaved through a river of tourists, around a corner, and down an alley. The maze of cobbled walkways was his only hope of escape.

Past *gelaterias* and pastry shops, clothing stores, galleries, and shops filled with masks. Deeper into the ancient city he fled. Heading northwest. Away from the lagoon. The crush of tourists didn't let up. Neither did the commotion of his pursuers behind him. He wedged through a Japanese tour group at an arch that bridged a canal. A raised fist, an irritated shout, and a gondolier's song cut off midchorus. He ignored it all. His focus ahead.

High-end jewelry shops lined either side of the next stretch. A throng of window shoppers narrowed the pathway. He pushed through, took the next alley, and found a less-busy straightaway. Renzo poured on speed. A vaporetto, or water bus, cruised across the end of the stretch dead ahead. It was the Grand Canal. A glance over his shoulder. Two men bobbed and weaved through the crowd. They were thirty paces back.

He skidded around the corner and kept moving. The Ponte di Rialto loomed a hundred meters ahead. Two inclined ramps covered by a portico with shops on either side. He recalled from his map that the ornate bridge was one of four that spanned the Grand Canal. It led to the less-crowded San Polo district. If he could make it across, he'd have a chance to pull away. He skirted past an artist chalking an image of the bridge, grinding his jaw over the loss of the peaceful life he'd embraced only twenty-four hours before. He was halfway to the bridge when a herd of uniformed children exited an alley ahead of him. They squeezed five deep between the sidewalk vendors and the water's edge. The path was blocked. Beside them, a row of docked gondolas bounced in the wakes of the water traffic.

An angry shout. The men behind him had turned the corner. Renzo leaped onto the bow of one of the gondolas and kept running, arms outstretched for balance, skipping from one boat to the next, thankful for the grip of his runners. Children shouted at the sight. They surged together like fans at a rock concert, cell phones held overhead. Their mass created an impassable palisade.

Three more leaps and he was past them and back on the walkway. A quick sprint and he turned the corner onto the bridge. The two men behind him had vanished, and Renzo assumed they'd detoured down the alley behind the children. This was his chance. Up the stone steps three at a time, sticking to the outer walkway along the balustrade. He dodged an arrangement of knockoff purses displayed on rugs and hurried over the top.

The sight of dark sunglasses and rubber-soled shoes stopped him cold. The man stood at parade rest at the bottom of the other side of the bridge.

Renzo sidestepped under the portico to the central walkway. Glittery shops lined either incline. Tourists were everywhere. The man ahead of him had followed his move. He stood at the base of the bridge. Another man joined him. A glance over his shoulder, and Renzo saw the two previous pursuers working their way through the crowd behind him. They spotted him, and one of them raised a finger to his ear. His lips moved as he coordinated the collapsing net.

Renzo was trapped.

Vendors hawked, a gondolier sang, and the motor of a vaporetto echoed below.

The men closed in on him from either side of the ancient bridge. Renzo felt a surge of anger. He was about to die and he didn't even know why. He squared himself to the two men moving up the incline behind him. They were closest. One of them gave a feral grin, and Renzo resolved that he wasn't going down alone. Determination balled his fists, and a rush of blood pumped through his limbs. They'd be on him in twenty steps. He was ready.

But when a family strolled past him and he saw the children licking gelato from cones, the wind left his lungs.

Collateral damage.

The echo of the motor spurred Renzo's feet even before the decision was half-formed in his consciousness. Three strides and he was atop the balustrade. The nose of a vaporetto pushed into the sunlight from under the bridge. The top of the passenger compartment was fifteen feet below. He prayed, jumped, and rolled when he hit its surface. Bullets puckered the rooftop beside him. He scrambled to the edge, dropped to the next level, and ducked under the roof. Passengers cried out in alarm, distancing themselves from him. Two more hammer blows from above, and then the shooting stopped.

The driver yanked back on the throttle and turned to identify the trouble. The boat slowed. Renzo rushed forward. Something in his expression caused the driver's eyes to go wide. He stepped aside and Renzo took the controls, slamming the throttle to its stops. The boat surged ahead. He steered around the sharp bend and out of sight of the bridge.

"The sooner I'm off your boat, the better for you, *sì*?" Renzo said.

The driver nodded three times in rapid succession.

Renzo pointed at a dock on the San Polo side of the canal. "Then drop me there," he said, stepping aside to allow the man to take over.

Barber-striped mooring poles framed the private dock. The four-story palazzo behind it stretched a full block. Its facade was obscured by a network of scaffolds. It appeared deserted. The boat approached, and Renzo moved toward the exit. Passengers edged away. He hesitated at a large wall map. They'd expect him to run to the train station, he thought. It was on the other side of San Polo. He placed a finger on the station, knowing that others were watching. But his mind traced a route that led to a marina in the opposite direction. He'd catch a water taxi there and disappear on the mainland. The vaporetto slowed. He unhooked the rail chain and readied himself. A quick look over his shoulder, and the passengers shrank back. They seemed to hold a collective breath.

"I'm sorry—"

He cut off when he saw a name on one of the posters on the opposite wall. It was an advertisement for a five-star hotel by Piazza San Marco. *The Hotel Danieli.*

A place, he realized with a start. Not a person! He swore to himself at the mistaken assumption. The kid had wanted him to go to the hotel. At noon. He checked his watch. Thirty past the hour. His mind raced. Maybe it wasn't too late.

The roar of speedboats shattered the thought. Two of them careened around the corner from the Rialto. Dark sunglasses locked onto him. Renzo turned his back to the threat and leaped onto the dock.

Chapter 6

Venice, Italy

TONY WAS THE FIRST TO ENTER THE HOTEL LOBBY. PRETTY damn posh, he thought, soaking it in. He'd been called in to plenty of lavish spaces as a senior cop with LAPD, but nothing compared with this. The lobby wasn't wide, but it was tall. A red-carpeted grand staircase hugged a mahogany wall as it twisted and turned up three open stories. The extended balconies above were edged with richly decorated balustrades, supported by hand-carved marble columns and gilded arches. Bouquets of fresh-cut flowers sprang forth from waist-high vases. Colored glass chandeliers reflected off marble floors that were polished to a mirror finish. The furniture was antique, the imported rugs luxurious, and the lighting subdued. It was glamorous, old-world, and it smelled like money. Tony couldn't have felt more out of place.

Seven impeccably dressed attendants bowed at his arrival.

Tony hesitated, unsure how to respond. Then Ahmed stepped past him. He approached the group with authority, issuing quick instructions in Italian. The attendants dispersed like a football team from a huddle. Two stepped outside to hold the doors for the bride and groom. Another rushed upstairs to prepare the waiting guests. The remaining four took usher positions at the base of the staircase. Tony respected the kid's take-charge attitude.

It made sense that he was comfortable in this environment, he thought. Before his incarceration in a medical-health facility years ago, Ahmed had grown accustomed to lush settings. He'd been raised by Luciano Battista—the wealthy international terrorist who had brainwashed the kid into nearly killing Tony and all his friends. Now the seventeen-year-old was like an adopted son to Francesca, and a big brother to Sarafina and Alex.

Ahmed's dark hair was swept back above a broad forehead, thick brows, black eyes, and a strong nose. He still had some filling out to do, Tony thought. But he looked dashing in his black tux. Tony ran a finger under the constricting collar of his own white shirt. The tailors had been able to adjust the penguin suit to handle his bulk. But the largest neck size on the fancy shirts was half an inch too small. Even so, he thought, his wife was gonna love the pictures. Of course, his two older kids were gonna laugh. He wished his family could've been here. But with the new baby and all, it hadn't made sense.

There was a round of applause outside, and Tony watched as Lacey offered a final wave to the crowd. Marshall stood stock-still. The red blindfold hadn't budged. Tony grinned at the sight. How his friend had allowed himself to be talked into that, he'd never know. But Lacey was worth it. She took Marshall's arm and guided him into the lobby. The hotel staff came to attention. Tony noticed several admiring nods.

"Dammit, girl," he said. "You are a breath-taker!"

Lacey tilted her head and batted her eyelashes. "You think?"

"Oh, yeah," he said. He patted Marshall on the shoulder. "You got a winner here, pal."

"If you say so," Marshall said, pointing to the blindfold. "Of course, I can't be sure. How do I know she hasn't been switched out for a different model?"

Lacey elbowed him.

"Ouch!" Marshall said with a feigned flinch. "Okay, it's definitely her."

They laughed.

Sarafina was next in the door, followed by Francesca and little Alex. Tony felt a twinge of sadness. The kid was Jake's spittin' image, and the sight of him reminded Tony of the best man he'd ever known. That Jake had died by sacrificing himself to save the rest of them left a hole in his gut. It was a loss that Tony and his friends would feel forever.

Alex looked worried. He stared at nothing, but it appeared as if his little brain was working overtime. It disconcerted Tony because the boy had always been oddly serene at get-togethers. Jake's kid had ranked off the charts on puzzles and other nonverbal tests, which had made a lot of sense in light of his pop's brain. The boy seemed to actively observe the world around him—via TV, the Internet, books, magazines, anything that provided input. It was as if he were soaking it into a vast library in his brain. Output, on the other hand, was limited. Alex seldom expressed emotions to anyone other than his mother. He never cried. Never laughed. Never spoke.

Tony shrugged off his concern, crediting the child's anxious behavior to the unusual pomp and circumstance of today's event. Hell, weddings loosened a few screws in everyone's emotions, he thought. It was nice to see that the kid wasn't immune to it.

Francesca's father, Mario, entered with several of his gondolier buddies. The gang was all here. It was time to get this show on the road.

They made their way up the staircase.

* * *

The panoramic view from the hotel's terrace stretched across the lagoon to the Isola di San Giorgio Maggiore, where sunlight glinted off golden-domed rooftops. Boats passed back and forth, and Tony could imagine noblemen of the past watching the arrival of merchant ships from the Orient filled with exotic wares. You couldn't find this kind of history in LA, he thought.

Marshall and Lacey held hands facing the guests. They were beneath an arched trellis of colorful flowers that cascaded to the floor. Tony and Alex stood beside Marshall. Francesca and Sarafina were next to the bride. Ahmed stood off to one side. The wedding party faced a gathering of guests who filled eight rows of chairs. A select group of photographers stood behind them. A string quartet played the last bars of the Bridal Chorus.

Even beneath her veil, Lacey's smile lit up the crowd. She'd waited long enough for this moment, Tony thought. He was glad to be sharing it with her and his best friend. Still wearing the blindfold, Marshall exhaled a slow breath. Tony noticed, and he couldn't help but crack a smile. Several guests must have caught the unconscious tell as well, because there was a roll of chuckles. It wasn't that Marshall didn't want to get married. He loved Lacey completely. He was in his thirties now and it was long past time. But still…

A priest stood on a dais behind the couple. "*Buon giorno, signore e signori,*" he said with a youthful sparkle in his voice. "Welcome, ladies and gentlemen," he continued in English, "to the ultimate celebration of love." He spread his arms to indicate the wedding couple. "Aren't they lovely?" The crowd erupted in applause. Lacey curtsied, Marshall blushed, and Tony felt Alex shift back and forth from one foot to the other. The boy had a thousand-yard stare that reminded Tony of Jake. He wondered what occupied Alex's mind.

At a cue from the priest, Lacey reached up and untied Marshall's blindfold. The crowd quieted. "As you have followed me to this altar," she recited from the old rite, "so shall I follow you in life."

The blindfold fell from Marshall's eyes. He blinked against the sudden brightness, staring at Lacey with an awestruck expression. The moment stretched, and Tony remembered that the groom was supposed to respond with a rehearsed line as well. Instead, Marshall dropped to one knee, cupped Lacey's hands in his, and said, "Lace, I can't imagine life without you. Marry me and make me the luckiest man in the world."

Lacey beamed. "Yes, yes, yes!" she exclaimed. He stood, lifted her veil, and dipped her into a long kiss. The crowd cheered, Sarafina jumped up and down, and Alex tugged at Tony's trousers.

The priest harrumphed at the premature affection. He tapped Marshall on the shoulder. "Shall we begin?"

Marshall grinned, and Lacey wiped lipstick from a corner of his mouth. It was her turn to blush, and Tony knew she wasn't acting. The couple turned their backs on the guests and faced the priest. He raised his hands and recited a blessing.

Alex tugged harder on his pant leg. Tony crouched down. "You okay, son?" he whispered. "You gotta pee or somethin'?"

Alex didn't respond. His fist gripped Tony's lapel and, for the first time since Tony had known him, the boy made eye contact with him. It was unnerving, as if Alex searched the caverns of his mind, looking for an answer to some profound question. When Tony leaned over to scoop him up, the boy stepped back to prevent it. But he held the stare and Tony sensed an intense internal struggle within him.

The priest stopped speaking at the interruption. Francesca and Sarafina hurried over to see what was wrong. Tony felt their presence, but he refused to break eye contact with Alex. The boy was on the verge of…something. He wasn't sure what it was, but he knew it was important. When Francesca crouched beside him, Tony palmed the air to keep her from breaking the connection.

She hesitated, and Tony suspected that she was using her empathic gift to read her son's emotions. "He's…excited," she whispered.

"Excited?" Tony said, holding the boy's stare.

"Is Alex okay?" Sarafina said.

Marshall and Lacey joined the circle. Ahmed had moved closer as well. "What's going on?" he asked.

Tony ignored them. Alex's gaze intensified. Tony allowed his mind to be the backstop for whatever was happening. Unbidden images of Jake suddenly pierced his consciousness. Alex had somehow teased the images from his memory. It shocked Tony, but he didn't look away. Alex's mouth curved up in a mimic of Jake's crooked smile, and Tony sensed a glimmer of satisfaction in his expression.

Without breaking the connection with Tony, Alex reached out his hand and pointed at a silver locket that hung from his mother's neck. Francesca let out a gasp, clutching at the keepsake. Alex extended his palm. She understood. She unclipped the necklace, opened the locket, and placed it in his hand. It was apparently a ritual they'd performed in the past.

Alex's eyes narrowed on Tony. He lifted the chain so that the locket was at eye level. Tony didn't need to break his stare to know that Jake's face was in the heart-shaped frame. But he looked anyway. The image brought with it a flood of memories—of friendship, battles, and sacrifice. Tony embraced them. When he looked back at Alex, the boy nodded as if he'd seen it all, too. Alex's eyes moistened, and Tony was taken aback by the flood of emotions they shared.

As if a terrible burden had been lifted from his shoulders, Alex drew in a deep breath. He held it a moment. Then he unclipped his tablet from its holster and made an entry on its screen. A robotic voice sounded from the device.

"My papa needs your help."

Chapter 7

Venice, Italy

The voice from Alex's tablet brought a collective gasp from the wedding party.

Francesca dropped to her knees and pulled her son into a smothering embrace. She cried out in joy, "My son!" Tears streamed down her cheeks.

Tony felt a mental jolt as his connection with the boy was lost.

Sarafina's eyes were saucers. She nearly stumbled as she lunged forward to join the embrace. Ahmed moved closer. His hands trembled, and Tony could sense the boy's desire to jump in. But his aversion to being touched held him back. Mario stood behind him, mouth agape.

"Holy cow," Marshall said.

"It's a miracle!" pronounced Lacey. Similar exclamations came from the guests. Cameras flashed, video cams panned, and the priest made the sign of the cross.

Tony's thoughts traveled a different path. Yes, it was incredible that the boy had finally communicated. But Tony's cop instincts pushed that piece of the puzzle aside as he asked himself why.

My papa needs your help.

He'd used English instead of Italian. The message had been directed at Tony. It had been a plea. The fact that he'd chosen this particular moment to make it lifted the hair on the back of Tony's neck. He rose and studied the huddled family as they rocked from side to side in their embrace. Alex turned his head around. Tony saw fear in the child's eyes.

Marshall and Lacey moved beside him. "Can you believe it?" Marshall whispered.

"Somethin' ain't right," Tony said.

"Of all the times," Lacey added.

"Exactly," Tony said, deep in thought.

"What do you think he meant about helping Jake?" Marshall asked.

"I don't know…yet," Tony said. He turned to Lacey. "I know this is the last thing you want to hear right now, but—"

He cut off as Lacey turned to the crowd. "Ladies and gentlemen," she announced. "A magical day has just become more wondrous than ever! Please enjoy some refreshments while we take a short break."

A few minutes later, the wedding party was gathered in a private salon.

"Everyone needs to calm down for a moment," Tony said. The room quieted. Ahmed and Sarafina sat together on a love seat. Ahmed spun a pencil on the coffee table. Sarafina sat as close to him as she dared. Her hands were in her lap. She rocked gently back and forth. Mario, Lacey, and Marshall stood nearby. Alex sat on his mother's lap on an antique lounger. He appeared agitated. He cradled the tablet. He hadn't used it again—despite a barrage of questions from Sarafina and Ahmed. Tony feared that he was retreating into himself. It seemed to Tony as if it had taken a lot of effort for the boy to communicate in the first place.

He pulled up a chair across from Alex and sat down. "Hey, pal."

Alex ignored him.

"So, that was pretty cool how you spoke using your tablet," Tony said. "How long you been doin' that?"

Still nothing.

Tony hesitated. He recalled the emotional connection he'd shared with Alex earlier. The experience had sparked difficult memories. His shoulders sagged. "I feel you, Alex," he said more to himself than to the boy. "I miss your pops, too. He was the best friend I ever had." He soaked in the gazes of everyone around him, settling finally on Francesca. "Aw, hell, kid," he added, "Jake was the best friend *any* of us ever had. We'd have done anything for him."

Alex shifted in his mom's embrace. He rested the tablet on his lap. His index finger traced the lines of a complicated fractal pattern on the screen.

The reaction fueled Tony's hopes. He continued softly, less the interrogator, more the friend. "You said he needs our help?"

The boy's fingers picked up speed across the screen.

The only sound in the room was the rustle of Lacey's gown as she edged closer to Marshall.

Okay, Tony thought. Keep it simple—yes-or-no questions only. "Umm…would you like us to pray for him?"

Alex's finger hesitated on the display. It was as if he was confused by the question.

Francesca opened her mouth as if to speak but evidently thought better of it. She didn't want to disrupt the connection. She arched her eyebrows at Tony. He got the message. *Keep it going.* He cut to the chase.

"O…kay," Tony said, drawing out the word. He was worried for the poor kid. But another part of him remembered that beneath the childhood veneer, Alex tested smarter than most adults. Maybe it was time to treat him as such. "Alex, do you know where he is?"

Alex glanced pointedly out the salon's picture window. Then back to his tablet.

"Outside?" Tony asked.

Alex swept the fractal image aside. His index finger moved across rows of application icons. Tony waited for him to pull up whatever app he'd used earlier to communicate. Instead, the boy opened an application that included a series of illustrated flash cards. He swept through them. The childlike images flashed by so fast that Tony could barely keep up. Each illustration included a word beneath it. He saw a television—TV; a boy in a bed—SLEEPY; a beverage—DRINK; and several others. When an image of two children RUNNING appeared, Alex stopped.

"He was running?" Tony asked. "Outside?"

Alex didn't look up. But the crooked smile was back. It was such a "Jake" expression that Tony found it unnerving. Apparently satisfied, Alex crossed his hands over the screen as if there were no further need for it.

"Nooo..." Francesca muttered, louder than she intended. The sentiment had come unbidden. She swallowed hard. Joy at her son's ability to communicate appeared to battle with her concern for his state of mind. After a moment her shoulders sagged. She pulled Alex closer. "I'm sorry, *caro*," she said softly. "But the man we saw could not have been your father."

Tony was immediately alert. "You saw someone running?" he asked Francesca.

"A man was being chased," she said. "Beyond the crowd. I saw him from behind. B—But it couldn't be..." Her voice trailed off, and Tony could imagine her replaying the scene in her mind.

Tony studied the boy. The connection he'd experienced in the other room with Alex had been extreme. True or not, Tony knew from the bond that the boy believed what he was saying. A sudden chase outside had likely triggered a reminder of stories about his father. His imagination had filled in the rest. Of course it couldn't be true, he thought. But that hardly mattered. He knew from his own experience as a father that there would be no peace—and no wedding ceremony—until he proved it.

He rose and whispered something to Marshall. His friend looked at him like he was crazy. "Just do it, Marsh," Tony said. He motioned toward Francesca's father. "And you better take Mario with you. Because they ain't going to give 'em up willingly."

Marshall nodded. He and Mario left the room.

Tony heard a commotion outside. A minute later, the two men returned. Three gondoliers acted as their rear guard. Marshall's face was red. He had a bruised lip. "Friggin' paparazzi," he mumbled. "I hope these are worth the trouble." He had a digital camera in either hand. Mario held two more.

"Pass 'em out," Tony said, taking one of the cameras. Marshall kept one, Lacey another. "Start with any video recordings. Scroll backward to when we were on the dock. We're looking for three men running at the back of the crowd."

Ahmed and Sarafina took the last camera back to the love seat. Francesca sat forward on the lounger. Alex stood beside her, his hand in hers. He watched Tony with an intense focus.

It was Marshall who spoke up first. "I've got something." Tony and Lacey gathered around the small screen. Marshall played it back. There were two men chasing a third. Their backs were to the camera. They ran over a short bridge. Marshall zoomed in and slowed the motion. But just as the first man turned his head to glance toward the camera, a group of tourists blocked the view. By the time the crowd passed, he was gone.

"Damn…" Tony muttered under his breath.

"Oh, God!" Sarafina's outburst chilled him. She and Ahmed gaped at the screen of the camera they held. Tony and the rest of them rushed over.

"*Allahu Akbar*," Ahmed said in a hushed voice. He turned the camera so the others could see.

Francesca's gasp accented the emotion everyone in the room felt.

Jake Bronson was alive.

Chapter 8

Swiss Alps

VICTOR CLOSED THE HINGED PANEL FOR THE FINAL TIME. The hidden room behind it had been his sanctuary since he was a child. Soon, the comfort it provided would no longer be necessary. He wiped the last bit of blood from his hand and pocketed the knife. The session had gone well.

The snowstorm had grown in intensity. A whistle of wind from an ill-fitting window pushed a chill breeze across his neck. He moved down the hall, and the crackle of burning logs drew him into the great room. He sauntered through the room, breathing it in, capturing the smells and memories of his life. The walls had been stripped bare. His footsteps clapped on stone floors that were no longer carpeted. He ran his hand along the burled edge of the pitted dining table that spanned the far wall. He wondered at the magnitude of power that had been wielded by the generations of men who had secretly gathered here. Men of science, art, politics, and influence. From across the globe, strategizing around a shared vision—all leading up to this moment.

There was much to do, he thought, and it bothered him that Hans had not awaited him here as instructed. Victor felt a tug of irritation. But a quick glance at a mirror revealed a calm expression. The reflection nodded back at him.

A distant hammering issued through a vent in the floor, reminding him of what was happening down below. The noise from the dungeons wouldn't have been heard hundreds of years ago, but the addition of a heating and ventilation system provided acoustic avenues for sound to travel in unusual directions. He made his way downstairs. The stone steps were worn smooth. They spiraled into the depths of the mountain. Sconce lights replaced ancient torch holders. Their illumination revealed a thin sheen of moisture on the rock. He felt the chill to his bones, but he didn't mind. He imagined his forefathers experiencing the same sensations, shrugging them off against the magnitude of their calling.

The reinforced steel door closed behind him, and a dozen men in heavy coveralls and hooded ski jackets jumped to attention. Heels clicked together with military precision. They stood among a stack of crates of various shapes and sizes. A few of them had yet to be sealed. Gears turned overhead in the cavernous space. Thick steel cable fed around a huge flywheel before disappearing through a wide gap in the cliff face. A gust of snow whipped into the room.

"As you were," Victor said, as he donned one of the fur-lined coats from a rack by the door. The men relaxed and continued their work. One of them stepped forward. He gave a slight bow and pointed at the receding gondola.

"That will be the last load today, *Mein Herr*," he reported. "We must wait for the storm to subside."

Victor watched as the last of the precious items was prepared for shipment. He knew that similar crates were being packed all over the world. Preserving mankind's culture was integral to their mission. "How many more loads?" he asked.

"Three more will take care of everything you see here." He motioned toward a secured double door at the far side of the room. "And one more..."

Victor nodded his approval. Everything was on track.

The entrance door opened. Hans rushed in. He didn't bother with a coat. "There's been a development," he said.

The surge of adrenaline Victor felt was no threat to his composure. His visage remained impassive. A glance at the guard, and the man turned on his heel and returned to work with the rest of the men.

"What is it?" Victor asked.

Hans explained.

Victor welcomed the news with a calculated expression that offered no hint of the excitement he felt inside.

"This changes everything," he said.

Chapter 9

Venice, Italy

JAKE'S FACE WAS EVERYWHERE.

Francesca stifled a sob. Marshall had used an application to snap-share the media from the camera to the personal devices in the room, including Alex's tablet. She watched as her son held the locket beside the displayed image. His fingers traced the outline of Jake's face on the screen. Alex was content. She envied the serenity he emanated. It was a stark contrast with the anxious emotions that otherwise filled the room.

Tony and her father huddled in a corner with two men from the Gondoliers' Guild. One of the gondoliers issued a string of orders into his phone. Marshall's fingers danced on his smartphone. Lacey hovered beside him. She was still in her wedding dress. The veil was on the floor. Her eyes were red, but her expression was determined. Sarafina played a haunting melody on a sixteenth-century clavichord at the other side of the salon. Her downturned face was hidden by her shoulder-length hair.

The fabric of Francesca's world unraveled with each passing thought. How could Jake have allowed her to go on believing he was dead? He'd been gone for six years. Yet still she woke every morning with an emptiness that was only partly filled by her children. Had everything she'd felt been one-sided? Had he ever loved her at all?

She watched as Alex flipped from one image to the next—the cameras had captured four shots of Jake's face. She wondered at the thoughts that must be traveling through her son's mind—and she fought to control a surge of anger.

Had he not cared about his own son?

The answer was in the question. The revelation startled her. She'd known of Jake's regrets over the turn of events in his life. Of his remorse at how his presence placed those close to him in danger. Of his belief that they'd all be better off if he had died in the MRI accident in the first place. She recalled his parting words in the jungles of Venezuela. *Instead of death, I offer you life!* he'd said. The words had haunted her. Only now did she fully understand their meaning. He'd chosen to disappear, to allow everyone to believe him dead, for their own sake. In his mind it would have been the ultimate act of love.

She hated him for it.

She loved him for it.

An elevation of tension from Marshall and Lacey brought her thoughts back to the present. The couple was focused on Marshall's phone. There was urgency in the whispers they shared. They moved toward Tony and her father, passing them the phone.

Tension doubled.

Francesca rose to join them. Her father was tight-lipped when he angled the device so she could see the screen. Marshall edged closer and tapped the PLAY button. The video focused on the two men racing after Jake. A passerby bumped into one of the men, causing him to stumble. As he caught himself, Marshall tapped the screen. The image froze. He zoomed in.

Francesca's breath caught. The man's jacket had flapped open. A pistol with an unusually long barrel was holstered underneath.

"It's a silencer," Tony said. "So he ain't a cop."

"Which means Jake is in trouble," Lacey said.

"He needs our help," Marshall added.

"Big surprise there," Tony said. He sounded disgusted. "Where Jake goes, trouble follows." He squeezed his hands into fists. His knuckles cracked. "Dammit, anyway!" he growled under his breath. "He shoulda told us he was alive."

"Take it easy, man," Marshall said.

"I'm pissed!" he said.

"*You're* pissed?" Lacey said, motioning to her gown.

A moment passed as each of them absorbed the enormity of the situation. Knowing looks were exchanged. Tony sighed, Mario nodded, and Lacey pointed an accusing finger at Marshall.

"Don't think for a minute that this is going to keep us from getting married!" she said.

Marshall pulled her close. "An early release of the latest iPad couldn't keep me away."

Lacey smiled despite herself. "But first we gotta pull our missing groomsman's butt out of the fire," she said.

"She is right, of course," Mario said. His English was good, though heavily accented. "We will help him."

Francesca mimicked their nods before catching herself. "But it's not safe!" she said, glancing at the children.

"We're past that," Tony said. "Because whoever is after him knows we're here. It's no stretch to figure they were watching us in case Jake showed up." He hesitated. His voice softened. "They already know where you live."

Her hand went to her throat. The truth of his words struck like a hammer blow.

Tony grasped her shoulders to steady her. "No worries, darlin'. Your pops and I already have a plan."

Francesca nodded dully. It was happening again, she thought.

Jake was back.

And her world was spiraling out of control.

Chapter 10

Venice, Italy

RENZO RACED DOWN ONE ALLEY AFTER ANOTHER. HE avoided the more crowded thoroughfares, hesitating at the next canal crossing, peering right and left before proceeding. The rumble of motorboats had faded, but he knew the chase was far from over. He suspected his pursuers had unloaded teams behind him. Others likely waited ahead.

The San Polo district was primarily residential. Though tourists still explored the area, most of those he passed appeared to be locals. He kept moving, recalling from the map how to make his way back to the Hotel Danieli. He hoped it was the last place they'd expect him to go. The next alley opened onto a small piazza where a group of young boys passed a soccer ball in front of a small church. Men played cards beneath an umbrella at an outdoor café. Two mothers rocked strollers as they chatted on a park bench. Renzo slowed. Foot traffic was lighter here, but there were still plenty of locals who would be more than happy to point the way to a crazy man sprinting past.

He was halfway across the piazza when the church bell rang. The reverberations stunned him, resonating in his skull, each clang like a doorbell on a locked memory. His feet kept moving, but his mind felt suspended in time. The sounds, the piazza, the church—they were all familiar, as if he'd been here before.

He grappled for the memory, startling when an image actually resolved itself. He remembered standing on a rooftop deck, a moment of peace as he watched the woman from his dreams through a pair of binoculars…

Renzo stopped midstride and turned toward a building at the opposite side of the square. A wreath of bougainvilleas framed the rooftop gazebo that he knew would be there. The sight of it shocked him. The doctor had said his memory might come back all of a sudden. Was that happening now? The possibility was intoxicating.

A startled shout, and the memory vanished like smoke in a breeze. Two men had bumped into a couple as they entered the far side of the piazza. They spotted him immediately.

Renzo swore to himself. He took off like a sprinter on a track. Any advantage he'd gained was lost. His brain's betrayal fueled a boiling rage. It spurred him forward. He ran blindly, numb to the scowls from those he rushed past. He ducked down the nearest walkway and poured on speed. Two more turns and the path dead-ended on a canal. An intersecting waterway stretched straight ahead. A gondola glided toward him. It slowed as it approached the turn into the waterway that blocked his path. The gondolier did a double take as Renzo skidded to a stop.

Renzo glanced both ways, immediately realizing his mistake. Buildings stretched up the sides of both canals. There were no sidewalks. He'd been corralled. A boat engine revved from the distance to his right, and a speedboat surged toward him. The man seated beside the driver pulled a pistol from under his jacket. The boat swerved around a second gondola, nearly swamping the slighter boat in its wake. The gondolier's angry fist stopped waving when he spotted Renzo. He pulled a phone to his cheek as the boat raced past.

The pad of running footsteps behind Renzo told him the jaws of the trap were closing. The gondolier in front of him confirmed the only choice he had left.

"*Vieni!*" the man shouted, motioning for Renzo to dive into the water. His boat had just entered the intersection.

Renzo plunged headfirst into the canal. He shallowed his arc to avoid any hidden pilings. His legs scissored, and he pulled through the murky water. He passed beneath the length of the gondola, broke the surface, and swam another twenty meters to the next dock. As he pulled himself out of the water, he took in the scene behind him. The gondolier's back was to him. He waved his hands about amidst a frenzy of angry shouts. His gondola wobbled kitty-corner in the intersection, blocking the speedboat. The man had bought him the time he needed.

Renzo's smile collapsed when he turned and saw two more men standing before him. Rubber-soled shoes. Dark glasses. Out of breath. Each of them held a pistol trained on his face.

"Good-bye," the shorter man said.

The life that flashed before Renzo's eyes was only four months long.

The squeak of a hinge bought him a few more seconds.

The taller man before him spun around at the sound. Green shutters swung open three stories above. A woman placed a basket of damp clothes on the sill. A clothesline stretched above the alley. She waved to two teenage boys standing on an opposing balcony. One of them aimed his cell phone down on the scene.

The two men in front of Jake were cut from the same cloth as those who had chased him in Focette. They were professionals. The taller man lowered his weapon. He flashed a badge upward.

"*Polizia*," he shouted. "Back inside." He spoke in Italian. His accent was Germanic. The woman retreated, slamming the shutters closed behind her. The two boys didn't budge. They spoke in excited whispers. The second one pulled a phone from his pocket, tapped the screen, and aimed it at the scene. Renzo could imagine the online hit-counter spinning ever faster beneath the live feed.

The shorter man kept his pistol trained on Renzo. He removed his sunglasses and slipped them into his shirt pocket.

His bald head shone. His glare was predatory. "If you try anything," he whispered in Italian, "they die as well. This will be your only warning, Mr. Bronson."

The name held no meaning for Renzo, but he had no difficulty understanding the threat. He was dripping wet and out of options. His shoulders sagged. "I understand."

The man held a finger to a point just beneath his ear and spoke. "We have him. Teams two and three, report to the evacuation point."

Two minutes later, Renzo was seated on the floor at the rear of the motorboat. Flex-cuffs secured his hands and ankles. A blanket had been thrown over his shoulders to hide the bindings from onlookers. The boat idled slowly down the canal. The driver was apparently searching for a secluded spot that would become Renzo's final resting place, at least until someone discovered the body. One guard sat in the open bow. Another sat beside Renzo. The bald team leader sat across from him. The windbreaker on his lap barely covered the pistol in his hand.

"You killed three of our brothers yesterday," he said. One of his shoes rested atop a cinder block. A rope linked the block to Renzo's ankle cuffs.

Renzo knew the end was moments away. The hopelessness of the situation brought a swell of emotions that issued from locked memories. Of loyalty, sacrifice, and loss.

And defiance.

The fear of death should not rule a man's actions, he thought. Rather, its rushing inevitability should inspire the moments of his life. He realized that the unbidden philosophy had come from the man he used to be. The brief glimpse of his former self emboldened him. He sat taller, gritted his teeth, and returned the man's stare.

"They died poorly," Renzo said. "I won't."

The bald man's face reddened, but he didn't react as Renzo would have expected. Instead, his eyes glazed over. As if reciting from a ritual, he said, "The death of a few for the many. *Cæli Regere.*"

"W-What?"

The leader ignored the question. He issued a sharp order in German, and the driver cut the motor. The boat drifted to a stop. A quick scan forward and back, and the driver nodded. One of the guards lifted Renzo to his feet. The other hefted the cinder block. The boat wobbled. Their leader stood to face him. Renzo's world narrowed to a close-up view of the silencer at the end of the man's pistol.

Cæli Regere? Renzo recalled the tattoo he'd seen on yesterday's lead assassin. It was Latin. Something about the heavens? He was about to die for a religious cause?

When the executioner brought his other hand up to shield his face from the splatter, Renzo took what he knew would be his final breath. He abandoned his confusion. He wouldn't carry the question into eternity. Instead, he closed his eyes and filled his mind with the image of the woman whose eyes haunted his portraits.

A smile found the corner of his lips.

In that final moment, when the mind shines its brightest and sensations increase tenfold, Renzo heard a faint beep. It was a digital alert. He opened his eyes.

The leader lowered the pistol. The index finger of his free hand pressed a point under his earlobe. The other guards did the same as the team listened to an incoming transmission. The leader stiffened. Protruding veins at his temples pulsed at double speed. "*Jawohl*," he said to whoever was listening at the other end of the implant. His tone was deferential. However, Renzo saw bitterness in the man's eyes as he holstered the pistol.

The driver pounded a fist on the dash. One of the others grumbled. Apparently, they'd all wanted to see him dead. But when the guard holding the cinder block removed a knife from his pocket and severed the rope linking it to his ankles, Renzo knew it wasn't going to happen right now. He blew out a breath he hadn't realized he'd been holding.

"Don't get too excited," the leader said. He stepped forward so that his face was inches from Renzo's. His breath smelled of sauerkraut. "There are worse things than dying with a bullet to the head." He shoved Renzo onto the rear bench seat.

The driver gunned the engine and the boat started off.

Chapter 11

Venice, Italy

RIDING IN THE GONDOLA BROUGHT TONY A FLASH OF MEMO-ries. The last time he' d been in one of these rigs had been more than six years ago, when he and Francesca's uncle Vincenzo had infiltrated the masked ball at Battista's palace. That mission and this one had the same goal—to rescue Jake. People had died, including Vincenzo. That's because shit happened when Jake was around, Tony thought. He patted the knife strapped to his shin. He was gonna make damn sure it happened to the other guy this time around.

He still couldn't believe that Jake was alive. He'd gone over and over it in his mind. His buddy had jumped off the V-22's ramp in Venezuela in order to put an end to Battista. Fifteen minutes later, there was a nuclear explosion. End of story. Or so he'd thought. He shook his head. If anyone coulda figured out a way to survive, it woulda been Jake. Hell, he'd gotten outta more fixes than a magician in Vegas. Tony was still pissed that Jake had kept him in the dark. But he buried the emotion under his determination to rescue the most selfless man he'd ever known.

Answers would come later.

The gondolier sang "'O Sole Mio" as he pushed the boat across the Grand Canal. A score of gondolas drifted nearby. Their gondoliers joined in the song. The tense tenor of their voices gave the tune an edge that sounded more like a soldier's call to arms than a romantic accompaniment. Each boat had one or more riders, several of them with cell phones to their ears. Although they were disguised as tourists, none of them were paying passengers.

The wake of a passing vaporetto rocked the boats as they converged near the entrance to an offshoot canal. A water taxi idled nearby. Francesca's father was at the helm. Marshall and two of Mario's gondolier buddies were in the back. They nodded to Tony. It was time to get wet.

* * *

Renzo's hands and feet were still bound. He sat in the port corner of the rear bench seat. The blanket draped around his shoulders disguised his predicament, but it did nothing to dampen the burning rage that grew inside him. He was tired of being in the dark, of running for his life. It was time to take charge. He may not have a past, he thought. But he swore to himself that the future would include sweet vengeance against the men around him.

And their leaders.

They'd made a critical mistake—they'd let him live. For how long, he didn't know.

Long enough.

He studied them. He saw hard edges and muscles. No strangers to violence. But there was something more. He sensed in them a calm strength of purpose. These men believed in a cause.

They passed under an arch. Pedestrians strolled overhead, but no one paid them undue attention. Renzo didn't have any options. If he shouted, innocents would die. If he jumped overboard, he'd drown. So he'd watch.

And wait.

The flat stares of his guards weren't encouraging.

The boat's motor reverberated between the buildings. He saw the Grand Canal up ahead. From there, the open water of the lagoon was minutes away. The driver slowed the boat as it neared the intersection. Traffic congested the large waterway, where a couple dozen gondoliers had joined voices in an impromptu group serenade. Their tourist charges held up cell phone cameras to capture the moment.

The guards pulled their jackets over their pistols, and the driver nudged the boat into the teeming mass. The perimeter boats gave way. The German leader edged closer to Renzo as the motorboat inched forward. Hulls bumped and tourists smiled. Gondolas bobbed all around them.

The motorboat wedged between them, slow but steady. They were halfway through when an altercation broke out on their starboard side. Angry shouts. A gondolier dropped his oar and leaped onto another's boat. Fists were thrown. A knife was pulled. A woman screamed. The singing stopped. All eyes followed the action.

Renzo gasped when a huge arm grabbed him from behind and yanked him out of the boat. Sunlight turned to a murky green swirl. A swallow of water, and panic took over. Arms and feet flailed, but the man behind him held him fast, pulling him downward with powerful strokes.

It was the initial signal of oxygen deprivation from Renzo's lungs that pulled the memory from the darkness of his mind—of a boy underwater at the community pool, holding his breath while all the others in the class pushed to the surface. Though many had challenged him, no one had ever beaten him. He clamped his mouth closed and stopped struggling. The big man behind him reacted by spinning him around and giving him a thumbs-up sign, signaling that he was there to help. The blanket swirled between them. The man pulled it loose, and it drifted away like a black wraith. Then his savior unclipped a soda can–size cylinder from his belt and pushed it toward Renzo's face. It had a mouthpiece. He clamped his lips around it and sucked in a deep breath. The man across from him did the same with a duplicate canister. He gave Renzo a questioning look, making an okay sign with the fingers of one hand. Renzo nodded. The man pulled a knife from a shin strap. Three or four quick saw strokes, and the plastic cuffs around his wrists and ankles were gone. Another okay sign, and the man motioned for him to follow.

Shadows passed overhead. Renzo saw that the gondolas had created a barrier around the motorboat. But the dam would break soon. Already, he heard the motor revving up and down as the driver pushed his way through the gaggle. Renzo and his new best friend swam in the opposite direction. Another powerboat idled just ahead. They passed beneath its hull and surfaced on the opposite side. Anxious faces peered down at them. Hands reached out. Strong arms pulled them into the water taxi.

The boat took off at full speed.

The trailing powerboat throttled forward, crashing through the line of gondolas, pushing them aside like flotsam before an ocean liner. Lacquered wood split. Men dove for the water.

The boat raced after the taxi.

The taxi driver was a middle-aged man. He had a Bluetooth device in his ear. He dodged and weaved through traffic with a deftness that could only have come with years of experience. The older man beside him issued orders into his cell phone. It sounded to Renzo as if he was coordinating the efforts of others who were part of the escape plan. Their eyes met. The old man's eyes glistened.

The man who had pulled Renzo into the boat wore patent leather shoes, black slacks, and an open white shirt with cuff links. Renzo recognized him as the groom from the wedding party.

"Su-weeet Jesus, Jake!" the man said, escorting Renzo into the taxi's covered seating area. He handed him a towel and smacked him on the shoulder. "I can't believe it's really you!"

The big man beside him was dripping wet. He dried his balding pate with his own towel and pulled a Yankees baseball cap over his head. He wore tux slacks and a gondolier's striped shirt. It appeared two sizes too small. "Damn, pal," he said. "You are a sight for sore eyes."

Renzo looked from one to the other. They spoke English. He didn't. He saw the recognition in their expressions, and he was glad for it.

But their faces—and their words—meant nothing to him.

The boat swerved to port. All three men braced themselves in the cabin. There was a seesaw of sirens behind them. Renzo looked back and saw that the trailing speedboat was being pulled over. The taxi driver eased off on the throttle.

Renzo breathed a sigh of relief. "*Grazie per avermi salvato la vita*," he said.

"Huh?" the groom said.

They all stared at one another.

The old man stuck his head into the cabin.

"Welcome back, my son," he said to Renzo in English. He'd been speaking in Italian on the phone earlier.

"*En italiano, per favore*," Renzo said.

"You can't speak English?" the old man asked in Italian.

Renzo shook his head.

The old man's eyes widened. He translated for the other two. They gaped.

"Do you know us?" the old man asked.

"No."

"What is your name?" he asked in Italian.

"Renzo."

Suddenly, the sirens started up again behind them. The taxi driver shoved the throttle to the stops, and Renzo nearly lost his balance as their boat lurched forward. The driver shouted something to the old man, who glanced quickly at his smartphone. A moment later he ducked into the cabin. He pointed sequentially at the big man, the groom, and himself. He spoke in Italian. "This is Tony, Marshall, and I'm Mario. I'm your son's grandfather, and they're your best friends."

Renzo's mind reeled. "I have a son?"

The boat swerved sharply. "There will be time for that later," Mario said, pointing behind them. "We have a complication."

The powerboat was still on their tail. It was farther back, but it was no longer alone. Two blue-and-gray police boats accompanied it. The wail of their sirens bounced off the buildings on either side of the water. Mario tapped a link on his smartphone and showed them the screen. The recorded ten-second video showed the powerboat being pulled over by the police. A flash of badges, a phone exchanged, and suddenly the police snapped to attention. The leader of the assault group jumped aboard one of the police cruisers and all three boats charged forward.

Mario leaned close so he could be heard over the roar of the taxi's motor. "The men who grabbed you have powerful friends," he said in Italian. "My people overheard Interpol being mentioned." He repeated himself in English.

"Son of a bitch," Tony said.

Renzo exchanged a worried look with the big man. The act felt familiar.

"Holy crap," Marshall said, grabbing the rail as the boat dodged traffic.

"Your people?" Renzo asked Mario. He was still trying to make sense of it all.

"The guild," the old man said. "There isn't a tracking technology in the world that compares to the eyes, ears, and smartphones of the gondoliers of Venice."

The boat bounced as it jumped the wake of a vaporetto. Traffic was heavy on the canal. There were over five hundred gondolas in Venice, and it seemed as if every one of them was on the water. They opened a path as the taxi approached, only to quickly fill the space in their wake. Renzo looked toward the stern. It was like the closing of the Red Sea. He heard shouted commands over the police loudspeakers in the chase boats. But the watercourse became more congested. The pursuers were forced to slow down.

The taxi pulled away.

Chapter 12

Swiss Alps

Victor's anger over the news that the American scientist had escaped the hospital unseen paled in comparison to the shock he'd felt when he learned that the young man had possessed the miniature pyramid. Victor had learned of the existence of the tiny replicas six years ago, following the unexpected launch of two of the parent objects. One of the miniatures had survived, and he'd wanted to get his hands on it ever since—that is, until he'd learned that it was useless without the help of the comatose American. In any case, he had given up hope of ever possessing it when his operatives within the US scientific agency had reported that it had been destroyed during the fire—the one ignited four months ago in an attempt to kill Jake Bronson.

But they had been wrong.

The failure stirred a cauldron in his gut. Had his agents been intentionally kept out of the loop? Or had the scientist named Timmy kept it to himself? If so, Victor wondered what other secrets the young man had withheld.

"Search his apartment," he said.

"I have already alerted the Washington team," Hans said. "They will be there shortly."

The device had untold potential, Victor thought.

He was determined to control its power.

That his men had uncovered it in the aftermath of the botched assassination at the beach had changed everything. The surviving team member had seen the object during the struggle. He had had the presence of mind to retrieve it. His foresight would be well rewarded.

Hans lifted a finger to his ear to receive a communication. "They've secured the American," he relayed. "The flight crew has been alerted. The boat is thirty minutes from the airport."

Victor permitted a flush of satisfaction to reach his features. Had news of the miniature's existence been delayed, then Jake Bronson—the only man on the planet with the knowledge to unlock it—would have been killed. Some would've called it a stroke of luck, he thought. But he knew better. Good fortune was nothing more than the logical outcome of layer upon layer of preparation.

"We may commence," Victor said. He sat at his desk in the castle, surrounded by rich wood paneling and leather furnishings. Hans stood beside him, a computer tablet in hand. He tapped the screen, and the wall of bookcases opposite the desk flickered. What had appeared to be a wall-to-wall collection of leather-bound first editions was actually a digitally created holographic display. The books dissolved into a three-dimensional image of a conference room. A dozen people sat at the table. Though they appeared to be gathered together in the same room, all of them were physically located at their respective home offices across the globe.

"Welcome," Victor said. He waited a moment as the attendees settled in for the meeting. Aides were dismissed, phones turned off, and each of them focused his or her attention forward. There was an eagerness about them that Victor appreciated. An Arabic sheikh, an African scientist, a Chinese magnate, a French museum director, and more—though they were from different parts of the world, they were all cut from the same dream. These were men and women of science, power, and influence from around the world, descendents of an order that stretched back a millennium.

"Our ancestors are smiling," Victor began. "For it is by their foresight and resolve that we find ourselves gathered here today, heralds of a new age."

The group responded with nods and smiles. Though they attempted to appear calm, Victor knew that all of them had dozens of tasks on their mind. At this stage, their homes and offices were likely as stark as Castle Brun.

"The end is upon us, my friends," Victor said. He paused for effect. "But so is our new beginning assured. We know our duty and we shall perform it with steadfast certainty. For it is only from the ashes of humanity's doom that we may mold a future of peace and prosperity."

Victor saw that his words fueled their fervor. He studied each of them in turn, hesitating only on the woman from Brazil. He tapped a keyboard set into the top of his desk, and her image zoomed to occupy the center of the wall screen. At forty-seven, she was the youngest of the group. Her family controlled a global shipping conglomerate. She was in charge of coordinating the South American exodus. Another tap and her face filled the screen—every freckle and wrinkle was revealed.

"Carla," he said. "Is everything ready on your end?"

"On schedule," she replied.

An eye twitch. A narrowed pupil. A tightening of the muscles around the lips. Victor caught the lie immediately. His external reaction was nonexistent, though he had little doubt that those watching him searched for one. He wondered how many of them had software analyzing his image even now. No matter. Even a computer could not find what didn't exist. He returned his focus to the group. He considered them one by one. Those who remained trustworthy would be rewarded. The others would not.

He tapped a key, and the rest of the attendees were once again on the screen.

"Are we ready?" he asked.

A man in a Russian military uniform responded first. "All the teams are in place. Codes are secured. Awaiting your orders."

The Russian's US counterpart was a navy admiral. "We had a slight hiccup on our end, sir," he said. Heads turned his way. "The sub commander died of a heart attack this morning. However, we've ensured that his replacement is one of ours. He's en route to the South China Sea as we speak. The executive officer and three of the crew are also with us."

Victor wasn't surprised that the admiral's resolution to the "hiccup" slid so easily into place. Each of the members of this council had been seasoned for his or her role since childhood. They were masters in the art of logistics.

Every plan has a backup, he thought.

All of the others gave their respective reports. Except for the inconvenience of Carla's lie, Victor was satisfied.

"Then we are ready," he announced. "The next time we gather, it shall be to mourn"—he paused for a beat and added—"and celebrate."

His eyes panned the group a final time, lingering for a moment on the attractive Brazilian. Their families had been allies for generations. They'd vacationed together on her sprawling ranch. He'd always enjoyed her company, especially after their relationship had grown intimate. But their time together had allowed him to learn more about her than she ever intended to reveal, and he had long ago sensed her lack of total conviction to the cause. It was a shame.

He returned his attention to the group.

"*Cæli Regere*," he said.

"*Cæli Regere*!" they responded in unison.

Victor nodded. Hans tapped the tablet, and the digital conference room morphed into an aerial video of a tropical island.

Victor relaxed into his chair and took in the scene. The familiar panorama was breathtaking. The island was at once foreboding and lush. White-water arcs skipped over treacherous volcanic reefs offshore. Two immense mountains centered the landmass. Their peaks disappeared into an umbrella of clouds. Tropical fauna sprawled above barren cliffs. Waves crashed below. The few beaches that sprang from gaps in the ragged terrain had little sand—dense foliage ran to the water's edge. Sunlight reflected off the mist that swirled in the upper reaches, and a rainbow formed.

Victor appreciated the island's beauty, but its hidden secrets were what he contemplated.

Hans stiffened suddenly beside him. Victor sensed his tension. "What is it?" he asked.

Hans lowered his finger from the comm implant. "The American has escaped."

Victor turned his gaze on Hans with slow precision. "How. Is. That. Possible?"

"He had help. It was well executed."

Victor's mind boiled and his stomach churned, but the muscles of his face remained relaxed. Every plan has a backup, he reminded himself.

"Gather his friends," he said calmly.

"Which ones?"

"All of them."

"The children as well?"

Victor didn't reply. It was a stupid question.

A click of the heels. "Immediately."

As Hans turned to go, Victor added, "And eliminate the Brazilian."

"*Jawohl, Mein Herr!*"

Chapter 13

Isola di San Michele

He was American. His name was Jake Bronson. He rolled the name over and over in his mind, sliding it into imagined keyholes in the hope of unlocking…something.

Anything.

What he got was nothing.

Renzo—Jake—struggled to deal with everything he'd learned during the past several hours. They'd told him he was smart, that he'd spoken a dozen languages. But he couldn't even speak the language that was supposedly native to him.

So Mario had translated as Tony and Marshall told him stories too wild to fathom—and too unimaginable to be anything but true. Especially the part about accidentally triggering the launch of a pyramid from an ancient cavern in Afghanistan. He thought back to the conversation:

"I was there, Jake—when you and Sarafina solved the riddle of the pyramid's glyphs," Mario had said in Italian, translating for Tony. "According to what you explained afterward, you used the solution to activate the device. It seemed to come alive, linking with your brain. You said there was a massive exchange of information and then the pyramid lifted from the ground, spinning like a top in midair. It produced a laser beam that bore an exit hole straight up through the mountain.

A second later, it launched itself out of the chamber and into space."

There had been a long pause before Jake finally said in Italian, "You're joking with me, yes?"

Mario had translated Jake's question for the two Americans. They had responded with grim expressions and shakes of the head.

"B-but why?" Jake had asked. "What was it all about?"

The three men had exchanged furtive glances before Marshall started to reply. But Mario cut him off with a wave of his hand. The old man knew the story for himself. Jake recalled his blowing out a long breath before saying, "You told us that the device had been left here thousands of years ago by an alien species. They had identified mankind's violent nature as a potential threat. The pyramid was like a testing station, or kiosk. Its purpose was to identify that point in time when man's intellect had achieved the level necessary to develop the capability for interstellar travel. Unlocking the device by solving the complex riddle of the glyphs was the first test; the brain scan was the second. With your enhanced abilities, you passed them both. That triggered the launch, sending the device back to its makers with the results."

Jake could barely imagine what he was hearing, much less accept it as truth. But he had seen from his friends' expressions that they believed every word.

Mario had hesitated before adding, "You explained that the aliens would later return to pass judgment on mankind. If our violent tendencies remained, then humanity would be eliminated."

Jesus!

Jake shook off the memory and returned to the present. He felt a kinship to these men. But it was a sensation born from the day's events, not from their shared past. He wondered at the bravery and loyalty they had exhibited by rescuing him today—six years after his funeral. Perhaps it was fitting that their reunion was to be consummated on the Isola di San Michele. The walled island was a cemetery isle.

It had also been the secret gathering place of the Gondoliers' Guild since the late sixteenth century.

They'd switched boats twice before arriving at the deserted dock. His wrinkled clothes were finally dry. Night had fallen, and a thin blanket of fog hung over the water. Bugs buzzed in endless circles around the lone lamp over the concrete pier. Two men appeared out of the mist. They wore windbreakers, knit caps, and wary expressions. Each carried a vintage assault rifle.

Mario motioned for them to lead the way. "Stay close," he said. They single-filed through an arched gate leading to an earthen path framed by cypress trees. A beam from one of the gondolier's flashlights strayed from the path and reflected off an expansive stretch of grave markers. Only a few were adorned with fresh flowers.

Death all around me.

"Creepy," Marshall whispered.

A white-haired monk awaited them at an open side door to the church. A rosary dangled from one hand, and his lips moved silently in prayer. He motioned them inside. Domed ceilings, carved arches, and marble columns dominated the space. Religious frescoes adorned the ceiling and walls.

They passed through a locked door and down a narrow staircase that led to the catacombs. Jake was taken aback by the expansiveness of the chamber at the bottom of the steps. A statue of Saint Michael on Judgment Day commanded the center of the circular room. He held the scales of justice in one hand and a spear in the other. Contemplation benches surrounded the figure. Five corridors spiderwebbed outward.

The monk ushered them down one of the dimly lit passages.

"The church was built in 1469," Mario said. "For a time, it also served as a prison." He pointed at the tombs inset into either wall. They stretched into the distance. "Each of the spaces was once a prison cell."

Jake shivered at the thought. The openings couldn't have been more than four feet tall. A bead of sweat slid from his forehead.

When the last of the tombs was ten paces behind them, Mario added, "One of those prisoners was a gondolier. He escaped with the help of a priest. His brother."

The line of caged overhead lightbulbs ended. The path ahead was shrouded in darkness. Flashlights flicked on. The beams danced off rough-cut walls. The tunnel made a sharp turn. Five paces later, it dead-ended into a wall of rock.

"The young priest was an archivist," Mario said. "He stumbled across drawings that revealed this." He placed his palm on an outcrop and pushed. There was a click, and the entire wall slid smoothly to one side. It barely made a sound. A wooden door stood behind it. It appeared ancient but well oiled. It was strapped in black iron.

"This part of the catacombs was God-made," Mario said. "It was used as a storage area during construction of the church. But it was long forgotten after a cave-in sealed the end of the tunnel. The priest toiled for six months to clear the path that eventually led his brother to safety." He patted the priest on the shoulder. "With the aid of brethren like Father Filippo, it became the guild's secret gathering place, protected through the ages."

There was a camera over the doorframe. Bolts were thrown from within. Jake flinched at the sound.

My family is on the other side of that door.

As it opened inward, Mario said, "Of course, we've made a few changes over the years."

The space was expansive and well lit. It resembled the interior of an eighteenth-century sailing vessel. The low ceiling was supported by stout beams, and the walls and floors were planked with polished wood. The furnishings were simple but inviting.

A leather couch and chairs formed a casual sitting area. Pictures adorned the walls, and a bowl of fruit rested atop a round dining table at the far end of the room. The space smelled of must, gun oil, and…pasta.

"There's a kitchen?" Marshall asked.

"Of course," Mario said.

"Smells like home," Tony said.

Voices traveled from a hallway at the far end of the room.

Jake braced himself.

Chapter 14

Isola di San Michele

SARAFINA PACED BACK AND FORTH IN THE UNDERGROUND room. The melody she composed in her mind reflected her anxiety.

"Stop it," Ahmed said.

She barely heard him. A full orchestra accompanied the frenzied music. A crescendo of drums, racing violins, and a crash of cymbals. Her fingers tapped imaginary keys…

"Stop!" Ahmed shouted.

It was as if the conductor had hurled his baton. The music ceased, she opened her eyes, and her hands went to her hips. She'd abandoned her bridesmaid dress and heels for a hodgepodge outfit that didn't fit. At least it was clean. The striped gondolier shirt was long-sleeved. The waistline of the black trousers wrinkled beneath a cinched belt. The cuffs were rolled up above a pair of deck shoes. "What's your problem?"

"Your humming was getting out of hand," Ahmed said. He was irritated. He still wore the white shirt and trousers of his tux.

"I was humming?"

"Dude, you're lucky the walls didn't come crumbling down."

"Shut up," she said. "And I'm not a dude."

Ahmed brought his palms to his ears. "My world for a pair of noise-canceling headphones."

"Shut—" She stopped herself. Getting angry wasn't going to help. Either of them.

Her shoulders dropped. "He'll be here any minute," she said, stopping in front of a dresser mirror to straighten her hair. "Where do you think he's been all this time?"

Ahmed sat on a lower bunk in the sparse bedroom. The pencil he was spinning on an empty chessboard came to an abrupt stop. "Bolivia, the Galápagos Islands, Siberia. Probably not Somalia. Too many pirates. Unless he was their hostage. Do you think he was captured by pirates? He'd have some stories to tell! If you ask me, I think—"

"Flip it," Sarafina interrupted. There was no anger in her voice. It was the signal they'd agreed upon long ago.

Ahmed clamped his jaw closed. He calmed. The mood change was instantaneous. He nodded. "Thanks. Sorry about that."

Sarafina shrugged. He hadn't blabbered like that in a long time. When they'd first met, years ago at the institute, it was the only way he knew to communicate. The way her mom had explained it, intense nervousness opened too many pathways in his overactive brain. He spoke whatever came to mind. Over the years, he'd learned to control it, slipping only during extreme circumstances. This had been the third time he'd lost it in the past hour.

"I don't blame you," she said. "It seems impossible that he's alive."

Alex's legs dangled down from the upper bunk. They swung back and forth in unison with his rocking body. His hands were in his lap. He still wore his black jacket and bow tie. The faraway look in his eyes was familiar, though Sarafina had little doubt that he absorbed everything that was going on. His tablet was on the bed beside him. He hadn't communicated through it again, despite everyone's encouragement. It frustrated her, but she knew there was nothing she could do about it. Life was complicated. She had learned that from her own experiences. It would happen when he was ready, she thought. Not before. That his first written words were in English was a shock. She and Ahmed stuck to the language, hoping to draw him out.

"Something compelled Jake to stay away," Ahmed said. There was no trace of his Afghan roots in his accent. He was a gifted linguist, due in large part to the brain implant he'd received years ago as part of Signor Battista's experiments. "It must have been for your safety." He pointed upward. "And Alex's."

The sentiment struck a chord. "I know," Sarafina said, wiping away a tear. "But it's not fair."

"No, it's not," Ahmed agreed.

They sat in silence for a moment.

"So, what are we going to do?" Ahmed asked.

"What do you mean?"

"I mean, regardless of why he was away, he's back now. And he's in trouble." He waved a hand to encompass their surroundings. "That's why we're all here, right? To help him?"

"I guess. But what can *we* do?"

Ahmed considered the question. His lips moved silently around the stream of thoughts that likely careened through his head. Finally, he captured her gaze and said, "Whatever we must."

The notion rendered everything in hard clarity for Sarafina. "Whatever we must," she repeated.

Alex's legs stopped swinging.

Chapter 15

Isola di San Michele

JAKE COULDN'T SHAKE THE SENSE OF FOREBODING. HE STILL had the envelope in his pocket.

Lives hinge on your ability to remain anonymous.

A striking blonde stepped into the underground hideaway, and Jake recognized her from the wedding party. She wore an ill-fitting outfit that appeared pieced together from a gondolier's wardrobe. The boots, baggy pants, blousy shirt, and leather vest were more fitting for a pirate than for a bride. Her eyes widened at the sight of him. She rushed forward.

"Jake!" she shouted as she threw her arms around him. "It's really you!" she said in Italian.

His return embrace was tentative. She noticed and pulled away. Her head canted to one side. Caribbean-blue eyes studied him. Marshall moved in and placed an arm around her waist.

"Oh, Jake," she said, her voice trailing off.

Mario stepped forward. He had called ahead to warn the others of Jake's condition. "This is Lacey," he said in Italian. "Marshall's fiancée."

"*Molto piacere, signorina*—" He cut off as the awkwardness of his formal greeting sank in. According to the stories he'd heard on the boat, Lacey had been one of his closest friends. Her courage had saved lives. He reached out and took her hands in his. He offered her a tight-lipped nod. Her features relaxed and she squeezed his hands.

"Welcome back, Jake," she said in Italian. "Don't worry. We'll figure it out."

"Damn straight," Tony said.

It was then that Jake noticed the woman behind her. She stood motionless beneath the hallway arch. One hand clutched a locket at her chest. She wore a white peasant dress that was belted around a small waist. Auburn hair spilled down her shoulders. It framed a face that was filled with hope.

The sight of her eyes took his breath away. Liquid chocolate—the eyes from his dreams. He'd sketched them a hundred times.

The room glided past him, and the next moment he was in front of her. He searched her depths, praying for the link to reveal itself. She respected the moment, drawing tentative breaths across parted lips. The delicate hand clasping the locket trembled. Neither of them spoke, and a distant part of Jake's consciousness wondered if his new heart would stop cold at the sight of someone who resonated with his very existence.

"I—I'm glad you're home," she said softly.

Her voice was music. He nodded dumbly. Her worried expression told him that she sensed the turmoil that simmered inside him. Instinct shouted at him. He *needed* his memories to burst forth and reforge his connection to this woman. His future—his life—depended on it.

One breath became two.

Then three.

Four…

Nothing.

His disappointment was reflected on her face. Her expression collapsed into itself and she moved into his arms. They embraced for a long moment before she finally pulled away. He'd expected tears. Instead her eyes were filled with a fierce determination that gave him strength. They moved into the room.

“What matters, my love,” she said, “is that you have returned to us. The rest will come with time.” She paused before adding, “It must.”

He nodded.

“But first,” she said, blowing out a deep breath, “I would like to introduce you to your son.”

Part II

Friendship is the only cement that will ever hold the world together.

—Woodrow Wilson

Chapter 16

Isola di San Michele

Francesca was a mother. She knew how to hide behind a wall of feigned strength. But if the man before her—the father of her children—had been able to sense her emotions as easily as she could read his, he would know she was petrified.

Yes, she'd been overjoyed that Jake was alive. It was a miracle. Then her father had called to warn her that his memory was shattered. She'd steeled herself, preparing for the worst. But while she awaited his arrival, a part of her had nurtured a secret belief that the strength of their former love would break through the veil. She'd thought, how could it not? If she and Jake didn't deserve a fairy-tale ending, then who did?

When he'd first sighted her, she had noticed a shadow of recognition cross his expression. Her heart had skipped and she had swelled with elation. Except for the hint of gray at the sideburns, he looked the same. The laugh lines, bold green eyes, and boyish mop of hair felt like home to her. Even his aura was the same.

But when she had searched his emotions, all she had found was a stranger's hope.

Not love.

She sensed his longing for something more, and she felt his disappointment when it wasn't there. It crushed her. But she couldn't show it. Instead, she called out over her shoulder, "Children!"

Alex was the first in the room. He approached without hesitation, stopping two paces in front of Jake. He held the tablet in his left hand. The room stilled as the boy and the man appraised one another. Francesca held her breath. Alex had a keen ability to sense the nature of those who came within his circle of consciousness. She knew that about him in a way that only a mother could. He shared her empathic gifts, and she sensed him calling on them now as he looked upon Jake.

Her heart was in her throat.

Ahmed and Sarafina stepped into the room. They gasped. Their wondrous expressions warned of a mad dash. But a simple gesture by Alex stopped them. His right hand hung loose at his side. His index finger carved lazy circles in the air, as if sending a silent appeal—or command. Something about the motion was mesmerizing. Francesca felt herself sway in concert with the gentle movement. Trepidation was nudged aside by a sense of serenity. The others must have felt it, too. They watched with rapt attention.

Jake crouched so that he was at eye level with his son. He appeared to be waiting for the moment to play out. They continued to study one another, and it seemed to Francesca as if invisible lines of packed emotion passed between them. After a moment, they both smiled. The crooked expressions were an exact match. Francesca sensed Alex's contentment and she felt joy.

Alex lifted the tablet.

Francesca held her breath.

He tapped the screen, and a robotic voice responded from its speaker. "*Hello, Father,*" it said in English. "*I've been waiting for you.*"

Jake's smile faded. "*Cosa?*"

Francesca stiffened. Her son had not expected the language barrier. He'd composed his message in English, knowing that was his father's native tongue. She sensed that the misunderstanding disturbed him. His normally confident expression was replaced by a little boy's sadness. His finger stopped twirling.

The spell was broken. Sarafina rushed forward and threw herself into Jake's arms. He nearly tumbled backward from the force of her charge.

"Daddy!" she cried out. She buried her face against his shoulder.

Ahmed moved beside them. Francesca sensed his desire to join in the embrace, but his touch phobia stopped him. "I'm so glad you're back, Jake!" he rattled off in Italian. "We've got so much to talk about. It's okay if you can't speak English, because I can teach you. I'm good with languages, remember? I taught you Dari. So much has happened. Do you still speak Dari? Where have you been? Wait until you hear about—"

"Flip it," Sarafina said between sobs.

"O-oh, yeah, sorry," Ahmed said. He clenched his fists.

"It's okay," Jake said in Italian. "I know there is much to talk about." He gave Sarafina a squeeze and pulled out of the embrace. He turned back to Alex. His features softened, and Francesca realized with a start that something had changed within him.

"My son," he said in Italian. He reached out. Alex holstered his tablet. Then he stepped slowly into the embrace. After a moment's hesitation, his fingers curled into the folds of Jake's shirt. A lone tear ran down his cheek.

A wave of relief crashed over Francesca. Only in her dreams had she ever imagined such a sight. Sarafina moved beside her, and they absorbed the moment together. Jake captured Francesca's gaze. She reveled in the emotions he radiated—loyalty, commitment, and the unbreakable bond of father and son.

It gave her hope.

Chapter 17

Isola di San Michele

His encounter with the boy—his son—changed everything for Jake. He felt warmth from the child that was unlike anything he' d ever known. It seemed to fill the room. A dam broke in Jake's mind, and a flood of emotions burst forth. He felt a sudden bond with the people around him—a depth of feeling normally possible only after years of association.

Francesca captured his gaze. It seemed as if she had sensed the change. The longing he saw in her eyes stirred him. It took force of will to break contact and take in the others.

They were family.

He trusted them.

He cared about them.

But he didn't remember them.

The link with Alex had unlocked doors to previously held emotions. But memories of his past remained hidden. The juxtaposition made him dizzy. A part of him wanted to rush forth and embrace them all. Another warned him to keep the revelation to himself.

The choice was made for him when a gondolier rushed in and shouted, "We've captured one of them!"

Thirty minutes later, the prisoner sat in a chair in the center of the room. His hands were bound behind him and there was a hood over his head. Blood leaked from a bandaged wound on his arm. The kids had been ushered back to their room. The rest of them surrounded the man.

"I'm goin' first," Tony growled. The knuckles on his ham-size fists were white.

Jake couldn't interpret the words, but he understood the sentiment well enough. The man in the chair represented everything that had gone wrong in the past twenty-four hours.

Francesca edged closer and translated the discourse.

"Take it easy, big guy," Marshall said, placing a hand on Tony's shoulder. "This is Mario's show."

The old gondolier stepped forward and removed the hood. There was a collective gasp from those around him. Including Jake. He recognized the man immediately. It was the American who'd saved his life in Focette.

The man blinked against the sudden brightness, grunting behind the strip of duct tape on his mouth. Mario ripped it off.

"Jeez!" the man said, sounding more like a teenager than someone in his late twenties. "Am I glad to see you."

Everyone seemed to speak at once.

"Timmy?" Marshall asked. "What the heck are you doing here?"

"Wait a minute," Lacey interjected. "I remember you!"

"Doc's friend," Tony said. "You helped get us out of Venezuela."

"You were at Jake's funeral," Francesca added softly. "But you knew he wasn't dead?"

The room stilled.

Timmy turned to Jake. He blew out a breath. "It's a long story."

Francesca's voice was choked as she translated his words.

Timmy's brow pinched in confusion. "Hold on," he said, studying Jake. "You spoke English just yesterday. Don't you remember what happened in the parking lot?" He rubbed his wrists after

Tony used his pocketknife to cut through his bindings. "You moved like a bat out of hell to lay into those dudes."

The knuckles on Jake's right hand were still raw. He recalled the fight.

Timmy continued, "Then you bandaged me up. Spoke English. Knew my name."

The scene was cloudy in Jake's mind. "I only remember you telling me to come to Venice," he said in Italian.

Timmy slumped. "I thought the mini had brought you back for good," he said. "Where is it, anyway?"

"The mini?"

Francesca continued to translate between the two men.

"Yeah," Timmy said. "The miniature pyramid. Let me see it."

"I don't know what you're talking about."

Timmy's jaw slackened. "Oh, no."

He told them what he knew. About Jake's new heart, the coma, and the top secret center where he'd been kept alive. About their inability to bring him to consciousness using conventional methods.

"It all came to a head six months ago," he said, "when the two pyramids appeared in orbit."

"I remember that," Lacey said. "It trended on Twitter for a couple days."

Marshall said, "Until the government explained them away as secret Chinese satellites."

"A cover-up," Timmy said.

"But the Chinese confirmed it," Marshall objected.

"They were a part of it. In fact, every major government in the world was a part of it. They still are."

Marshall's eyes widened as if a sudden realization dawned on him. "Wait a second," he said. "Are you saying those satellites are actually the same two pyramids that Jake launched from Afghanistan and Venezuela?"

"Afraid so."

A chill fell over the group. Francesca summed it up for Jake in Italian, but he was having difficulty absorbing what he was hearing. *I launched a pyramid from Venezuela, too?*

Marshall was the first to speak. "I thought it was supposed to take them forty years to travel back and forth between Earth and their home planet."

"You're right," Timmy said. "And we've rechecked the numbers over and over. Forty years is accurate. Returning any sooner defies the laws of physics."

Marshall's shoulders slumped. "You mean the laws of physics as we know them."

"Yeah," Timmy agreed sullenly. "That's what scares the crap out of us."

"Which explains the cover-up," Tony said.

"Exactly," Timmy replied. "Sure, the level of cooperation was unprecedented. But the alternative was world panic. They needed to buy time while they figured out what to do. The result? They built a device—a chair—that they hoped to use to communicate with the pyramids. It incorporated the mini—a small component of the first pyramid Jake had launched. But they couldn't make the device work. They tried for weeks. Its design required the use of a human brain as a conduit. They had plenty of volunteers, but their minds simply couldn't handle the load. That's when they decided to proceed with an experimental method to revive Jake. It was risky. Very risky. But in light of his"—he paused as he looked at Jake—"*history* with the objects, they felt they had no choice. They needed his help. If he didn't make it through the procedure, so be it. They'd be no worse off."

He paused until Francesca had completed the translation. Jake was having trouble grasping the magnitude of what Timmy was saying. No wonder his brain had decided to close off his memory.

Timmy continued, "But someone didn't want Jake revived. The night before the procedure, an assassin started a fire in the room beneath his. Jake's bed was engulfed within minutes. If I hadn't been working late…"

"My God," Francesca added after she translated. Mario moved beside her and placed an arm around her shoulder.

Jake was shocked. "You saved my life," he said in Italian.

"Just returning the favor," Timmy said. "I'd been analyzing the mini in the lab. I unplugged you, wheeled you out, and hoped for the best. I nearly had a heart attack when you came to in the back of the van."

"Speaking only Italian," Tony said.

"Uh-huh. With total amnesia."

"I don't remember any of it," Jake said.

"Why would you? You were delirious. Anyway, I knew about the problems they were having with the chair. Three people had died already trying to use it. In your state, there was no way you'd survive it. So I hid you in the one place I knew they'd never look—a place where you spoke the language."

They all stared at Timmy in amazement. As if he could see the dumbfounded question they wrestled with, he said, "Hey, transporting him to Italy was easier than you'd think. I've got skills."

Marshall harrumphed, Lacey smiled, and Tony crossed his arms and hiked an eyebrow.

Jake liked the way they melded together in the face of everything that spiraled around them. He felt fortunate to call them friends. He moved to Timmy and offered his hand. "*Grazie*," he said.

Timmy shook it. "No prob." His face flushed. After a moment he said, "So…I assume you guys are using off-grid protocols down here."

Marshall said, "Of course."

"But you still have secure Internet access?"

A nod from Mario.

"Then I've got some good news."

Ten minutes later, the blip on Mario's laptop screen settled on a point in the Swiss Alps. Timmy hovered over the keyboard.

Marshall sat beside him. "Zoom it," he said.

"Chill, man," Timmy said. "I'm three steps ahead of you."

Marshall bristled, Lacey chuckled, and Francesca translated.

Jake watched the screen. The satellite image tightened on a tenth-century castle. A blanket of snow covered the surrounding terrain.

"The radio frequency identification—RFID—chips are microscopic," Timmy said. "My own design. I floated them in a metallic coating that matched the mini's finish. They latch onto any cell or wireless signal within a quarter mile."

Marshall sat back in his chair. He nodded. "Respect."

"Thanks," Timmy said. They fist-bumped.

Lacey rolled her eyes. "Oh, brother."

"So that's real time?" Tony asked.

"Yeah."

"Do you really think that thing will restore my memory?" Jake asked.

Francesca's hand clasped her locket as she relayed the question in English.

Timmy turned around to face Jake. "I can't be sure. But it seemed to work when you held it yesterday. Besides, what other options do we have?"

Jake nodded. "Then we've got work to do."

"Here we go again," Tony said.

Chapter 18

Swiss Alps

VICTOR TIGHTENED THE FUR COLLAR AROUND HIS NECK. He watched as the ten-person gondola swung to a stop at the far side of the space. The suspension cables creaked. The storm had dumped two feet of snow on the surrounding terrain. But the weather front had broken, at least temporarily. Sunlight lanced through the opening in the cliff face. All but one of the crates of precious cargo had been taken off the mountain. Four men and a hand-operated lift waited patiently for access to the final package.

Victor turned to face the steel door behind him. "Open it," he said.

Hans entered a code on a panel beside the door. The lock clicked and they stepped inside the small room. The door closed behind them. Halogen track lights illuminated a single five-foot-square crate. Its hinged top was open. An ink-black upside-down pyramid was supported inside. The artifact had been found by Victor's ancestor a thousand years ago.

"The time is upon us," he said softly. He removed his gloves and ran his hand over the smooth surface of the object. It felt cool to the touch. The detail of the etched images around the perimeter of its upward-facing base never ceased to impress him. Each laser-like engraving depicted ancient man raining violence upon his brethren. Clubs crushed skulls, sharpened stones pierced bellies, and infants were smashed underfoot. His hand stopped on the final glyph. Three hairless humanoid figures stood on an outcrop of rock above a tribe of ancestral fur-clothed *Homo sapiens*. Their backs were turned, and Victor imagined expressions of serenity on their faces. A small pyramid hovered over their outstretched hands. Lances of light shot from the object and pierced the heads of those below. Their wild-eyed expressions were frozen in anguish.

There was a series of embossed shapes and patterns inside the track of perimeter images. Over the centuries, the Order's scholars and scientists had been unable to solve the riddle they represented. But Jake Bronson had done so in a matter of minutes. Victor shook his head, marveling at the irony. His gaze traveled to the center of the pyramid. There was a four-inch square etched into it, its surface untouched by engravings. Victor reached into his coat pocket, removed the mini, and placed it on the square.

It was a perfect match.

Chapter 19

Swiss Alps

LACEY NOTICED JAKE SCRATCH HIS FAKE WHISKERS AGAIN. He said they'd itched almost as much as the silicone nose he wore.

"Even your mother wouldn't recognize you," she said in Italian. She sat across from Jake in the utility van. The motor idled. Marshall, Tony, and Timmy were inside with them. The vehicle was parked on an overlook off an alpine highway in Switzerland. They'd driven through the night in two vehicles. It was midmorning. The outside temperature was below freezing. The sky was clear, but dark clouds gathered on the horizon.

"My mother?" Jake asked.

"Oh, yeah," Lacey said in Italian, realizing that no one had mentioned anything to Jake about his immediate family. "A sister, too. They're both terrific." She combed one last strand of his slicked-back hair into place. "That'll do."

Her acting background had proved to be a critical asset. A dark wig, clever makeup, and a coquettish attitude had changed her from a blushing bride to a clingy middle-aged mistress. Her tight-fitting traveling clothes finished the look. The men had been duly amazed at the transformation. She appreciated it. For Jake's part, the facial disguise needed to be more extensive. But he was perfectly typecast for the acting role of an Italian artist on vacation. The Fiat sedan parked behind them would provide the ideal cover.

In the van, Tony and Marshall sat in the driver and front passenger seats. They each had binoculars pressed to their eyes.

"Once we clear that outcrop beneath the gondola, we're home free," Marshall said.

Lacey translated for Jake.

"Christ," Tony said, adjusting the focus knob. "I'm gettin' too old for this crap."

Lacey and Jake turned their attention to the computer station that Timmy had set up in the back of the van. The young scientist had connected one of two monitors to the electronic image on Tony's binoculars. When the image zoomed tighter, Lacey understood Tony's reservations. The snow-dusted cliff face looked treacherous.

"No worries, dude," Marshall said. "I'll blaze the trail."

Lacey explained to Jake that Marshall had been an avid rock climber since childhood. It was the only form of exercise he practiced besides finger-dancing on a keyboard.

The mission wouldn't have been possible if it hadn't been for the safe house in Geneva. Timmy had explained that US government agencies had over a dozen of them scattered around the city. Between Timmy's access codes and Marshall's hacking abilities, it had been a simple matter to initiate what appeared to be an executive order to prep one for the arrival of a clandestine team. They'd gone there first. Weapons, disguise kits, and tech equipment—it was all there. The clothes and climbing gear, they purchased along the way.

"Man, oh, man," Timmy said. "I still can't believe we're doing this."

"It's like we said," Lacey reminded him. "What choice do we have?"

"Even so," Timmy said. "This is way out of my league. I'm not what you'd call an outdoorsman. Besides, I can't even imagine the shit storm that's waiting for me back home."

Marshall chuckled. "Welcome to the club, dude. This sort of thing is par for the course when Jake's around. The rest of us learned that the hard way a long time ago."

"I should've been home by now with Mel and the kids," Tony said. "She's gonna be pissed."

Lacey said, "Yeah, well, I'm supposed to be on my honeymoon. So shut up."

Jake waited for Lacey to translate the interchange. She chose not to. He shrugged. She figured he got the drift of it anyway. She hoped they were making the right move with this plan. After all, when they'd first discovered that the owner of the castle was Victor Brun, Timmy had said he was one of the good guys.

"Heck, he's the one behind the Geneva conference," Timmy had said. "Without his political savvy and connections, world leaders would've never gotten together."

"Then why not simply knock on the door and ask for the mini?" Marshall had asked.

It was Lacey who had pointed out what a bad idea that was.

"Think about it," she had said. "Jake shows up out of the blue and suddenly people are trying to kill him. Next thing you know, Interpol is involved and they decide they want him alive. Then the mini shows up in this guy's basement? From everything Timmy has told us about it, it's critical to what is going on with the pyramids up above. This Brun character is probably examining it as we speak. As important as it is, why on earth would he let us borrow it just so we can try to restore Jake's memory?"

"Well, they might," Marshall had said.

"Yeah, but they might not," Tony had said. "We can't take that chance. We know how important Jake's memory is to what's going on up there." He had pointed to the stars. "But nobody else does. Nope. Lacey's right. We've gotta go get it. No matter what. And a quick smash-and-grab is the surest way. They'd never expect it."

The castle loomed dark on the ridge. Lacey glanced at the second display on Timmy's console. A 3-D digitized image of the ancient structure rotated on the screen. A blinking light on one of the lower levels identified the location of the mini.

She blew out a breath.

It was a crazy plan.

Chapter 20

Swiss Alps

The Fiat slowed as Jake made the final hairpin turn on the private road. There was no guardrail. The drop-off was sheer. Woodsmoke hung over a village 1,500 meters below. Snow blanketed the surrounding peaks.

The château was impressive. It was a five-story, thirty-five-thousand-square-foot medieval castle, complete with deep-set lancet windows, crenellated ramparts, and twin keeps that framed the arched entrance to an expansive courtyard. Two sides of the curtain wall rose flush with the promontory cliffs that supported it. A fistful of antennae sprouted from one of the pinnacles.

Jake pulled to a stop at the gate. He and Lacey were bundled head to toe. Icy condensation coated the sedan's windows. Lacey shivered. It wasn't an act. A wall camera swiveled on its mount, and Jake rolled down the window and waved with his hand. "*Buon giorno.* Ciao!" he said. His breath fogged around the words. The internal camera lens rotated, and he imagined his image being zoomed on a monitor.

A stiff voice replied from an inset speaker. "*Guten tag.*"

"*Mi scusi. Parli italiano?*" Jake asked.

"*Sì.*"

"Thank God!" Jake said in Italian. "The car heater is broken. W-we need help."

There was only a slight hesitation. "Of course. Come. Come!" The voice sounded genuinely concerned. The gate swung open and Jake drove through.

The cobbled courtyard was half the size of a soccer field. The surrounding curtain wall supported a covered parapet walk. Snow banked on its pitched roof. There was a six-passenger helicopter in the center of the bailey. Two sedans and four SUVs were parked in front of a five-door garage that had likely been barracks hundreds of years ago. The towering residence commanded the far end of the courtyard. Jake stopped the car at the front staircase. A stout main entry door swung open, and two men rushed out. The taller man wore pleated slacks and a thick sweater that failed to conceal his athletic build. His face was all planes and angles, with blue eyes and a blond flattop. He seemed to take in the scene much like a tank commander would a battle zone. But it was the shorter man who captured Jake's attention. He wore a velour housecoat and wool scarf over corduroy slacks. His thick mane of silver hair was swept back over a broad forehead. His face was filled with concern. He rushed to open Lacey's door.

It was stuck.

Nice touch, Jake thought. It had been Tony's idea to drip water in the latch. It had since frozen solid.

The taller man moved in. "Allow me, *Mein Herr*," he said. Thick fingers gripped the handle. A sharp tug, a crunch of ice, and the door swung open.

"Thank you s-s-sooo much," Lacey said, taking the shorter man's proffered hand. He escorted her up the steps.

Jake shouldered open his own door and followed them inside. The taller man appraised him warily as he passed by. The man was four inches taller than Jake and carried at least thirty more pounds. All muscle. Jake maintained his meek composure. "*Grazie, grazie*," he said, rubbing his gloved palms together.

Jake and Lacey cuddled in a love seat by the grand fireplace. Their gracious host had introduced himself as Victor

Brun. He sat across from them in a wing chair. His man, Hans, stood beside him.

Lacey cradled her teacup in both hands. She took a sip. "I feel so much better," she said in Italian. "I don't know how to thank you enough."

Victor waved it off. "It's nothing. We're only too glad to help. Hans has called for a mechanic." He motioned out the picture window. The sun had disappeared behind gray clouds. "The storm may delay him, but no matter. If so, it will allow me the pleasure of your company a while longer. Perhaps you'll stay the night." He winked and tipped his cup in their direction. "After all, we do have the room!"

Victor couldn't have been more pleasant, Jake thought. The man showed a genuine interest in their well-being. It was hard not to like him. Jake wondered how he was mixed up in all this. According to their online search, the owner of Castle Brun was a respected philanthropist and peacemaker.

"You're very generous," Jake said. "But once I've warmed up I think I can repair it myself. Assuming I can borrow a few tools from your garage."

"Of course."

Lacey sneezed.

"Gesundheit, my dear," Victor said.

"Excuse m—" Her words were cut off by another sneeze. Then another.

"Goodness!"

She sniffled and collected herself. "Do you by any chance have a cat?"

The shadow that flitted over Victor's face was so brief that Jake decided he imagined it.

Victor's expression softened. "Actually, my pet passed yesterday morning. I apologize if his presence lingers a bit."

"Oh, dear me," Lacey said. "I'm so sorry."

Lacey kept the conversation lively. As she and Victor exchanged pleasantries, Jake studied the expansive mural on the wall. The family tree was an artful piece of work. It stretched back for generations.

Jake's went back a few months.

Victor's portrait was the most recent addition. The face was twenty years younger, but the pleasant expression was a perfect match to the one he wore now. Jake felt the man's eyes on him and wondered what untold secrets hid behind his mask.

Then Jake checked his watch and his stomach tightened.

He should have received Tony's signal by now.

Chapter 21

Swiss Alps

TONY WATCHED AS MARSHALL SET ANOTHER SPRING-LOADED cam into a crack on the cliff face. Tony clung to the wall five feet behind him. His size 13 boots were double the width of the ledge they traversed. The shoulder-high rope Marshall had strung between anchors meant the difference between life and death.

Tony checked the time. He whispered into his comm unit, "Can't you move any faster?"

"Shut up," Marshall said in a hushed voice. "How was I supposed to know the cliff face was smoother than a baby's butt?"

"Hey, you're the sucker who's supposed to be the rock star," Tony said.

"Cool it with the quips. No worries. I'll get us there."

Tony appreciated his pal's confidence. The sooner he got off this rock, the better. It wasn't that he was afraid of heights. He just didn't like falling.

The wind had picked up, whistling up the cliff face. The sky was cloudy and the temperature had dropped ten degrees. Despite his thermal climbing gear, Tony's joints were stiffening. The cavern that housed the gondola station was twenty feet beneath them. But activity inside ruled it out as an access point. Instead, their target was on the opposite side of the cliff.

Marshall tugged on the cam. Satisfied, he attached the rope and crabbed ahead. Tony followed.

Timmy was in the van. It was hidden in a copse of snow-leaden pine trees. His voice intruded over the headset. "I lost sight of you guys when you cleared that outcrop. How much farther?"

"One more clamp should do it," Marshall said.

Tony was glad to hear it.

"Damn," Timmy said. "I don't like monitoring you guys without streaming sat video. No visual. No infrared. It's like the friggin' Stone Age."

"More like the Ice Age," Tony said with a shiver. "Just sit tight and keep an eye on the mini's locator beacon. If it moves, scream." He shared Timmy's trepidation. This harebrained scheme was nothin' like what he was used to in SWAT.

It was rushed.

There was no backup.

He felt a tug on the rope. Marshall had jumped off the face onto the footfall that led to the castle's ski shed. He sank into the snow up to his knees. He gave the okay sign and waved Tony forward. "Your turn," he whispered.

Tony crabbed to the edge, bunched his muscles, and made the leap.

He landed short.

Chapter 22

Swiss Alps

Tony's boots landed half-off the ledge. The cliff's edge had been hidden by a projecting snow shelf. It calved from his impact and plunged down the mountain. His arms windmilled in a desperate attempt to shift his center of gravity forward.

It wasn't enough.

But Marshall's mighty tug at the rope around his waist did the trick, and Tony face-planted in the thick powder.

"Watch your step next time," Marshall whispered.

Tony spit snow from his mouth. He rose and brushed himself off. "Just checkin' to see if you were payin' attention."

"Oh? How'd I do?"

"Not bad," Tony said. He pulled out a four-shot tranq pistol. "Let's go."

Marshall flinched as Tony chambered the first hypodermic round. "Hell of a honeymoon," he said.

Tony nudged him as he walked past. "Consider this part of the bachelor party."

Marshall stuck close behind him. Snow crunched underfoot. The downward-sloping trail wound through a thick stand of snow-covered pines. Tony paused as his friend used his smartphone to link with Timmy's computer. The castle's 3-D image had shifted since their relative position had changed.

Thirty paces later, Marshall whispered, "Around the next corner."

The ski shed was the size of a two-car garage. It abutted the base of the castle. Two feet of snow covered its sloped roof, and icicles rimmed the eaves. A double set of boot prints led from the side door. They trailed past the front roll-up door and disappeared around the other end of the structure. There were voices.

"Wait here," Tony whispered.

He moved forward in a crouch. A puff of cigarette smoke drifted from behind the building. Men's voices. German.

Tony hugged the wall and listened. A lull in the conversation marked the vulnerable inhalation break.

Shoulda paid attention to the surgeon general's warning.

Tony leaned around the corner and took two quick shots. The first ballistic syringe struck the smaller of the two men in the neck. The man yelped, slapped at the dangling needle, and folded into the snow.

The second man was Tony's size. His oversize jawline and protruding snout reminded Tony of a pit bull. The dart impacted just above his clavicle. He ripped it out. A chunk of bloody skin and fabric trailed from the barbed tip. He bared his teeth and started toward Tony.

Another shot to Pit Bull's broad chest failed to penetrate the man's thick jacket.

But the third to his forehead stopped him cold.

The three-inch dart hung limp down the man's nose. His stunned eyes crossed on it. The hydrated chemical spread instantly from the sinus cavity to his brain. He teetered, then slumped to the ground, his back to the wall. His half-mast eyes glowered, and his slack jaw drooled spittle. But the stubborn dog was still in the hunt. His fingers fumbled with a radio at his belt.

He managed to raise it to his lips. By then, Tony had switched weapons. He stepped forward and aimed the MP5 submachine gun at the man's face.

"Down, boy," Tony whispered, shaking his head.

The man's glassy gaze took in the seven-inch suppressor.

He grunted and dropped the radio. A beat later his eyes rolled into the back of his head and he slumped to one side.

Tough son of a bitch, Tony thought. He noticed the man's rubber-soled boots. They were the same as those he'd seen on the video of the two men chasing Jake in Venice. It could've been a coincidence, but it set off a warning flare in his LAPD gut. It was a feeling he'd learned long ago not to ignore.

When he searched the two men and discovered weapons, he knew they were in trouble.

He pocketed the radio and tossed the weapons in a copse of trees. They disappeared beneath the powdery snow.

Then he motioned Marshall forward. He reloaded the tranq pistol and handed it to him. "This is all yours, pal," he said. "From now on I'm sticking to this." He patted the MP5.

"What the hell?" Marshall said, motioning at the assault rifle. "I thought no one was supposed to get hurt."

"Don't worry about it. This is just an insurance policy."

Marshall inspected the pistol. He handled it with more ease than Tony would have given him credit for. Tony hiked an eyebrow.

Marshall noticed. "I may prefer shooting via a game controller," he said, "but that doesn't mean I don't know what's up."

"Best news I heard all day," Tony said.

They checked the blip on the screen. They were less than fifty paces from the mini. Tony reported over the headset, "We're going in."

Chapter 23

Swiss Alps

VICTOR STUDIED THE MAN SEATED ACROSS FROM HIM. THE disguise was clever, but the eye movement, forehead fasciculation, and body language spoke volumes. The man was nervous. Victor had expected much more from the formidable legend that was Jake Bronson—a supposed master of a dozen languages, with Einstein's brainpower and unparalleled physical skills. The discrepancy was a concern. Had a lesser man awakened from the coma?

Victor leaned forward, switching to English. "Dear me. There's a spider on your shoulder." He studied the American's reaction.

A pinched brow. A tilted head. Confusion.

The man hadn't understood. He didn't speak English.

Victor brushed the imaginary insect from Jake's sweater. He said in Italian, "I'm afraid the castle is riddled with them."

The woman had kept her composure during the exchange. She was a consummate actress, Victor thought. He admired her talent. But that didn't change the fact that she and Mr. Bronson were amateurs on the stage they attempted to play on now.

Victor had been expecting a visit. His men in Washington had uncovered the tracking receiver in the young scientist's apartment. The signal pointed to the castle. The mini had been tagged. Victor had been alarmed, but his initial shock had dissipated when he recognized the opportunity it presented. He was certain that the authorities weren't aware that the mini existed—much less that it had a tracker on it. Only the scientist knew. And when Victor's men spotted him being taken prisoner by gondoliers outside the Hotel Daniele in Venice, and later taken to the island of San Michelle, Victor knew it would be only a matter of time before Bronson and his friends came knocking.

So Victor had ordered the assault team to stand down. After all, why chase the mouse with a broom when you can lure him with cheese? Of course, the entire exercise would prove futile if the American had lost his abilities. It was time for a test.

He rose and said, "There is something I would like to show you."

Chapter 24

Swiss Alps

JAKE ROSE SLOWLY FROM THE LOVE SEAT, PUSHING ASIDE A wave of light-headedness. He took Lacey's arm in his and followed Victor down the hall. Hans was close behind.

There was a brief squelch of static from his earbud—both he and Lacey wore the hidden devices. Tony's voice sounded in his ear. "We're going in."

Though Jake couldn't translate the words, Lacey's double squeeze of his forearm confirmed that it was the signal they'd awaited. Tony and Marshall were in the castle. If everything went as planned, they should be back out in a few minutes. Another ten to make it to the van. Then Jake and Lacey could bid farewell to their host.

They followed Victor into his study.

Rich wood dominated the coffered ceiling and walls. A hand-carved mahogany desk centered the room, framed by a leather sofa and coffee table on one side and a pair of wing chairs on the other. The French-paned window behind the desk presented a view of Mont Blanc. It had begun to snow. The room smelled of books. However, most of the surrounding bookshelves were empty—all but those opposite the desk. That wall-to-wall shelf was filled from end to end with a colorful assortment of old editions.

"It's a 3-D video wall," Victor said. He tapped a tablet and the image changed to a panoramic view of New York City. "It's linked to live feeds around the world." He switched the image a couple more times. The effect was dizzying. Lacey must have felt it, too, because she seemed to lean into him for support. Victor made an entry on the tablet, and the original bookcase image reappeared. They turned their backs on the scene, and Jake escorted Lacey to the chairs opposite the desk. They sat down, but the dizziness didn't settle. Each time he blinked, the room spun.

"Ah," Victor said. "I see you're feeling the effects of the tea. It is a wonderful blend, yes?"

The man sounded so reasonable, Jake thought. Even Lacey seemed to smile at his words. She'd relaxed considerably, leaning into him.

"Wooo," she said. "I feel a bit tipsy."

Marshall's voice came through Jake's earbud. It was sharp. But when Jake turned to Lacey for a translation, he saw immediately that her thoughts were elsewhere. Her expression was sultry. Her eyes dreamy. She stared at Jake.

"I love you, Marsh," she said.

And before Jake realized what was happening, she kissed him. Her lips were soft.

"Now, now," Victor said with a chuckle. "There will be plenty of time for that later."

Jake pulled away.

Reluctantly.

Lacey's words were slurred. "But I'm on my honeymoon," she said with a pout.

Marshall's voice was in Jake's ear again. Sharper this time.

"Huh?" Lacey said. She looked confused.

Victor shook his head from side to side. His expression was condescending. "You have been naughty children," he said. "Isn't that right?"

Jake wondered why Lacey was nodding. Then he noticed he'd done the same.

"But you'd like to make up for it," Victor said. His voice was soothing. "Wouldn't you?"

They nodded again.

I didn't mean to be bad, Jake thought.

Victor continued, "In that case, there's something you can help me with."

Jake and Lacey leaned forward in their chairs.

Gunshots in Jake's earbud jolted his senses. The fog in his mind cleared for a moment.

That's when he noticed the metallic container that Victor cradled on the desk.

Chapter 25

Swiss Alps

TONY FLICKED ON HIS UNDER-BARREL TACTICAL LIGHT AND swept its beam around the shed. The floor was paved. Skis, poles, and snowshoes lined the back wall. There was foul-weather clothing on pegs. Shelves were stacked neatly with helmets, climbing gear, and flashlights. A treaded Sno-Cat was parked in the center.

An interior roll-up door was open. It led to a larger garage. They wound their way through a dozen or more snowmobiles and exited into an eight-foot-wide tunnel that had been carved out of the rock. The symmetry and smooth-cut walls suggested that it had been machine-drilled. Tony figured it had been added in the last century as part of the gondola installation. Thick conduit hugged the ceiling, and fluorescent lighting hung overhead. The air felt crisp and ventilated. Voices echoed around the corner to their left.

"That's the gondola station," Marshall whispered, studying the image on his screen. He pointed in the opposite direction. "This way."

They moved swiftly, the rubber soles of their boots muffling their footfalls. Around the next corner, Marshall pointed down a narrow offshoot to the right.

"Not far," he said.

The tunnel narrowed, and the ceiling height dropped sharply. Tony had to duck his head to clear it. The air was suddenly dank and musty. There was no lighting. Tony's tac light bounced off ragged walls of rock. Not machine-made, he thought. Ten paces later, the passage widened to an oblong chamber that stretched thirty feet ahead. A score of child-size spaces lined the perimeter of the room. Tony shone his light in the first one. It was only six feet deep.

Prison cells, Tony thought with a chill. Where iron gates once existed, only a scatter of rust-colored granite remained. "I gotta bad feelin' about this," he said. He swept his rifle back the way they had come.

It plunged the room into darkness.

"Wait a minute," Marshall said. "There's a light up ahead."

Tony swung the weapon's light back around. The distant flicker faded beneath the intensity of the beam.

"Douse it a sec," Marshall said.

Tony clicked off the light. They both saw it. A faint glow from one of the cells. Marshall held the smartphone in front of him. The blinking signal corresponded with the position of the light up ahead. They shuffled to the opening and looked inside. There was a small lantern in the far corner.

The cardboard box beside it was about six inches square.

"Bingo," Marshall whispered.

He crab-walked into the cramped cell, grabbed the box, and crawled back out.

Tony illuminated the box with the flashlight. Marshall unfolded the top flaps. They peered inside.

A tiny pile of black shavings was all they found.

"Oh, crap," Marshall said.

"What is it?"

"The party's over, dude!" Marshall said too loud. "We need to be out of here now!"

"Marsh!" Tony growled under his breath. He grabbed his buddy's shoulder and gripped him hard. "Settle down. Talk to me."

Marshall had a thousand-yard stare that told Tony that he hadn't heard a word. But whatever had crossed his mind had sobered up his buddy faster than an oncoming freight train. Marshall's eyes widened. He keyed his mike. His voice was calm but authoritative. "Lace, it's time for you and Jake to leave. Don't linger. Do it now."

When he unkeyed the mike, all the breath went out of him. "It's a trap," he gasped. "They scraped the RFID coating off the mini to draw us in. They knew we were coming!"

Tony didn't hesitate. He reached into his jacket and came out with a 9mm Glock. "Dump the tranq gun," he ordered, handing the Glock to his friend. "Follow me."

They ran toward the corridor.

Tony skidded into the main tunnel and ran toward the exit. Marshall was right behind him. There were multiple footsteps around the corner behind them. Moving fast. Tony moved faster. If they could make it to the garage, they could bar the door.

He reached for the door handle just as another guard rushed into the corridor ten paces in front of them. He'd come from the gondola station. The man raised an assault rifle. Tony reacted instinctively, lunging to shove Marshall from the line of fire. Marshall tumbled to the floor just as the weapon's barrel flashed. Rounds ricocheted in the narrow space. The blast from the weapon reverberated off the walls. Tony swung the MP5 on the target. He squeezed the trigger. The suppressed weapon chattered, and the guard flew backward.

The trailing group took cover behind the bend in the corridor. "*Feuer einstellen*!" one of them shouted.

Tony understood the *cease fire* command.

There was a terse response from someone in the gondola room. Then more words behind them. The two teams were coordinating their efforts over their radios.

Tony grabbed the strap on Marshall's climbing harness and hauled his stunned friend to his feet. "Let's go!" he said. He opened the door to the snowmobile garage and bolted inside.

The click of the door's electronic lock was the first sign that they'd made a mistake.

That the internal roll-up door was closed was the second sign.

Strike three came in the form of a voice over the intercom: "Drop your weapons or the woman dies."

Chapter 26

Swiss Alps

Jake felt giddy. It seemed as though Lacey felt the same. Her eyes fluttered and her smile was soft. Her head leaned into the wing of the high-backed chair beside him. The tea had been very good, Jake thought.

Victor sat across from him at his desk. His voice was soothing. The man was a generous host. And he really wanted Jake to see what was in the metal box on his desk.

Why not?

Victor's attention was drawn over Jake's shoulder. Jake followed his glance and saw two men standing inside the doorway. They wore crew cuts and coveralls. Their hands were clasped behind their back. Jake suspected they were friendly, too. He wished they'd brought more tea with them.

Han stepped forward and rested a hand on the back of Jake's chair.

"*Alles ist in ordnung,*" he said to Victor.

"Wonderful!" Victor said.

Jake hoped they were referring to food. He was getting hungry.

"Now then, Mr. Bronson. Shall we take a look?"

"Sure." He leaned forward and propped his elbows on the desk.

The box was eight inches square. The metallic surface shimmered under the desk lamp. Four latches secured the lid. Victor used two hands to slide it forward.

Jake grinned in anticipation. He reached out and pulled it closer. "Whoa," he said as he felt its weight. "Is this thing filled with gold?"

"Better," Victor said. "Go ahead. See for yourself."

Jake unsnapped the latches. He cradled the heavy lid and hefted it upward.

The instant the seal was broken, Jake felt a surge of energy. It was numbed by the drug coursing through his veins, but not enough to keep his head from clearing. His mind snapped to attention, and he suddenly remembered why he was here—his friends were down below, and Marshall had issued a warning that they should leave immediately. Victor had played them.

"*Schifoso*," Jake said.

Victor grinned.

Jake's rage boiled over. He started to rise, but Hans's thick hands pressed down on his shoulders, pinning him to the chair. Jake swiveled and launched the lead-lined lid of the box into the man's shin. The giant yelped. His leg folded. Jake shoved his chair backward, and the man toppled over. Jake kept moving, barreling into the first guard and launching him into the wall. The man's head impacted the bookcase with a thunk. He slumped to the carpet. Jake ducked a blow from the remaining guard and responded with a palm strike to the man's chin. Teeth crunched. Jake finished him with a vicious chop to the throat.

When he turned, Hans was on him. The big man's eyes were cold steel. He lifted Jake from his feet and hurled him back into the room. Jake shielded his face with his arms, barely missing Lacey's chair as he crashed into the front of the desk. A computer display went flying, and Victor's tablet toppled to the floor. The shielded container landed on top of it, crushing the screen and activating a new image on the video wall.

The mini tumbled across the carpet.

The shock of the impact with the desk stole the wind from Jake's lungs. He pushed himself to all fours and gasped for air. When he looked up, Hans's hulking frame was backdropped by a wall-to-wall aerial video of a lush, twin-peaked volcanic island. It was as if the man were suspended in midair. The sight brought on a wave of vertigo. The drug in Jake's system made it worse.

Jake shook his head and focused on the man's feet. He was glad to see they were still firmly planted on the carpet. He coiled his muscles for the tackle, but movement to his right stalled the effort. Victor had picked up the mini. He placed it in the lead case and closed the lid.

Jake's world clouded over.

"Excellent," Victor said.

Chapter 27

Swiss Alps

THE START-UP WHIR OF THE PROPS BROUGHT JAKE BACK TO his senses. He was upright on a bench seat in the passenger section of a plush helicopter. Hans sat beside him, and Victor occupied the seat across from him. A stern-faced guard climbed into the cabin and sat next to his boss. He cradled the shielded metal box on his lap. The ground crew closed and latched the door, and the heavy throb from the overhead blades was muted to a rumble. Snow swirled around them as the props came up to speed.

Victor and Hans each wore a headset. Victor pointed to a third set dangling beside Jake's seat. Jake donned it. It felt comfortable, and he recalled that his friends had told him he'd been a pilot in his previous life.

"Mr. Bronson," Victor said. His voice came across loud and clear through the noise-canceling headphones. "I'm glad you're feeling better. You gave us quite a scare back there."

Jake felt woozy. His head ached, and a sharp pain throbbed in his shoulder. He blinked several times as he struggled to recall what had happened. He remembered having tea by the fire. Lacey had been with him. Everything was a blur after that.

"It was as if the mini took control of you," Victor said.

The mini! Jake thought. That's why they'd come here. To find it. So he could restore his memory. He glanced at the metallic box in the guard's lap.

"I—I remember getting dizzy."

"More than that!" Victor said. "You opened the container and your eyes went wild. You toppled forward like a felled tree. Hans tried to catch you, but you dropped the lead case on the poor man's foot and he missed. You cracked your head on the corner of the desk."

Victor's words helped the puzzle pieces fall into place. It wasn't a perfect fit, but it felt right.

"It's obvious that you have an intense connection with the object," Victor added. His voice was smooth as silk. "And I believe you and your friends are right."

My friends? Jake thought. "About what?"

"About restoring your memory. I think it can work. We simply need a more controlled environment, that's all. That's why we're going to Geneva. Remember?"

Jake didn't remember.

"Where *are* my friends?"

"They're worried about you. Sorry there wasn't room for them in here. But it's only a two-hour drive. They'll be following by car." He pointed out the window. "There they are now."

Jake saw Lacey, Tony, and Marshall walking toward the snow-covered SUVs at the far end of the courtyard. Several of Victor's men accompanied them.

"Hans," Victor said. "Please let them know we're watching."

Hans swiveled the mouthpiece of his headset to one side. Then he placed a finger to a point under his ear and said something. The action sent a chill through Jake. He flashed on the men in Focette communicating the same way. Those men had tried to kill him.

A coincidence?

Jake couldn't hear what Hans said over the prop noise, but the group by the SUVs paused. There was an interchange between them. Then Lacey, Marshall, and Tony turned and waved.

Jake sighed. They were okay.

False alarm.

He waved back.

Victor leaned forward. "Mr. Bronson, restoring your memory is as important to me as it is to you. You have my word that I will do everything in my power to make it happen." He reached out and offered his hand.

Jake shook it. The man couldn't have been more sincere, he thought. He felt lucky to have his help.

Everything's going to be okay.

* * *

Victor was pleased with himself. The hypnosis drug coursing through the American's system worked wonderfully. Very few could resist its charms, he thought. The suggestions he'd planted in Bronson's memory had taken root. As long as he kept them well watered, the deception would continue. Using the restoration of Jake's memories as the key motivation had been Hans's idea, garnered after he'd overheard the American captives speaking about it. It was brilliant.

The helicopter lifted off. As it banked west toward Geneva, Victor saw a pillar of smoke rising from beneath a copse of trees. He smiled. His men had located the Americans' second vehicle.

Yes, he thought, sitting back in his chair. It was all coming together nicely.

All that remained was to tie up a few loose ends.

Chapter 28

Swiss Alps

TONY GRIMACED WHEN HE SAW THE TRAIL OF BLACK SMOKE rising from the location where Timmy had parked the van. The kid had gone silent on their comm net since Tony and Marshall had been nabbed an hour ago. Now Tony knew why. Timmy wouldn't have stood a chance against Victor's thugs.

The helicopter disappeared from view. "Show's over," the guard said in guttural English. It was Pit Bull. He had a lump on his forehead the size of a golf ball. A Band-Aid hid the puncture wound from the hypo Tony had shot into him. He jabbed his pistol into the small of Tony's back. "Move it."

The remaining guards pulled out the weapons they'd hidden during the charade. They corralled Tony and his friends and escorted them back to the castle.

Ten minutes later Marshall said, "We're in some deep shit this time."

"Could be worse," Tony said.

"Yeah? How'd you figure?" After a beat he added, "I mean, other than being dead."

"They coulda crammed us in those tiny cells in the dungeons."

Marshall's shiver was real. He rattled his head as if trying to shake off an encounter with a ghost.

They were in a ten-by-ten storage room within the gondola station. Other than a few slivers of wood on the concrete floor, the space was empty. A cluster of new halogens on the ceiling suggested something important had been stored here. The temperature had continued to drop as a new storm front moved in, and they'd been allowed to keep their coats. Tony had taken that as a sign that the guards wanted to keep them alive. At least for a while.

"Quiet down, you two," Lacey said. "I'm trying to listen." She had her ear pressed up against the steel door. There were faint voices from the other side.

"Lacey," Tony said gently. "Remember, you don't speak German?" The drug from the tea she'd drunk had worn off for the most part, but Tony was still worried about her.

She shook her head. "No. But I can interpret inflection and tone well enough. The guys on the other side sound pretty relaxed."

"Why shouldn't they be?" Marshall said. "They've got Jake. We're locked in a room surrounded by granite and steel. And once they receive the order, all they've gotta do is heave us over the cliff. It'll look like a climbing accident."

"If that's the case," Tony said, "then they've got another thing comin'." He clenched his fists. "Because a few of them will be going down with us. I can promise you that."

The trio grew silent at the prospect. Tony cracked his knuckles, Marshall paced, and Lacey listened at the door. None of them had spoken of Timmy. It was too painful.

They'd all seen the smoke.

"Hey," Lacey whispered urgently. "There's something happening."

They pressed their ears against the door. Shouts echoed from the adjoining chamber. They were followed by a rush of fading footfalls. Then all they heard was the swirl of wind from the growing storm.

"I think they're gone," Lacey whispered.

"What do you think happened?" Marshall asked.

"Shhh," Lacey said.

There was a shuffle outside the door. A moment later, the electronic lock disengaged. All three of them jumped back. Tony braced himself for the worst. He took three rapid breaths, tensed his muscles, and prepared to charge.

The door swung open.

The sight took his breath away.

"Timmy!" Lacey said. She rushed forward and threw her arms around the scientist. He wore a climbing harness around his waist and thighs. "You're alive!"

Timmy blushed. "I had to stay alive. Tony told me I was the only backup."

Tony and Marshall patted the kid on the shoulder so hard he nearly fell over.

"Dude, am I glad to see you," Marshall said.

"I was scared shitless on that cliff face," Timmy said. "I can't even believe you do that for fun."

"Let's get the hell outta here," Tony said. He moved toward the exit.

"Hold on," Timmy said, checking his watch. "We can't leave for another sixty seconds."

Tony didn't want to wait, but the kid had just infiltrated a fortified position entirely on his own. He had to trust him. "So what the hell happened, anyway?" he asked as they counted down the seconds.

Night had fallen, the wind howled, and snow sprayed into the cavernous space. Timmy moved to the gondola control station while he explained. "I knew something was wrong when I couldn't reach anyone at San Michelle."

"Oh, no," Lacey said.

Timmy studied the placard beside the controls while he spoke. "I tried both protocols we set up. I couldn't get through on either of them."

Tony said, "If anything's happened to those kids—"

Timmy cut him off. He'd apparently already compartmentalized the emotional "what ifs" of the situation. His mind was a thousand miles beyond them. "When the van's perimeter alarms went off," he said, "I knew we'd been found out. I had just enough time to gather a couple things and hightail it out of there before the patrol showed up." His hands slid from one control to another.

"They took Jake," Marshall said.

"I know. I saw the helicopter take off. But I think I know where they're going."

"Where?" Marshall asked. They all waited intently for Timmy's reply.

"Geneva. The conference. Victor has a residence there. That's where they'll hold him until Victor' s ready to stick him in that damn chair."

"We've got to stop him," Lacey said.

Tony said, "Damn straight."

"I know," Timmy said. "But first things first." He turned to face Marshall. He blew out a long breath before continuing. "Marshall, there's something I need you to do."

"O...kay," Marshall said, drawing the word out.

Timmy pointed sequentially to two buttons and a throw switch on the control panel. "As soon as you hear the signal, I need you to press this button. That's going to send a warning signal to the gondola station down below."

"Huh?"

"Then wait five seconds and press this one. That'll start up the motor."

Marshall cocked his head and looked at Timmy as if he were crazy.

"Then lift this safety guard and throw the switch. That'll send the gondola on its way."

Marshall hesitated as he absorbed the intent behind the instructions. The interchange from that point forward was faster than the disclaimers at the end of a pharmaceutical commercial.

"Will I have time to jump on?"

"Yes, but you don't want to do that."

"I don't?"

"No. You want to run like hell to the garage."

"I do?"

"Uh-huh. That's where we're going to be."

"But the bad guys will think we went down the mountain?"

"Exactly."

"What's the signal?"

"A revving snowmobile."

"When do we start?"

"Right now." Timmy woke his smartphone. The active application presented a glowing red button in the center of the screen. The countdown beneath it was at six seconds.

"I lured them to the front gate with an explosion," he said.

Three...two...one.

He pressed the button. There was a series of muffled explosions. "I figured a few more blasts in the surrounding tree line ought to keep their eyes front for a few more minutes. Let's go!"

He took off running.

Lacey kissed Marshall. "I love you," she said. Then she and Tony sprinted after Timmy.

Tony glanced back at his pal. Marshall's hand hovered over the first button. The toes of one foot tapped the pavement faster than a woodpecker on a pine tree.

"Go!" Marshall said behind clenched jaws.

Tony nodded and ran after the others.

Stay alive, Jake. We're coming!

Chapter 29

Swiss Alps

TONY SPRINTED INTO THE SHED AND PUSHED THE PALM button beside the outer door. The motor hummed and the door rolled upward. A blast of frigid air charged through the widening gap. Timmy and Lacey donned thick snow jackets, helmets, and ski gloves. Tony did the same. He grabbed the largest helmet he could find. It was snug. He stuffed gloves in his coat pocket and looped a ready-made emergency backpack over his shoulders.

Lacey moved with calculated efficiency. She grabbed a spare coat, helmet, and gloves, straddled the lead snowmobile, and cranked the engine. It started immediately. She redlined it three times in succession. The high-pitched whine echoed through the space. Her head swiveled to watch the rear door.

Timmy's helmet dwarfed his slight frame. He held out two mini bricks of C-4. "These are the last two," he said, offering them to Tony.

Tony palmed the plastic explosives. Each brick was the size of a butter cube.

"You'll need these, too." Timmy handed him two wireless blasting caps.

"Uh-huh," Tony said absently. He pocketed the caps. His eyes scanned the surrounding structure with the expertise of a seasoned demolition expert. “Taking out the studs will do the trick,” he said, more to himself than to Timmy. He started toward the front corner of the shed.

A hail of gunfire halted Tony midstride. Marshall dove into the room and slammed the door behind him. “They’re coming!” he yelled.

Tony pocketed the explosives and straddled another snowmobile. He turned the key. The engine responded. Timmy clambered up behind him.

“Marsh!” Lacey’s scream was drawn out. Tony looked back. Marshall was still by the door. The guards would be on him any second. Tony didn’t have a weapon to cover his retreat.

What the hell was his friend doing?

Marshall’s back was to them, but Tony could see his fingers making entries on the ten-digit keypad beside the steel door. His head shook back and forth as he discarded one option after another. Finally, he glanced desperately about, grabbed a wrench from a nearby toolbox, and smashed the keypad.

The plastic shattered, the circuitry sparked, and a thin trail of smoke rose from the remains.

Marshall spun on his heel and ran toward them. “Fail-safe,” he said as he jumped on the back of Lacey’s sled. “Locks engage automatically when the keypad’s tampered with.”

“Shut up and put on your helmet,” Lacey said.

“How much time did you buy us?” Tony asked.

“No clue.”

Automatic fire jackhammered the door. The steel held.

Lacey gunned the engine and took off.

Tony followed.

They were only twenty meters into the blustering night when Lacey’s snowmobile jerked to a stop. Tony pulled up beside her.

“I can’t see a thing!” she shouted over the wind, lowering her face shield. Visibility was horrible. Wind-driven snow slanted across their headlight beams.

Timmy shifted behind Tony as he unzipped the side pocket of his backpack. "Use this," he said, handing Marshall his smartphone. The 3-D real-time image revealed the path down the mountain. "The GPS will keep you on track, but it won't show trees or other obstacles. So go slow. I'd do it myself, but I can't see around Tony."

Tony only half listened. His focus was on a copse of trees to his left. "I'll be right back," he said, jumping off the sled. Sinking up to his knees in the snow, he frog-stepped to the base of the trees and plunged his hands into the drift.

Pay dirt!

He pulled an assault rifle and a pistol out of the powder. He brushed them off and high-stepped back to the sled. The pistol went into his pocket. He handed the HK G36 assault rifle to Timmy. "Hold this," he said. After a moment he added, "Don't drop it."

"Way to go!" Marshall said.

They were Pit Bull's weapons, Tony thought. Or his sidekick's. Either way, it felt good to be armed again.

"Move out," Tony ordered.

They kept their speed up as much as they dared, weaving their way down the mountain, wary of the deceptive terrain, constantly checking over their shoulders. Pit Bull and his buddies should be on their tail by now.

Eventually, the thickening tree line forced them closer to the cliff. Tony reckoned the edge was less than ten feet to his right. The drop was 1,400 meters. They slowed to a crawl.

Ten minutes later, the wind died and the snow stopped falling. The moon shone through a gap in the clouds. They pulled to a stop. The engines idled.

"I don't like the looks of that," Lacey said, pointing ahead.

A string of crossed poles blocked their path. Their metallic yellow paint reflected off the beams from the snowmobiles' headlights. The *X* where the poles crossed was only a few inches aboveground. The top half of a stout warning sign stood in front of it.

"Anybody read German?'

"A little," Timmy said. "It basically says *go around*."

He didn't need to unbury the rest of the sign to figure out why, Tony thought.

Avalanche area.

Chapter 30

Swiss Alps

MOONLIGHT ILLUMINATED THE MASSIVE BOWL BEYOND the stakes. It was two hundred meters wide and stretched double that distance up the mountain. There was a sharp overhang above it that shadowed the top third of the bowl from the moonlight. No trees grew within its borders.

Marshall held up the smartphone. "The trail leads straight across," he said. "According to this, there's a ranger station on the other side."

"Kill the engines," Tony said. "Turn off your headlights." He and Lacey both switched off.

He slid open his helmet visor and dug through the emergency pack. There was a thick coil of rope, duct tape, flashlight, med kit, radio, and below that, binoculars. He used them and spotted the cabin immediately. "It's on a promontory on the opposite side. About thirty meters back from the bowl. There's a rocky clearing ahead of it, and…"

Tony refocused the lens. There was a second structure. It was an open-air platform supported by a thick column of concrete. Its base was about ten feet off the ground. A metal staircase provided access. The object on top of it captured his attention. It was wound in canvas, but the silhouette was unmistakable. "It's a cannon."

"A cannon?" Timmy repeated.

"Sure," Marshall said. "They use them for avalanche control."

"The ranger station looks empty," Tony said. A plan formed in his mind. He kept it to himself. "It looks like there's a fire road on the other side. Once we're there, we can full-throttle it to the bottom."

Right after I take care of the assholes behind us.

Lacey startled. She swiveled her head behind them. "Do you hear it?"

It was like the faint buzz of angry hornets. Flickers of light—at least eight pairs meant eight snowmobiles, eight men, maybe sixteen if they had doubled up—appeared over the ridge they had crested ten minutes ago. Tony didn't need the binoculars to confirm who was coming. He and Lacey cranked over their engines at the same time.

"We're going for it," Tony shouted over the sputtering rumble of the motors. "Stick to the low side of the bowl. No sudden turns. Keep it straight and steady, but get enough speed to make it up the other side." He flipped down his visor, steered around the protruding stakes, and dipped the nose down the slope. Lacey and Marshall's sled followed in their tracks.

It was like waterskiing on Lake Placid. No bumps. No waves.

Smooth.

Tony opened the throttle, and Timmy's grip tightened around his waist. By the time they were at the bottom of the swale, the speedometer was at fifty mph. As they climbed up the other side, Tony held full throttle to keep their speed up. His mind was already working through the details of the ambush.

They were twenty meters from the crest when the ground sloped abruptly upward. What had appeared from a distance to be a single smooth slope was actually broken in two by a sweeping upheaval of snow-covered granite. It was Mother Nature's version of a ski jump.

By the time Tony realized his mistake, the snowmobile was already airborne.

The nose was pointed at the moon. Its upward momentum stopped in midair, and Tony felt his stomach in his throat. Then gravity took over. The engine whined, Timmy yelped, and the sled fell backward.

There was a mighty whiplash when the machine hit the snow. The back of Tony's helmet cracked against Timmy's.

Then the world stood still.

The sled's rear end had impaled itself in the snow at a forty-five-degree angle. The front skis were suspended aboveground. The engine had died. Timmy clung to his waist tighter than a pallet strap on full torque. But there was no need. The kid's back was against the snow. Tony's full weight was on top of him.

"Are you all right?" Lacey shouted from the crest fifteen feet above them. They'd avoided the obstacle. She was bathed in the beams of Tony's headlamps. She rose on the footrests of her sled to get a better look. Marshall stood nearby. He was in front of a row of crossed warning poles. Snow-covered pines towered behind them.

Tony waved. He raised his visor and turned his head as far as the big helmet would allow. "Hey, kid," he said. "You okay?"

"I—I think so. Nothing feels broken."

Marshall shouted. "I'm coming down!"

"No. Wait!" Tony shouted. Something didn't feel right.

Marshall hesitated.

The sled shifted. Then it sank backward another three or four inches.

"Get off me!" Timmy cried. He threw his arms out to arrest the slide. Two-thirds of his helmet was under the snow. He wriggled beneath Tony's bulk. Tony grabbed the handlebars and shifted his weight upward.

The sled dropped another few inches. It was like quicksand.

Timmy panicked. His arms and legs flailed.

"Don't *move*!" Tony ordered with drill-sergeant authority.

The command broke through Timmy's fear. He stilled his limbs. The sled stopped shifting. But Tony heard a crackling sound beneath them—like the wadding of a piece of cellophane. He felt Timmy's chest heave in short, rapid breaths. The kid's helmet was completely submerged. If not for the visor, he'd be sucking snow.

Timmy's voice was muffled. "Jesus Chr—"

"Don't talk," Tony said. "Conserve your wind. I've got a plan."

He saw Marshall take a tentative step forward. His foot sank to his knee, and a short wave of snow cascaded toward the sled. He backed up and shook his head.

"No way I can make it down there," he shouted. Tony noticed that Lacey's attention was up the mountain. Their pursuers were getting closer. Time was running out.

"Timmy," Tony said, "I need you to slide the rope out of my backpack. No quick movements."

Tony still gripped the handlebars. He stiffened his arm muscles and eased his weight upward to create a pocket of air between them. Timmy shifted beneath him. There was a tug on Tony's shoulder straps. The sled shifted a fraction and Timmy stilled. But when the machine steadied, he resumed his task.

The calmness in Tony's voice didn't reflect his churning gut. "Secure one end to your harness," he said. Timmy's movements were slow and steady as he performed the task. Half a minute later, the fifty-foot coil of rope sprouted into view.

"Way to go, kid," Tony said. "We're halfway there. Prepare yourself, 'cuz I gotta let go of the bars. You ready?"

A tap on the shoulder told Tony he was. He lowered his weight back onto him. The kid's body shivered.

"You ready up there?" Tony shouted.

Marshall stood as close to the edge as possible. He rubbed his gloved hands together like a receiver before the opening kickoff. "You get it here. I won't miss."

Tony avoided any jerky movements as he slowly unwound a six-foot length of slack. He tied a slipknot and gently looped the rope down over his head and around his chest.

The sled inched downward despite his precautions.

He readied the coil of rope and gauged the distance up the slope. "We're gonna drop like a tank when I toss this," he said. "So secure it quick."

"I'm on it," Marshall said. Lacey stood ready beside him.

Tony cocked his arm, gritted his teeth, and hurled the rope up the hill.

The snowmobile sank three feet.

Tony's world went pitch black. Snow covered his face and mouth. He sensed the sled continuing to slip farther into the depths. He punched a fist upward. It didn't break the surface. Timmy struggled beneath him. Thirty seconds passed. Then forty. His lungs cried for release. There was a loud crack, and he felt the ground suddenly give way beneath them. A curtain of snow cascaded around them. The rope snapped rigid, and suddenly he and Timmy were swinging in midair. They hit the mountain wall, watching in shock as their snowmobile tumbled into an abyss below them. Its headlamps illuminated the walls of the natural fissure. It struck an outcrop and spun end over end until it crashed into the ground in a fiery explosion.

"Get with it, you guys," Marshall shouted from above. "I've secured the rope. But we can't haul you out together. Move to that shelf and we'll go one at a time."

Timmy was suspended four feet below Tony. The assault rifle was still slung across his shoulders. "You still with me?" Tony asked.

"Hanging in there."

This kid's growing on me, Tony thought.

The five-by-ten-foot shelf was within easy reach. They climbed up. Tony disconnected from the rope so that Marshall and Lacey could haul Timmy up. When they threw the rope back down,

Tony saw that the bottom third of it had knotted loops at eighteen-inch intervals. Good thinkin', Marsh, Tony thought, as he stepped onto the first rung of the makeshift ladder—there was no way the three of them could've hauled his dead weight out of there. On the way up, Tony studied the geological gash that had almost become his tomb. It was as if God had cleaved into the mountain with an ax and then covered the blemish with a land bridge. But erosion had carved a ten-foot-wide hole in the bridge. A protective guardrail encircled it. Ice and snow had hidden it until Tony's ski-jump stunt shook it loose. The crossed poles had apparently warned of the danger—as had the half-buried warning sign they'd ignored earlier.

As soon as Tony got to his feet next to the others, he heard the faint buzz of snowmobiles. Discarding his helmet, he stared up the mountain. The flicker of headlights in the distant trees told him that their pursuers were only three or four minutes away.

He pointed to Marshall and Lacey. "You two get the cover off that cannon. Aim it at the top of that bowl. Timmy, you're with me."

He high-hurdled through the snow toward the ranger station. Timmy followed in his trail. Marshall and Lacey climbed onto the snowmobile and carved a path toward the platform.

The door to the station was padlocked. Two shots from the pistol drilled through the hasp. Tony shouldered through. The main room was furnished like a combination hunting cabin and office. Couch, sitting area, fireplace, desk, and equipment. A door led to a small bedroom and bath. He grabbed two walkie-talkies from the desk and threw one to Timmy. Then he pointed to a rack of skis and poles. "Grab two sets and get to the platform."

The skis went cockeyed when Timmy slung them over his shoulder. He repositioned them with a determined grunt and trotted out the door. Tony beelined to an equipment cabinet. Another padlock. Another 9mm bullet. He swung open the door and breathed a sigh of relief. He cradled the 105mm Howitzer round and raced outside.

By the time he scaled the platform, the cannon was uncovered and pointed up the mountain. Tony handed the heavy round to Marshall. “Don’t drop it.”

He raised the big gun’s elevation with two turns of the adjustment wheel. Satisfied, he opened the breech. Marshall slid the round into the chamber. Tony closed the breech and pointed to Marshall and Lacey. He knew they were avid skiers. “You two are on skis. Get going. Tim and I will catch up on the sled.”

The couple nodded. They hurried off the platform.

Tony and Timmy watched the headlights grow closer on the opposing ridge. Tony figured they’d clear the trees in about ninety seconds.

“They’re all going to die, aren’t they?” Timmy asked.

“It’s them or us. Go down below and get out of sight.”

Tony ducked behind the cannon and grabbed the lanyard. He was gonna wipe the bastards from the face of the earth.

It couldn’t be any easier than this, he thought.

That’s when he heard the distant thrum of the chopper.

Chapter 31

Palais des Nations
Geneva, Switzerland

"DROP US AT THE WEST GATE," VICTOR SAID TO THE limousine driver.

"Of course, sir."

Victor pressed a button overhead to close the driver partition. "We might as well enjoy a last look."

"*Jawohl*," Hans said with a sharp nod. He sat tall in the plush leather seat beside Victor. With calculated precision, his gaze alternated from one side of the vehicle to the other.

The stretch Mercedes turned down a broad street lined on either side by poles bearing the flags of nations from across the globe. News vans were parked up and down the adjoining streets. Staging areas for network and affiliate crews had been cordoned off in the greenbelts. TV cameras followed the limo's progress. A photographer stepped forward in the hope of getting a glimpse inside. He was quickly warded back by the UN security team that lined the curbs. There were others in sniper positions on neighboring buildings. Victor ignored them all. Instead he contemplated the scores of colorful banners that flapped in the breeze as they drove by—each one a symbol of independence born from the blood of countless souls.

Soon there will be only one.

The Aisle of Flags led to the stately west entrance of the Palais des Nations. The immense art deco complex was situated in Ariana Park overlooking Lake Geneva. It was built between 1929 and 1936 to serve as the headquarters for the League of Nations. It later became home to the United Nations, and was known as the largest and most active center for conference diplomacy in the world. For the next three days, it was hosting a summit on world hunger.

At least that was what the public had been led to believe, Victor thought. Yes, world leaders would put on a good show during the general assemblies. But the real work would be addressed during breakout sessions that were sealed from the public.

When the car pulled up to the circular drive, a network of ropes and portable barricades kept the reporters and onlookers at bay. Hans exited first. Victor waited patiently while his man confirmed that the path was clear. Victor straightened his tie and brushed the front of his tailored blue suit. That's when he noticed the random strand of white cat hair on the seat. The pet had been with him for ten months—far longer than its many predecessors. Remembering his session the day before brought on a flash of remorse, and he realized he missed the animal. It was an unexpected emotion, especially in light of the lack of any such feelings after the final childhood session he'd had with his father.

"All clear," Hans reported, interrupting his reverie.

Victor shook off his emotions and exited the car. There was a collective sigh of disappointment from the crowd. Photographers lowered their cameras, and spectators dropped from tiptoes. A few of the more seasoned reporters seemed to recognize Victor, but none of them were interested enough to shout out any questions. They'd come for bigger fish, most of whom should have already arrived by now.

The anonymity suited him.

He walked through the security checkpoint at the west gate passageway. Hans was at his side. The first courtyard stretched a hundred meters ahead. Its central greenbelt was lined with mature trees.

The rectangular structure surrounding it towered seven stories tall—and this expansive section represented barely a third of the entire complex. Two dignitaries appeared to be having a heated discussion up ahead. Their respective entourages shifted uneasily behind them. Victor steered a course around them. One of the men speaking noticed him pass. He offered a subtle nod. Victor kept moving.

It would be a ten-minute walk before they navigated the lobbies, hallways, and galleries between here and their final destination. Normally, Victor would have been dropped off at the opposite end of the property. But this diversion was important to him.

The *palais* was home to a unique collection of art from around the world. Donations were made by governments and individuals alike, as expressions of their commitment to human rights and the well-being of mankind—a sentiment he appreciated despite the naïveté of those who expressed it. The property was stocked with rare treasures that included paintings, engravings, sculptures, tapestries, frescoes, and even caricatures.

It was a Russian painting by Mikhail Romadin that Victor had come to see. He stopped before it, his hands behind his back. It was titled *Staring Indifferently.* The colorful oil-on-canvas creation depicted an endless mass of people—from all walks of life—gazing with total indifference upon a distant nuclear explosion.

Worth a thousand words, he thought. The image evoked memories of his childhood—of a father who believed that external expressions of emotion opened the door to exploitation by those around you.

It was a week after his fifth birthday. Victor awakened to discover his pet lying dead at the foot of his bed. The Swiss Mountain Dog had been his guardian and playmate since birth. He was devastated. The castle was nearly empty. The staff was at church in the village, and his mother was in Paris on a shopping trip. He ran to his papa's study. Tears flowed. Papa sat in his reading chair. There was no book in his hands. It was as if he'd been waiting for him. He opened his arms, and Victor tumbled onto his lap. It was a rare moment. Joseph Brun was an intimidating presence—and not given to outbursts of emotion.

"Let the tears flow, my son. They shall be your last."

Victor brushed off his confusion over his papa's words. He sobbed and curled tighter in his father's embrace.

It was only a minute or two later when Papa reached beside the chair and retrieved the leather riding crop. The sight of it frightened Victor. He'd seen Papa use it on the horses.

Papa moved forward in the chair, and Victor slid from his lap and stood before him.

"It is time for your first lesson," Papa said. He gripped his son's wrist with his free hand.

Victor stiffened.

"Listen carefully, my son, because what I'm about to teach you has been passed down from father to son for nearly a thousand years." Papa's eyes seemed to glaze over as if he recalled a distant memory. "It won't be pleasant. I'm sorry for that. But you must trust that it is necessary. Eventually it will become the cornerstone of your strength, helping to mold you into the man you must become before you can take your rightful place as leader of Castle Brun."

"I—I don't understand."

"I know," Papa said, his attention still seemingly in the past. "I didn't either, until I was much older. But it is the single most important thing that I must teach you...and you must learn. Regardless of the toll."

Victor was frightened by his father's intensity. He tried to pull away, but Papa's grip tightened.

"Regardless of the toll," Papa repeated under his breath. He refocused his gaze on Victor.

"You cry too much," Papa said. "It is a weakness." He held the crop aloft. "You will stop now."

Victor was overwhelmed. Instinctual reactions took over. His face contorted, and he burst into tears.

His father struck him for the first time in his young life. The crop whipped across his buttocks. A wave of fire spread through his system. The physical pain was horrible, but the emotional anguish was all-consuming. Victor was terrified.

Papa's face remained neutral as he studied Victor's reaction. When Victor sobbed louder, Papa struck again.

And again.

Each swipe of the crop was separated by a brief pause, giving Victor a chance to compose himself.

Finally, Victor found the strength to hold his breath. He choked back his tears. His body trembled, but he didn't cry. He hid his terror and did his best to return his father's calm stare.

At the end Joseph Brun said, "Your outward expressions speak louder than words, my son. They can reveal your vulnerabilities. Or they can be a valuable tool. Do not underestimate their power."

It was the first of many lessons.

It wasn't long before Victor took to practicing on his own in front of the mirror. When self-infliction of pain brought too much attention from his mother, he took to including small animals in his sessions.

He was a fast learner.

Victor studied the images on the canvas. He doubted that the artist intended that the indifference on the faces of those in the painting be feigned. No, he thought, this was a depiction of the true nature of modern-day man—with no concern for the devastation wrought in his wake, so long as it didn't affect him.

The painting had moved Victor since the first day he'd seen it, years ago. Unfortunately, the original had not been available for sale. So he'd commissioned a reproduction. It was one of his prized possessions. He'd even considered a plan to swap the two, but in the grand scheme of things it hadn't been worth the risk. Still, it was a shame that the original would remain here.

Hans checked his watch. "It's time, *Mein Herr*," he said.

Victor sighed.

A few minutes later he was in a private viewing room, looking down upon the grand assembly. The fan-shaped room was designed to hold 880 people. There were over one thousand in attendance. Extra chairs had been brought in to accommodate the overflow. Statesmen and ministers of every major country were present. But it was the unprecedented presence of the leaders of the fifteen permanent and temporary members of the UN Security Council that had drawn the world's eyes to the summit. Members of the media lined the back of the room. Video cameras streamed. Security agents from a joint task force were positioned at strategic points throughout the auditorium.

Twin video screens on either side of the room depicted a stream of images of starving families and children. The event was hosted by the Food and Agriculture Organization of the United Nations. Its director general spoke from the center-stage dais. Victor flipped a switch on the speaker under the window.

"Previous summits helped to identify the problem. But in hindsight, they did little to resolve it. As a result, it is estimated that more than a half billion children will grow up physically and mentally stunted over the next fifteen years. It is our job to prevent that!" Applause erupted. When it settled down, the speaker said, "So let's roll up our sleeves and get to work. The breakout sessions shall begin in thirty minutes."

A final round of applause. Then people rose from their chairs. Security agents peeled from their positions to accompany their respective charges.

It was all very calm and organized, Victor thought, as people began to file out of the room. Of the thousand people milling about, fewer than sixty knew the real purpose of the summit. They departed through a separate door near the front of the stage. It led to the secure basement levels. He marveled that the cooperating regimes had been so successful in keeping the secret of the twin pyramids. Of course, the alternative would have been world panic. And everyone wanted desperately to avoid that.

Well, he mused, not everyone…

Chapter 32

Palais des Nations
Geneva, Switzerland

THE UNDERGROUND BUNKER HAD BEEN CONSTRUCTED AS A bomb shelter. It currently resembled a futuristic NASA launch center. The expansive chamber consisted of a central floor space surrounded by a mezzanine balcony with offices and meeting rooms. The main floor was the size of two basketball courts. Technicians and science engineers worked at concentric rows of computer stations surrounding a ten-foot-square electronic platform—above which rotated a car-size 3-D hologram of one of the pyramids. A forty-foot-wide display occupied the two-story wall at the end of the room. The streaming video showed images and clips of mankind's heroes of peace: the Dalai Lama, César Chávez, Mother Teresa, Reverend Martin Luther King Jr., and many others. There were videos of people from every faith as they celebrated and prayed in their churches, mosques, synagogues, and temples. There were baseball and soccer games, New Year's and Carnival celebrations, and even scenes from the free-love generation at Woodstock. It was like watching clips from the History channel—with all hints of violence edited out.

The scenes and accompanying narrative were intended to depict humankind as a species that embraced life and begged forgiveness for its past transgressions. The stream was being transmitted from Earth to the twin pyramids that orbited overhead.

"Has there been any response?" the British prime minister asked. He'd hesitated on the balcony as the delegation was being escorted into the meeting room behind them. A few others stopped as well, including the US and Russian presidents and the general secretary of the Communist Party of China. Victor stood among them.

"Nothing yet," Victor said. "But Dr. Finnegan believes there is hope that a new combination of signal wavelengths might get through. It's a bit over my head, to be honest. However, he will explain it during the briefing."

"And what of the chair?" the Chinese official asked.

"It gathers dust in a room down below. I'm afraid that without the mini and Mr. Bronson, it's quite useless." Each of the delegates was familiar with the role that Jake Bronson had played in launching the pyramids in the first place. When the objects had returned six months ago, they'd all been a party to the decision to bring him out of his coma—at any cost. It had been a terrible blow to their plans when both Jake and the mini had perished in the fire. Victor motioned toward the meeting room. "Shall we proceed?"

They filed into the room and took their chairs around the racetrack-shaped conference table. Victor stayed near the door.

The man at the lectern had a salt-and-pepper beard and longish gray hair that curled over his collar. Unlike everyone else in the room, he wore no tie or sport coat. The sleeves of his white shirt were rolled up. His clothes were wrinkled.

"For those of you who don't know me, my name is Albert Finnegan. People call me Doc. I've been responsible for the Obsidian Project for seven years. The fact that I still hold the position after my good friend—former President Jackson—lost his bid for reelection tells me I must be doing something right." He was awarded with a nod from the current president.

The sixty-six-year-old scientist removed his frameless glasses and rubbed his bloodshot blue eyes. Despite his exhausted appearance, his friendly demeanor seemed to soften the tension in the room. He sighed, replacing his glasses. "I notice some new faces in the crowd," he said. "For their sake, I'll start with a summary brief." He blew out a breath. "There's still so much we don't know about the objects. How could they possibly have returned from their home planet so quickly? What is their timetable? Are they operating independently? Or are their makers controlling their actions? If so, why have they not opened a dialogue with us? We learned six years ago from Mr. Bronson that their purpose is to be the judge, jury, and executioner in the mother of all trials—with nothing less than the fate of mankind hanging in the balance." He motioned with his hands to indicate all of the people in the room. "We are the court-appointed advocates whose job it is to fight on humanity's behalf." He paused before adding, "And it's time for closing arguments."

Doc pointed to the wall monitor behind him. A video image of Mahatma Gandhi was on the screen. One of his quotes scrolled beneath him. *You must not lose faith in humanity. Humanity is an ocean; if a few drops of the ocean are dirty, the ocean does not become dirty.*

"That's what our video stream is all about," Doc said.

"And how have the pyramids responded?" someone asked.

Doc's shoulders sagged. "They haven't. But that doesn't mean the message isn't being received. Their technology is too advanced to assume otherwise. The question is, are they paying attention? The answer lies in our ability to establish two-way communications. That's what we're working on now."

"Any progress?" the Russian president asked.

Doc shook his head. "Conventional approaches have failed. Currently, we're experimenting with various combinations of musical chords embedded within the transmissions. That's how Mr. Bronson originally solved the riddle that unlocked the pyramids in the first place. Unfortunately, the fire that killed him four months ago also destroyed portions of the record of his debrief. Our team is still trying to piece together the remnants. Given enough time, we'll solve it. So we remain…hopeful."

Doc paused while he let the information sink in. Victor wasn't surprised when all he got in return was a number of somber expressions. Finally, Doc added, "Any questions?"

By the time the barrage of questions began, Victor had left the room.

It was time to look in on Jake Bronson.

Chapter 33

Isola di San Michele

Francesca wasn't hungry, but she needed to keep up appearances for her children's sake. Dinner had always been a strong ritual in her family, so observing it here in the underground hideaway was only fitting. She used her fork to wind another clump of spaghetti into the spoon she held with the opposite hand. She took a bite. The sauce was her mother's recipe—her father's favorite. He'd become expert at cooking it since his wife had passed so many years ago. He sat across from her at the round table. The children sat between them. The other gondoliers ate in the adjoining kitchen.

"Shouldn't they have left a message by now?" Sarafina asked, referring to Jake and the team. She'd barely touched her food.

"No, no," Mario said calmly. "It's much too soon." He took a sip of red wine, glancing at Francesca over the rim of the stemmed glass.

Ahmed used his napkin to wipe a dribble of sauce from his chin. "I wish I could have gone with them. A castle in the Swiss Alps? What an adventure! We're stuck here surrounded by the dead."

And we're safe, Francesca thought. She prayed that Jake and her friends were as well. She shared Sarafina's concern. Their inability to use their cell phones to reach out to the others was frustrating. But for safety's sake the phones had all been disabled. They were too easy to track. Instead, Marshall and Timmy kept in contact with them by leaving messages at a third-party website. The last update had indicated they were about to enter the castle.

"Mind that you respect the dead, Ahmed," Mario said in response to the teen's comment. "The spirits have ears."

Ahmed swallowed a forkful of spaghetti. A lingering strand dangled from his lip, and he sucked it in. His expression was thoughtful. He seemed to be contemplating Mario's words. "I meant no disrespect, Grandfather. However, I must disagree with your statement. The Koran clearly states, *And behind them is a barrier until the day they are raised*. This barrier is known as the world of *Barzakh*, where the dead will stay until the Day of Judgment. Scholars interpret this to mean that no living person can communicate with the souls of the dead."

"I see," Mario said. "And what of your dreams, my boy? Do not the spirits of our ancestors speak to us, then?"

Ahmed thought about it a moment. He nodded. "Yes, but this is only because the soul of a living person, when sleeping, departs the *Dunyā* and experiences a brief death." He closed his eyes as he retrieved the quote. "Allah—exalted be He—says, *And He it is that takes your soul at night*. In other words, your soul tastes death while the body sleeps. But it is only during these short periods when both souls are dead that they can communicate."

"Ah, so you agree, then? The spirits have ears."

"No, that's not what I said. Actually…"

The friendly debate continued.

Sarafina shrugged and began to eat.

Francesca knew that her father had intentionally drawn Ahmed into the conversation. The table needed the distraction. She loved him for it.

She watched as Alex broke a piece of bread in half and mopped sauce from his plate. He hadn't needed the diversion.

He'd already finished his pasta. There had been a dramatic change in her son since he had met Jake. He radiated a sense of confidence that was resolute. It was as if he'd peeked into the future and knew that everything was going to be all right.

Francesca wished she shared the sentiment.

She'd always found wonder in her son's unusual nature. He faced the challenges of the world in his own special way. When he was an infant, it was the movement of a multilevel mobile over his crib that had grabbed his attention. She'd noted the markers for spectrum disorder not long afterward—lack of eye-to-eye contact, limited facial expressions, delayed vocal ability, and more. As a specialist in the field, she'd conducted her own tests. It seemed as if each one revealed an additional layer of depth that was indefinable by ordinary standards. Early on, Alex had exhibited a strong affinity for fractals. Something about their geometry offered him an appreciation for the patterns that his brain observed in the natural world. Science had discovered that many things previously considered as chaos were now known to follow subtle mathematical laws of behavior. Alex had apparently known this all along. It provided order to his world.

Eventually, Francesca had stopped testing and simply embraced his unique qualities. He didn't need a psychologist, she'd thought. He needed a mother. His fascination with fractals continued. When he wasn't studying images he'd retrieved from the Internet—snowflakes, fern leaves, galaxies, and the like—he was drawing his own. When he did neither, his screen saver generated one evolving digital fractal after the next.

Until today.

Alex's tablet was on the table beside him. Jake's face was the only image on the screen.

Her thoughts were shattered by the sound of gunfire.

Chapter 34

Isola di San Michele

FRANCESCA'S SHOCK WAS MIRRORED ON HER FATHER'S FACE. Mario lurched to his feet. The dining chair toppled behind him. There was a muffled explosion outside.

Sarafina screamed.

Three armed gondoliers rushed into the room from the kitchen. One of them tossed a double-barreled shotgun to Mario. He snatched it out of the air like a pitched oar from a boat. "How many?"

"Too many!" one of the men shouted as he and his compatriots stacked in front of the entrance door. "They are already in the tunnels!"

Mario's face went ashen.

Francesca knew why. If the assault had reached the tunnels, then those above were already dead.

Alex rocked back and forth in his chair. His eyes were closed. He hugged his tablet against his chest. Jake's image peeked out from beneath his arms. She picked up her son. Sarafina was already at her side.

Ahmed rushed to join the three men at the door. Francesca gasped when he pulled a switchblade from his pocket and flicked it open. The boy was seventeen years old, but he was ready to stand and die with the men.

The staccato cracks of automatic weapons echoed from the hallway beyond.

Mario took charge. He rushed beside the two gondoliers closest to the door. One of them had a white-knuckled grip on the handle. His enraged expression left no doubt about his intent to charge out. Mario stayed his hand. "You cannot go out there, my friend."

"My cousin was guarding the docks." The man's voice was strained.

"I know. We will avenge him. But we must wait until they break through. Then we shall kill them all."

Francesca shivered at her father's ruthless intensity.

The man nodded, grim faced. He and his partner stepped back and took cover positions on either side of the room.

"Rico," Mario said to the third man. "I need you with me in the back." He spun Ahmed around and aimed him toward the kitchen. "You, too. Let's go!"

"But—"

"And keep that knife handy. You may need it yet."

The acknowledgment had an immediate impact on the teenager. He stood taller. He folded the blade into the handle but kept the knife in his hand. Then he raced after Rico toward the kitchen.

Sarafina reached for Alex's tablet. "I'll hold that for you," she said breathlessly. He let her take it. Then he tightened his grip around his mother's neck and the three of them rushed after Ahmed. Mario brought up the rear.

They moved through the kitchen, past the bedroom, and down a hallway. It ended at the base of a narrow staircase. Its upper reaches were shrouded in darkness. Mario squeezed past them. "Stay here," he whispered. "Keep quiet." He followed Rico up the steps.

As a child Francesca had accompanied her father to the guild's hideaway many times. She'd loved sharing the secret with him. Each visit had seemed like an adventure. But in all those times she'd never been through the rear exit. It opened somewhere in the cemetery.

Ahmed edged closer to Sarafina. "It's going to be all right," he whispered. His firm disposition belonged to a man twice his age. She sensed the comfort it gave her children.

There were hushed voices above. Then the creak of a door.

Gunshots blistered the silence.

A yelp was followed by a cascade of thumps. They dodged to one side as Rico tumbled down the steps and landed at their feet. Blood gushed from two holes in his chest. He wasn't breathing.

Sarafina's scream was buried beneath two shotgun blasts. The reports reverberated throughout the corridor. A door slammed above, and Francesca heard bolts slide into place. Mario ran down the steps. His face was crimson. Smoke trailed from the twin barrels of his weapon.

He leaned over and pressed a finger against Rico's neck. He shook his head.

"*Bastardi!*" he growled.

More gunshots hammered against the door up above. Both exits were blocked, Francesca realized with a shudder.

They were trapped.

Mario turned to his daughter. "Quickly, child!" he ordered. "You know what must be done!"

Francesca's feet were moving even as her mind processed the full impact of her father's words. She couldn't believe this was happening. But there was no time for mournful consideration.

The children's lives were at stake.

Chapter 35

Isola di San Michele

THE STORAGE ROOM WAS SIX FEET DEEP. THE SHELVES ON either side were sparse. There were jars of pasta, a couple boxes of cereal, bottled water, and a scattering of canned goods. A wine rack filled the back wall from floor to ceiling. Only a dozen of the cubbyholes contained bottles. Mario removed the few that occupied slots in the bottom third of the wall. Then he reached into one of the empty holes and pulled a lever. A section of the rack abutting the floor shifted.

Francesca flinched. She knew what lay behind the false front.

Mario pulled the thirty-inch square of rack forward. The paneled wall behind it looked no different than those backing the rest of the room. Her father approached on hands and knees. He pounded on a section of the wall. It sounded solid. He shifted his aim and pounded again. There was a click as the spring-loaded locking mechanism disengaged. He pushed the hinged panel forward. A waft of stale air leaked out. It smelled of moisture.

And decay.

Sarafina and Ahmed shifted to get a better look. Even Alex was intrigued. He twisted in her embrace, and she allowed him to slide to the floor. He retrieved his tablet from Sarafina. Mario shone a flashlight into the cramped space. The batteries were old. The dim light reflected off cobwebs. He reached inside and flicked a switch, but the bare bulb that hung from the ceiling had burned out.

Francesca shivered. Her mind flashed on the childhood memory. She had been seven. Her father and his friends had revealed the hidden space to an initiate. She'd been watching, and when they had retired to the main room with a bottle of wine, she'd snuck back into the secret room. The interior light had worked then.

Until she'd closed the panel behind her.

The lock had engaged, and she'd had no idea how to release it from the inside. Her screams had gone unanswered. It was the need for a second bottle of wine that had led to her rescue a half hour later. It had seemed like days.

Her mouth went dry at the memory. "They will never find you in there," she said.

"I can't go in there!" Sarafina said. She appeared horrified.

"You will survive, daughter," Francesca said flatly. She was too unnerved to say much else.

Ahmed said, "Where does it lead?"

"Nowhere."

"Huh?"

The distant gunfire ceased abruptly.

Her father apparently didn't take that as a good sign. "We must hurry," he said, stepping aside. "Do not worry, you cannot get locked in. There is a pocket above the door with a release lever. Push it and the door will spring open."

"It leads nowhere?" Ahmed repeated. "Are you sure? A door to nowhere makes no sense. Why build it at all? This doesn't sound like a good escape plan to me. I wish Jake was here. Where is—"

"Quickly. Inside!" Mario said, pressing his hand into Sarafina's lower back to usher her forward.

She resisted. The fingers of both her hands played an unheard melody in the folds of her dress. Her intake of breath hissed as it crossed her bared teeth. It stopped abruptly when Alex stepped calmly forward. He turned the tablet so that Jake's image illuminated the way. Then he pushed aside the cobwebs and moved into the space. The top of his head missed the burned-out ceiling bulb by less than an inch.

Mario motioned again to Sarafina. "There is room for all three of you. But remember, sound travels through the walls. So you must remain absolutely quiet. Do you understand?"

Sarafina's mouth was agape as she allowed herself to be led into the space. Francesca's heart raced at the sight. Sarafina sat beside her brother. Her eyes glistened in the darkness.

Twin explosions shook the room. Blast waves from either exit rushed inward and took Francesca's breath away. Her ears popped, Sarafina screamed, and Mario shouted at Ahmed.

"Hurry!"

The boy hesitated. Mario grabbed him by the shoulders and captured his gaze. "It's up to you to keep them safe."

The order struck a chord. Ahmed nodded. He pocketed his knife and scrambled into the space. Sarafina and Alex had to shift to make room for him. Ahmed swiveled around and stared at Francesca as he closed the door between them. His expression was grim but determined.

She drew strength from it.

The sounds of assault rifles resounded down the hallway.

Each ricochet snapped a nerve, but it didn't stop her. She moved quickly to help her father shove the wine rack into place and redistribute the wine bottles.

Then she ran out of the room with her hands in the air. "Don't shoot!"

Three minutes later, Francesca sat on the sofa beside her father. Their hands were bound behind their backs. Her father had duct tape across his mouth. His nostrils flared with each rapid breath.

The main room was in shambles. The thick door had been blasted in two—one splintered half lay charred on the floor, the other hung limp from its bottom hinge. A veil of smoke hung in the air. It smelled like burned matches…

…and blood.

The two gondolier guards lay in bloody heaps on either side of the room. The walls behind them were puckered with bullet holes. Three more bodies were sprawled near the doorway. Each was dressed in a black assault uniform.

The man in front of Francesca wore black on black. The webbed belt at his waist supported a holstered pistol and spare magazines. He had a crew cut, dark eyes, and a thick bandage over his nose. "I'll ask you one last time," he said with a nasal twine. "Where are the children?" A strip of duct tape was stretched between his hands.

Francesca said nothing.

He shrugged. He leaned forward and wrapped the tape across her mouth. He took his time massaging the ends into the skin of her cheeks. His eyes never let go of hers. His breath was on her face. She sensed his lust.

"I met your boyfriend yesterday," he said softly. "He killed my friends." He tapped the side of his bandaged nose and added, "And he gave me this."

She glared at him.

His grin was feral. "I'm looking forward to returning the favor." He brushed a lock of hair from her forehead.

She flinched.

"Perhaps you and I can teach him a lesson…together."

But his words were lost on her. She'd heard something from the kitchen. It sounded like splashing.

"Take them," her interrogator said to the uniformed men standing at either side of the couch.

She craned her neck to see what was happening behind her. Rough hands pulled her and her father to their feet. The splashing grew louder.

They were halfway to the exit when she smelled the gasoline.

Francesca twisted violently in her guard's grasp. She saw three men backing into the room from the kitchen, each of them dispersing liquid from a ten-liter gas can. They systematically covered the walls, furnishings, floors, and bodies. The pungent odor filled the air.

Her shouts of appeal were backstopped by the duct tape. Her father grunted as well. He struggled to get free, and another guard clipped the back of his head with the butt of an assault rifle. Mario's eyes rolled, and he was dragged into the hallway. Francesca was pulled after him. Her breathing was ragged.

The interrogator was the last to step out of the room.

Her wide eyes connected with his. Her head nodded in time with the rapid beat of her heart. She pleaded frantically with her muffled voice and expression, trying to tell him, *Yes, yes! I'll tell you where they are!*

He simply smiled.

Then he removed a small device from a pouch on his belt. It was the size of a ring box. He flipped up the lid, twisted the underlying knob, and tossed it into the room.

The guard yanked her forward. She was propelled down the corridor. The interrogator was right behind her. There was a sudden rush of air, and she felt a blast of heat at her back.

Her scream was nothing more than a pitiful whine.

Chapter 36

Palais des Nations
Geneva, Switzerland

When Jake awoke, his mind was groggy. He blinked against the brightness from the fluorescent lights. The crust in his eyes told him that he'd been asleep for a long time. When he tried to bring his hand up to rub it away, he discovered it had been restrained on the arm of a chair. There was a butterfly needle taped to the inside of his elbow.

"Careful, please," the man standing in front of him said. He appeared to be in his midforties, with a bald pate, bulbous nose, and oversize horn-rimmed glasses that reflected Jake's image. He wore a lab coat with a pocket protector that held two identical silver-topped pens. He spoke in Italian with a German accent. "Please use your other hand, Mr. Bronson."

Jake did as he was told, taking stock of his situation as he wiped his eyes. An IV bag overhead metered clear liquid into his arm. It felt cool as it coursed into his system. An electrode was attached to his index finger. Several others were attached to his bare chest. A medical device beside him monitored his vitals. His heartbeat was slow and steady.

He shook his head in an effort to clear the cobwebs. The small, windowless room was stark, its white walls unadorned. A large flat-screen display had been wheeled in on a chest-high cart.

It was turned off. A tripod supported a camera that was aimed at Jake—the red light indicated it was recording. Two technicians sat at computer consoles on one side of the room. Jake noticed that both of them had the same silver-tipped pens clipped under the button seam of their polo shirts. They watched him.

"The wooziness will pass," the man said smoothly, offering him a glass of water.

He seemed friendly, Jake thought. He drank it down and handed back an empty glass. "Thanks." There was no label on the IV bag. He pointed at it. "What's in there?"

"Saline. It's nothing to worry about."

"Oh, okay."

The leather cushioning made the chair comfortable, but when he swiveled in order to get a better look at it, the hairs behind his neck stood on end. The back of the chair extended two feet over his head. There was a pyramid-shaped inset in its center. It was empty. A skullcap was suspended from the high back. It hovered over his head. It appeared to have been molded from a fine mesh of fiber optics. A forest of wires extended from the cap and the back of the chair. They came together in a bundle and disappeared into the ceiling.

Alarm bells went off in his mind, and he tried to rise. The man's firm hand on his shoulder stopped him. He brought his face close to Jake's and spoke softly.

"Everything is fine. Please relax." The man's voice was soothing. It drove other thoughts aside. Jake settled back into the chair.

"That's better. My name is Dr. Strauss. I was part of the team that cared for you during the coma. Do you recall?"

Jake shook his head.

"There is a friend outside who would like to speak with you," Strauss said. "Is that okay with you?"

Jake nodded.

The man turned to face the camera. He said something in German that Jake didn't understand.

The door opened and Victor entered. He was accompanied by Hans and two guards. Hans proceeded to the back of the room. He held a satchel. The others took up positions on either side of him, and something about them tugged at a corner of Jake's mind. But before it resolved, Victor moved forward and clasped his free hand. The handshake was firm.

"I'm so glad to see you, my boy," he said jovially. "We were worried about you!"

"W-worried?"

"Apparently the crack on your head was more serious than we thought. You've been out for quite a while."

Jake's eyes blinked several times as he tried to think back to what had happened. He remembered the helicopter ride and seeing his friends in front of the castle. But whatever happened before that was a blur. "Are my friends okay?"

"Of course," Victor said. "They are guests at my home on the lake. We'll be going to see them as soon as we're finished here."

"Good. Good," Jake said dully. "What is it we need to finish?"

"We're going to get your memory back, of course."

"Oh, good."

Chapter 37

Palais des Nations
Geneva, Switzerland

DR. STRAUSS'S DRUG WAS WORKING PERFECTLY, VICTOR thought. It had erased Bronson's short-term memory and made him compliant to suggestion. The American's infamous brain was his to control.

It was like a dream come true—his ancestor's vision coming to pass after nearly a thousand years. The story had been passed down from father to son for generations:

Andreas Brun was a pious man. He was also a savant. He saw patterns in the world that were invisible to others. It made him a master strategist and tactician, skills that drew him into the quest to rescue the Holy Land. But the violence of the Crusades had left him hollow. He returned home a wealthy man with no soul.

It was during the construction of his castle that he discovered the pyramid hidden in the mountain. He found personal salvation in the message of the glyphs that only he understood: Man would be punished for his violence. Judgment Day would come. Heaven's wrath would be meted out from an unearthly species wielding the power of the pyramid. Only the righteous would be spared. He made it his mission in life to prepare for that day.

The Order was born.

Yes, his ancestor's prediction was about to come true. Judgment Day *was* coming. Victor would see to it.

Unbeknownst to Doc Finnegan, the Order spies on the scientist's team had long ago hijacked the signal being sent to the pyramids, replacing it with one of their own. They'd hacked into the stream using the chair as an interface. Now—with Mr. Bronson's assistance—Victor suspected that they would finally be able to establish two-way communications, paving the way for a dialogue with the judges above. What better way to ensure that the Order would remain buffered from the holocaust?

Like Noah before the flood.

"I'm your friend, Jake," Victor said.

"My friend," Jake repeated.

"You can trust me."

"I trust you."

"Would you like to begin?"

The American nodded. He seemed eager to please. Victor motioned to the doctor.

Strauss stepped forward. "All right, Mr. Bronson. For your safety, we must secure your hands and feet to the chair. Is that okay?"

"Uh-huh," Jake said, moving his free hand and ankles closer to the sheepskin-lined straps.

The doctor buckled them. Then he lowered the flexible cap onto Jake's head. It flattened his hair and covered his skull from his brow to the top of his neck. There were half-moon cutouts for his ears. It appeared to be a perfect fit. Bronson seemed to stiffen as it was fitted into place. The doctor noticed.

"Are you okay?" he asked. His voice was silky. "If this is making you uncomfortable, I'll be happy to remove it. But you don't want that. Do you?" The last words came out as more of a suggestion than a question.

The American relaxed. "You're right. I'm okay."

"That's good. Next, I'm going to turn on the chair. You'll feel a slight vibration." Strauss reached around the back of the chair.

Victor stepped back. He recalled that Doc Finnegan had told him there was considerable risk in the procedure. Three had died already. Strauss threw the switch. There was a soft hum, and the bundle of fiber-optic wires filled with light.

None of it seemed to bother the American.

Strauss picked up a tablet from a shelf behind him. He made an entry, and the high-def video screen in front of Jake turned on. A real-time image of one of the two orbiting pyramids was centered on the screen. Stars sparkled in the background. Strauss handed the tablet to Victor.

"That's our target, Jake," Victor said, angling the tablet so the American could see the screen. He expanded his thumb and forefingers on the display, and the image zoomed in. The pyramid was ink black. It rotated slowly in an off-axis tumble. Its etched surfaces glimmered under the sun's reflected light. He tapped the tablet to freeze the frame when the base of the pyramid was visible. Then he zoomed in farther and the perimeter images of violence-wielding *Homo sapiens* came into focus. "Does any of this look familiar?"

* * *

Jake's mind was still foggy. The cool flow of the fluid dripping from his IV hadn't helped to clear it. His thoughts wandered to his friends. He was happy that he would be seeing them as soon as they were finished here. Afterward, he could get back to Francesca and the children. He missed them. He might not remember their past together, but the emotional attachment was as strong as ever. It was nice to know they were safe.

"Does it look familiar?" Victor asked. The man seemed dedicated to helping him retrieve his memory. That was nice. Jake liked him. Everyone around him seemed nice as well.

He stared at the video monitor. The images etched in the pyramid's surface had a photorealistic quality to them. He recalled the conversation he'd had with Timmy and his friends about the alien artifacts. They'd explained that he had been responsible for launching them into space six years ago. Now they'd returned. He narrowed his eyes and studied the glyphs in the hope they would trigger a recollection.

It was no use. He couldn't remember a thing.

"I'm sorry," he said. He shook his head and felt the tug of wires sprouting from the skullcap.

"That's quite all right," Victor said. "We're going to fix your memory soon enough. First step is to make the link."

"The link?"

Victor hesitated a moment before answering. He sighed. "Jake, the chair you're sitting in was designed by the people who kept you alive all those years. Good people, with your interests at heart. It's tuned to the unique wavelengths emitted from your brain. Its purpose is to allow you to communicate with the pyramids."

Even though Timmy had told him pretty much the same thing, Jake struggled to grasp the concept. "Really?" Having a unique history with the pyramids was strange enough, he thought. But they were inanimate objects. How was he supposed to communicate with them? He shrugged. The only thing he knew for sure was that Victor was a friend.

He could trust him.

"That's right," Victor said. "You see, it was your last contact with one of the pyramids that gave you amnesia. We believe the link will restore it."

Finally, Jake thought. "That would be great."

* * *

The lies rolled easily from Victor's lips. In actual fact, he couldn't care less about restoring the man's memories. Quite the opposite.

The true purpose for today's session was simply to determine if a two-way link could be made. If not, the man would be killed and Victor's team would continue to use the chair to transmit a one-way signal. But if so, Mr. Bronson would accompany the chair to the island—where his memories would be erased permanently and his brain used to provide an ongoing conduit with their benefactors above.

At Victor's signal, Hans opened the satchel. He reached inside with both hands and removed the lead-lined case holding the mini.

Chapter 38

Palais des Nations
Geneva, Switzerland

JAKE'S FOCUS WAS IMMEDIATELY DRAWN TO THE SQUARE metallic case. Something about it tickled a memory. It wasn't a good one. Hans stepped forward, and Jake grew uneasy. He shifted in the chair.

"Keep that away from me."

Victor held up a hand. Hans hesitated.

"What's the problem, Jake?" Victor asked.

Jake glanced from the case to Victor and the doctor. They both seemed to be studying him intently. He appreciated their concern. "I—I'm not sure. Something doesn't feel right."

The two men in front of him exchanged a curious glance. After a moment Victor said, "It's a key part of the process, Jake. Without it the chair won't work." He motioned Hans forward.

"No!" Jake pleaded. He struggled against the wrist and ankle restraints.

Hans held out the case, and Victor snapped open the four latches securing the top. "Don't worry, Jake. Everything's going to be just fine." He lifted the lid.

Jake felt a surge of energy course into him from the box. It scared him. He panicked. His body tensed and his heart beat double-time. "Put it back!" he shouted. Warning bells rang through his mind. He didn't comprehend why, but every fiber of his being told him that death waited inside that box. Instinct took over. Adrenaline shot into his system, and his body went into fight-or-flight mode.

But he could do neither. The straps held him fast. Terror overwhelmed his senses.

Victor hesitated. The lid was only an inch above the box.

Strauss rushed forward and placed steadying hands on Jake's forearms. Jake noticed a filled hypodermic syringe jutting from the folds of his lab-coat pocket. The sight of it fueled his dread.

"It's okay, Mr. Bronson," Strauss said. "The box can't harm you."

But Jake wouldn't listen. He bucked at the restraints. He felt a bead of sweat dribble from his forehead.

Strauss moved closer to capture his gaze. But Jake twisted his head violently from side to side as if someone held a poisonous snake before him. Finally, the doctor turned to Victor and ordered, "For God's sake, close it!"

The words seized Jake's attention faster than an aircraft's fire-warning light. He watched with stilled breath as Victor lowered the lid. It was in that brief instant of time that it dawned on him that he'd likened his reaction to something that only a pilot would understand. It had come naturally. In his mind's eye, he saw himself in a cockpit. The memory rushed back:

He was on his first solo flight in the T-38 during USAF pilot training. A multiple-bird strike during takeoff had killed engine number two. The fire warning light illuminated. The aircraft was only one hundred feet above ground level. The plane sank, the stall warning buzzed, and his hands moved instinctively on the controls as he executed the memorized boldface commands: throttles—max; flaps—60 percent; airspeed—attain setos minimum. He recovered just before impact...

Victor secured the latches on the container. Jake's eyes saw the action, but his brain latched onto the memory:

By the time he rolled to a stop after the emergency landing, the entire squadron was on the tarmac. Fire crews surrounded the blood-streaked plane. Cheers erupted as he stepped out of the cockpit. He saluted his commander, who said, "From the looks of your plane, Lieutenant, I think you must've nailed at least half a dozen of the bastards. It only takes five kills to make Ace. So congratulations!" The officer returned the salute with a wink. There were more cheers and gibes from his fellow airmen as they hoisted him on their shoulders and carried him to the tank—a recycled hot tub that had been donated to the squadron for the purpose of dunking students after their first solo flight. They threw him in. He'd never felt more proud.

Jake harbored the memory like a miser would his only coin.

It didn't fade.

When he refocused on his surroundings, all eyes in the room bore into him. The metal container was back in the satchel. He breathed a sigh of relief. Its presence still disturbed him.

But he was no longer afraid.

Chapter 39

Palais des Nations
Geneva, Switzerland

VICTOR HAD SEEN IT. THE AMERICAN HAD BEEN PETRIFIED when the lid was removed. The abject terror on his face hadn't been feigned. It seemed as if the man's mind had snapped. At one point Victor had even worried that they'd lost him for good. But as soon as he resealed the box, Bronson's fit had abated. And for a moment the man's thoughts had appeared to be a million miles away. However, when his attention finally returned to the room, Victor had seen a flicker of defiance cross Jake's features.

He didn't like it.

He stood outside the door with Strauss and Hans.

"What happened in there?" he asked.

Strauss said, "I've never seen anything like it. Did he react that way when you showed him the mini at the castle?"

"No. He seemed invigorated by it. To say the least."

"Then it had to be the drug."

"But he'd been drugged at the castle as well. With the tea."

"That's like comparing nicotine to heroin. The narcoanalysis drug is eminently more powerful. Yes, it's highly effective, but there can be serious drawbacks with some patients. Key among them is paranoia."

"Can we lower the dose?"

"It wouldn't help, especially after what just happened. The paranoia associated with the mini would outweigh the benefits of any hypnotic effects."

"What if he's blindfolded?"

"Normally, that might work. But not in this case, since he obviously senses something from the object. He'd know the instant it was no longer shielded."

Victor nodded. The American was fast becoming more of a nuisance than he was worth. He checked his watch. Phase two of his plan would be initiated in less than thirty minutes. By then, they needed to be in the air. To Hans he said, "Gather the extraction team. I want the chair—and possibly Mr. Bronson—out of here as soon as we're finished."

"*Jawohl.*"

He turned back to Strauss. "How long after the IV is removed before the drug wears off?"

"Less than five minutes."

"Very well. In that case, we shall give Mr. Bronson one last chance to cooperate. However, this time we'll use more conventional means to convince him."

Victor caught the glimmer of a smile from Hans.

He shared the sentiment.

Chapter 40

Swiss Alps

THE TACTICAL SITUATION HAD DONE A 180, TONY THOUGHT. The clearing weather had allowed Victor's men to call in air support. The thrum of the helicopter's rotors echoed off the distant slopes. There was no telling if it was right around the corner or three minutes away. Whenever it arrived, the copter would spot them easily with infrared. They were outmanned and outgunned. There was no way to escape without a fight.

Unless…

He rushed down the metal staircase. Marshall and Lacey had just started off on their skis. "Hold up!" he shouted. "Change of plans!"

Ninety seconds later, Tony's snowmobile steered around the crossed posts and nosed into the bowl. He was in plain view of Pit Bull and his pals, who peered down from the opposing ridge. He angled the snowmobile toward the apex of the bowl and poured on the gas. The treads dug in, the machine leaped forward, and a rooster tail of powder trailed in his wake. Three sleds dropped down the other side and accelerated on an intersecting course.

The bowl was four football fields in length from cliff to apex. Tony was two-thirds of the way to the top when he entered the shadow of the outcrop that towered above it. His headlights pierced the darkness. The slope steepened, and he stood forward on the sled to keep from flipping backward. When he felt the snow loosen beneath the treads, he switched off his lights and made a ninety-degree turn to the left. The deep shadows hid the change in direction from his pursuers.

He dropped the first of the C-4 charges and accelerated across the top of the bowl. The three attack sleds continued toward his original position. But after three or four seconds, they turned back in his direction. They sped into the mountain's shadow, and their silhouettes were replaced by three pairs of headlights.

Tony dropped the second package.

Then he faced the sled downhill and raced directly for the approaching headlights. He crouched low and opened the throttle to the max. He'd been tempted to bring along the assault rifle, but he knew if it came to a shoot-out, he and his friends would be done for. Instead, he brought a walkie-talkie. It was duct-taped to the handlebars. The talk button was locked in the ON position.

"Get ready!" He shouted the order to make sure Timmy would hear him over the rushing wind.

The handlebars vibrated. The speedometer indicated seventy mph. He shot through the oncoming trio faster than a stock-car driver past a checkered flag. Heads swiveled. He steered down the center of the bowl. When he broke from the shadow, four more sleds dropped from the ridge and took up the chase. They'd be on him in thirty seconds.

Then the helicopter popped up from the cliff ahead. It dipped its nose and flew directly at him. Its spotlight illuminated Tony like a Broadway star. Gunfire would follow any second.

"Now!" Tony shouted into the walkie-talkie.

The high-velocity plastic explosives blasted deep into the overloaded snowpack. It sounded like twin thunderclaps. The air trembled, the ground shook, and Tony's heart climbed into his throat.

He angled the snowmobile toward the jump, checking the scene behind him in the jiggling side mirror.

It takes only a pebble to start an avalanche, which meant that two quarter-pound bricks of C-4 were more than overkill. Twin spouts of snow blasted into the air. The shock waves loosened the hardpack, and a thundering white tidal wave barreled down the mountain. It sounded like the deep rumble of a hundred bass drums.

Then a thousand.

The three snowmobiles chasing him were overwhelmed in seconds. Those on his right skidded into 180-degree turns. The helicopter veered away.

Tony's sled hit the natural ramp, but this time around he was ready for it. He launched himself to one side as soon as the machine was airborne. He hit the snow and rolled. He was three feet outside the guardrail that encircled the crevasse. The sled's sky-bound momentum ended abruptly. It vanished tailfirst into the abyss.

Tony scrambled over the guardrail. The ground shook, the air filled with snow crystals, and visibility dropped to inches. His hands searched desperately for what his eyes could no longer see. The roar intensified.

A yank on his ankle startled him.

"This way!" Marshall shouted.

Chapter 41

Swiss Alps

THEY WAITED FOUR HOURS BEFORE DIGGING OUT OF THE snow. Tony figured that by then any of Victor's men who had survived the avalanche would presume them dead. The lack of infrared signals on the chopper's scope would have confirmed it.

They'd huddled on the shelf near the top of the cleft. The rope that Marshall had secured to the guardrail had provided access. When the mountain of snow rushed past overhead, a raging torrent had poured through the gap. But the huddled foursome had been spared the worst of it. Within seconds the opening above had clogged and their world had been plunged into silence.

And safety.

Marshall and Lacey had grabbed some additional gear from the ranger station—including hand warmers, snowshoes, and more rope, plus hand and foot ascenders to simplify the climb back up. They'd also brought a folding shovel. Tony used it now to burrow a forty-five-degree tunnel through the snowpack. When he broke the surface, he squinted against the brightness of the rising sun. The sky was clear and blue.

He popped his head over the lip and did a quick 360. The slide had contained itself within the bowl. There was no movement on either ridgeline.

"Looks clear," he whispered to Marshall.

He pulled himself to the surface and brought the assault rifle to the ready position. He scanned for threats. When he was satisfied they were alone, he said, “Shoes first.”

Marshall passed up four sets of snowshoes. Tony donned a set. “Give me sixty seconds to get to the tree line. I’ll cover you from there.”

Tony made it there with time to spare. He breathed easier. It appeared as if their ruse had worked. Lacey was the first out of the tunnel. She donned her snowshoes as Timmy crawled out. By the time Marshall made it to the surface, she was crouched beside Tony in the trees.

“Boy, am I glad to be out of that hole!” she said.

“You and me both.”

Timmy appeared to be struggling with the buckles on his snowshoes. Marshall knelt down beside him to give him a hand.

Tony motioned toward the ranger station. “Why don’t you go on ahead and see if you can rustle us up some coffee or hot chocolate?”

“Sure,” she said. She hesitated a second. “Hey, I hope you’re not trying to stereotype me with that request.”

“Wouldn’t dream of it. But keep your eyes peeled for a bagel and cream cheese while you’re at it.”

She harrumphed, winked, and trudged off. A minute later, Marshall and Timmy crested the ridge.

“Breakfast is thataway,” Tony said, motioning with his thumb.

Marshall grinned. Timmy breathed a sigh of relief. They made their way past him.

That’s when Tony noticed the flash of reflected sunlight from the overhang above the bowl.

He reacted instinctively. “Sniper!” he shouted, tackling his friends. They landed in a heap as the first round dug a fist-size chunk out of the tree in front of them.

“Run!” Tony shouted. He spun around and pulled the trigger even before the G36’s reflex sight came to bear on his target. He loosed three short bursts. The weapon's effective range was eight hundred meters. The rocks above the overhang were only four hundred meters.

That was the good news.

But the tango was firing from an elevated position. And he likely had a scope. Tony triggered one more burst and dodged behind a tree. He felt the disturbance of air beside his ear before the sound of the rifle shot registered in his brain.

Dammit!

At least he'd drawn the fire away from his friends, he thought. He saw them stick to the trees as they ran a dodge-and-weave pattern toward the cabin.

Tony jerked around the side of the tree and triggered two more bursts into the rocks. He somersaulted forward to get behind the next tree. By the time he realized his mistake, it was too late. His bulk was bigger than the tree he now crouched behind.

That's the bad n—

The bullet grazed his shoulder blade and impacted something solid in his backpack. It jackhammered him backward into the snow. His stomach leaped when he saw the clear sight line between him and the rocky ridge. He opened up on full auto.

The magazine clicked empty after two rounds.

He was a sittin' duck. His shocked brain froze for the fraction of time that it took for the faces of his wife and kids to flash before him.

There was a booming retort from behind him, and the stand of rocks surrounding the sniper exploded from the Howitzer's 105mm round. Boulders and body parts flew into the air. The blast echoed between the alpine summits. Tony rolled onto his stomach and stared at the cannon platform behind him.

Lacey waved back.

Chapter 42

Isola di San Michele

"THE SHOOTING STOPPED," SARAFINA WHISPERED. AHMED nodded. He sat beside her in the cramped space. They each had an ear pressed against the panel. Alex sat cross-legged behind them.

"What's going to happen?" Sarafina asked.

"Nothing good."

"How long before they get us out?"

Ahmed remained silent.

"How long?" she insisted.

Ahmed pulled away from the door, and she turned to face him. Her grandfather's flashlight was dim, but she could still see the grim expression on his face.

"You're asking me questions," he said softly. "But you already know the answers."

Her eyes moistened, but she shook her head, refusing to allow her mind to go there. Neither spoke for several moments.

She pressed her ear against the panel. The wood felt cool. She closed her eyes and listened. When they'd first entered, she'd heard her mother shout, "Don't shoot!" But the thick door and their location deep in the storage room made it impossible to discern the faint sounds Sarafina had heard since. All she knew for sure was that the shooting was over. But what did that mean? She stifled a sob.

Ahmed whispered to her. "It smells like something died in here."

She screwed her face into a question mark. "W-what?" He seemed to be studying her. That's when she realized his words were intended as a distraction. She appreciated the effort, but he could've picked a better topic. "Don't remind me," she said.

"There are dead people buried all around us."

"You said that before. Grandfather told you to show respect."

"It's like we're in a coffin."

"Are you kidding me right now?"

"Did you ever read 'The Cask of Amontillado' by Edgar Allan Poe?"

"You're sick."

"What? Creepy is the new cool, right? And this place is definitely creepy." He still had the folded knife in his hand. His fingers absently rolled it over and over again against his palm. It was one of his tells.

Somehow the sight of it calmed her. He'd risen above his own fears in order to soothe hers.

"Alex doesn't seem to think it's so creepy," she said.

Ahmed turned to follow her gaze. Alex had his back to them. He held his tablet face-out in front of him. The glow from its display illuminated the wooden slats in the back wall. They were discolored with age. One of them had a trio of wormholes in it. There was a tiny pile of dirt on the floor beneath them.

An abrupt roar came from the storeroom. The door trembled. The trio jumped.

"What was that?" Sarafina asked.

"Shhh," Ahmed said. "Listen!"

It began as a distant but constant rumble. It quickly grew in intensity, and it felt as if the air was being sucked from the room.

There were sounds of breaking glass and the smell of wine. The temperature rose.

Dear God!

"Fire!" Ahmed said.

"Out!" Sarafina screamed. Her hand went to the recessed pocket over the door.

"No!" Ahmed shouted, grabbing her hand. He placed it against the door. "Feel."

The door was warm under her touch.

"The fire's in the storeroom," he said. "We'll never get through."

Her first instinct was to embrace Alex. She turned toward him. His attention was still on the wall behind him. The palm of one hand hovered over a slit between two of the slats. She placed her hand beside his and felt a flow of air.

"Ahmed!" she said urgently.

But he was already one step ahead of her. He edged forward, flicked open his knife, and plunged it into the center of the wall. The five-inch blade sank to its hilt in the dry-rotted wood. He pulled the knife out, and a thick stream of dirt spilled into the room. He thrust again, higher on the wall. This time no soil rushed from the gash.

"Yes!" he said, jabbing the knife like an ice pick against the wall. Each impact dug a new hole. Wafts of cool, earthy air crept from the shadows beyond. He poked holes in a widening circular pattern.

The door at their backs felt like an open oven. Sweat poured from Sarafina's brow.

Ahmed widened a few of the holes with levered twists of the knife. The aged wood crumbled under the assault. When several of the holes converged into a fist-size opening, he dropped the knife and began to wrench pieces away with his hands. Parts of it came away easily. Others did not. When the opening was about eight inches wide, Sarafina aimed the flashlight within.

It was more of an oblong depression than it was a tunnel. It appeared to be about eighteen inches wide and a foot high at its center. She shivered at the prospect of crawling through it. The weak beam penetrated only five or six feet, but the rush of cool air filled her with hope.

"We can do this," she said.

Ahmed nodded and continued tugging on the wood.

She handed Alex the flashlight and moved in to help. Alex aimed the light at the opening. She grabbed the jagged edge of a slat and pulled with all her might. The wood resisted. She shrieked in frustration and brought her other hand to bear. The weakened wood cracked, and she tugged it loose. The opening in the wall widened. They kept at it. Both of their hands bled.

Steam began to rise from the inside surface of the storage room door. The flames could eat through any second. Ahmed grunted as he yanked on another slat. It ripped free. More of it came away from the wall than he'd expected, and a soccer ball–size chunk of earth fell from behind it. He kicked it aside.

"That's good enough," Sarafina said, measuring the width of the opening against Ahmed's shoulders. The hole was about thirty inches above the floor. "I'll go first. Then Alex."

"That won't work," Ahmed said, taking the flashlight from the child. "If there's more digging to be done, I'm going to have to handle it." He didn't wait for a reply. He pocketed the knife, pushed the flashlight ahead of him, and pulled himself into the opening. The beam of light led the way as he wiggled forward. He stopped when his ankles were still suspended in the room. Sarafina wiped sweat from her eyes as she strained to see past him. The dim light reflected on a tangle of white roots a few feet ahead of him.

"There's debris in here," Ahmed said over his shoulder. His voice sounded hollow in the tunnel. "But it's nothing to worry about." He scooted forward and said, "Okay, Alex. Your turn."

Her little brother tucked the slim tablet in its holster. He reached his arms and head into the opening, and she boosted him the rest of the way. His shirt was soggy with perspiration, but he'd never complained. He crawled forward on all fours but was forced to stop after a couple feet.

She stuck her head into the space. "What's going on?"

Ahmed seemed to be wrestling with something. "Some of this"—he grunted as he pulled something free—"stuff is embedded in the dirt. I'm working to clear it!"

The door at her back radiated waves of heat. The room was like a sauna. The exposed skin on her face and arms stung. An amber glow formed around the perimeter of the door, and smoke leaked into the space.

"Hurry!" she shouted.

"Almost there!"

Suddenly, the entire surface of the door seemed to blacken at once. A crack formed up its center. A thin flame licked the wood. In the half heartbeat that followed, the oxygen-starved flames drove through the crack and jumped to the ceiling. Shadows were cast aside, and the chunk of earth on the floor was revealed as a dirt-encrusted skull.

Primal panic electrified Sarafina. She dove into the tunnel. "Move!" she screamed. But the boys had already sensed the danger. Alex was several feet ahead of her and moving fast. There was a bright flash behind her, and heat singed her ankles. She scampered forward, clawing with her hands, pushing with her feet, and praying with every ounce of her being. She passed the pile of bones that Ahmed had dislodged. It was a rib cage. Remnants of rotted pine dotted the walls. The tunnel shifted every six or seven feet. More bones, scraps of clothing, an iron cross.

The guttural moan she heard was her own—prompted by the realization that the burrow they uncovered had been formed from rotted-out coffins.

The shaft twisted left. Then right. She followed on Alex's heels. Finally, she heard a splash up ahead. Ahmed's voice echoed. "Come on. We're clear!"

They'd dropped into a sewer tunnel that ran the length of the island. Heading north, they climbed the first exit ladder they came across and found themselves in a maintenance shed near the docks. Moonlight shone through the sole window. It cast a pale glow on the space. There was a workbench, a tool chest, and several shovels. But it was the twenty-four-pack of bottled water that drew her attention. She ripped open the shrink-wrap and they drank their fill. With a moistened rag, she wiped Alex's hands and face. Then she did the same for herself and passed the cloth to Ahmed.

The view through the window stretched across the lagoon. It was around 10:00 p.m. Boats crisscrossed the water. The lights of the ancient city glowed in the distance. Ahmed put his back to a wall and slid to his butt on the concrete floor. Alex sat beside him. He unholstered his tablet and flipped through images until he found the one he wanted. It was a photo of their mother. Sarafina snuggled next to him. She wrapped an arm around her brother and pulled him close.

"She's okay," she said. "So is Grandfather." She prayed it was true.

Alex nodded.

"I've thought about it," Ahmed said. "Those men came for Jake. They wanted him alive, remember? When they didn't find him, they would have taken Mother and Grandpa Mario as leverage. That means they won't be harmed. If they'd have found us, we would have been held hostage as well."

What he said made sense, she thought. She took comfort from the logic. "So if they find us, they will have even more leverage," she said.

"Exactly." He paused before adding, "We cannot let that happen."

They sat in silence for a while. There was a chill in the air.

"We can't stay here," she finally said.

"I know."

"We can't go home."

"No."

Her frustration got the better of her. She raised her voice. "So what the heck are we going to do?"

Ahmed didn't answer right away, but she could sense that the wheels of his brain were in full motion. When he finally replied, his first words were slow and calculated, as if he were still formulating the balance of a plan in his mind.

"There was a man in the old city," he began, "who was a good friend to Signor Battista..."

Mention of the terrorist's name brought quivers to her skin.

"He was an artist," he continued, "and a photographer. He created documents for the signor. Passports. Identification. They were friends. He even dined with us on occasion. Once, we visited him in his home on the canal. He will remember me."

"What use is he to us?"

"Don't you see? He will provide us with everything we need for our trip."

"Our trip? Where are we going?"

"To the safe house, of course. To meet up with Jake and the rest of them."

"What are you talking about? Father is at a safe house? Where?"

The voice that answered came from Alex's tablet. It was robotic. "*Avenue de Miremont.*"

Both of them gawked at the device. A Google satellite image of Geneva filled the screen.

Alex smiled.

Chapter 43

Geneva, Switzerland

"I HOPE YOU LIKE IT STRONG," TONY SAID, POURING A steaming cup of coffee. "You may wish you made this yourself."

It was 10:30 a.m. They were in the Geneva safe house. They'd made it off the mountain in less than an hour. A rental car from the village brought them into the city. Timmy drove. The rest of them napped for the two-hour drive.

"Not likely," Lacey said, reaching for the cup. "Trust me, you don't want me anywhere near the kitchen."

"No kidding," Marshall said from the other side of the room.

"Shut up!" Lacey said. "My vows never said anything about cooking. Besides, I like a man who knows how to take care of a lady." She took a sip and wrinkled her nose. "Uh…what else are you serving?"

Tony pulled a pastry out of a bag. "Here, I baked it myself."

"I'll bet."

He placed the glazed croissant on the plate and slid it across the kitchen counter. The two- bedroom apartment wasn't big, but it had everything they needed—including a hidden closet with weapons, comm units, and reconnaissance gear. The main room included a kitchen, living room, and dining area. The curtains were closed.

"You saved my butt out there," Tony said.

"Mine, too," Timmy chimed in. He and Marshall were huddled over a laptop at the dining room table. A city map was spread out beside them.

"Hey, I didn't have much choice," Lacey said with a deadpan expression. "We can't very well have a wedding without a best man." She took a bite of the pastry.

Tony shook his head. She was somethin', he thought. Kinda like one of those Russian nesting dolls. Layers beneath layers. "If you ever decide you wanna give up acting and join up with LAPD SWAT, you let me know."

The comment inspired a smile. She wiped a crumb from her lip and said, "Yeah, and when you decide to give up being a cop, we could always use a good pastry chef on the set."

"Hey, you two want to get a room, or what?" Marshall said. "While you guys are flirting, we're starving over here."

"Yeah, yeah," Tony grumbled. He placed a few assorted pastries on a serving dish. He'd purchased them from a shop across the street. "Comin' right up, boss." He was glad for the friendly banter. They needed the stress relief. Because as soon as Marsh and Timmy isolated the location of Victor's residence, they'd be going in guns blazing.

Chapter 44

Venice, Italy

THEY APPEARED TO BE TOURISTS—TWO TEENS WITH backpacks and a boy clicking photographs with his tablet—just like the hundreds of others who crowded the Venice train station. They wore T-shirts, jeans, and tennis shoes. Ahmed had a black sweatshirt draped over his shoulders and a baseball cap on his head. Sarafina's hair was pulled back in a ponytail. Her sweatshirt was tied around her waist.

She lowered her oversize designer sunglasses to get a better view. "That way," she said, pointing to the train on track number 4. She held Alex's hand as they maneuvered through the throng of people. He wore a child-size Bavarian fedora adorned with pins from a dozen locales across Europe. He'd been drawn to it like a magnet when they'd met the old man yesterday.

"It was my son's, may he rest in Paradise," the man had said, pulling the keepsake from an upper shelf in his living room. "But I think it will suit you well on your journey."

After hitching a water-taxi ride from San Michelle to San Polo the night before, they'd rung the buzzer at the old man's home at midnight. Lights had flicked on, and a hunched-over, gray-bearded man had cracked open the door. It had taken only a moment for Battista's former associate to recognize Ahmed.

His sleepy eyes had widened in fear. After furtive glances in either direction, he'd rushed them into his apartment.

The man had worked through the night and most of the morning on their documents. They were perfect, right down to the notarized letter from Alex's fake parents authorizing him to travel with his older brother and sister. He'd also given them a bundle of euros. They'd used some of it this morning to buy clothes, backpacks, prepaid cell phones, and personal items. He'd been very friendly, but Sarafina had sensed his relief when they'd waved good-bye.

It was late afternoon. The setting sun cast a rusty glow on the few clouds that hung over the skylight stretching over the tracks. They boarded the train and settled in their private compartment. The 6:05 p.m. train was scheduled to arrive at 8:35 p.m. in the Milano Centrale station, where they'd wait to switch trains.

Ahmed studied their tickets. "We'll arrive at the downtown station in Geneva at nine eighteen a.m.," he said. "From there it will be a short taxi ride."

Which would take them to the apartment building on Avenue de Miremont, Sarafina thought. She wasn't surprised that Alex had recalled the address of the safe house. She'd learned to expect the unexpected from him. This time it had been a blessing. He'd been on the couch playing with his tablet when Jake and the rest of them had discussed their plans. She suspected he remembered every detail.

The train had been delayed for nearly two hours while crossing the Alps. They arrived in Geneva at 11:00 a.m. A late-season snowstorm had blanketed the surrounding mountains through the night, but the sun was back in command. The remnants of snow on the city streets and sidewalks had melted under the assault. Water dripped from the snow-covered eaves of the train station.

The taxi took them over the Rhône River and into the Champel district within the city. They passed rows of luxurious apartment structures, each separated by well-kept parks and open spaces. Trees lined the streets and greenbelts in the posh neighborhood. They pulled to a stop in front of a pair of six-story apartments with gabled roofs, pristine landscaping, and tons of old-world charm.

"It's the building in the back," Ahmed said.

They paid the driver and donned their backpacks. Traffic was light, but there were plenty of people out and about. Couples sauntered arm in arm. Others filled a pastry shop across the street. A group of teens gathered at a park bench. The pace was easy. It felt good to Sarafina. Alex held her hand and Ahmed led the way. The walkway leading to the rear building was lined with ivy-covered lampposts. The path opened onto a manicured greenbelt that stretched between the two structures. A family enjoyed a snack at one of four picnic tables. Beyond them, trees towered over three sides of the second building. It appeared as though the woodland behind it stretched back for an acre or more. The chalet-like lines of the structure reminded her of a gingerbread house—but a lot bigger. She guessed there were three dozen apartments inside. Staring at the dormer windows on the upper floor, she wondered, was Father looking down at them even now? She felt Alex cross his fingers within her grip.

It was an unusual gesture from him. To her knowledge, he'd never done it before. "Yes," she said with a smile. "I hope he's there, too." But doubt nagged at her. In the past she'd been able to sense when Jake was nearby. She'd felt it during their reunion on San Michelle.

She didn't feel it now.

Two awning-covered staircases led up to split lobbies at the front of the building. Each of the entrance doors was protected by a touch-pad entry system. There was a video camera mounted beside each one.

Ahmed led them to one of the picnic tables. "I'll be right back," he said. He did a quick reconnaissance of each of the doorways and returned to join them.

"Apartment 6B is on the right. Top floor. I didn't recognize the name on the tag. We need a code to get in."

Alex turned his tablet around so they could read the number he'd entered on the screen: 7-5-2-3-8.

"Way to go," Ahmed said. "Wait here."

He went to the entrance, entered the code, and tried the door. It didn't open. He tried again, with the same results. Then he tried the other entrance. Nothing.

"Wrong code," he said, slumping down beside them.

They both looked to Alex. All they got in return was a blank stare.

"Now what?" she asked.

"Let me think." Ahmed pulled out his pocketknife and twirled it on the table. His eyes narrowed on the spinning handle as it moved faster and faster.

After a few moments, Alex slapped his hand over it. His gaze was focused on a woman and two children who approached the door. When the woman reached toward the keypad, Alex tilted an ear in her direction. He closed his eyes. The tones were faint. The door clicked open and the family disappeared inside. Alex was halfway up the steps before Sarafina and Ahmed caught up to him. The keypad was an image on a touch screen. Alex stood on tiptoes to reach it. He tapped each of the digits sequentially, 1 through 9, and then 0. Each responded with a different two-note chord.

Sarafina smiled at her brother's ingenuity. She patted him on the shoulder. He'd memorized the tonal sequence he'd heard from the woman. She knew his mind was now matching it to the numbers on the screen. He entered the code. The door clicked open.

Chapter 45

Palais des Nations
Geneva, Switzerland

THE FACT THAT THEY HADN'T REMOVED HIS RESTRAINTS was Jake's first clue that something wasn't quite right.

Dr. Strauss replaced the IV bag, switched off the chair, and left the room. The pyramid rotated on the video monitor. The computer techs and two guards were still in the room. The techs were talking about how glad they were to be finally leaving the cramped confines of this cellar after two months. He ignored their banter. His mind was on the black satchel.

The object inside the metallic container had scared the crap out of him. He'd experienced an overwhelming sense of foreboding as soon as Hans had removed the box from the bag. Some distant part of him didn't want anything to do with it.

Until its energy unlocked the memory of the in-flight emergency.

He nurtured it and details clarified: the familiarity of cockpit controls and instrumentation, the tightness around his abdomen and thighs from the G suit, the sudden impacts from the flock of birds. He'd been scared then, too. His initial impulse had been to pull the ejection handle and save his ass. But his training had taken over.

That's what needed to happen now.

He studied the two guards. Earlier, they'd seemed so…*nice*. Just like Victor and his doctor. Had he actually thought that? These dudes had him strapped to a chair, for Christ's sake. That didn't make them *nice*! But thinking they were sure as hell made him a weak-minded pansy.

Pansy?

That was an American colloquialism, Jake thought. And that's when it dawned on him that he was actually thinking in English. The tantrum prompted by the exposure to the mini had dislodged a blockage in his brain. His language ability had returned. Not just English, but French, German, Spanish, and others. They were back. Just like that. And the contact with the mini had been brief. The lid on the lead-lined container had been lifted for only a few seconds.

Imagine what could happen if…

The fog in his head was clearing. The new IV seemed to be helping. *Allahu Akbar*, he said to himself, recalling Ahmed's request that he speak to him in Dari. That had been two days ago in Venice. Other memories cleared as well. There was nothing more from his distant past, from pilot training, or otherwise. But the events of the previous four months—and especially the last couple days—clarified like a defrosted windscreen.

The guards in front of him wore the same rubber-soled boots as the men who had first tried to kill him in Focette—the same guys who had murdered the girl at the beach. They were Victor's men. He'd been behind it all along. The haze lifted further, and he remembered the details of the confrontation in Victor's office. He and Lacey had been drugged. A shiver crawled up his back when he thought of her. She and Tony and the others had waved to him from the castle courtyard. But they'd been surrounded by Victor's men…

Victor and Strauss walked into the room.

Jake glared at them.

"Ah," Victor said. "I see you're back with us."

“Where are my friends?”

“How intriguing. You’re speaking English.”

“Where. Are. My. Friends.”

Victor’s English accent was cultured. “Buried beneath twenty feet of snow, I should think.”

The words vaporized Jake’s hopes. His mouth hung open, but no air could get in. Victor’s face revealed no reaction to the news he’d just delivered. No satisfaction. No concern.

No regret.

Jake clamped his jaw closed. He drew a long, hissing breath across bared teeth. His eyes bore into the man.

“Now, now, Mr. Bronson. Don’t despair. They would have been dead by tomorrow in any case.”

Jake didn’t know what he meant by that. And he didn’t care. Right now all he could think about was getting his hands around the man’s throat. That was impossible as long as he was tied in this chair, so he played along. He didn’t bother to disguise the anger beneath his words. “What the hell are you talking about?”

“I’m in a bit of a hurry, so I’ll give you the short version. I wouldn’t bother except for the fact that it was you who started it all. And depending upon what happens in the next few minutes, you may play an even more important role in the next few days. In fact, you might possibly end up being responsible for saving the lives of thousands of people. Including one or two that are important to you.”

That last tidbit stoked the fires. Francesca and the children were still hidden in Venice. Whatever Victor had planned would likely impact them. Jake needed to keep them safe. He kept his mouth shut and listened. He needed intel.

Victor gazed upon him as a scientist would a lab rat. “You don’t remember everything yet, do you?” Victor asked. He pointed to the pyramid on the video display. “Judgment Day is upon us, Mr. Bronson. The men and women of the Order have known the glorious day was coming for over a thousand years.

We've prayed for it. Prepared for it. And thanks to you, it has all but arrived. The planet balances on the brink, and all we need to do is tip the scales."

Jake didn't like where this was heading. He knew about the implied threat from above—not from his personal recollection, but from what his friends had recently told him: an alien race was going to wipe out mankind if they determined that we posed a threat to the universe. But Victor hinted at something more. Jake sensed the fanaticism beneath the man's neutral facade. It was disturbing. It needed to be dealt with like a poisonous spider underfoot.

"Tip the scales?" Jake asked, hoping to learn more.

"Yes. A series of events that will cleanse the planet and set the stage for a new world order of peace, culture, and prosperity."

A new world order, Jake thought. Isn't that what Hitler had said?

"And I suppose you and your pals will be in charge, right?"

Victor didn't take the bait. He was at his lectern, and Jake's heckling wasn't going to interrupt him. The speech was one that Jake suspected he had practiced many times.

"It's too late for mankind as a whole," Victor continued. "We are doomed. It's only a matter of time. Even without the involvement of an alien species, the world as we know it will not last much longer. The population grows at a staggering pace. People die of starvation in record numbers. Already, in many regions of the world, the food stores cannot supply the masses. Soaring prices have left a third of parents unable to properly feed their children. One in six skips school in order to work for food. In the next fifteen years, half a billion will grow up physically and mentally stunted. Already fourteen percent of the world population suffers from malnutrition. That will double and double again. By 2050 population growth will outstrip food output. Food riots and global war will follow. No one will be immune. Our world will end."

He added, "That is unacceptable." He struck his palm with a fist for emphasis. Then he tensed for a moment as if he regretted the act. He rubbed his hands together and lowered them to his side. His face was impassioned but not angry. He was the picture of the peacemaker. A Swiss Mother Teresa. It was creepy.

Jake wanted to keep him talking. The more he learned, the better. "And you have a way to prevent it?"

Victor hesitated before answering. His green eyes searched Jake's. Finally, he said, "Not just me, but people like me from around the world. Men and women of influence…and faith. The ruling nations of our planet hide behind the veneer of cultured society, ignoring the realities of the world at large. They bicker and feud while the masses struggle. They can't even agree on how to deal with global warming, much less world hunger. In the meantime, the planet crumbles. Only when the personal interests of their own nation-states are at risk do they act. And how has every tribe or empire or nation of the world dealt with such circumstances since the beginning of time? Through force. At first it was village against village using clubs and fists. Now, our methods of meting out violence are more efficient—with enough destructive power to deal with the direst of circumstances…or enemies. And the worst of these are controlled by a series of cross-checks and backup systems that ensure what governments blithely refer to as *mutual assured destruction*. Who would dare attack, they ask themselves, knowing that their own nation would perish as a result? The belief allows them to sleep comfortably at night. But it's a false confidence—one that will sooner or later lead to man's downfall. We prefer that it be sooner."

"How soon?"

Victor looked at his watch. "Very."

"And what do I have to do with it?"

"Nothing, really. It happens with or without you. People are in place. Everything is in motion. Nobody can stop it. Certainly not you."

The man was a megalomaniac, Jake thought. "There are far better men than me in the world," he said. "Men who are probably three steps ahead of you already. Whatever convoluted plan you've got up your sleeve, you'll never get away with it."

"Ah, but the beauty of our plan lies in its total *lack* of convolution. It's quite simple. It relies on the one thing that can be counted on in this world—man's nature. Let me ask you, Mr. Bronson: What would *you* conclude if a group of NATO-allied countries—the USA and all of its puppets—miraculously survived an attack that killed every one of their enemies?"

The sheer magnitude of the premise shook Jake. The results of such an event would be cataclysmic. The world already hated America. Such an act would send it over the edge. He had no clue how Victor would pull it off. But the man's confidence was absolute.

"You're a sick bastard," Jake said.

The man's smile was warm and friendly. "I am neither the trigger nor the weapon. I'm merely a facilitator."

"And an asshole."

"Such vulgarity. But I suppose it's to be expected from an American. I liked you better as an Italian." He walked to the back of the room and crouched beside the satchel.

Jake didn't care any longer about his lost memory. Whatever it was that Victor wanted from him, it wasn't good. He might die in this chair, but he sure as hell wasn't going to help the bastard with his little experiment. He braced himself.

Victor removed the metal container and placed it on the floor. He unsnapped the lid, lifted it off, and retrieved the mini. The surge of energy was immediate. It was like a jolt of electricity. Jake's heart pounded, adrenaline pumped, and his brain came alive.

Chapter 46

Palais des Nations
Geneva, Switzerland

MEMORIES FLOWED LIKE WATER FROM A BREACHED DAM. A childhood of traveling from country to country, school to school, waving good-bye to friends who came and went. The initial flashes were general, each one replaced by a dozen more, then a hundred, a thousand. Pilot training, his deceased wife and child, cancer once, and then again, the accident in the MRI…

He thought of Battista, the implant subjects, and dancing at a masquerade ball with Francesca.

Then he remembered the accidental triggering of the pyramids—the one in Afghanistan *and* the one in Venezuela—and the false message they'd taken to their otherworld makers. He recalled the number of lives lost, and the billions more at risk because of his carelessness.

The rush of returning memories faltered.

Lives hinge on your ability to remain anonymous.

The true meaning behind the words impacted him with the force of a sledgehammer. It staggered his consciousness. He was suddenly consumed with guilt. The feeling was all too familiar. He recalled going over and over it in his mind. And no matter how he'd looked at it, he'd always arrived at a single inescapable conclusion: his friends—if not the world—would be better off if he were dead. He'd tried to sacrifice his life in Venezuela, not only to cover his friends' escape from the jungle, but to eliminate the threat of his presence forever.

He'd failed.

The government hadn' t wanted him to die. So they had patched up his body. But they couldn't control his unconscious mind, and he suddenly realized that it was that part of him that had then taken it upon itself to complete the mission. It built a wall that neither doctors nor his own consciousness could scale, triggering amnesia and sending him into an irrecoverable coma.

Those walls no longer existed.

Jake was back in charge.

The question was what to do about it. *Life…or death?*

That's when he flashed on the moment when he and Battista had shared a link with the second pyramid—just before it was launched. The flow of information hadn't been solely between them and the object. He had sensed hundreds of other streams of data flowing from other points on the planet. He'd realized that he and Doc and the science team had been wrong about how long it would take for the visitors to return to cast judgment. They'd estimated it would require a minimum of forty years to travel back and forth between Earth and their home planet.

But the visitors didn't need to make that trip. The long arm of their justice was already here—in the form of hundreds of pyramids buried across the planet. He didn't know how the remote-enforcement devices worked, but his brief connection with them six years ago left him with zero doubt in their ability to decimate humankind.

The memory sparked a fierce inner resolve in Jake. He needed to do whatever he could to prevent the coming destruction. And he could start right here, by stopping Victor's insane plans—whatever they were—dead in their tracks. To do that, he needed to be whole again.

He chose life.

The floodgates reopened. Memories bombarded his consciousness. His brain embraced them as a father would a lost child.

He remembered them all: Tony, Marshall, Lacey, and all his loyal friends. Becker, Papa and the fire team, Street and his bangers, the prince, Cal and Kenny, Josh and Max, Ahmed, Sarafina, and Mario.

His son. *Alex.*

Francesca...

Emotions tangled with one another. He felt loss, longing, fear, rage, love, and more. One by one his brain cross-linked them to the kaleidoscope of life events that flowed across his consciousness. The pieces of the puzzle slipped into place, and the essence that was Jake Bronson—the man who he had grown to be before the coma—reclaimed its rightful place.

As his frontal lobes cataloged a lifetime of memories and emotions, his visual cortex registered the fact that Victor now stood directly in front of him. He held the mini. He leaned forward and placed it into the inset in the high back of the chair.

Dr. Strauss stood beside him. At a nod from his boss, he reached around the back of the chair to throw the switch.

Jake readied himself.

Bring it on!

Chapter 47

Palais des Nations
Geneva, Switzerland

JAKE FELT THE CHAIR VIBRATE WHEN STRAUSS SWITCHED IT on. When the doctor stepped back to study his reaction, his glasses reflected the bundles of pulsating lights that streamed from the skullcap and toward the ceiling. The doctor appeared satisfied with the results. He removed the syringe from his lab-coat pocket and stuck the needle into the injection port below Jake's IV. He didn't press the plunger, but his thumb rested on it.

"Ready," Strauss said.

Victor didn't react immediately to the doctor's signal. Instead, he appeared to be appraising Jake's reaction.

Jake's jaw was clenched tighter than a torqued vise. The connection with the mini suffused him with energy. It was the only weapon he'd need. He flashed on the interrogation he'd undergone when Battista had kidnapped him. He'd survived then using his new abilities. He'd do the same here. It was time for payback.

He focused on Victor's forehead, imagined the spongy coils and swirls of his brain. Then he ordered a release of power into the man's skull.

Nothing happened.

He tried again, grunting beneath the effort.

Nothing.

Victor appeared amused. "What exactly are you trying to do?"

Jake ignored him. Instead, he focused his thoughts on unlatching the buckle on his wrist strap. He projected the tendrils of his mind around the leather and thought, *Pull!*

It was no use. His abilities to affect objects remotely had not returned. His fast reflexes had kicked in during his confrontation with Victor's thugs at the beach, but those wouldn't do him any good here. He yanked at his restraints in frustration.

Victor arched an eyebrow. He shook his head as a parent would to an obstinate child. With a shrug, he turned to the men at the computer stations. "Proceed."

The technicians tapped a series of entries into their keyboards. After a moment they both looked over at Jake. Their eyes widened in unison.

The guards at the corners of the room shifted uneasily. Victor's expression portrayed calm and confidence. But when he took two steps backward to position himself by the exit, Jake knew he'd grown suddenly anxious.

Jake glanced at his reflection in Strauss's glasses. The intensity of the light from the fiber optics had brightened. The pulses increased in speed, and he felt a tingle at the back of his head. It was gentle at first, like the tug on a line when a fish nibbles on bait. There was a gasp from one of the technicians, and Jake's attention was drawn to the video screen.

Both of the pyramids had stopped rotating. They glowed with a pulsating luminescence that seemed to match the pattern of light surging from the chair.

Suddenly Jake noticed the undeniable presence of something else in his head. It was a feeling that he'd experienced twice in the past—just before the pyramids had been launched.

Jake prepared for the worst. He closed his eyes and tightened his grip around the chair's armrests. He felt the familiar probe of his brain. Except this time it wasn't accompanied by the mind-numbing information transfer. Instead, it felt as if the pyramids had recognized him in a fashion. They'd already gleaned whatever knowledge they'd needed from his brain in order to be triggered in the first place. Now, it seemed as if they were in more of a monitoring mode. It was as if the intelligence on the other end was waiting for something.

Victor's words interrupted his thoughts. "Dr. Finnegan said it would be like an open telephone line."

Jake opened his eyes. He remembered Doc. He'd been a friend.

"The machine was built specifically for you," Victor said. "Tuned to your unique brain patterns. It didn't work very well when others tried it."

Timmy had told Jake about the deaths. The young scientist had been worried that the same might happen to Jake. So far, so good, he thought. Of course, it wasn't over yet. He was still hooked up to the damn thing.

Victor continued, "I'd like you to send a simple test message. That's all we need from you today. If it works, you shall live. If not…"

"Go to hell."

"You are nothing if not predictable, Mr. Bronson. I've heard the stories about you. You have exhibited your willingness to sacrifice yourself for what you believe to be the better good. I admire such conviction. I won't challenge it." Victor's expression reflected a compassion that Jake knew wasn't really there.

Victor continued, "However, the tales also revealed a weakness. One that I'm afraid we must leverage now." He motioned to one of the technicians, who made a quick entry on his keyboard.

The image on the large video display went black. A moment later it was replaced with a close-up view of a man and woman seated side by side in hardback chairs. They were gagged and tied. The head of the man who stood beside them was cut off by the tight camera shot, but the automatic weapon that he aimed at the woman's torso was in plain sight.

The woman's eyes were wide with fear.

Francesca!

"At the risk of being somewhat redundant," Victor said, "let me start again. I'd like you to send a message. If it works, they live. If not…"

Jake let out a shuddering breath. His gaze darted from Francesca to her father and back again. They'd been with the kids. He was filled with a sudden dread.

His voice cracked. "W-where are the children?"

"It was a shame, really," Victor said. "You see, there was a fire. I'm afraid they didn't make it out in time."

Ice rippled across Jake's skin. He'd reconnected with his friends and loved ones less than thirty-six hours ago. In that time, all but two of them had been killed by the man who stood before him. Jake felt a rage unlike any that he'd ever felt before. His chest seized, his body trembled, and his mind began to unhinge.

Only the sight of Francesca and her father prevented him from leaping into the abyss of mindless hatred. As he teetered on the brink, he sensed a sudden intensity from the orbiting pyramids. Invisible tentacles latched onto his thoughts. A surge of energy from the mini coursed through his limbs, and he felt as though he might pop like an overfilled balloon. It was as if it was lending him the power so that its parents might see what he would do with it. He held his breath.

Francesca is alive, he thought, staring at the screen.

"I see we have your attention," Victor said, watching the high-def display. His voice was a million miles away. "Are you ready to cooperate now, Mr. B—"

His words cut off when the video image suddenly dropped to Francesca's bound feet. The scene was skewed ninety degrees. The remote camera had toppled over. A shadow passed across the screen, and a man's boot stepped in front of the lens. The sound of automatic gunfire spilled forth. Blood splattered on Francesca's flinching legs. A man's shout. More gunfire. A rush of movement. Francesca's chair toppled backward, her torso hidden from view. She was motionless. Blood flowed from beneath her chair and spread across the hardwood floor.

The image went black.

"Nooo!" Jake yelled. His bloodlust rose, his body seized, and fury erupted from his core. The scene around him slowed as he unleashed a wave of primordial rage.

In one beat, the doctor's thumb hovered over the syringe's plunger; the next, his palms were pressed to his temples. He screamed in agony as Jake focused his thoughts on the folds of the doctor's brain. Strauss's eyes bulged, and blood leaked from his ears. He twisted and shriveled to the floor. The guards were next. The muzzles of their weapons made it only halfway to bear before Jake directed his fury at them. He sent a mental command that loosed a laser beam of energy from the mini into their foreheads. Their brains boiled, and they collapsed in a heap. When the door swung closed, Jake realized that Victor had left the room.

"Die!" Jake shouted after the man, sending his wrath at the door. But he could tell it hadn't worked. Victor had escaped. However, his two techs were still in their chairs, and they were every bit as guilty as their boss. Jake ignored their wild-eyed appeals. He killed them where they sat.

It felt good.

The power surging within him made Jake feel invincible. He yanked on his restraints, expecting them to rip free. They didn't. He refocused his thoughts on the clasps, drew in a deep breath, and…

The connection with the pyramids suddenly waned. It felt as if they had learned all they needed to. Tentacles unlatched, fiber optics stopped pulsing, and energy drained from his system faster than jet fuel from a bullet-ridden wing tank.

It was in that moment that he sensed another presence in his mind. It seemed filled with concern. It was a familiar sensation—one that he' d last felt in the underground hideaway on San Michelle. Jake embraced it.

Alex?

Then he sensed Sarafina and he knew instantly that they were alive. He swelled with hope…until he looked around and realized what his rage had wrought—all while linked to the pyramids.

What have I done?

The last drop of energy leached from his system, and Jake collapsed into unconsciousness.

Chapter 48

Geneva, Switzerland

THERE WAS A KEYLESS-ENTRY DIGITAL KEYPAD BESIDE EACH of the doors. Apartment 6B was halfway down the hallway. Ahmed knocked, but nobody answered. He tried the handle.

It was locked.

Sarafina noticed that Alex's eyes targeted the keypad. "Go for it," she said.

He reached up and entered a code. Sarafina recognized the number sequence that he'd first suggested they use downstairs—the one that he'd apparently overheard in San Michelle. The lock clicked. He looked up and smiled.

She was taken aback by the rare eye-to-eye contact. He'd done it once on the train ride as well. She placed her hands on his shoulders and savored the moment. "I'm proud of you."

"As am I," Ahmed added. Then he pushed open the door.

"Hello," he called out. No one replied. They stepped inside.

Sarafina's excitement rose as she took it all in. There were signs everywhere that the apartment was occupied. The main room included a kitchen, dining, and living area. There were dishes in the sink and half-empty coffee cups in the sitting area. A map was spread out on the dining table. There was a laptop beside it. Lacey's perfume lingered in the air.

"They were here," she said.

"The coffeepot is still warm," Ahmed said from the kitchen. "They must have just left." He rummaged through a paper bag on the counter and came out with a lone pastry. He broke it into thirds and gave each of them a piece. It was fresh and sweet. Alex scarfed his down so fast that he finished it before Ahmed took his first bite. Ahmed noticed, and he relinquished his piece to Sarafina's little brother. The sacrifice moved her. She knew how much Ahmed loved his pastries. Two days ago the gesture wouldn't have crossed his mind, she thought. But the challenges that had been thrust upon them had changed him.

"Nothing in the fridge," he said, closing the door. He checked the food pantry. The shelves were bare. He opened and closed several other cabinet doors but came up with nothing. He shrugged and poured himself a cup of coffee. "Breakfast of champions," he said with a wink. He motioned toward the dining table. "Come on. Let's figure out where they went."

Alex and Sarafina followed.

The map on the table incorporated only the city. There was a felt-tip pen beside it.

"I thought the castle was a long way from here," she said.

"A couple hundred kilometers," Ahmed said as he sat down. He picked up the marker. One hand spun it like a top while he studied the map. "They would have arrived at the castle yesterday, which means they came here afterward. When they left this morning, they were headed someplace else—someplace on this map." The finger of Ahmed's free hand tapped an area that had been *X*'d with the marker. "Right h—" He cut off as he studied the location. His finger traced a route from the nearby train station to the marked area. "Oh, that's where we are now. Give me a second." He did a grid search of the rest of the map. The felt-tip pen spun faster while he worked. Alex watched with keen interest.

The pen came to an abrupt stop. The only other mark on the map was a rust-colored circle made by the bottom of a coffee cup. Ahmed sat back and crossed his arms. "You've got to be kidding me," he said. "Who marks the starting point, but then doesn't bother marking the destination?"

"Good question," Sarafina said. "But a better one is who uses a paper map these days?" She settled in the chair beside his and slid the laptop over.

He nudged her with his elbow. "Good thinking."

Alex gave a subtle nod as if agreeing with the statement. It was both odd and wonderful to see him so actively engaged in what was going on around him, she thought. His tablet was turned off.

Sarafina hit the laptop power button, and the display came to life instantly. It had been in sleep mode. An icon in the upper-right corner indicated they were logged in as GUEST. Google Maps filled the screen. It featured a close-up satellite image of an estate overlooking Lake Geneva. There was a mansion and three outbuildings. A private lane twisted through the surrounding trees. She zoomed out in order to get their bearings, cross-referencing the mansion against their current location. Then she clicked GET DIRECTIONS. It was only four kilometers away. A ten-minute taxi ride.

"Let's go!" she said, standing up.

Ahmed blocked her path. "No."

"What do you mean *no*?" she asked.

"It's not safe. We need to remain here."

"But they don't even know we're here."

"Neither does anybody else."

"But we have to catch up to them. What if they don't come back?"

"We cannot follow them," Ahmed insisted.

She hesitated, sensing that he was holding something back. "What are you not telling me?"

He ignored the question. "We must stay here."

Her hands went to her hips.

He threw a sidelong glance at Alex, and she got the hint. There was something going on that Ahmed would rather not share with her younger brother. Alex must have noticed the gesture as well, because he switched on his tablet and buried his focus into the device.

Ahmed sighed. He rose and led Sarafina to the kitchen. He opened the cabinet under the sink and pulled out a plastic trash bin.

It was filled with empty ammunition boxes.

"Wherever they went," he whispered, sliding the bin back into place, "they expected trouble."

The wind went out of her. She nodded. "You're right. We need to—"

Alex's yelp cut her off. His chair crashed to the floor as he rushed to the window and placed a hand on the glass. Sarafina rushed beside him. She'd felt it, too—Jake's cry of anguish had filled her mind. It wouldn't have been any louder had he been standing in the room. She embraced Alex and followed his gaze. Their sixth-floor view looked out the front of the building. The city skyline peeked over the rooftops. Ahmed had moved to their side.

"It's Father," she explained. "He's in trouble."

"W-what?" Ahmed asked. "How do you know?"

"I heard him. In my head," she said. Alex rocked forward and back on his heels. She tightened her arms around him. "He heard it, too."

"You mean like before?" Ahmed asked. He sounded shaken. "When we first met him at the institute?"

"Shhh," she whispered. She could still sense the connection, but the emotional tone had shifted. There was a sudden explosion of fury from her father. Her blood chilled from the intensity. It lasted about ten seconds. Then the connection was lost.

"Oh, God," she said. "Did you feel it?"

"No!" Ahmed cried out. "I didn't feel anything. Or hear anything." His words spilled forth with increasing speed. "How come you felt it but I didn't? I heard him in my head before, so why can't I hear him now? What's the matter with me? Why are you two looking over there? The mansion is in the opposite direction. If Jake is in trouble, I want to help him. But how can I help if—"

"Flip it," she interrupted, avoiding his questions.

But he didn't miss a beat. "—I can't hear him? Why didn't he go with Tony to the mansion? What did I do wrong? There's got to be some reason why I—"

"Please, Ahmed!" Sarafina shouted. She choked back tears. "We need you right now!"

The words broke through. Ahmed bit down on his tongue. He balled his fists and paced circles in the room. His breaths were heavy.

Sarafina was thankful that she didn't have to deal with his questions head-on. Ahmed had been changed by the intense treatments he had received during his two years of "protective care"—following his attempt to blow up the airplane in Afghanistan. He looked at the world from a more logical perspective than before, but he had lost his intuitive nature in the process.

Right now she had her own crushing emotions to deal with. Her daddy's rage was disturbing. She closed her eyes and allowed her body to sway in motion with Alex's. The metronomic movement brought with it an unbidden symphony. It washed over her and replaced her thoughts, pushing away her fears. She allowed the music to take her away.

It was Ahmed's encircling arms that tipped the balance in favor of reality. He'd overcome his touch phobia in order to make the physical contact.

"I'm sorry," he said firmly. "That. Will. Never. Happen. Again." His determination anchored her.

"Where is he?" he asked.

She motioned outside the window. "That way."

"Can you narrow it down?"

She shook her head. "Sorry."

What happened next surprised them both. Alex pulled from the embrace and walked quickly to the laptop. By the time they joined him, he had scrolled the satellite map to a position north of downtown Geneva. He zoomed in on a magnificent multistory structure. With its numerous wings and offshoots, the complex spread out more than a third of a mile. It was surrounded by parks and greenbelts. It overlooked the lake. A final zoom filled the screen with a 3-D image of the front of the main building. It was stately and immense. The label named it the PALACE OF NATIONS.

Alex placed his index finger on the lowest floor of the building. Then he looked up and captured their gazes.

"Are you sure?" Ahmed asked.

A sharp nod told them he was.

A few minutes later, Ahmed stood by the door. He was ready to leave. He wore a backpack and a ready expression. Sarafina thought he had never looked better.

"They say everything happens for a reason," he said. "Perhaps that is true. But I was taught that each person is a master of his own fate. I take charge of mine now. And I do so with the belief that it is the right thing to do. Not only for Jake, who needs my help, but for all three of us as well."

"I'm scared," she said.

"I understand. But you'll be safe here. If I didn't believe that, I wouldn't leave."

But he hadn't understood at all, she thought. She wasn't scared for herself or Alex. She was scared for him. She'd sensed the danger surrounding her father. And Ahmed was heading straight for it. What could he do all by himself? How could he even find Jake within the immense complex?

Ahmed turned to go. She grabbed his arm to stop him. He flinched, but he didn't pull away. He steadied himself and returned her gaze.

The moment stretched.

Alex stood beside her. He reached out and placed his small hand on hers. His intervention was another first. Her grip loosened, but she didn't let go.

Ahmed smiled. "Can't you see it, Sara? He has his father's strength. And his mother's wisdom. He wants me to go. We must trust him."

She knew Ahmed was right. The changes manifesting in her little brother weren't coincidental. Something powerful was at play within him. She dropped her hand to her side. "Please be careful," she said softly.

"Keep your cell charged," he said. "I'm only a phone call away." Then he leaned forward and kissed her cheek. The gesture shocked her. Her face flushed.

To Alex he said, "Take care of her."

Then he opened the door and was gone.

Chapter 49

Geneva, Switzerland

THE THREE-STORY RESIDENCE WAS SITUATED ON A FORESTED rise overlooking Lake Geneva. A cleared area stretched from the house to the surrounding tree line. Patches of lawn peeked through the melting snow. A private lane curved from the coastal highway, up the hill, through a hundred meters of dense pines, and terminated at the driveway circling the house. There was a lone SUV in front of the detached four-car garage. A helicopter was parked on a nearby pad. Similar residential plots dotted the rolling hills around the mansion. It was like a Swiss Beverly Hills, Tony thought, with four times the acreage per home.

He lowered the binoculars. He was crouched in a dense copse northeast of the house. The elevated position provided him with a panoramic view of the lake and the surrounding snowcapped mountains. The landmark Jet d'Eau fountain was a mile upshore. It shot a powerful jet of water more than three hundred feet into the air. Tour boats crisscrossed in the distance.

He scanned the grounds again and shook his head. Something didn't feel right. He'd expected an army of defenders. Instead, there were only five. If he hadn't recognized the chopper as the one from the castle, he would have worried they were in the wrong place.

He spoke into his headset. "Still nothin'?" he asked.

Timmy had moved through the trees in order to get close to the garage. The location also gave him a good view of the other side of the house. He'd taken their only infrared scope with him. "I'm still only seeing six heat signatures," he said. "Two in the bedroom, with a third posted in the hall. Two more in the kitchen. Plus the guy on the front porch."

Any way you cut it, Tony thought, that's six total. Jake and five guards. His pal was being held upstairs under close guard. That's where it would get tricky. Any alert on the way in and the upstairs guards could take out the hostage. But would they? Or were they still intent on keeping him alive? There were too many unknowns and not enough time. His instincts told him to wait, but the urgency of the situation wouldn't allow it.

"Damn," he said to himself. This would have been difficult enough with a full SWAT team. Instead, he was being backed up by an actress, a scientist, and a computer geek—in broad daylight.

He'd considered one tactical approach after another, discarding each in turn. In the end, he'd decided to keep it simple.

"I'm in position," Marshall said.

Finally, Tony thought. "Sixty seconds," he said into his headset.

"Ready," Lacey said. She was in the car on a road behind him.

"Timmy, you're up."

"I've got movement on the scope," Timmy said. "One of the guys from the kitchen is heading for the front door."

"It don't matter. We've got to make our move before they spot Marsh. Do it."

He watched Timmy break cover and run to the backside of the garage. A moment later, the kid sprinted back to the trees.

So far, so good.

He kept his eyes on the man at the front door, who was smoking a cigarette.

Tony had planned the assault so that the killing would be left up to him. But in his gut he worried that it wasn't gonna go down that way. Sure, his friends knew that the men inside were part of the same team that had tried to murder them on the mountain. And they were holding Jake. However—justified or not—taking a life up close and personal wasn't something they'd trained for. He suspected they could if they had to, but it would change them in ways he'd rather not think about.

You never forget the faces of the men you kill.

A trail of smoke rose from the rear of the garage. It thickened quickly. The incendiary charges would make quick work of the wooden structure. Tony raised the P90 submachine gun to his shoulder. He and Marshall each carried one of the compact weapons. With a fire rate of more than nine hundred rounds per minute, it was the ideal "spray and pray" weapon for his friend. But in his own experienced grip, it would be the men guarding Jake that should be talkin' to God right about now.

The front door opened, and a second guard stepped outside. He stopped abruptly and pointed to the garage. He shouted something in the open door. The first guard threw his cigarette to the ground, and both of them rushed toward the detached structure.

Tony tracked them in the P90's reflex sight.

Lacey spoke over the comm net. "I made the call. The fire department will be here in five minutes."

"Going up," Marshall said from the back of the house.

As soon as the pair of guards turned the corner around the house, Tony opened fire. The two suppressed bursts sounded like muffled firecrackers. Both guards went down hard.

"Hold on!" Timmy's excited voice sounded in his headset. "Two more heat signatures just popped up out of nowhere in the center of the house. Must've come from a basement. One of them's headed toward the door!"

But Tony was already on his feet and running across the circular drive. The guard saw him from the foyer. He ducked to one side just as Tony squeezed the trigger. The door began to swing closed.

"No!" Tony roared. He charged forward and let loose on full auto. Craters erupted in the door. It flew backward as a dozen rounds hammered into the wood in less than a second. He slid feetfirst into the grand foyer like a ballplayer into home plate. The man behind the door was slumped on the floor. His eyes blinked once. Blood splattered on the ground around him.

There was a flash of movement at the top of a broad circular staircase.

Tony rolled behind the marble fountain centering the foyer, just as slugs stitched a line into the polished stone floor beside him. Chips of granite bit into his back. The weapon above him lacked a suppressor. The gunshots reverberated through the house. Tony rolled back and triggered a burst of his own. But the upstairs guard had vanished. He heard footsteps pounding down the second-floor hall.

"Guard coming for Jake!" he shouted into his headset.

There was a crash of glass upstairs. An exchange of gunfire. A woman's scream.

Over the comm net Marshall shouted, "Oh my God."

Tony pushed to his feet and started up the stairs. *A woman?*

"Halt!" The voice behind him carried a calm authority that froze Tony midstride.

"Drop your weapon. Remove the headset."

Tony released the P90. It bounced down the three steps below him and clattered to the bloody stone floor. He heard the seesaw of sirens in the distance. The fire department would be here soon. At this point he wasn't sure if that was good or bad. They'd planned to use the commotion of the fire to distract the guards and cover their exit. The only thing he knew for certain was that something wasn't right upstairs. He kept his back to his captor and slowly raised his hands over his head. "I give up. Don't shoot!"

The shotgun blast shredded the wooden banister beside him. Tony flinched. His ears rang, but he didn't try to run. If the guy had wanted him dead, he'd already be bargaining at the gates. He was out of options. If his SWAT team had been with him, his last words over the comm would've triggered a coordinated—and lethal—response.

But with Lacey and Timmy backing him up—and no idea what had happened to Marsh…

"Remove the headset," the man repeated. His German accent sharpened the words. "Or I end you now."

Lacey's voice whispered over the net, "Two minutes." It was the last comm he'd receive. He used a hand to drag the headset from his scalp and drop it to the floor.

"Turn around. Slowly."

It was Pit Bull. He exuded a casual confidence. He held the shotgun at waist level. Smoke drifted from the barrel. He had a golf ball–size lump on the bridge of his nose—where Tony's third tranq dart had struck him the day before. The swollen skin contorted his intersecting eyebrows into a confused expression. The guard beside him glared at Tony. Tony recognized him as the one who'd been with Pit Bull outside the ski shed at the castle. The man held a machine pistol.

Need to stall.

"We meet again," Tony said.

"You were naive yesterday," Pit Bull said. "You should have killed us."

The words struck a chord. "Trust me, I won't make that mistake again."

"Correction: you won't be making *any* mistakes again." Pit Bull raised the barrel toward Tony's chest. His smile was half formed when something crashed through the kitchen window behind him.

Both guards spun to face the threat. By the time they saw the boulder rolling across the floor, it was too late for them to react to the true danger.

An engine whined.

Tony leaped to one side when the Volkswagen rental car crashed through the foyer's bay window. Glass, wood, and drywall exploded inward. The guards dove for cover. The vehicle careened into the fountain. Cherubs toppled, water sprayed, and the car lurched to a stop. Air bags filled the cab, and a fog of debris filled the air.

The guards rose to their feet. Pit Bull's growl was ferocious. He rushed to the driver's-side window. The air bags had collapsed. Lacey's face was bloodied and bruised. She spit at him. He raised his shotgun.

Tony dove for the P90. He whipped it around and strafed over the top of the VW. A line of bullet holes stitched Pit Bull from shoulder to shoulder. His body flew backward. Tony swiveled the weapon and loosed the last of the magazine into the startled second guard. His body jerked and danced with each impact.

Moving quickly to the other side of the car, Tony slammed home a new fifty-round mag and stood over Pit Bull. The man's breathing was ragged. His eyes were at half-mast. He sat with his back to the wall, his feet splayed out before him. He had a one-handed grip around the shotgun in his lap.

"No more mistakes, eh?" the German muttered. There was a gurgle in his voice.

Tony answered with a short burst into Pit Bull's heart. He turned his back and buried any further thoughts of the man.

For now.

He rushed to the car.

Lacey was conscious but shaken. One side of her face was swollen. A trail of blood snaked from a cut on her forehead. In spite of it all, she managed a wink. He tried the door. It was jammed. He startled when Timmy appeared in the front doorway. The young scientist held a pistol in a shaky double-handed grip. He still wore his headset.

"Try the other side," Tony ordered.

Timmy hurried over and opened the front passenger door. "Marshall's trying to reach you on the comm," he said.

Tony met the words with a sigh of relief. His friend was alive.

"He needs help," Timmy added. "Hurry. The fire brigade will be here any minute!"

"I'm okay," Lacey said, unclipping her seat belt and crawling across the seat. "Get up there!"

Tony sprinted up the stairs. He checked the corner with a quick out-and-back glance. A guard lay sprawled in the hallway. The doorway to his right was open. Tony held the P90 in ready position as he stepped over the body and into the room. What he saw shocked him.

"Tony," Francesca said. Her voice was weak. Her face was drawn and haggard. She looked broken. The sight of her hopeless expression widened the hole in his gut.

He moved quickly even as his mind reeled over the scene. The glass doors leading from the balcony had been shattered inward. Marshall's P90 hung loose from its shoulder sling. He hovered over Francesca and her father. Mario's head was in her lap. He had been shot in the chest. A video camera and tripod lay on the floor.

Where the hell was Jake?

"I—it's my fault," Marshall said. "I wasn't fast enough. The guard got off a shot…" His voice trailed off.

Tony inspected Mario's wound. It was bad. "We can't move him." His mind raced through options. Mario needed a hospital, but the rest of them couldn't risk being taken by the authorities. The sirens grew louder. A horn blared outside.

"I sensed my children nearby," Francesca said dully. "But that can't be. Because they're dead. I felt Jake, too."

She's obviously in shock, Tony thought. Delirious. But her words still made his skin ripple. He lifted Mario's head from her lap. She didn't resist. Her mind was miles away.

"Let me take him for a moment," he said.

She scooted back.

"Pillow," Tony said to Marshall, motioning to the bed. Marshall grabbed one and Tony lowered Mario's head onto it. The old man groaned, but his eyes remained fierce. He grabbed Tony's wrist. His weathered grip was strong.

"You must protect my daughter," he whispered.

"With my life."

Marshall's hand went to the earpiece of his headset. "We've got thirty seconds."

Mario turned to Francesca. "You must leave, child. I will be okay." His voice was calm and soothing—despite his pain. Tony felt a flush of admiration for the gondolier.

"Yes, Father," she said. Her manner was childlike.

The car horn grew more insistent.

Tony took Francesca's hand and guided her to her feet. She hesitated as they moved toward the door. She looked back at her father, and Tony saw a flicker of realization grow in her eyes. Her legs wobbled. Tony reached around, picked her up, and moved quickly down the hallway. "The ambulance will be here any second," he said. "The emergency teams will take good care of him." He prayed they'd get Mario to the hospital in time.

They raced out of the house. Smoke billowed from the garage. Flames roared upward from the side window. The sirens were loud, and Tony saw emergency lights flashing through the distant trees. The confiscated black SUV was pulled up to the entrance. The rear doors were open. Timmy was at the wheel. Lacey sat beside him. Their eyes widened at the sight of Francesca.

Marshall sprinted around to the other side. He carried a hefty laptop and backup drive under one arm. Wires dangled beneath them. Tony set Francesca on the seat. He jumped in, slammed the door, and shouted, "Go!"

Timmy floored it, and the BMW X5 leaped forward. It jumped the curb surrounding the circular drive and made tracks through the patchy snow-covered lawn. They spun around the backside of the house and headed uphill. By the time they made the tree line, the first of the fire trucks was arriving on scene. Tony caught a glimpse of a black SUV among them. It was an exact match to the one they'd just hijacked. Timmy wove the vehicle through a hundred meters of forest before reaching the road. No one followed.

They were halfway to the safe house when amber lines of light suddenly crisscrossed the sky all the way to the horizon.

"What the hell?" Lacey said, leaning forward in her seat to look skyward.

Traffic pulled over on both sides of the streets. Timmy did the same. He thumbed a switch overhead to open the panel covering the moonroof. They all gazed upward at the unearthly sight.

It was Francesca who spoke first. "It was Jake," she said. "He did a very bad thing."

Chapter 50

Geneva, Switzerland

VICTOR CHIDED HIMSELF FOR THE INCESSANT TWITCH IN HIS leg. Less than five minutes had passed since he'd escaped the room. He sat in the backseat of the limo. It was parked outside the rear exit of the palace.

Hans leaned in the open rear door. "Strauss and the others are dead. The American is unconscious. But we have him."

"And the chair?"

"It's intact. The men are bringing it out now."

Victor nodded. There was no question that the American had been able to link with the pyramids using the device. The death of the woman had turned the experiment on its end, but that didn't mean something couldn't be salvaged the next time around. They may have lost their leverage over the man, but there were other methods. Either way, he would leave neither the chair nor the American behind.

Hans said, "You must go, *Mein Herr.* The men and I will follow in a couple minutes." He closed the car door.

As the limo drove away, Victor had to fight to hold his anger in check. The loss of Dr. Strauss and the men inside was regrettable. But the news he'd just received that the American's friends had apparently survived the avalanche—and his suspicion that it was they who had raided his residence—was infuriating. It wasn't a common emotion for Victor. Unforeseen events—and the extreme emotions they can sometimes spark—were a rare occurrence in his structured life. He allowed a part of his mind to embrace the rage. He clicked on his tablet, activated the front-facing camera, and examined his features. He saw the micro-twitch at the corner of his right eye. It was his tell. His weakness. He despised it.

Then he glanced at the clock in the top corner of the display, and he realized that none of the things that had happened would have any impact on the trigger that was about to be activated.

In less than fifteen minutes, 90 percent of the people in attendance at the Palace of Nations would be dead.

The twitch in his eye vanished, and Victor watched the corners of his lips lift in a smile.

Chapter 51

Palais des Nations
Geneva, Switzerland

A sudden pain on the side of his skull woke Jake up. He felt cold linoleum against his cheek. Two sets of boots filled his vision.

A muffled voice in German. "Careful!"

"A lump or two on the head won't kill him. Besides, he's not our first priority."

They were in a hallway. Two men had dropped him on the floor. There was an urgent command from up ahead. "Quickly. You can return for him in a moment."

Jake recognized Hans's voice. The realization sent a wave of adrenaline through his system. But he remained still. They thought he was unconscious.

The memory of what he'd done in the chair rushed back to him, and the sudden wave of guilt threatened to pull him under.

He wouldn't allow it. His children were alive. They needed him. He pushed his guilt aside.

The two men who'd been carrying him ran ahead. Jake followed their movements through slit eyes. They rushed toward a heavy-looking exit door that opened to an exterior stairwell. A wedge of sunlight sliced across the landing, suggesting the hallway was situated less than one floor from street level. Hans propped the door open with his foot. He held a compact submachine gun with a suppressor screwed onto the barrel. A part of Jake's brain cataloged the weapon as an IWI Micro Tavor (MTAR-21) assault rifle, considered one of the most compact 5.56mm weapons around. At least that was the case six years ago, when his eidetic memory captured the stats of just about every weapon on the market. The memory flash confirmed that his faculties were back.

He'd need every one of them.

A thin trail of smoke snaked from the tip of the weapon. The bodies of two security guards lay slumped nearby on the hallway floor. One of their legs twitched in the final throes of death. It supported Jake's suspicion that only a few minutes had passed since he'd fallen unconscious. Shadows interrupted the wedge of sunlight, and he heard grunts in the stairwell. It sounded as if men were lugging something up the steps.

It had to be the chair, Jake thought. And the mini with it.

Hans motioned up the stairs. "Help them." The two men moved past him and disappeared from view. Hans stared at Jake's limp form, cocking his head as if it might give him a better view. But from ten paces away he wouldn't be able to tell that Jake's eyes peeked at him from behind a curtain of lashes.

Ten paces, he thought. With his superspeed, he could cover the distance in less than two seconds. He waited for his chance.

An angry shout in the stairwell drew Hans's attention upward. It sounded as if the men were struggling at their task.

Jake tensed in anticipation.

"*Dummkopf*!" Hans said to someone above. He kept one hand on the outward-swinging door as he lowered the weapon and leaned up the stairwell.

Jake sprang to his feet and sprinted toward him.

It took only two steps to realize he'd not regained his enhanced reflexes. But by then he was committed. He poured everything he had into the mad dash. Fear brought the sequence of events into clear focus. His body wasn't superfast, but his brain was.

Measure distance against speed.

At six paces, Hans's torso began to lean back into the doorway.

Analyze angles.

At four paces, the German turned his head.

Deduce reaction.

At two paces, Hans was raising the weapon.

Jake launched himself into the air feetfirst. The silenced weapon was already spitting as the barrel rose. The rounds passed beneath him as Jake's stiffened legs torpedoed into the German's solar plexus. Hans was propelled against the back wall of the stairwell while Jake broke his own fall with his hands. He scrambled into the hallway on hands and knees, yanking the door closed behind him. The electronic lock engaged. There was a loud thud against the door, and Jake could imagine Hans's foot kicking it in frustration. But the German and his men had accessed the rear exit to the facility once before, so Jake knew it would be only seconds before they entered the code again. He jumped up and ran like hell toward the door at the opposite end of the hallway.

He was halfway there when ear-piercing Klaxons sounded throughout the facility.

Door locks engaged up and down the hallway. He passed an elevator, noting that the push-button lights flashed on and off in concert with the sirens. The facility was on lockdown.

Jake spun around at the sound of a sudden jackhammer staccato at the exit door behind him. It sounded as if Hans had loosed his weapon on the door lock. That meant his entry codes no longer worked. A second weapon opened up, and Jake saw a pencil-thin beam of sunlight peek through a hole in the door. The multiple projectiles were working their way through like termites on a two-by-four. They'd break the lock any moment.

Jake made it to the far door. It was thick, it was steel, and it was locked. He pounded on it. It felt as sturdy as a bank vault's. There was an entry keypad and a retinal scanner beside it.

And a camera above it.

"Open up! I need help!" he shouted, jumping up and down and waving his arms at the camera. There was no response. The hammering at the other end of the hall got louder. He risked a quick look over his shoulder. Several beams of sunlight poked through the door. He was out of time.

He focused his thoughts on the keypad, imagined its inner workings in his mind, compared the wiring against the vast database of information he'd memorized years ago. He needed to bypass the entry code. He imagined shorting wires in the same way that he'd scrambled Strauss's brains. But the instant he tried it, he realized it was no use. Those abilities were lost to him.

Perhaps forever.

Jake pounded on the door. "You've got armed terrorists at the back door! They're about to break thr—"

There was a loud crash behind him. Jake spun to see two of Hans's men rushing toward him. They carried assault rifles. Hans was silhouetted in the doorway behind them. He had a finger to one ear.

Jake was out of options, but he wasn't going down alone. They hadn't fired on him, which meant they wanted him alive. That was going to cost them. He lowered a shoulder and charged. The distance closed. Suddenly, the two men went wild-eyed. They skidded to a stop and raised their weapons.

"Kill him!" Hans shouted.

"Down!" someone ordered from behind Jake.

Jake dropped to the floor as automatic weapons opened fire from both directions. Bullets ricocheted all around him. Victor's men were thrown backward from a hail of rounds. Hans ducked from view. Several uniformed security guards leaped over Jake from behind and ran toward the exit. Then a knee dug into his lower back and he felt the hot muzzle of a weapon at the nape of his neck.

"Don't move," a man's voice commanded.

There was a squeal of tires outside, and Jake knew Hans was gone.

"Hands behind your back," the voice said.

Jake complied. He sensed other men standing nearby. Strong hands held his wrists together and cinched plastic cuffs around them. He was jerked to his feet and escorted toward the open interior door.

"Thanks for—"

"Shut the hell up," the man walking in front of him said in English, holstering his weapon beneath a sport coat. He had a tight haircut and a curlicue earpiece. "You're lucky as shit that somebody recognized you. Save the talk for him. Now get a move on!"

They prodded him forward, winding down two flights of steps. A fire map indicated they were headed toward the bunker. The echo of a dozen pairs of boots followed them down the stairwell. The men surrounding him appeared to be hardened combatants. But Jake sensed an elevated level of tension from them that didn't jive with what had just happened upstairs. The firefight had ended quickly. They'd won. So what the hell else was going on?

The Klaxon still sounded.

Chapter 52

Geneva, Switzerland

THE FIFTEEN-MINUTE DRIVE FROM THE PALACE OF NATIONS to Geneva International Airport passed through a manicured scattering of high-end apartments and condominium complexes, separated by vast stretches of forested greenbelts. Victor rolled down his window to enjoy the pleasant view.

They were seven minutes into the trip when the driver suddenly pulled to the shoulder. The privacy screen behind him was halfway down even before the car came to a stop. The driver turned around, his face drained of color. "*Mein Herr.* Something terrible has happened!"

Victor checked his watch. The attack wasn't supposed to commence for another six minutes.

"What's wrong?" he asked.

"I-it's happening all over the world, sir," the driver said in a panic. "I heard it on the radio."

"*What's* happening, man?" Victor asked, switching on the television monitor embedded above the liquor cabinet. "What are you talking—"

The scene on the TV stopped him cold. The wide-eyed reporter stared dumbfounded at a video window that was inset on the screen beside her. It revealed a glowing object of some sort rocketing into the sky. The window became smaller in order to make room for three more insets, showing similar missiles launching from different locations. Captions on each read TOKYO, NEW YORK, LONDON, and BEIJING. He turned up the volume.

"…the objects appear to have been launched simultaneously from points all over the globe…"

Victor was taken aback by the images. His mind reeled with the implications.

"…burst forth from hidden locations beneath the earth, causing widespread damage."

Could it be? Victor wondered.

"We've just received close-up footage of one of the orbs." A single video filled the screen. It was a video of the object as it shot upward. It looked like a glowing ball of light with a rotating dark blur at its core. It jiggled and danced on the screen as the camera zoomed tighter. The reporter continued in voice-over.

"This footage was taken with a super-high-speed camera. Here's what was discovered under freeze-frame."

The image froze. The darkness within the glow was no longer a blur.

It was a pyramid.

Victor disregarded the reporter's ongoing ramblings. He stared spellbound at the object. After several moments he began to laugh—softly at first—as the realization hit him. Bronson had done it! His rage had triggered the end more efficiently than all of Victor's plans put together. Nothing can stop us now, he thought.

"…huge death toll. Widespread panic in the streets…" the reporter announced.

Victor laughed louder.

The driver couldn't help but relax. Color returned to his face. "What does it mean, sir?"

Victor spoke between chuckles. "It means that traffic is about to get very bad. So we better get going!" He burst out in laughter. He couldn't remember when he'd felt so good.

"Yes, sir!" the driver said. He turned around, raised the privacy barrier, and accelerated onto the road.

Victor pursed his lips in an attempt to hold back a renewed bout of laughter. But when he glanced at his watch and realized that the attack at the palace was less than three minutes away, he erupted into a full-out, belly-jerking guffaw.

Chapter 53

Palais des Nations
Geneva, Switzerland

THE EIGHT-INCH-THICK STEEL DOOR SWUNG CLOSED BEHIND him, and Jake heard a series of hydraulic bolts slide into place. The Klaxon alarm no longer sounded, at least not here in the bunker. The scene before him was pandemonium. The buzz of loud voices and exclamations reminded Jake of an angry hornet's nest. The main floor was the size of a high-school gymnasium. Men and women worked feverishly at computer stations that fanned out around a central platform. Dignitaries and their military countertypes gathered on the balconies that skirted three sides of the room. Several of them appeared to be in heated arguments. A movie theater–size screen on the far wall streamed videos that Jake knew instantly were an intended message of peace to the pyramids above. Armed security personnel were everywhere.

But Jake's gaze was fixed on the holographic image that hovered over the center dais. It was a three-dimensional real-time view of Earth. The eight-foot-wide planet—cloud patterns and all—rotated slowly overhead. Hundreds of bright missiles rocketed outward from all points around the planet's surface, like a slow-motion exploding firework.

A woman's voice sounded from a loudspeaker. "The final count is one thousand twelve objects, not including the two already in orbit."

Jake's stomach tightened.

"Out of my way!" a man shouted in French. He pushed toward the door Jake had just entered through. He was well dressed and flanked by two bodyguards with bulges under their jackets. Three soldiers blocked the door. Two of them raised their assault rifles to port arms. The third held his hand out like a stop sign. "I'm sorry, sir. No one is permitted to leave."

"That's preposterous. I'm the president of France!"

"Respectfully, sir, it doesn't matter who you are. We are on lockdown."

"But the door was just open!"

"Sorry, sir."

The man seemed about to explode when he noticed Jake. His eyes narrowed and he pointed a trembling finger at Jake's chest. "It's you!" He spoke in English. "You're the American." The French president hesitated a moment. His face reddened. His lips twitched as if searching for which words to form next. He reeked of fear.

Finally, as if throwing all of his energy into the act might ease his pain, the president of France lunged forward with outstretched hands. He screamed at the top of his lungs, "This is your fault!"

Jake shrank back, his escort stepped forward, and the president's bodyguards restrained their furious boss.

A rush of footsteps sounded from a staircase leading to the balcony. A white-haired scientist led the pack, and the crowed parted before him. His blue eyes twinkled behind frameless glasses. He wore a white shirt with rolled-up sleeves—and a Santa Claus smile. "Jake, my boy," he said, throwing his arms around him. "It's really you!"

"Hi, Doc," Jake said. He was genuinely pleased to finally see a friendly face. He and Doc went way back to the Area 52 days. He'd saved the man's life. And Doc had then been instrumental in rescuing Jake and his friends from the jungles in Venezuela—not to mention keeping him alive for the past six years.

Jake said, "I'd shake your hand, but..." He held up his cuffed wrists.

"Get those off of him!" Doc ordered.

One of Jake's escorts produced a zip-cutter and snipped through the plastic. Jake rubbed his wrists and offered his hand.

"Oh, come here, son!" Doc said as he pulled Jake into another embrace.

After a pat on the back, Jake broke the hold. "We need to stop Victor Brun."

Doc seemed startled by the statement.

Jake continued, "That son of a bitch—"

"Not here," Doc interrupted. He motioned at the crowd.

Jake got the point.

"Follow me," Doc said. He led Jake up the stairs.

As they moved off, Jake noticed a man rush to the French president's side. He whispered something into the leader's ear, and the president immediately relaxed. The aide pointed to a door at the far corner of the room. The Frenchman nodded, and he and his bodyguards hurried in that direction.

When Jake reached the mezzanine balcony, Doc motioned toward several of the dignitaries who stood at the rail, watching the hologram. He whispered, "That's the general secretary of the Communist Party of China, the prime minister of India, the president of the Russian Federation, the prime minister of the United Kingdom..." A few of the men and women glanced at Jake as he walked past. Some seemed to recognize him. One high-ranking Russian military officer appraised him warily. He maintained his stare as he whispered something to his aide. But the bulk of the group wasn't interested in Jake. They couldn't peel their focus from the holographic scene that unfolded in the center of the room.

The missiles had been launched from all corners of the globe. From their speed and trajectories, it was apparent that they'd taken off simultaneously. Jake's gut went hollow when he realized that must have been when the Klaxons had first sounded. It didn't take a genius to conclude that he'd been the cause.

"They're exact duplicates of the pyramid from Area 52," Doc said. "They were buried everywhere. Something triggered them."

*Make that some*one...

The singular stream on the huge video wall suddenly split into eight separate screens. Each contained television broadcast coverage of the event. Footage flowed in from around the globe. The pyramids had bored upward from their underground resting places—many in populated areas—leaving death and destruction in their wake.

Jake felt his knees go weak. Alex and Sarafina were out there somewhere. Alone.

He felt Doc's hands on his shoulders. His friend must have sensed his despair. "Don't lose it now, man. We need your help to fix this." A few of the men and woman around him turned to follow the exchange. He felt the burden of their combined stares.

World leaders were looking to him for answers? What the hell could *he* do?

Doc grew excited. "Don't you see? You can communicate with them. Reason with them. We've built a device precisely with that purpose in mind. You may be our only hope!"

Jake shook his head. They had no clue about what had happened earlier. "Then we're in deep shit," he said. The words came out of his mouth before he had the sense to stop them.

He was saved from immediate reproach by a loudspeaker announcement: "The objects are slowing."

Everyone turned toward the center of the room. The chamber quieted. The rocketing pyramids slowed abruptly. Within a few seconds they came to a complete stop. Each was at the same altitude as the original two. The symmetry of their spacing was exact. The entire globe was enveloped.

Everyone stared in awe—except the Russian officer, who dared a quick glance at his watch before bracing himself on the rail to see what happened next. It was an odd gesture, Jake thought, to say the least. What appointment could possibly be so important as to distract him at a time like this? Alarm bells went off in Jake's gut.

He allowed his mind to step away from the immediacy of the scene and to instead take in the room as a whole. Everyone appeared transfixed on the rotating 3-D image. He studied the leaders who stood around him, connecting the faces to the few introductions he'd heard earlier. They were all there except for the British prime minister. He'd disappeared. Many others stood nearby whom Jake hadn't met yet. They each wore a name tag bearing the emblem of the flag of their home country: Pakistan, South Africa, Colombia, Venezuela, Iran, Azerbaijan, Indonesia, North Korea, Syria, Jordan…

And then it hit him. There wasn't a NATO ally among them. Or even any non-NATO countries that had been granted MNNA—major non-NATO ally—status. Where was Japan, Canada, Israel, or the good old USA? What about Italy, Germany, Fr—

France!

Movement at the far end of the chamber drew his attention. Jake saw the British prime minister and a small entourage being escorted out the same door that the French president had gone through earlier. Then he remembered Victor's question. *What would you conclude if a group of NATO-allied countries miraculously survived an attack that killed every one of their enemies?*

The Russian officer checked his watch again. His gaze suddenly lost focus—and he and his aide simultaneously placed fingers just below their left ears. Jake's heart dropped. He flashed on Victor's boast. *People are in place...*

The Russian officer's eyes locked on Jake's. The man seemed to be holding his breath. He pulled a silver pen from his pocket that Jake recognized as a duplicate of those that Strauss and the lab techs had carried. The Russian plunged it into his thigh as if it were a hypodermic.

Jake's brain went into hyperdrive. Meeting rooms circled the balcony. He pointed to the nearest one.

"Everybody needs to get into the conference room *now*!" he shouted.

The people around him exchanged confused glances.

But none of them heeded the warning...

...Until several people on the opposite balcony grabbed their throats and collapsed to their knees.

Chapter 54

Palais des Nations
Geneva, Switzerland

People stampeded the doorway to the conference room. A Syrian woman fell to the floor. Jake shouldered two men out of the way and stooped to help her up. The Chinese communist leader noticed. He nodded to Jake, took the woman's hand, and helped her inside. Jake stood by the door as the throng pressed past him. When he saw that Doc was waiting beside him, he grabbed him by the shoulders.

"Brun is behind this!" Jake whispered. Then he shoved the older man into the stream of people. Over their heads he shouted, "Everyone hold your breath as long as you can. Once you're inside, lie on the floor!"

Jake felt a tickle of irritation at his throat. It began to swell. He tightened his lips and stopped breathing. Then he scanned the perimeter of the crowd, found his target, and charged.

The Russian aide was oblivious to Jake's onrush. He appeared to be fumbling to remove the cap from the end of his silver pen. His face was red. The cap snapped loose and he raised the fisted pen, now open, over his thigh. Jake tackled him just as he started his downward thrust. They landed in a tumble, and Jake grabbed the man's wrist. The Russian twisted loose, but Jake kneed him in the groin just as the aide plunged the pen through his pant leg. The man gasped, and Jake ripped the pen from his grasp. Liquid dripped from the tip of the half-inch needle. Jake jabbed it into his own thigh, pressed the plunger the rest of the way, and felt a cool rush spread across his skin. He'd received a half dose at most, but it would have to do. He rolled away and pushed to all fours. The Russian rose to his feet, his back to the balcony rail—he reached under his jacket for a weapon. Jake stayed low, launching himself like a blitzing linebacker. The pistol came into view just as Jake's arms bear-hugged the Russian's thighs. He heaved upward and the man flew back-first over the rail.

His scream ended abruptly.

Jake's lungs told him to breathe, but he refused to open his mouth. He'd already ingested some of the gas. His throat was nearly closed, and he worried that any more would be the end of him. He raced toward the staircase.

His mind blazed through a jungle of possible solutions to the disaster that unfolded around him. Victor had loosed a deadly gas into the facility. The pens provided an antidote for Order members. No one else was safe.

Except the NATO folks who were taken to another area.

Which meant the gas was being selectively delivered to some rooms but not others, he thought. That could be managed only through ventilation-control systems.

Computer operated.

He leaped down the staircase three steps at a time.

Men and woman collapsed around him. Eyes bulged, hands clasped throats, and bodies writhed in agony. Some didn't move at all. A number of people had dodged into the meeting rooms on the perimeter of the main floor. Several watched him with wild-eyed expressions, apparently unaffected by the gas in the enclosed rooms. Jake suspected their reprieve was temporary. If he didn't do something to prevent it, the gas would invade the salons any second.

His mind continued to flash-sort solutions. This was a fallout shelter. Which meant it had to contain extensive fire-suppression systems. That would include the ability to isolate areas within the facility that were divorced from the building proper, and to provide a separate source for respirable air.

One computer station was still manned. The tech cast a furtive glance toward Jake. He entered a command into his keyboard and then ran toward the far exit—where Jake saw a group of five or six people slipping through an open doorway. The Russian officer was at the head of the pack.

Bastards.

Jake sprinted toward the tech's station. His lungs felt as if they were going to burst. He couldn't ignore their demands much longer. When he reached the screen, he knew it was all over. He skipped to the next station, and then the next. But every screen was the same. The cursor flashed inside an empty space that read ENTER PASSWORD.

He was out of options.

His body trembled. It demanded oxygen. In the end, he knew he'd have no choice but to unclench his jaw, suck in the poisonous air, and pray that the dose he'd received would be enough. He looked up at the 3-D hologram that hung suspended in the air. One thousand fourteen pyramids hovered overhead. He knew their purpose, but he wondered how it would be accomplished. Would they suck the oxygen from the atmosphere? Melt the ice caps and flood civilization? Or would they simply blow them all to hell?

As if in answer to his question, each of the pyramids started to glow. And in a sudden flash, they burst forth with laser beams of light that connected one to the other—until together they formed a geodesic envelope of light that imprisoned the globe.

The world was out of options.

He staggered at the base of the platform, horrified by the immensity of what he'd caused. It had all started with an accident during an MRI, he thought. The changes in his brain had seemed magnificent at first, but they'd come with a heavy price tag. Everyone he cared about had been drawn into the deadly vortex that surrounded him. And now the entire world was at risk.

He dropped to his knees.

God forgive me.

That's when he noticed the fire panel embedded in the platform wall. The placard was in English. Foggy brain or not, Jake saw that the instructions couldn't have been simpler. There were two buttons. One was red. One was blue. Each had a hinged Plexiglas cover. They were labeled ALARM and SPRINKLERS.

Jake flipped open the covers, pressed both buttons, and prayed.

Chapter 55

Geneva, Switzerland

Ahmed had been gone only ten minutes when Sarafina heard the noises.

Doors slammed in the hallway outside the apartment. There were anxious voices and rushing footsteps. She looked through the peephole and saw a family run past. They were headed toward the staircase. She heard the blare of several automobile horns in the distance. Then an emergency-vehicle siren.

She and Alex rushed to the window. A throng of people gathered in the park out front. More flowed from their apartments to join them. Others stood on balconies in the opposing building. They all looked upward, many pointing at the sky. It was the sort of scene she'd have expected to see if someone were about to jump from the rooftop. She slid open the window and heard astonished outcries drifting up from the crowd. She leaned out and looked up.

It wasn't a jumper.

It was the sky.

A series of intersecting beams of light stretched from one horizon to the other, creating a symmetrical pattern of triangles that lit up the sky. It was as if God had used neon lights to paint the heavens.

Fear gripped her throat. She grabbed Alex's hand, moved to the couch, and switched on the TV.

The woman reporter's voice was frantic. "Reports are coming in from stations all over the world. The phenomenon circles the globe. The grid—that's what scientists are calling it—appeared just minutes ago after hundreds of missiles exploded from beneath the earth and were launched into the atmosphere. This footage was taken in Tokyo."

The screen split. The video beside the reporter centered on a busy downtown intersection. The image began to jiggle as if the ground shook under the cameraman's feet. Suddenly, a spinning black orb burst from the pavement. The camera barely caught up with its track as it rocketed into the sky and disappeared. The only exhaust plume in its wake was a brief rippling of the air. When the camera panned back down, there was a six-foot-wide hole in the street. Steam issued forth. A motorcycle and its rider skidded too late and disappeared from sight. Cars swerved to avoid the hole. Traffic came to a standstill. Just as it appeared that the worst was over, the entire intersection caved in on itself.

"It's the same everywhere," the reporter said. "States of emergency have been declared around the world."

Sarafina squeezed her brother's hand. They watched in awe as the video stream switched from one location to another. The quality of the picture varied as scenes came in from cell phones, traffic cams, and other sources. There was a mall in America with matching holes in its floor and ceiling. Children scattered from a launch that exploded through a playground in New Delhi. Buildings toppled in Johannesburg and Beijing.

"The death toll is in the thousands, if not the tens of…"

The reporter hesitated. She placed a hand to one ear.

"I understand we have some new footage. It was captured via satellite. Our scientific consultant, Thomas Goodfellow, is on the line from our London bureau. Tell us what we're looking at, Tom."

This time the video filled the entire screen. It was a side-angle shot of one of the orbs as it streaked into Earth's upper atmosphere. It had taken on a luminous glow.

The British reporter's voice was authoritative. "This shot was taken two minutes after launch. At this point, the object's estimated speed has accelerated to over fifteen thousand kilometers per hour. By comparison, that's three times faster than the speed of a space shuttle launch during the same time period. Although we're only looking at one of the objects in this video, we've been told that all of the other missiles matched its speed and launch timing exactly."

The computerized high-speed camera steadied on the object's flight path. It zoomed in to reveal a glowing mass that appeared to be spinning on its axis. As the object's altitude above Earth exceeded that of the satellite's camera, the backdrop image of the cloud-covered planet disappeared from view off the bottom of the screen. It was replaced by the star-filled expanse of space.

"At three minutes after launch, the object decelerated abruptly, as did all the others across the globe. They each stopped at an altitude of five hundred kilometers. That's three hundred ten miles above the earth."

The camera zoomed and the object filled the screen.

"That's when they stopped rotating."

The orb stopped spinning in the blink of an eye. The luminosity faded, and the blurred mass resolved into a hovering black pyramid.

Sarafina gasped. She'd seen one before.

"Two minutes later, this happened."

Six beams of light burst from the peak of the pyramid. The camera zoomed out as the beams stretched outward to meet with those from the other orbiting pyramids. They connected one to the other in a symmetrical pattern that encircled the globe. When the last of them was linked, the beams seemed to triple in intensity. It was as if an illuminated geodesic dome had been wrapped around the planet.

Sarafina felt the air crushed from her lungs. She knew immediately that this event involved her father. I can't handle this alone, she thought. She switched off the television, grabbed the cell phone from the backpack, and dialed Ahmed.

All she heard was a rapid busy signal. The cell network was overloaded.

Her body trembled, her eyes fluttered, and she heard the first notes of a symphony form in her mind. But a squeeze of her hand by her little brother prevented the music from carrying her away. She glanced down at him. He seemed to be gauging her reaction. His worried expression tore at her, and just then—in that vortex of panic and fear—she knew what they must do.

A few minutes later, they were swerving through the panicked crowds on a stolen Vespa motor scooter.

Uncle Tony will know what to do.

Chapter 56

Palais des Nations
Geneva, Switzerland

THE FIRE ALARM BLARED, THE COMPUTER DISPLAYS BLINKED off, and a deluge of water rained from the ceiling.

Jake was on all fours. He opened his mouth, and his chest heaved with the effort to draw air through his constricted throat. At first it was like sucking a milkshake through a cocktail straw. His airways squeaked with the effort, but the water-scrubbed air tasted sweet. Each breath was easier than the last—oxygen got in. His head cleared and his throat opened. He heard the whine of exhaust fans overhead. They were designed to switch on as soon as the temperature in the room indicated that the fire was extinguished. With no fire in the first place, they kicked on instantly. The poisonous air was evacuated out the top of the chamber, replaced by fresh air drawn from vents along the base of the walls.

Rising to his feet, Jake blinked through the shower. He took in the scene around him. There were bodies everywhere. Only a few of them moved. An office door opened and two techs walked through. They hesitated a moment, sniffing the air. Then they rushed to help their fallen comrades. More doors opened and people flowed out. Jake looked up to see Doc standing with a two-fisted grip on the rail. The Chinese leader stood beside him.

He pointed at Jake and said something to two Asian security types. They started for the stairs.

Jake could guess what that was about. At the very least, they'd want answers as to what he had to do with the pyramids. At worst, they'd assume he was behind it all. Either way, it was going to be a long time before he ever saw the light of day. By then the Russian officer and the rest of the Order's men would be long gone.

He ran in the opposite direction, surveying the area in front of him with the precision of a combat pilot on takeoff roll. Water continued to rain down. The floor was flooded. He skirted computer stations, leaped over bodies, and aimed for the doorway the Russian had used. The bodies of two guards blocked the exit. He skidded to one knee beside them, pulling a lanyard from the neck of the first man. Then he scooped up each of their machine pistols.

"You there. Halt!" someone shouted behind him.

Jake swiped the lanyard's dangling key card across the door's security pad. The lock clicked. He shouldered through, slammed the door behind him, and fired a short burst into the security pad on the opposite side.

The air was dry and fresh. The short passageway led to another blast door. It was open. He rushed through, up three flights of steps, and found himself in a long hallway. It was a mirror image to one he'd been dragged through earlier—right down to the dead guards at the far exit. The Russian officer and his cohorts had likely killed them on their way out. He moved to the exit and tried the key card. It didn't work. A quick search of the downed guards turned up nothing. He checked the evacuation placard. The only other way out was through the main lobby one floor up.

He raced up the emergency staircase and cracked the door leading into the lobby. He knew from the placards that he was in a structure called the Palace of Nations. But he'd never read anything about it, so he had nothing to draw on. It had to be big. He knew that much. And given the range of dignitaries who were in attendance, he had no doubt that the main floor was teeming with people. Most of them would be innocents.

But not all of them.

He checked the weapons slung over either shoulder, his mind flashing on the specs: Steyr TMPs—*Taktische Maschinenpistoles* or Tactical Machine Pistols. Eight-hundred-fifty-rounds-per-minute fire rate. Limited range. Good stopping power. He flicked off the safeties and kicked through the door.

The first thing he heard was sirens.

The first thing he saw was mayhem.

He stepped onto the ground floor of an expansive lounge that wrapped around the perimeter of the largest window-wall he'd ever seen. Each glass panel stretched three stories tall. The entire curtain wall was as long as a football field. It stretched away in a quarter-moon arc, overlooking a park that was overrun by news reporters and television crews. Small groups of well-dressed men and women stood among them. Many of them pointed up at the sky—it glowed with an amber cast. In the distance, crowds of people made their way toward the building. A line of emergency vehicles wound its way through them like an armed division on an assault charge. The frightened population knew world leaders were gathered here.

They wanted answers.

Jake returned his attention to what a sign referred to as the DELEGATES' LOUNGE, where coffee tables and sitting areas fanned outward from a serpentine bar. The space was empty. Half-eaten sandwiches and drinks covered the tables, and chairs were overturned. Whoever had been here had left in a hurry, and Jake suspected they'd joined the crowd outside. He heard voices overhead. There was a mezzanine balcony above, where a group of men and women were making their way toward the main entrance.

They didn't run.

They didn't panic.

Members of the Order.

He trailed them from one story below, steering clear of the windows and hugging the curved inner wall. When he rounded the bend beyond the lounge, he hesitated. The main lobby was dead ahead. Reporters were stacked three deep outside the locked entrance. Three security guards shifted nervously inside the glass wall. Their backs were to Jake.

But it was the roped-off entrance to the main conference room that shrank the skin around Jake's spine. A pedestal supported a sign that read MEETING IN PROGRESS. A placard by the door read CAPACITY 880. He realized that the Order group he'd seen up above must have exited the large assembly room from the upper level.

Jake sprinted forward. He was one pace from the roped-off entrance when he heard the screams.

Hundreds of them.

The doors flew open, and a wave of people bowled him over and knocked him to the floor. People gasped, coughed, and clutched their throats. The rush of air exiting the room was sour. Jake felt his throat close up.

A woman collapsed onto his legs. Several others fell nearby. A few made it as far as the lobby exit before succumbing. Jake went into a coughing fit of his own. He freed himself from under the woman and crawled toward the exit. Reporters stared wide-eyed from the other side of the glass. Cameras flashed and a TV crew pressed close. The group from the balcony stepped into the lobby from a nearby stairway. They walked briskly toward the exit, where two of the three security guards had clasped their throats. The third nodded to the approaching group. He escorted his fellow Order members toward one of the side doors.

Jake felt a fit of rage. Hundreds of people were dying because of them. An explosion of adrenaline brought him to his feet. His weapons hung loose from their shoulder slings. He grabbed them in either hand and did the first thing that came to mind.

He aimed at the crowd of newspeople on the other side of the glass. He waited a beat.

The publicity hounds lurched backward, raising their arms defensively.

Another beat.

They turned and ran.

As soon as the last of them cleared the steps, Jake adjusted his aim and opened fire. Twin lines of bullet holes raked across the middle of the massive curtain wall above and beside the doorway. The tempered glass shattered into a million pieces, cascading like a massive waterfall. Two Order members jumped clear. The rest were buried in the deluge.

Tons of glass piled onto the floor.

Tons of fresh air rushed in.

Jake was still coughing. He discarded the weapons and ran back into the assembly room. Fewer than a quarter of the attendees were still standing. He urged them into the lobby as his own throat closed further.

An older gentleman struggled to help a woman to the door. Jake lent a shoulder and helped them out. Then he staggered back in and grabbed a man just as he was about to fall. They were halfway to the lobby when the fire crews and EMTs arrived with gas masks. When one of them finally relieved him of his burden, he collapsed to the floor. The men and women lying beside him were dead or dying.

He couldn't save them all.

Chapter 57

Palais des Nations
Geneva, Switzerland

STRONG HANDS PINNED JAKE'S SHOULDERS. HE WAS ON HIS back. His chest was on fire, and his heart jackhammered against his ribs. The muscles of his diaphragm heaved—but only a small amount of air squeaked through his choked windpipe.

His vision was blurred. A shadow crossed over him. He felt a finger to his neck. A voice said, "He's still alive. Shoot him!"

Jake tried to roll away, but his muscles seemed devoid of strength. His limbs were lead. The hands holding him down were relentless.

He felt a sharp stab of pain in his thigh and a rush of coolness spread from his leg. Then hands ripped his collar open and there was the cold press of a stethoscope on his chest.

"Hand me the trach kit," the voice said. It sounded robotic. And female. Jake ignored her, instead focusing on the slip of air that leaked into his lungs. He told his body to relax. The figure above him shifted, and he felt something cold and damp swab the area just beneath his Adam's apple. A part of him realized what was about to happen. There was an external pressure against his neck, and he could imagine the woman holding his skin taut while she readied a scalpel. Jake twisted his head violently to one side. He felt a sharp nick on his neck.

“Jesus, Kurt. Hold him!” the woman said.

Jake felt blood dribble around the side of his neck. He sucked inward, and more air rushed in. He harbored the sweetness of it. Then he slowly exhaled.

“Wait,” the man holding him down said. “He’s breathing.”

“Please don’t struggle,” the woman’s voice said. “I’ve put the scalpel away.” Moving one hand beneath his neck and the other onto his forehead, she gently straightened his head and strapped a clear plastic oxygen mask over his nose and mouth. He felt the air passage open up. A beat later, his lungs filled with air.

Jake took several deep breaths. His vision cleared. He was in the assembly room. It was crowded with prone forms and emergency personnel dressed in hazmat suits. The EMT released the pressure on his shoulders.

The second EMT—the woman—knelt beside Jake. She leaned over so he could see her features through her faceplate. “Can you hear me?” she asked through the hood. Her voice sounded tinny through the suit’s amplifier.

He nodded.

The woman squeezed his arm. “You’re going to be all right,” she said. Her tone was professional. “Your breathing mask is connected to this tank.” She looped a strap over his shoulder and showed him the pony tank that was cinched to it. She placed the unit on his belly and moved his hand onto it. The steel cylinder was about the size of a liter water bottle. It was hefty. “Hold on to this. Don’t remove the mask until you’re well outside. I’ve injected you with epinephrine. Side effects are headache and anxiety. Do you understand?”

He nodded again.

Her hands moved efficiently as she bandaged the wound on his neck. She shook her head. “Thank God it’s just a shallow cut. A few butterflies and a wrap will take care of it. Wow, a half inch closer and I might have slit your jugular.” Then, as if realizing she’d just gone off-script, she went on to explain. “The epi didn't work fast enough for the first two victims I treated. That's why I went so quickly for the trach." She hesitated before adding, "I—I'm sorry." When she was finished with the final wrap on his neck, her eyes softened. She stooped closer and whispered, "There are people who want to talk with you. They're angry. I don't know what that's all about. But I do know this: from what folks have told us, you saved a lot of lives today by blowing out those windows. Whatever else happens, I want to thank you for that." She patted him on the chest, then stood and motioned to her partner. "He's ready," she said, moving on to the next victim.

The man helped Jake to his feet. The room spun once or twice, and he felt wobbly at first, but his strength returned with each step. He kept one hand wrapped around the oxygen tank to prevent it from banging against his pelvic bone. In the lobby a trail had been swept between knee-high mounds of popcorn-size glass. Escorts and their charges walked in a single-file line toward the exit. Volunteers waited outside to take over for the EMTs. One by one, victims were handed off so that the hazmat-clothed medics could move back inside. Jake was passed to two men with strong frames and crew cuts. They appeared to have been waiting for him. They were dressed in dark slacks and white shirts. Their ties hung loose, and their sleeves were rolled up. Jake suspected their sport coats weren't far off.

Along with their weapons.

He'd recognized the unique style of their rubber-soled shoes right away. His suspicions were confirmed when the white fabric of one of the men's shirts stretched over a muscled shoulder. The outline of the tattoo was the same as that of the assassin he'd encountered in Focette. These were Victor's men.

But Jake didn't let on. He was done playing the patsy. Victor and his creeps weren't dealing with the same befuddled man they'd dealt with yesterday. His memory was back, his thoughts were clear, and his mind was made up.

He was going to stop them if it was the last thing he did.

The park was awash with victims and emergency personnel. In order to make more room, the news vans had moved aside. The mood was somber, but the normal feeding frenzy one would expect at a time like this wasn't present. Yes, film crews continued to capture the moment, and some reporters held private court with the lenses of their TV cameras, the disaster providing a grim backdrop for the stories they relayed to the world. But others had abandoned their microphones and equipment in order to help the victims.

It gave him hope.

A massive crowd had formed on the outskirts of the park. Men, women, children, families—they huddled in groups. Hugging. Holding hands. Crying. Some watched as victims were escorted from the Palace of Nations. Many more simply stared at the glowing amber stripes in the sky.

Very few of them held up their cell phone cameras.

The world would never be the same, Jake thought. The existence of life beyond the borders of our planet was no longer conjecture. It was a reality. He supposed it shouldn't have come as a big surprise, recalling something he'd read after his encounter with the first pyramid. When the Hubble telescope had been launched years ago, scientists had used it to study one tiny piece of the universe. Within it they had discovered *tens of thousands* of galaxies that they hadn't known existed before. And each of those galaxies contained *hundreds of billions* of stars like our sun. And around those stars orbited planets. He remembered discussing it with Tony. His friend had said that it hurt his brain to think about it.

Jake understood. There's only so much a mind can handle. It wasn't man's arrogance that led him to believe that he was the sole form of life in the universe. It was his inability to grasp the alternative.

Jake felt better. His airways had cleared, his strength had returned, and his rage had a target.

Two targets.

But first, he needed to use them to get clear of the palace… and the authorities.

The two men led him across the grass toward a tented care center. But instead of stopping, they kept walking. He sensed an increase in tension through the grips on his arms, but he didn't resist. His shoulders were slumped, his feet dragged, and he still wore the oxygen mask.

I'm not a threat.

They approached a copse of trees. The road beyond was lined with parked vehicles. Traffic in either direction was bunching up. A siren sounded as an ambulance tried to push through. A Swiss motorcycle cop dismounted and waved traffic aside. A man exited a parked SUV on the opposite side of the street. Cars passed slowly in front of him. He stood beside his vehicle and glanced from Jake to the cop and back again. One of the men holding him gave the man a subtle nod.

Jake readied himself. He absorbed the scene, sorting out the angles, the moves, the timing. The ambulance weaved its way toward the SUV. The copse was dead ahead. The trio crossed into the shadows of the stand of trees at the same moment that the ambulance blocked the view of the man by the SUV.

Jake faked a stumble, leaning to the left. The guard on that side brought his other hand around to catch him. Jake twisted his torso and thrust the oxygen tank upward in a savage strike to the base of the man's chin. Bone cracked. The man toppled backward like a felled tree. The motion caused the other guard to lose his grip. Jake reversed direction to face him. He ripped off his oxygen mask, freed the cylinder strap from his shoulder, and swung the steel tank like a mace. The startled guard dodged backward to avoid the blow, but Jake pressed forward, whipping the tank around in a figure eight. The guard was ready for it. He blocked it with a forearm. But by then Jake had already abandoned the weapon, releasing it midflight as he initiated his next strike. It came from below—under the man's guard—as he drove his heel into the man's knee. The joint gave way. The man spilled to the grass with a howl.

That's when a third man stepped from behind a tree and leveled a silenced pistol at Jake's head. He stood less than three paces away. "We were told to kill you if we couldn't—"

He cut off when a teen on a bicycle streaked into the trees from Jake's right. The cycle rocketed straight at the man with the gun. By the time he realized that the cyclist was an active threat, it was too late. He swung to face the bike just as the front wheel struck him between the legs. His eyes went wide, he folded in half, and the teen went flying over the bars.

It was Ahmed.

Jake rushed forward, overlaying the new chess pieces onto the evolving tactical schematic in his mind. He grabbed the pistol from the stunned gunman and swiped its butt across the man's temple. His eyes rolled into the back of his head, and he fell still. Jake spun around toward the guard with the ruined knee. The man was still on the ground, a finger pressed to one ear. He spoke urgently to someone on the other end of the connection. Jake's aim was instant and instinctual. He squeezed the trigger. The pistol spit, and the man's ear and finger disappeared in a spray of blood. A part of Jake's mind marveled at the fact that the bullet had impacted at the exact spot that his mind had been trained on. He may have lost his super reflexes, but his brain-and-body coordination was better than ever. He fired again, and the man spun from the slug that entered his shoulder, eliminating him as an immediate threat. The first guard was out cold, so Jake didn't worry about him. He turned to Ahmed as he unscrewed the suppressor from the end of the pistol. The kid had pushed to his feet. He had a bloody nose and an eager expression.

"You ready to run?" Jake asked.

Ahmed nodded.

Jake pointed the pistol at the sky and squeezed off three rounds. Ahmed flinched at the first shot, but not the second two. The gunshots echoed across the grounds. Jake dropped the pistol beside the gunmen, grabbed Ahmed by the arm, and took off at a sprint.

There were shouts from the park. Several people pointed in their direction.

"Stay close," Jake said as they exited the tree line. On the other side of the street, the man by the SUV spotted them immediately. He had his hand inside his windbreaker, craning his neck from one side to the other as traffic passed in front of him. Jake ignored him. The motorcycle cop had heard the shots. He moved in a crouch down the sidewalk. His gun was drawn. Jake saw two more policemen running his way from down the street. Then he heard another cop's whistle from the park. The alert had been sounded. He and Ahmed ran toward the motorcycle officer.

"Help!" Jake shouted, waving his hands back and forth.

The cop spotted them and hesitated. He held the pistol in both hands. It was pointed at the ground.

Jake whispered to Ahmed, "Act scared."

Jake skidded to a stop in front of the cop, ducking down between two parked cars. He pulled Ahmed down beside him. The kid was crying. "Some guy's shooting people!" Jake screeched. He pointed to the trees. "Over there!"

The policeman crouched beside them. He bought the act without question. "How many?"

"One shooter," Jake said, panting. "Two bodies. S-so much blood!" Then his eyes rolled, his shoulders drooped, and he collapsed into the cop. The officer braced himself and steadied Jake. Ahmed's sobs seemed to take on an edge of panic at the sight.

"You're going to be all right," the cop said. "Just stay down." Then he relayed the information into his helmet microphone and ran toward the copse of trees.

As soon as the policeman's back was turned, Jake grabbed Ahmed and took off. They ran in a crouch in the opposite direction, being careful to keep the line of parked cars between them and Victor's last gunman. A quick glance confirmed that the man mirrored their track on the opposite side of the street. Jake caught a glimpse of a weapon beneath his jacket.

But I bet you don't have one of these, Jake said to himself, squeezing the set of keys he'd lifted from the cop's belt ring.

The motorcycle was parked in front of the next car. He grabbed the handlebars, released the kickstand, and jumped onboard. By the time he turned the key and started her up, Ahmed had his arms locked around Jake's waist. Horns honked, and Jake saw the gunman in the bike's mirror. The man raced between traffic. He held a machine pistol.

"Hang on!" Jake shouted. He kicked it in gear, revved the engine, and popped the clutch. The BMW R1200RT motorcycle leaped across the sidewalk and onto the grass. Bullets ripped into the parked car behind them. Jake opened the throttle and steered a course that paralleled the walkway. He and Ahmed ducked low on the seat. They were at sixty mph in 3.5 seconds. He saw the jittering image of the gunman receding in the mirror. The muzzle of his weapon flashed, and Jake felt the disturbance of air as bullets whizzed past them. There was a deep thud in the rear saddle, and Jake reacted with a skidding turn across the sidewalk and into traffic. He rode the centerline between opposing vehicles, speeding past startled drivers. He didn't slow until the gunman was out of sight.

"Are you okay?" he asked over his shoulder.

"Yes!" Ahmed said. There was no fear in his voice. Jake wondered at the boy's courage.

"You did really good back there," Jake said.

It seemed as if Ahmed sat taller in response to the comment. But his words were humble. "Allah was with us."

"I'm grateful."

"It was my duty. We are family," Ahmed said.

Jake was proud as hell of the kid. Ahmed was right, he thought. They *were* family. In fact, Jake was the only family Ahmed and Sarafina and Alex had left now. He dreaded that he was going to have to break the news about Francesca to them. But first things first. "Where are Sarafina and Alex?"

"At the safe house."

Jake breathed a sigh of relief. He thanked God they were safe. He remembered the address from his visit there two days ago with Tony and the rest of them.

Also dead.

He entered the location into the bike's nav system.

"It's good to have you back," Ahmed said. "There aren't many around me these days that can speak Dari with me."

Jake hadn't even realized he'd been speaking in Ahmed's native language. It had come naturally to him.

Ahmed added, "Are you all back, Jake? I mean, are you back to the way you were? Do you remember everything?"

Am I all back? Jake asked himself. Sure, if you don't count the huge hole in my gut from the loss of the woman I love and my best friends in the world. He flashed on Victor's nonchalant manner when he had shared the news of their deaths. Jake's blood boiled at the thought of it.

"Yeah, Ahmed," he said. "I remember everything."

Chapter 58

Thirty-Two Thousand Feet over Northern Italy

VICTOR GAZED THROUGH THE PORTHOLE WINDOW OF THE luxurious Gulfstream IV. It climbed toward its cruising altitude of thirty-two thousand feet. Beneath him, a scattering of white clouds stretched to the horizon. Above, the blue sky was stitched with a network of glowing lines of light. It was the most beautiful thing he'd ever seen.

Cæli Regere, he recited to himself, absently rubbing the fabric that covered his tattooed shoulder.

The heavens shall rule.

A thousand years of preparation had finally come to a head, he thought. All doubt could now be buried. The events unfolding around the world were proof positive that all their planning had been justified. Mankind's judgment was at hand. The alert had gone out to Order members everywhere. The gathering time was upon them. Many were already settled on the island. The rest were en route.

The birthplace of the new world.

Hans sat stoically beside him. He seethed. The American had escaped him. Even worse, he'd escaped the gas attack and severely reduced the death toll of those in attendance. To Hans, such failure was inexcusable. He'd not rest until he righted it. Victor had shared his anger at first, at least inwardly. But it had dissipated quickly in light of what had happened since. They may have lost the American, he thought, but that didn't mean they couldn't control him.

He recalled the urgent phone call he'd received while waiting for Hans and his men to load the chair into the cargo hold. It had been the leader of the backup team that he'd sent to the residence—one of his agents from Interpol. His report had been brief and to the point. By the time they'd arrived on scene, police and firefighters were there. The blaze in the garage had been extinguished. The guards stationed at the house were dead. The old gondolier had been critically wounded and rushed to a hospital. There was no sign of the Italian woman.

Then the man had given Victor the good news. He and the backup team were en route to the plane—and they weren't coming empty-handed.

Victor turned to look at the two young guests seated in the lounge area at the rear of the cabin. They stared back at him. The young girl was the picture of defiance. Her jaw was clamped, her lips pursed, and her eyes shot daggers. But it was a transparent veneer. He sensed her fear. Her fingers tapped a rhythmic pattern on the armrests.

The young boy was another matter. He resembled his father in more than physical features. He exuded a calm confidence that was disturbing. The boy tilted his head to one side, and it felt to Victor as if his eyes bore right through him. Then, as if the child realized he'd won the staring contest, his lips turned up in a crooked smile.

Victor turned away.

The boy's expression chilled him.

Part III

Any intelligent fool can make things bigger, more complex, and more violent. It takes a touch of genius—and a lot of courage—to move in the opposite direction.

—Albert Einstein

Chapter 59

Geneva, Switzerland

Jake ducked out of view of the peephole. Ahmed did the same. They were in the hallway outside the door to the safe house. Voices inside the room had startled them. They flattened themselves on either side of the doorway and listened. The voices were muffled. Male and female. Jake edged forward in a crouch and placed his ear against the wood. It took a second for his belief system to acknowledge what he was hearing. He stared wide-eyed at Ahmed.

Then he rose and knocked on the door.

There was a woman's yelp inside, pounding feet, a man's warning shout, and then the door flew open.

Jake was stunned. He had never seen a more beautiful sight. Francesca stood framed in the doorway. Her gaze had been aimed downward, as if she'd been expecting someone shorter. When she realized it was him, the hopeful expression on her tear-streaked face turned to shock. Her body tensed and her eyes darted to Ahmed. She lurched forward and looked down either side of the hall. Then she grabbed Ahmed and drew him into a desperate embrace.

"I thought you were dead!" she said. Ahmed stiffened under the assault, but he didn't push her off. "Where are Sarafina and Alex?" she asked.

"They're not here?" Ahmed replied.

Francesca's face turned pale. She turned to Jake. Her expression pleaded for an answer.

Jake shook his head, tight-lipped.

She rushed into his arms and buried her face in the crook of his neck. Her shoulders hitched from silent sobs. The rest of his friends stood in a semicircle behind her. He could hardly believe it. He'd thought everyone in this room had been killed. He took them in one by one, awash with an overwhelming sense of hope. Tony nodded, Marshall grinned, and Lacey wiped away a tear. Timmy fidgeted like he wanted to exchange a high five.

Jake's next words were intended for Francesca, but he spoke loudly enough for everyone to hear. "We'll find them. I promise."

The words stilled her. She sniffled once and pulled back. Her eyes narrowed.

"Y-you spoke in English," she said in a throaty voice.

"That's right!" Ahmed said, pushing into the room. "Jake is back!" He stepped clear as everyone else surged forward with hand pats and hugs.

* * *

Francesca's emotions roiled like opposing tidal wives. The only man she had ever loved stood next to her. He remembered everything. She clung to his arm. It should have been a joyful moment. Instead, her elation was smothered by concern for her father and fear for Sarafina and Alex.

"It wasn't my fault," Ahmed said. He paced back and forth among the group. He stared at the floor and shook his head from side to side as he spoke. "I told them to stay. Why would they leave? Where would they go? Why didn't they listen? I told them I'd call. It's not my fault. I shared my pastry. They should be here. It was my job to take care—"

He stopped abruptly when Francesca stepped forward and blocked his path. She knew he was reverting. She'd witnessed it many times before. Stress took him back to a time when he was a child.

He sidestepped her. "How come they could hear Jake but I couldn't? It's not fair. I'm the first one he ever talked to that way. I taught him Dari. Why—"

She moved in front of him again. He started to move around her.

"Flip it," she said softly.

Ahmed stopped midstride. He lifted his gaze and glanced awkwardly at each of them. It was Tony who spoke first.

"I'm proud of you, pal," he said, leading Ahmed toward the sitting area. "Let's chill a minute over here." The rest of them followed, except Timmy, who returned to the dining room table to examine the laptop and backup drive they'd taken from Victor's residence.

Tony said, "How about you start by telling us how you got out of Venice?" He settled into one of the overstuffed chairs. His posture and demeanor made him appear relaxed and patient, but Francesca sensed the boiling anxiousness beneath the facade. The former special-ops sergeant knew a thing or two about interrogation, she thought. The others had picked up on it, too. Tension leaked from their expressions as they took their seats. She and Jake sat on the couch. Lacey and Marshall pulled up chairs from the dining room.

Ahmed preferred to stand. Sometimes, being center stage seemed to help him collect his thoughts.

"Start at the beginning," Tony said.

Ahmed blew out a breath. Then he gave them the highlights of everything that had happened: the tale of their harrowing escape from the fire in the cellar, the old man who'd helped them with money and fake IDs, the train ride to the safe house. Francesca was amazed at their ingenuity. She'd always been proud of their intellect, but the determination and courage they'd exhibited went beyond her expectations. She remembered something her father had told her long ago. *A person's true character is revealed in the face of great danger.*

Ahmed turned toward Jake. "We'd only been here a few minutes when Alex and Sarafina felt you…in their heads. They knew you were in trouble."

Jake seemed to tense at the comment. Ahmed didn't notice. Francesca did.

"Somehow Alex knew you were at the Palace of Nations," Ahmed continued. "That's why I left. I told them to stay here…" His voice trailed off. His head dropped.

"You saved my life," Jake said. Ahmed looked up and locked eyes with him. Francesca felt his swell of pride.

"What about before that?" Tony asked.

Ahmed looked to the ceiling as he recalled events. "We got here right after you left," he said. "The coffeepot was still warm. We saw where you went on Google Maps."

Francesca's breath caught in her throat. The others exchanged furtive glances.

Tony said, "You're talking about Victor's residence?"

"I guess. It was a mansion by the lake." When he seemed to sense the mood change in the room, he quickly added, "I told them we *couldn't* go there! We saw the empty ammunition boxes in the garbage. Why would they…" His voice caught, his eyes widened, and he looked out the picture window.

But Francesca was already three steps ahead of him. Her children had been alone when the sky had erupted in light. They would have known Uncle Tony was close by. They would have run to him.

Ahmed's voice was pained. "But they shouldn't have gone there. I told them it was dangerous. If anything went wrong, they were supposed to call me on the phone."

"Phone?" Marshall and Timmy said simultaneously. Marshall stood so fast that Ahmed took a sudden step back.

"Uh, yeah. We picked up two pay-as-you-go phones before we left Venice."

"Let me see," Marshall said. The fingers of his hands twitched like a kid about to get a chocolate bar.

"It's in my backpack," Ahmed said, leading him toward the dining room.

Timmy's fingers moved quickly over the computer keyboard as he hacked into the site he needed. He didn't look up when he asked, "Do you remember their phone number?"

"Yes," Ahmed said. "It's programmed on that phone."

"Excellent," Marshall said, examining the phone. "Good, it's GPS enabled."

While the three of them huddled over the computer, the rest rose to their feet in the sitting area. Francesca leaned into Jake for support, one arm entwined in his.

"I thought the cell service was down," Francesca said.

"It may be overloaded," Jake said. "But that doesn't mean it's down."

"As long as the battery is installed, they'll be able to lock on to their location," Lacey said. "They did that in my last film." She took Francesca's free hand. "Don't worry. We'll find them."

The swell of hope she felt was cut short by the grim expression on Tony's face.

"What is it?" Francesca asked.

His lips thinned.

Tony's hesitancy made her angry. She let go of Jake and Lacey and stepped to face him, hands on her hips. "The world is on fire, my father may be dead, for all I know, and my children are lost. I have no feelings left to spare, Tony. So don't try. *Avete capito?*"

"Yeah, I understand. And you're right. We're all in this together, come hell or"—he pointed out the window toward the sky—"high water." He waited a beat before continuing. His tone stiffened. "As we were leaving the residence, more of Victor's men were coming up the drive. Sarafina is a resourceful young girl, so I'm hoping she steered clear. But if she didn't…"

Lacey said, "If those creeps took them, there's no telling where they could be."

"It doesn't matter where they are," Jake said evenly. There was a menacing edge to his voice that caused Francesca to flinch. His eyes seem to be focused a thousand miles away. The room quieted. Even the guys at the dining table stopped what they were doing.

"We'll find them," Jake said. "You have my word. If they avoided being taken at the residence, so much the better. But if Victor's men did take them, know this—they won't be harmed. At least not until Victor's got me strapped in a chair to watch. And that's okay, too. Because I intend to sit in that chair one last time anyway. I *will* save the children. And I *will* stop Victor Brun."

Jake's steeled gaze focused on each of them, one at a time. Francesca imagined it was the same expression that a defiant prisoner might have when spitting in the face of his executioner. His eyes didn't soften until they settled on hers. He gripped her shoulders. The connection was instantaneous. He was in her mind; she was in his. It had been six years since she'd last been linked to him like this. But she hadn't forgotten what it felt like: the power of his life force, the sense of peace, the intense attraction of spirit and body. Squeezing her flesh, he said, "Whatever it takes."

He released her. The spell was broken. But the promise still warmed her blood.

Tony placed a hand on Jake's shoulder. "And this time you ain't going in alone," he said.

"That's right," Lacey said, hands on her hips.

"Hell yes!" Marshall chimed in from the dining table.

Timmy high-fived him and said, "I'm in!"

Francesca wondered at Ahmed's hesitation. He squared his shoulders and watched her. There was no fear emanating from him. Instead, she saw in him a strong sense of purpose. He seemed to be looking to her for something. She thought she understood. He held his fervor in check, awaiting her lead. Out of respect. Out of love. She nodded, more to herself than to him. Her jaw tightened. She wiped both eyes with a rough pull of her wrists. The time for crying had passed. She fixed her resolve, balled her fists, and said, "Whatever it takes!"

"Whatever it takes," Ahmed said, his fist clenched overhead.

"Whatever it takes!" the rest of them shouted.

Chapter 60

Geneva, Switzerland

HERE WE GO AGAIN, JAKE THOUGHT. I'VE BEEN BACK IN THEIR lives for less than two days, and already Mario is critically wounded, the children are missing, and the rest of them have gathered around me to face down a challenge better suited for a world of armies.

They were spread out around the dining room table. Timmy was attempting to hack into the laptop that they'd grabbed from Victor's residence. Marshall hovered over the other laptop. He'd taken on the task of isolating the location of Sarafina's phone. Though nothing had been said between them, Jake sensed the underlying competition to see who'd be finished first. Their fingers blurred over the keyboards. Lacey filled cups from a fresh-brewed pot of coffee.

Francesca sat on one side of Jake, with Tony and Ahmed on the other. They listened intently while Jake filled them in on what had happened at the Palace of Nations. He told them what he'd learned about Victor Brun and the Order. Each layer of information added weight to the tension in the room. At one point Francesca felt compelled to get up and pace around the table, arms crossed, deep in thought. Jake lowered his eyes when he got to the part about his rage at the sight of her death. But he didn't leave anything out, including the ease with which he'd taken the lives of the men in the chair room. They deserved to know it all.

When he was finished, it was Lacey who spoke first. "Sounds like the son of a bitch has got his fingers in a lot of pies."

"Sure," Tony said. "Brun and his pals have had a thousand years to get ready. We already know he's got plants at high levels in some governments. The Russians, for one."

Timmy didn't stop typing when he added, "The US, too. Remember, they didn't have any trouble getting an assassin into our top secret facility in order to try to kill Jake."

"Not to mention Interpol," Francesca added.

Ahmed was looking out the window. "Something's happened!" he said. "Everybody's running."

Lacey moved beside him. "He's right. It looks like chaos just graduated to pandemonium."

"Switch on the TV," Jake said.

"Already done," Marshall replied, holding the remote.

They gathered in front of the fifty-inch flat-screen.

The images and videos that filled the screen were horrific. It was an ever-changing slide show that depicted death and destruction on a massive scale: gruesome images of heaping piles of dead bodies, drawn from the archives of recorded history. There were battlefields ridden with the mangled ruins of life, and endless lines of victims being herded for slaughter, toward gas chambers, firing lines, or worse. There was no sound track. None was necessary.

Francesca and Lacey collapsed onto the couch. Francesca had a hand to her mouth as if to prevent some evil from reaching inside. Marshall shrank to Lacey's side, pulling her close. Ahmed moved beside Francesca.

Jake couldn't join them. His focus remained glued to the screen. He knew what was coming.

Marshall pointed the remote at the screen, switching from channel to channel. It was the same on every station: burned-out villages and towns. Smoke-filled streets strewn with bodies. Dogs licking at the charred and curled remains of children. Gut-wrenching scenes of abuse and murder from ethnic cleansing in Bosnia, Nigeria, Rwanda, Kosovo, Sri Lanka, Indonesia, and elsewhere. Several sketched images depicted the slow but steady slaughter of American Indians by US settlers. It went on and on. No deplorable secret was left uncovered. All was revealed for the world to see.

"Where are they getting all this from?" Lacey muttered, referring to the alien objects.

"If they can override broadcast signals around the world, it'd be a piece of cake for them to access our databases," Marshall said. "Hell, they're probably tapped into the Library of Congress."

The sad truth was that it could stream for months and never show the same image or video twice, Jake thought. And that was the lesson of it. It was as if the lead prosecutor for the mother of all trials was laying out his evidence.

Jake felt hollow inside. Who was he in this macabre play if not the "inside man" who'd betrayed his people to the court?

The theme of the images shifted to wars. Embedded videos of modern battles mingled with artistic renderings of ancient conflicts. In either case, it was still violence on an immense scale, veiled in the name of country or religion, but motivated by greed and the hunger for power and wealth. The Crusades, the "Holy" Roman Empire, the Mongol invasions of Genghis Khan. The World Wars, Vietnam, Korea, Iraq, Afghanistan, and so many more. Chemical warfare, carpet bombs, napalm…

The nuclear blasts at Hiroshima and Nagasaki.

The message was clear: No country on Earth had been spared the violence. And none could claim innocence from wielding it.

Judgment cast, Jake thought. Mankind has been found guilty.

As if to accent his conclusion, a digital timer suddenly appeared in the top-right corner of the screen. It glowed with the same color as the lines in the sky. It read 40H:00M:00S.

They all held their breath.

A beat later, the clock switched to 39H:59M:59S.

Seconds continued to tick off.

The countdown to the annihilation of mankind had begun.

Jake walked to the TV and switched it off. He turned to face his friends. He crossed his arms, kept his mouth shut, and waited.

Eyes narrowed, bodies shifted. Francesca locked gazes with Jake. He sensed her probing his emotions, and he welcomed it. He had nothing to hide. The others respected the moment with their silence. Jake caught the subtle changes in her expression. Her lips tightened, her jaw jutted forward, and the fear in her eyes was replaced with fierce determination. She riveted him with a fervent stare.

Finally, she rose to her feet. "This changes nothing," she said flatly. "I'm going to make another pot of coffee. We've much planning to do."

Her unflinching reaction seemed to fuel the fire within them all.

Jake used his thumb to point at her as she strode to the kitchen. "That's *my* girl," he said with more than a little pride.

Ahmed mimicked the motion and said, "That's *my* mom!"

"You go, girl," Lacey said.

Tony nodded in agreement. "So where were we?" he said, making his way back to the dining table. The others followed. Marshall and Timmy resumed their work on the computers.

"Talking about Victor," Lacey said. "He figures that his group—the Order—is going to be spared extermination. How is he going to make that happen?"

"Good question," Jake said. "But he seemed real sure of himself on that score."

"They'd need an isolated location," Tony said. "To keep their population out of harm's way."

"You're talking about a mass exodus," Francesca said from the kitchen. "Entire families."

“There could be hundreds of them,” Lacey said.

“More like thousands,” Jake said.

Marshall made a final keystroke entry. Then he sat back and clenched and unclenched his fingers. He watched the screen as if waiting for a program to load. He glanced up and said, “Which means they’d need an effective means of telling friend from foe. They can’t possibly know everyone personally, especially if they’re scattered across the globe.”

Timmy seemed oblivious to Marshall’s comment. His keystrokes seemed to grow more frantic. He was totally engrossed in the machine.

Ahmed said, “Sort of like a secret handshake?”

“Yeah,” Tony said, catching on. “But higher-tech. Facial recognition or something like that.”

Jake recalled how Victor’s men communicated. “They have some sort of embedded comm devices. I’ve seen them press a spot just beneath their ears when they communicate.”

“Military-grade implantable comm units,” Tony said. “Very high-tech.”

“They can do that?” Lacey asked.

“Are you kidding?” Marshall said. “Intel is working on a brain-implant chip that will allow you to enter data into a computer simply by thinking it. They expect it to be ready by the year 2020. It won’t be long after that until it’s adios, cell phones.”

The mention of a brain implant sparked a knowing look between Jake and Ahmed.

Marshall continued, “But for now, the communication implant you’re talking about is still a serious surgery. No big deal for the field operatives, but overkill for the families. They’d need something simpler than that for tracking and identification purposes.” His computer beeped. He made a quick entry and added, “Something that would provide each individual with a unique identifier.”

Lacey said, “What’s wrong with an ID card?”

"Too easy to forge," Ahmed said, drawing on his recent experience.

"I'm in!" Timmy said excitedly. His fingers tapped in an organized frenzy on Victor's computer. He paused a moment, his eyes scanning a document. Another entry, another document, then he started typing again. This went on for several moments. Finally, whimpers leaked from his throat, increasing in frequency with the speed of his keystrokes. Then all at once he lifted his hands in the air. His jaw was set, his eyes burned with intensity, and he pointedly dropped an index finger on the ENTER key. A beat later, he did a Tiger Woods–style fist pump and shouted, "Yes!" He spun the laptop around so everyone could see the screen. "And I know just how they're doing it!"

Jake leaned forward to get a closer look. It was a satellite map of Geneva. There were several clusters of blinking lights overlaid onto the map.

"It's a tracking system," Timmy said. He placed the cursor over one of the lights, and a rectangular window popped up with an alphanumeric string. "Military-grade RFIDs. The same sort of thing that they use in consumer products. Except this is an active system, meaning it transmits a wireless signal. They have a limited range, but if they're piggybacked onto the cellular system, then they can be tracked anywhere there's coverage. They're easily embedded under the skin using a modified vaccine gun."

"Each of those dots is a person?" Ahmed asked, pointing to the screen.

"Yep."

Tony pointed at a small cluster of four lights. "That's Victor's residence."

But Jake was focused on the twenty or more blips bunched within the Palace of Nations. "This isn't a live feed."

"No," Timmy said, pointing at the digital clock in the corner of the screen. "This was recorded about an hour ago. But I can fast-forward." He made an entry, and the blips started to move.

They watched as the scene unfolded: Several blips of light at the palace sped northward toward a waiting cluster of blips at the airport. The four lights at the residence jiggled somewhat but remained on the property. Three more lights traveled to the residence, hesitated a moment, and departed on a track toward the airport. The remaining lights at the palace were starting to exit the complex, when every light on the screen suddenly disappeared.

"What happened?" Lacey asked.

"That's gotta be just after the launch," Timmy said. "When the cell system was overloaded." He rewound to the point just before the lights vanished.

Tony said, "They were hightailing to the airport—"

"Oh, no," Marshall interjected, staring at his own laptop. He looked as if the wind had gotten knocked out of him. "I located Sarafina's cell phone," he said softly. He slid his laptop around so that it was alongside Timmy's. It depicted the same Google map of Geneva. He pointed to a glowing icon containing the phone number on the disposable phone. "This was her last location before the overload."

There were gasps around the table. It was the exact same spot as that of the three blips that had departed the residence toward the airport.

Victor's men had grabbed the children.

The room grew silent. Eyes turned to Francesca. Jake squeezed her hand, but the tremble he expected wasn't there. He sensed the despair that boiled beneath the surface of her stern expression. But she pushed it aside like an army general planning his next move after a failed battle.

"So how do we find them?" she asked evenly.

Jake compartmentalized the swell of admiration he felt for her. He'd act on that later. For now, another part of his mind had already grasped the solution. He pointed at Timmy's screen. "Zoom all the way out."

Timmy placed the cursor on the minus-sign end of the zoom bar and clicked six or seven times. With each click, the satellite image zoomed outward to capture a larger view: the snowcapped Alps, Switzerland, Europe, Asia, and Africa, the world…

Blinking lights covered the globe.

"Son of a bitch," Tony muttered.

"Holy crap," Marshall said.

Jake tuned them out as he studied the icons representing the members of the Order. His brained captured, sorted, and analyzed the data. Nine hundred fifteen lights. Unevenly distributed. Fewer in the Americas. A higher concentration in Asia. Many of them over water—which meant aircraft or ships.

The exodus had begun.

He reminded himself that the freeze-frame he looked at was just before the lights had blinked off. "How far back can you rewind?" Jake asked.

"Twenty-four hours," Timmy said.

"Do it."

Timmy made the entry. The blinking icons repositioned themselves. The change was dramatic. They were evenly distributed across the populated areas of each continent. Only a small percentage of them were over water. But what Jake found most intriguing was the fact that there were 322 additional markers. That brought the total to 1,237.

"Now fast-forward at maximum speed."

The lights jiggled and danced in place at first. Then suddenly, as if they had been activated by a simultaneous signal, they started to move in concert with one another. Like scattered fish gathering in schools, they began to migrate. Jake imagined them on trains and planes and ships, all heading toward the same destination—converging on a body of water near Indonesia. But as the lights at the front of the pilgrimage neared the destination, they disappeared. It was as if a spatial black hole were drawing the lights into its vortex.

"Zoom in on that point," Jake said, pointing to the void.

Labels indicated it was the Banda Sea. It was surrounded by the eastern portion of the Indonesian island chain, about 350 miles north of Darwin, Australia. The disappearing lights described a circle two hundred miles in width. Something within that circle was jamming the signal so the markers couldn't be tracked to their final location.

The area was dotted with hundreds of islands.

"A needle in a haystack," Tony said.

"If we could get hold of one of the trackers, I might be able to narrow it down," Timmy said.

"By backdooring into whatever is jamming the signal," Marshall added.

Timmy nodded. "We'd have to counterloop the signal in order to—"

"Work it out later, guys," Jake interrupted. "Did this place come with a sat phone?"

"Sure," Timmy said. "It's in the backpack."

"Let me have it. And let's gather all the rest of the equipment and weapons, too. We need to hit the ramp running."

"Run where?" Lacey asked.

"To the island. Where else?"

Lacey blinked twice as she put two and two together. "The one we saw in Victor's study," she said, more as a statement than as a question.

"Yeah, where we had our first kiss," Jake said.

Lacey's eyes widened. She blushed.

Ahmed grinned.

"Huh?" Francesca and Marshall asked in unison.

Jake's comment achieved the desired result. He needed everyone to lighten up a bit—despite the enormity of what they faced. He knew from working with them in the past that tension relief was the key element in keeping them sharp.

Tony was the only one who didn't take the bait. "Aren't we gonna need an army to help us?"

"Nah," Jake said, taking the sat phone from Timmy and dialing the first number from memory. "Just a few friends."

After a moment, he added, "And a prince."

Chapter 61

Grid Countdown: 18h:01m:30s

Darwin, Australia
1:30 p.m.

THE SIX-VEHICLE MILITARY CARAVAN WOUND ITS WAY FROM the international airport toward Darwin Harbour. It was midday. The temperature was in the high nineties. The streets of Australia's Northern Territory capital were desolate. Gone were the street vendors, bicyclists, and casual pedestrians—replaced by stalled cars, smoking buildings, and looted storefronts. The population of 128,000 had committed their worst deeds during the initial panic twenty-four hours ago. Now they huddled in their homes, glued to their computers and TVs, awaiting their doom. Many had ventured inland, hoping for refuge in the wilds of the outback.

It was the same the world over.

"Is she ready to go?" Jake asked. He was dressed in an Australian SASR—Special Air Service Regiment—multicam-pattern uniform, the same as everyone else in the caravan, including the women and Ahmed.

"Right as rain, Jake," Becker said in his rich Aussie accent. "Gassed up, well guarded, and most of the equipment Cal and Kenny brought with them should be onboard by now." Despite the six years that had passed since the last time Jake had seen him, Becker hadn't hesitated when Jake had asked for his help.

"Why am I not surprised?" Becker had said on the phone after he got over the shock of finding out Jake was alive. "Pyramids launched into the sky across the globe, and the world is about to come to an end. Who else but my old pal Jake Bronson could make an entrance like that?"

Becker's uniform bore a squadron leader insignia. It suited the blond-haired, blue-eyed, chocolate-skinned ranger from the outback. He'd been a city boy until the age of twelve, when his parents had died. Then his aboriginal grandfather had taken over. He wore the coveted sand-colored beret affixed with a badge shaped like a black shield and topped by a silver dagger with gold wings, as did the sixty fully kitted operators who accompanied them. It distinguished them as the best of the best.

Darwin Harbour was nearly empty. All serviceable civilian vessels had disappeared within hours of yesterday's event. Three military tenders waited at the end of the loading dock. A trio of armed operators was posted at the dock's entrance. They held F89 Minimi Para light machine guns. Becker slowed the jeep long enough for them to acknowledge his presence with a sharp salute.

Jake stared at the ship that would become their mobile command post. It was moored outside the confines of the harbor.

"She's a beaut. That's for sure," Becker said.

Jake couldn't disagree. The 296-foot megayacht was the picture of luxury, with sweeping lines, four decks, and a rooftop sporting an array of domes and antennae that hinted at the state-of-the-art command-and-control center underneath. The only thing that looked out of place on the white vessel was the matte-finish stealth chopper that rested on its stern. Jake suspected it could only have come from Kenny's arsenal of "toys."

"Damn," Tony said from the backseat. "The prince don't mess around when he lends a helping hand. First the private jet to get us here, and now this."

No question about that, Jake thought. It seemed like only yesterday that he'd met the young Kuwaiti royal at the Grand

Casino in Monte Carlo. The two of them had won a small fortune at the roulette table—with a little help from Jake's rewired brain. The prince had later played a key role in bringing down the international terrorist Luciano Battista. In light of the current stakes, Jake wasn't surprised at the man's eagerness to help in any way possible.

"You don't know the half of it," Jake said. "Both of his personal yachts were too far away, so he *bought* this one for us."

"Bloody hell," Becker said. "That must have run him a pretty penny."

"Yesterday morning it was listed for sale at one hundred seventy-five million euros," Jake said. "But after the sky lit up, he had to fork out four hundred twenty-five million to get the owner to let it go."

Tony whistled.

"How do you feel about the crew?" Jake asked.

"Top-shelf," Becker said. "Most of the original crew stayed on, including the captain. They were too far from their home port of Johannesburg to make it back before zero hour anyway. They don't know any details of the mission, but they understand they're sailing into harm's way."

Jake glanced at the ominous grid overhead.

The entire planet is in harm's way.

Jake, Tony, Becker, and the rest of them were greeted with hugs and slaps on the back from Cal and Kenny. They met up with the men on the compass bridge deck after stowing their gear. The ship was just getting under way.

"What the hell kinda mess have you got us into this time, flyboy?" Cal said. The blond-haired, blue-eyed airman was a crack pilot, avid surfer, and party animal. Jake had known USAF Major Cal Springman since pilot training. He and his copilot, Kenny, had been part of the assault and rescue missions in Afghanistan, Mexico, and Venezuela. Without their help, Jake would've died two or three times over.

"Aw, you know," Jake said. "Rescue the kids, defeat a megalomaniac intent on ending the world. Same ol', same ol'."

"Rad," Cal said with a grin. "It's been pretty boring since your funeral."

"Yeah, for me, too."

"It's really you!" Kenny said, holding his hand up for a high five. Jake obliged the freckle-faced redhead, taking care not to smack the slender man's hand too hard. He had to be close to thirty years old, Jake thought, but he still looked like he was in his late teens. He wore a faded USAF flight suit that had seen better days.

Jake pointed at the dark spot on the shoulder where a rank insignia had apparently been removed. "Did you get demoted or what?"

"Heck, no," Kenny said with a boyish Midwestern lilt. "I got out five years ago and started my own toy company. I brought a few of 'em with me." Kenny was a genius with remote-control aircraft.

"Now he's raking in the dough as a big-time government contractor," Cal said. He threw an arm around Kenny's slim neck and knuckled his hair. "But he's still just a kid copilot to me."

Kenny grinned under the abuse. But when he pulled away, he was all business. "A lot's changed since you've been away, Jake. The stuff I've been working on lately is top secret. I brought it anyway." He pulled a smartphone out of his breast pocket and tapped the screen. "Here's a quick preview."

The group gathered around. It was a live aerial shot of the bridge deck. Another tap on the screen, and it zoomed to an overhead view of the four of them talking. The definition was incredible.

Jake said, "That's from a drone?"

Kenny chuckled. "A very low drone."

"How low?"

Kenny pointed to a spot in the sky. Jake followed his gaze, expecting to see a tiny dot in the distance. But he couldn't spot it. From the squints and headshakes of the rest of the group, they couldn't either.

"Keep watching," Kenny said. He slid out a tiny keyboard from the body of his phone and tapped a quick entry.

There was a brief shimmer of light above their heads. It was as if a part of the sky suddenly shifted in color. And then it was there. Twenty feet overhead. A hovering square platform no larger than two side-by-side shoe boxes. It was held aloft by four inset fans that spun without a whisper of sound. Suspended twelve inches beneath it was a convex mesh sheet that appeared to support a thousand tiny reflective surfaces. There was a similar umbrella of mesh above it.

"This is our latest urban stealth surveillance drone. The hemispherical webs surrounding it provide the camouflage that makes it invisible to the eye. Each of those sparkles is a miniature video screen. Switch 'em on, and each depicts what its slaved minicam sees on the opposite side. When you look at it from below, all you see is the sky above.

Timmy and Marshall were particularly engrossed by the technology. Ahmed, too.

"Whoa," Marshall said. "What else you got?"

"That'll have to wait," Jake said, as he felt the engines kick into full speed ahead. The ship had just cleared the outer reef. "We've got work to do."

As they made their way to a lower deck, Jake overheard Kenny answer Marshall's question.

"Have you ever heard of robotic swarms?"

"Dude!" Marshall and Timmy said in unison.

Chapter 62

Grid Countdown: 13h:01m:30s

Banda Sea
6:30 p.m.

By now Jake had stopped being amazed at the incredible opulence he encountered around every corner. The ship was a floating testament to self-indulgence, with rooms and amenities that rivaled the finest suites in Trump Tower. There were three VIP suites, ten guest cabins, and a variety of salons and dining areas. Unfortunately, the ship was built for luxury—not speed.

"It's going to be another ten hours before we reach the center of the target zone," Jake said, as he and Tony made their way down the corridor. Marshall had paged them over the ship's intercom to meet in the boardroom.

"Just before dawn," Tony confirmed.

Jake checked his digital watch. Its timer matched the countdown being transmitted by the grid. "That'll give us three hours to identify our target, infiltrate its security, rescue the kids, and stop Victor from doing whatever it is he's got up his sleeve."

"Three whole hours?" Tony said. "That's a lot to do on an empty stomach. I hope they have decent grub on this tug."

The boardroom was decorated in polished teakwood, plush carpet, and seafaring oil paintings. It was dominated by a racetrack-shaped conference table surrounded by fourteen cream-colored leather chairs, all but three of which had been pushed up against the perimeter wall to make it easier to walk around. Kenny, Marshall, and Timmy sat along one side of the table. Each huddled in front of his own self-made command-and-control center. There was an impressive arrangement of computer equipment and displays. A waterfall of wiring spilled through the oval slit in the center of the table. Soda cans and energy drinks dotted the tabletop. The three men were intent on their work. None of them looked happy.

Without looking up, Marshall said, "Me first."

"Go for it," Timmy muttered without breaking the cadence on his keyboard.

Jake and Tony moved behind the trio.

Marshall's central screen showed a satellite map of the Indonesian island chain. His finger described a two-hundred-mile-wide circle east of Sulawesi—formerly known as Celebes—and west of New Guinea and north of Timor. "This is the target area. Dead in the middle of what used to be called the Spice Islands. There are nearly one thousand islands here." He pointed to an area at the eastern edge of the Banda Sea. "By projecting the trajectories of the tracking signals that disappeared, we've narrowed the target down to this region." He hesitated a moment before adding, "It's composed of nearly five hundred islands. Even after eliminating those that are too small to accommodate Victor's plans, there are still ninety remaining."

"You can't do better than that?" Tony asked, glancing nervously at the flat-panel display dominating the wall at the end of the conference table. The sound had been muted, but the slide show of damning evidence against mankind continued to stream—as did the countdown clock.

Timmy's eyes were bloodshot. He pointed to a pill-size capsule that he'd wired into an open circuit board connected to his computer. "I thought I could do something with the bloody present you got for me. By the way, the man's name was August Schmidt." He was referring to the RFID that Tony had extracted from under the tattoo on Pit Bull's shoulder. He and Jake had made a side trip to the morgue on the way to the Geneva airport. In the midst of the mayhem, it had been a simple matter to find time alone with the body. "I've been able to reactivate it," Timmy said. "But backtracking it to the jamming source simply isn't working. I've still got one or two things to try, but I'm not hopeful."

If Timmy couldn't do it, nobody could, Jake thought. They'd have to find another way.

Marshall switched to a different screen. It depicted the same map of the Spice Islands region without the satellite overlay. Islands were highlighted in green. "This is a static image from ten days ago. The black dots on the water represent vessels." There were hundreds of them. It looked like a still shot of an army of ants moving from point to point. The majority of them seemed to be traveling single file along trade routes between the major islands.

Marshall continued, "I thought maybe we could learn something from the traffic patterns. You know, look for an island that boats were heading toward. But when I go to a live feed, here's the problem." He tapped a key and the image shifted. Hundreds of dots were replaced by thousands. "It's as if every boat in the region had taken to the water, scattering in every direction. And that's not the worst of it. Watch this." He zoomed in on a random cluster of about a hundred ships. Several of the blips jiggled on the screen and disappeared—only to reappear an instant later somewhere else.

"What the hell?" Tony said.

Kenny took over. “They’re using random signal generators. The same type we used to cover our entry into and exit out of Mexico six years ago. But this is on a scale like nothing I’ve ever seen before. Heck, until we get overhead with the drones, I can’t be sure that some of the islands we’re seeing are even there. These dudes must have been setting this up for years.”

“How long before the drones are on scene?” Jake asked. Kenny had brought three vertical-takeoff reconnaissance drones onboard. Unfolded, the gull-shaped aircraft had twelve-foot wingspans, rotating nacelles that allowed for both vertical and horizontal flight, and a full complement of recon equipment. It had taken a few hours to unpack and assemble them above deck. Jake had watched them take off an hour ago.

“They’re built for endurance, not speed,” Kenny said. He rolled his chair to one side so that he sat in front of a tri-screen remote-control center. It was compact and ruggedized, designed for field use. He checked a readout on the center screen. “They’ll hit the edge of the target area in forty-seven minutes.”

“That’s good, right?” Tony asked.

But Jake already knew that wasn’t the case. His mind had already completed the calculation. The circular target area was approximately 150 miles wide. That was 17,662.5 square miles of search area. “Three birds can’t complete a grid search quickly enough,” he said.

Timmy’s lips tightened. He nodded. “He’s right. There’re thirty islands for each bird to inspect in order to isolate the real ones from the red herrings.”

Sitting next to him, Marshall shook his head. “That’s why we called you in here, Jake. We’re running out of ideas.” With a glance at the wall screen, he added, “And time.”

“Maybe if we called in some help…” Kenny suggested.

“Believe me,” Jake said, “I’ve thought about that. But who do we call? Who can we really trust besides those of us on this ship?

No," he said, pulling up a chair next to Kenny's. "We've got to figure this out on our own."

Twenty minutes later, one of the crew brought in food and drinks. Tony was two bites into a sandwich before the platter made it to the table. Jake was reluctant to interrupt their brainstorming session, but they were still at an impasse. Maybe the break would help.

Kenny grabbed a Coke and offered it to him. Jake popped it open and took a long pull.

"Thanks for coming, Kenny," Jake said, leaning back and stretching his neck. "We wouldn't have had much of a chance without you and your toys."

"Wouldn't have missed it for the world," Kenny said, taking a bite of his turkey sandwich. "Besides, I can't wait to examine the tech on this top secret chair you've been talking about. It sounds like you guys are several generations ahead of Intel on thought guidance and communication."

"It's some pretty cool stuff," Timmy confirmed with a full mouth.

"We're damn lucky they only got the chair when they beat feet out of the Palace of Nations," Tony said, hefting a scoop of potato salad onto his plate. "If they'd got our fearless leader here along with it, we'd be up a creek."

The comment triggered a question in Jake's mind. Why would Victor go to the trouble of taking the chair in the first place—if it wouldn't work without him?

He wondered why he hadn't considered it before. Victor had said that *our* scientists developed the chair. Timmy had told him previously that the chair had been developed at a secret facility in the United States. Timmy and Doc had both been involved. But what if one or two Order scientists had been part of that team? He thought back to his narrow escape from Hans and his men, replaying the sequence of events in his mind. When the hypnosis drug had first begun to wear off, the techs in the room had been discussing how glad they were *to be leaving the cramped confines of this cellar after two months.* Then later—when two guards had dumped him on the floor in order to help their comrades heft the chair up the staircase—one of them had said, *He's not our first priority.*

Which meant the chair was Victor's first priority. They'd planned to take it all along, even before they knew that Jake was alive. But why? Timmy had explained that the chair was originally designed with the intention of establishing communication with the pyramids. But without Jake's brain as a conduit, they couldn't receive…

Then it hit him. "They're using the chair to transmit," he said. "They've probably been sending messages to the pyramids for months. That's why Victor is so confident that the Order will be spared. He's been prepping them with his own custom message."

The comment silenced the room—except for Tony's chewing. Timmy was the first to pick up the ball. "Which means we need to be looking up. Not down—"

"Toward the first two pyramids," Marshall interjected.

"There are thousands of signals streaming outbound from the grid to Earth's communication networks," Timmy said.

Marshall finished the thought. "But there would be only one inbound."

"Which we *can* back-trace to the source," Timmy said, high-fiving Marshall.

"How long?" Jake asked, standing up.

"Thirty minutes," Marshall said, pushing his plate to one side.

"Maybe twenty," added Timmy, his fingers moving faster on the keyboard than a pianist's playing "Flight of the Bumblebee."

Chapter 63

Grid Countdown: 3h:01m:30s

Banda Sea
4:30 a.m.

FRANCESCA WANTED TO MOVE, BUT SHE DIDN'T. JAKE HAD asked her to remain still.

Neither one of them had slept. They stood on the upper deck. Her arms rested atop the railing as she gazed toward the front of the cruising yacht. The warm equatorial breeze pulled the hair from her face. It was 4:30 a.m. The amber grid illuminated the night sky, its light casting an eerie reflection off the rippling surface of the water. Jake stood beside her. He wore a camouflage uniform. A combat vest, backpack, and assault rifle rested on the deck beside him. His green eyes shone bright behind the dark face paint that covered his skin. She watched as his focus shifted from her face to a sketch pad and back again. He'd borrowed the pad and pencil from one of the crew.

"I could do this with my eyes closed," he said softly, his hand moving back and forth across the canvas. A corner of his mouth turned up in a brief smile as if his words had sparked an ironic memory. He kept drawing.

She hadn't questioned his odd request to sketch her. It had been important to him. That's all that mattered. He was a warrior. Her warrior. About to thrust himself into untold dangers to rescue their children.

The man standing before her was so much more than he had been when they'd first met in the library in Redondo Beach. Gone were the boyish manners, abrupt quips, and hidden insecurities—replaced by a man who embraced the changes that had been thrust upon him, and who was anchored in his belief that he could make a difference. The walls that he had so often used to shield his emotions were gone.

She reveled in his trust.

As he drew, she allowed her empathic gift to embrace him. She sensed his guilt, knowing that he felt responsible for all that had happened. But though he harbored those feelings, he didn't seem compelled to nourish them as he'd done in the past. There was fear there, too. As well there should be, she thought. But most of all she saw in him in an overwhelming sense of purpose—and a calm certainty that reassured her.

The ship slowed. There was activity at the stern, and she knew that the boats were being readied for the infiltration. She sagged at the realization that their time alone was about to come to an end.

"Finished," Jake said, tearing the page from the pad and rolling it up. He handed it to her. Then he pulled her gently against his chest. His face was inches from hers. A brief chill rushed up her spine.

"I survived the last six years because of you," he said softly. "I've carried you in my thoughts ever since that day we connected on the roof of the institute. I didn't realize it then, but it was in that moment that you became a part of me. You gave me strength. And the will to live."

His words caressed her.

He continued, "It seems as if everywhere we turn, circumstances conspire against us. Venice, Afghanistan, Mexico, Venezuela…" He looked to the sky. "And now this."

She shivered and buried her face in the crook of his neck.

"Yet despite it all," he said, "here we stand. Arm in arm. Together."

He pulled back and cupped her face in his hands. She stared at him through moist eyes, and his thumbs wiped away her tears. He kissed her. His lips were gentle. She melted into him, and for several moments the rest of the world disappeared.

When he finally pulled away, he took both of her hands in his and lowered himself to one knee.

Her breath left her.

Jake stared into her soul and said, "Francesca Fellini, I pledge myself to you, in spirit and in body. I promise to honor and protect you and our family from this day forward, to have and to hold, in sickness and in health, in good times and bad, to love you and cherish you all the days of my life."

Her body trembled. The purity of love and devotion that poured from him was absolute. She lowered herself to both knees before him. Her heart thrummed in her ears. She fought to control her breathing. "J-Jake Bronson, I've loved the thought of you since I was a little girl. A part of me dared to believe that you truly existed. So I prayed for it. And now here you are, kneeling before me, everything and more that I have ever dreamed of. You are my life, Jake. I've known it since the day we met. I've never wavered in that belief, and I never will."

She took a deep breath before continuing. "Now, under the eyes of God, I pledge all that I am—and all that I will ever be—to you and our family. I promise to honor and protect you from this day forward, for better or for worse, to have and to hold, in sickness and in health, to love and to cherish you to the end of my days and beyond."

His face beamed. He pulled her into his arms and showered her with kisses.

"My wife," he whispered.

"My husband…"

They turned to the sound of heavy footfalls. Tony trotted around the corner. He spotted them on their knees and came to an abrupt halt. Ahmed skidded to a stop behind him. Jake and Francesca shared a final squeeze and then rose to face them. She used a sleeve to wipe away the last of her tears.

Tony cleared his throat, "Uh…sorry, but we gotta go."

"Yeah," Jake said with a sigh. "I figured."

Ahmed moved around from behind Tony, and Francesca's muscles tightened when she saw the submachine gun slung from his shoulder.

"What is that?" she asked.

He pulled the weapon up to his chest and held it as if it were second nature to him. He answered the question as a soldier would a drill sergeant. "It's an M4 carbine. Standard SAS patrol weapon. It is a gas-operated, air-cooled, magazine-fed, selective-fire, shoulder-fired weapon with a telescoping stock. It fires a 5.56mm NATO round and—"

She cut him off. "That's not what I meant!" she scolded. "I mean, what are *you* doing with it?"

He didn't shrivel under her glare. Instead, he remained calm. "This was issued to me. I've been training with it all night."

She'd heard frequent bouts of gunfire since they'd been onboard. She'd assumed that it had been Becker's troops getting warmed up for what was to come. It had never occurred to her that Ahmed was involved. Tony and Jake didn't interfere in the discussion. Instead, they seemed to be appraising her reaction. She was about to give them an earful when Ahmed took another step forward.

"Whatever it takes," he said. "Remember?" His eyes were steel.

She hesitated.

Jake stepped forward and faced the would-be soldier. "Eyes on me," he said.

Ahmed snapped to attention and returned the stare.

Jake appraised him for several moments. Man to man.

Then to Tony he asked, "How'd he score?"

"Well above average."

"Is he ready?"

Tony nodded. "He wouldn't be carrying a weapon otherwise."

Jake turned back to Ahmed. "You will protect Francesca at all costs," he ordered. "Do you understand?"

"With my life," Ahmed said.

Francesca gasped. She hoped they hadn't heard.

"You're to stay on the ship," Jake added. "Don't leave her side."

"Yes, sir!"

Jake placed a hand on the boy's shoulder. "*Shohna ba shohna*," he said.

Ahmed nodded at the Afghan sentiment. Francesca had heard Battista's soldiers use it. She believed it meant shoulder to shoulder.

Jake turned around and pulled her close. He planted a hard kiss on her mouth. As he pulled away, his lips brushed her ear and he whispered, "My wife."

Their hands lingered a moment. Then Jake grabbed his gear and slung it over his shoulder. He turned on his heels and disappeared with Tony around the corner.

Ahmed moved to her side. "They're going to be all right," he said. "I can feel it." Then he pointed to the scroll in her hand. "What's that?"

She'd forgotten that she was holding the sketch. She unfurled it.

"Wow!" Ahmed said. "It is beautiful."

He was right. Jake had captured her essence in the portrait. The love she felt for him shone in the expression on the page. She marveled at the artistry. The gentle curves, the subtle shading, the fine detail…

Her throat caught when she saw the dazzling extra feature.

He'd added a diamond wedding ring on a finger of her left hand.

Dear God, she prayed. Please keep him safe.

Chapter 64

Grid Countdown: 2h:30m:30s

Banda Sea
5:01 a.m.

THE TWO INFLATABLE RAIDING CRAFTS SPED ACROSS THE water. The hums of the fifty-five horsepower outboard motors were muffled. The low-profile boats were used for clandestine surface and extraction. Each carried five fully laden troops. The elite SAS operators surrounding Jake were a tough lot, he thought. They held their weapons with easy familiarity. Each wore a black balaclava that covered his head, nose, and chin. The oval opening around the eyes revealed face-painted skin and the iron expressions of combat-hardened veterans. Like Jake, they each wore a tactical bone-conduction headset and boom mike. They leaned forward in the boat in order to maintain the lowest possible profile.

Tony hunched over behind him. There was no one whom Jake would rather have along on a mission like this. The big man had pulled Jake's butt out of the fire more times than he'd like to remember.

Becker sat to Jake's left. He studied the flexible display strapped to the inside of his wrist. Each of the operators wore one, as did Jake and Tony. Various data and video were available on the device, streaming from satellite, weapon cams, or the drone that circled overhead. "I sure hope the geek crew knows what they're talkin' about," Becker said. "Because except for that tiny hot spot near the base of the peaks, I'm still showing nothing bigger than wildlife on that island."

"It's the right place," Jake said. "I'm sure of it."

Jake knew everything rode on that conviction. He'd better be right, he thought, recalling the sequence of events that had led him to believe that Victor was on the island ahead of them. Marshall and Timmy had found the signal that was being transmitted to the grid. They'd isolated its source to a cluster of volcanic islands at the southeastern edge of the target area. Unfortunately, a network of jammers and repeaters had apparently been positioned on several of the islands. Without more time, it had been impossible to identify all of their hidden locations. So they'd had to isolate their target by process of elimination. There were five major islands and a dozen smaller islands in the Lesser Sunda chain from Bali to Timor. The bigger islands had been discounted because of increased visibility when attempting to hide that many newcomers. Of those that remained, only three were large enough to house the Order, yet still small enough to keep their massive influx secret. Timmy had sent a drone over each. Both the visual and the infrared revealed nothing unusual—except for the single hot spot that Becker had just pointed out. The drone's cameras had zoomed in. However, scattered interference from nearby jammers prevented a detailed inspection.

It didn't matter. Jake's mind had raced into autopilot the moment he saw the circular blob of heat. Even as his brain went through the machinations of estimating size against surrounding vegetation, analyzing its position relative to ideal construction sites, recalling geological composition of the landmass, and more, his gut had already told him what it was. He'd seen it before on a mountain in Afghanistan—a perfectly round hole bored through the earth—laser-drilled by the pyramid he'd launched from its depths. He remembered Battista's vast underground facility, and he imagined the same thing here. It was the perfect hideaway for Victor and his friends—well hidden, electronically protected, and far enough away from the mainland to avoid fallout.

Yes, Victor was here. And so were Sarafina and Alex. They had to be.

The imposing twin-peaked island was silhouetted a half mile ahead. It had been formed around two side-by-side volcanoes with peak elevations that stretched two thousand meters. Clouds ringed the peaks. The mountainous landmass was five miles long and three miles wide. It appeared as if the backside of the island had suffered a cataclysmic calving from an ancient eruption. Sheer cliffs thrust hundreds of feet from the water, making landing from that side impossible. However, the lush frontal plain on the side of the island they sped toward was an ideal landing spot. A river flowed from the natural canyon between the two peaks, twisting and turning beneath the lush overgrowth to eventually spill into the sea.

Becker raised a hand overhead and made two chopping motions. The second boat peeled away. It was headed for an insertion point a hundred meters downshore. The target hot spot was two miles inland.

Becker said something into his mike. Then he tapped his headset. "We've lost comm with the ship."

"Kenny said that would happen," Jake said. "We must have passed through the island's electronic shield. What about the drone and sat feeds?"

"Nothing," Becker said. He pressed an icon on the screen, and the image shifted to show a close-up overhead shot of their five-man squad. "But *Mother Ship* is still working fine."

Tony and Jake both looked upward. But Timmy's minidrone remained invisible.

Thirty minutes later, the two operators in front of Jake were using machetes to chop a path through the dense vegetation. It was daybreak. Clouds of insects swarmed around them. Jake removed his balaclava. His hair was matted with sweat. He swatted the back of his neck, and his palm came back with a bloody mosquito.

He heard another slap behind him. It was Tony. "If there's an underground facility on this island," he grumbled, "they sure ain't getting into it from around here. Nobody's been through this brush in years."

They circumvented a grove of sixty-foot-tall bamboo. The impenetrable wall of thick stalks clicked and clacked as they swayed back and forth in the morning breeze. When the group came across a game trail, the going got easier.

Tony pointed overhead. "So why'd Kenny name it *Mother Ship*?" He'd been training with Ahmed when Timmy had provided Jake and Becker with a demo of the drone's capabilities.

"Let's just say she's pregnant," Becker said. "Besides that, she's cradling us in an electronic blanket that should shield us from video surveillance." He pressed a selector on the side of his wristband and issued a verbal command into his boom mike. "Scout forward. One hundred meters."

They watched their images recede on their wrist screens as the little drone rose above the tree line and proceeded forward. The river was just ahead. Jake saw the other five-man squad on their right, crouched low as they studied their own screens. The drone continued upstream. Its camera panned from side to side. At one point the image hesitated. Its sensors picked up a heat signature. It zoomed in on a small boar rooting its muzzle through the soft undergrowth.

"Disregard," Becker commanded.

The image zoomed out, and the drone continued upstream. Both teams followed. When the stream widened to a large rippling pool, the drone slowed. Its camera panned forward. A towering wall of water blocked the path. Mist blurred the scene, and water droplets formed on the lens. The drone backed off, and the scene clarified. The waterfall reached taller than a twenty-story building. The rock walls on either side glistened.

"Hold position. Scan for threats," Becker commanded the drone. Then to the teams he said, "Move out."

Water tumbled into the cul-de-sac-shaped pool with a constant roar. Lush vegetation and exotic flower–covered vines spilled from the steep walls on either side. They glistened in the sunlight. The moist air was sweet with their fragrance. Under different circumstances, Jake would have been awestruck by the beautiful scene. Instead, he was filled with despair. Their target was two hundred meters beyond the falls.

The path was blocked.

The two teams joined up. Becker motioned to one of his men. "Sergeant, I think a four-man perimeter should suit our needs. Then let's get three of the chaps on a scouting mission along the base of the cliff. Check for cracks, fissures, hidden pathways. Anything that can get us past or over these falls."

"Sir," Sergeant Fletcher said sharply. The scowl-faced Aussie could back off a crocodile in a staring contest. He issued several quick orders, and the team hustled to their positions.

Jake and Tony stood near the edge of the pool. "You thinking what I'm thinking?" Jake asked.

Tony harrumphed. "Ha! What are the odds of that?" He cocked an eyebrow when he noticed Jake peeling off his backpack, combat harness, boots, and socks. "But I guess it doesn't take a genius to figure out you're goin' for a swim."

Becker said, "A little cliché, wouldn't you say, Jake? The proverbial passage behind the waterfall?"

"You never know," Jake said, patting his pockets to make sure there was nothing there that the water would ruin. His hand came out of his breast pocket holding a folded slip of paper. It had been his constant companion since he'd awakened from the coma four months ago. He handed it to Tony. "Save this for me."

"What is it?" Tony asked, starting to unfold it.

Jake stayed his hand. "Let's just call it my good-luck charm, okay?"

Tony slipped it away and palmed his pocket. He offered Jake a broad grin. "In that case, I'll guard it with my life."

Jake sighed. He was certain this was destined to be a one-way mission for him. He wouldn't survive it. That's why he'd said his heartfelt good-bye to Francesca the way he had. He patted the shoulders of the two men standing before him. They'd been through hell together.

And back again.

"Thanks for being here, guys," he said.

"Wouldn't have missed it, mate," Becker said. He pointed up at the grid overhead. With a wink he added, "Not for the world."

Tony cocked his head to one side. His eyes narrowed into that what-the-hell-are-you-up-to expression that Jake had seen so many times before. But before his pal could voice his concern, Jake turned and dove into the rippling pool.

Chapter 65

Grid Countdown: 2h:30m:30s

Banda Sea
5:01 a.m.

"This standing around doing nothing is driving me crazy," Lacey said.

Francesca couldn't agree more. Her children had been taken, Jake was heading into danger, and the world was coming to an end. They needed to do *something*. They were in the ship's boardroom. She and Lacey stood behind Marshall, Kenny, and Timmy. Each of the men was focused on a workstation. The supersize wall monitor streamed scenes of atrocities and death during the Vietnam War.

Ahmed stood nearby. He'd refused to leave her side since Jake had left. His assault rifle was slung over his shoulder. He'd been intently scanning the web with his smartphone for the past several minutes.

One of Becker's men stood beside him. The uniformed soldier was built like a tank, with a tanned face that was all angles and planes, broken in two by a swarthy mustache. Sergeant Major Abercrombie was in charge of the force that had remained onboard. It seemed to Francesca as if he was a wound spring straining to be released. His steel-gray eyes stared at Kenny's screen.

Francesca shared his focus. Dark forms huddled low in the two inflatable boats as they skimmed across the water. One of those forms was Jake. The video signal was being transmitted by one of Kenny's over-the-shoulder minidrones. "How much longer?" she asked.

Kenny said, "They'll make land in two minutes." He wore a headset and boom mike. It was his job to coordinate the insertion.

"What if it's the wrong island?" Lacey asked.

"Then we're screwed," Marshall said, more to himself than to anyone else. He leaned forward, his fingers flying over the keyboard. His eyes narrowed on his screen, where an endless stream of computer code scrolled. He hit the ENTER key, and his hands hovered a moment. A window opened with an ERROR code. "You bastard," he growled. He pulled an MP3 player from his pocket, selected a song, and donned earphones. Then he cracked his knuckles and began typing, faster than ever. "You can run but you can't hide," he said, his body rocking to the music.

Francesca could hear the tinny crescendo of music from his earbuds. It sounded like the film score from *Star Wars*. He was lost in his own world, Francesca thought, leveraging his unique expertise to help his friends and her children.

Lacey nudged her. "He's got that song on a loop," she said. "He'll listen to it over and over again until he figures it out."

"What's he working on?"

"Anybody's guess," Lacey said. "He won't talk about it until he's finished. Hell, when he gets in this mode, he won't talk about *anything*."

"Hey, wait a second," Timmy said, his hand gripping a joystick that controlled one of the larger drones. Kenny had given him a quick training session on the equipment. The avid video gamer had taken to it like a fish to water.

Kenny leaned over to get a look at Timmy's screen. "Whad'ya got?"

"It vanished," Timmy said.

Kenny nodded. "Yeah, that's their random signal generator."

Francesca recalled that the drones had revealed thousands of blips loitering around the archipelago, many of which were false signals.

"Man, I know that," Timmy said, showing his frustration. "This was infrared, not radar. I was tracking a boat headed around the other side of the island."

"Rewind it," Kenny said.

"Already doin' it."

Francesca edged over to get a look. Lacey joined her. Ahmed had taken a seat along the far wall. He continued to scroll through scenes on his smartphone. Marshall was oblivious—his keyboard tapping had increased to a feverish pace.

The infrared image on Timmy's screen revealed the tiny outlines of dozens of boats cruising in the vicinity of the island. Timmy made an entry, and the screen split in two. The left side continued to show the infrared view. The right side depicted radar signals. He overlaid the two screens. All the positions matched. He pointed to a boat that was on a course that would skirt the cliffs on the far side of the island. "Now watch this one."

The infrared image suddenly turned to port. It was headed directly toward the face of the cliff. But its radar signal continued on its previous course. Timmy zoomed in on the infrared image. The drone's grayscale thermal imaging camera revealed the outline of the hundred-foot yacht. It glowed pale white against the gray waters, maintaining its speed. Francesca held her breath as the bow was about to impact the rocky shoreline. But instead of an explosion of debris, the ship's glow simply vanished from bow to stern. It was as if the island had swallowed it up.

"Looks like we found the front door," Lacey said.

"We gotta let 'em know!" Timmy said, looking to Kenny.

But Kenny had already diverted his attention to his own screen. The landing team had reached the shore and was pulling the craft into cover. "Raider One, come in," he said into his headset. His voice was urgent.

The raiding team continued on as if they hadn't heard a thing. Francesca felt a jolt of adrenaline churn her stomach. The Aussie sergeant major edged closer.

"Raider One or Raider Two, come in," Kenny repeated, tapping the up-volume arrow on his console.

Jake and his team disappeared under the foliage.

Then the screen went blank.

Kenny made several entries on his console. When the image didn't return, his face screwed tight.

"What's happening?" Francesca asked.

"They're inside the island's electronic shield," he said. "We've lost contact."

Francesca steadied herself on the back of his chair. She drew her lower lip through her teeth.

Lacey said, "But we have to warn them!"

"We can't," Kenny said. "Not until they launch a homer-relay from *Mother Ship*." His voice trailed off as he returned his attention to the tracking image on Timmy's screen. It appeared as if Timmy was studying the ship's track in reverse.

Kenny leaned closer. "Are you seeing what I'm—"

"Hey, wait a minute," Lacey said, cutting him off. "What's a homer—"

"Can it!" Kenny said, spinning his chair around so fast that Francesca flinched backwards and nearly fell. The Aussie caught her. Lacey crossed her arms and stood her ground.

Kenny's frustration vanished when he thought he'd hurt Francesca. "I—I'm sorry. You okay?"

Francesca shouldered herself free of the Aussie's grasp. "Of course. I'm fine," she said. "But Lacey's right. We have a right to know what's going on. So, what are you talking about?"

Kenny blew out a quick breath, and Francesca sensed his frustration ease.

"Short version," he said. "We knew we'd lose contact. It was part of the mission profile. When they arrive at the target spot, they'll launch a drone that will allow us to relay information. Until then, they're on their own." He looked to the Aussie for confirmation.

"He's right, ma'am," the sergeant major said. "Squadron Leader Becker was prepared for this."

"But in the meantime," Kenny continued, "we've got a lot of work to do." He pointed to Marshall, who was still hunched over his keyboard with his earphones on. Light from his computer screen reflected off his narrowed eyes. He was grinding his teeth. Kenny added, "We need to go into Marshall mode."

"I've isolated a pattern here," Timmy interrupted. Everyone except Marshall and Ahmed turned toward his screen. He traced his finger across the image. "This is the track the ship took before turning into the cliffs. See how it made three tacks, here, here, and here?"

"Like an airport approach pattern," Kenny said.

"Except there's no need for one on open water," Timmy said.

Francesca sensed their excitement as they spoke back and forth.

"Unless you're avoiding reefs," Kenny said.

"Of which there aren't any on this side of the island."

"Or underwater mines."

"Which they would never use if they wanted to maintain the secrecy of their location."

They paused a moment while they thought it through.

It was Lacey who spoke next. "It's like a secret door-knock at a speakeasy."

Both men turned toward her at the same time. Their slack-jawed expressions morphed to grins.

"Exactly!" Timmy said.

"It's an ID-track," Kenny added. "A simple friend-or-foe pattern that they can track with underwater acoustical equipment. As long as the boat follows the track, the bouncers will open the door and let you in."

"And here's the next customer," Timmy said, pointing to a blip on the screen. He switched to infrared mode and zoomed in. It was a smaller boat, maybe thirty-five feet. There appeared to be three people onboard. "They're five miles out. Just made the first tack."

"We need that boat," Kenny said.

The sergeant major didn't hesitate. He rushed toward the exit, speaking into his boom mike. "Team three at the ready!"

Kenny switched frequencies on the communication console and said, "Cal, fire up the chopper. It's time to go to work!"

Chapter 66

Grid Countdown: 2h:15m:30s

The Island
5:16 a.m.

VICTOR'S SMILE WAS GENUINE. HE'D EARNED IT. GENERATIONS of planning were coming to a head. He glanced up at the wall monitor. A new world was a couple hours away. Nothing could stop them now.

He was in the plush underground viewing lounge—so named because of the wall-to-wall video screen at one end. It currently streamed a live feed of the inlet and the picturesque landscape and structures surrounding it. It was dawn, but the scene was still cast in shadows from the surrounding peaks. Lampposts illuminated the walkways and dock area. Light shone from windows. There was an old-world feel to the scene that Victor found soothing. The captivating city was a far cry from the village of huts that his ancestor had discovered here two hundred years ago.

"It is truly glorious," said the Pakistani statesman standing beside him. The bearded man was dressed in a *sherwani* and *salwar kameez*, a shin-length doublet over pajama-like trousers that narrowed at the ankle.

Victor was surrounded by an international ensemble of Order leaders. Many of the men wore suits and ties like he did. A few wore military dress uniforms. The women's elegant dresses were overshadowed by an assortment of rich jewelry. Not everyone in the Order was wealthy, but those in this room represented the elite. Several nodded at the statesman's comment.

"Centuries in the making," Victor said, thinking about the countless resources that had been dedicated to the task. Since the island's discovery, each adult Order member had been required to live here for a minimum of two years. Many stayed longer. Some never left. All of them contributed to the design and construction of the complex. The most intriguing accomplishment had come in the past several decades—when their scientists had perfected the art of electronic camouflage. As a result, their activity had been kept hidden from overflying aircraft and satellites. Coupled with its well-honed lore of venomous snakes and lethal gas plumes that could "suck a man's soul to the depths of hell," the island was seldom troubled by outsiders.

Victor watched the screen. The city pathways were scattered with folks migrating toward the entrance to the underground complex. Despite the countdown, they were calm and orderly. He was proud of them. He noticed a few late arrivals at the dock. There were likely others yet to come. If they didn't make it by the time the doors were closed…

Victor shook his head at the shame of it. They were like his children. He'd mourn them.

He wondered what it would be like up above when the end came. Would the grid destroy all sign of civilization in a massive explosion that consumed the planet? Or would the ancient visitors have devised a more elegant solution, one that targeted humans alone, allowing the animal kingdom to once again rise to the top of the food chain? He prayed it was the latter. He'd hate to see their aboveground utopia decimated by the process.

His thoughts were interrupted when he noticed Hans making his way toward him. His man didn't need to say anything for Victor to realize something was wrong. The purposeful stride and stiff jaw spoke volumes. Victor took a couple steps back from the crowd.

"What is it?"

"Activity in the south quadrant," Hans reported.

"Pirates?" Victor asked. There had been three incursions in as many months from the brazen bandits. Officials had been tightening up on them in nearby populated areas. Many groups were looking for new homes.

"Perhaps," Hans said. "But I can't confirm it. We're having an issue with video imagery on that side of the island. Some sort of static interference. But IR and motion sensors have been activated. I've sent a squad to deal with it."

Victor felt a brief chill of alarm, but it faded quickly. If it wasn't pirates, it was likely evacuees seeking shelter from the apocalypse. Thousands had fled to the seas. Many would seek shelter on an island. A few would ignore the warning signs that ringed the beaches on the south end of the island. They had been a nuisance in the last few days. But at least they'd provided live-fire training for their security forces. Whoever they were—pirates or refugees—they would not be permitted to leave the island alive.

A squad, Victor thought. That's only ten men. "Send more than one squad," he said, waving off his concern. "I don't want any hiccups right now."

"*Jawohl*," Hans said with a snappy nod.

Chapter 67

Grid Countdown: 2h:10m:30s

Banda Sea
5:21 a.m.

FRANCESCA HELD HER BREATH AS SHE WATCHED THE SCENE unfold.

The grayscale infrared image of the thirty-five-foot cruiser filled the screen. The bow wave rippled and jumped as the boat pushed through the water. The three occupants were on the compass bridge of the yacht. Suddenly, the glow of the helicopter obscured half the screen. Its nose rocked upward as it braked to a hover over the cruiser's bow. In the same instant, four soldiers slid down ropes to the deck. The occupants scattered, and there was a flash of gunfire from one of them. The fire was returned, and the occupant flew backward and lay still on the deck. The other two huddled in a corner. They were quickly surrounded.

Francesca cringed at the efficient ferocity of the attack. She sat at the boardroom table with Lacey and Ahmed. Kenny and Timmy had worked together to coordinate the hijacking. They sat back and shared a collective sigh.

"Wow," Timmy said. "They're good."

"Some of the best," Kenny said. "They have to go through hell to earn those berets."

Ahmed said, "They killed that guy, didn't they?"

Francesca cringed. She hated that Ahmed had watched that. She placed her hand on his.

He twitched but didn't pull away. Instead, he returned her concerned gaze with an expression of calm determination. "I'm okay," he said, patting her hand. "Truly, I am."

She searched his emotions and knew that he was.

"Yes!" Marshall suddenly shouted behind them. He punched both fists overhead, standing up so fast that his chair toppled behind him. Then he jabbed his index finger at his computer screen like a boxer taunting a felled opponent. "I own you!"

Lacey rose and made her way behind him.

"Yeah, you think you're all that," he shouted at the computer.

She gently removed his earbuds.

He didn't seem to notice. He remained focused on his screen. "But you ain't nothin'!"

Lacey slowly positioned herself in front of him. She laced her hands around his neck.

Marshall leaned to one side in order to maintain eye contact with the flashing icon. "Who's the man?" he said, sticking out his chest.

Lacey lifted to her toes and leaned forward.

"I own you! You're my b—"

Her lips covered his. There was a moment of wide-eyed shock. Marshall blinked several times. Then his shoulders sagged. His arms embraced her and he closed his eyes.

They kissed.

Even though Francesca recognized their behavior as a learned ritual, she was transfixed. So were the guys.

After several moments, Lacey pulled away. "Better?" she asked.

Marshall grinned. "Oh, yeah." He grabbed her shoulders and pulled her into a passionate full-on kiss. Lacey melted into it. When he pulled back, he said, "Much better."

He took in the rest of the room, and his face flushed at the gawking stares from Kenny, Timmy, and Ahmed. But any embarrassment he may have felt was washed away by his eagerness to share the news.

"Dudes!" he said, spinning around his screen so everyone could see it. The window in the center of the screen read ACCESS GRANTED. "We now have one hundred percent control of the outgoing signal to the grid. Let's put together a message of our own, and then we'll hit 'em broadside!"

"A message of our own?" Francesca asked.

"Yes," Ahmed said, stepping forward and pulling out his smartphone. He turned it on, tapped an icon, and held the screen so the others could see. "Like these."

Everyone moved closer to get a better look. It was a video of a large African tribe—men, women, and children, eyes glistening, joined in song, their faces to the sky as they appealed to the matrix of light overhead. Ahmed tapped the screen to reveal a similar scene taking place in what Francesca recognized as Piazza San Pietro in Vatican City. Ahmed swept through several more. It was the same the world over, the videos live-streaming to the Internet from smartphones. They depicted what Francesca held to be the true nature of mankind—the loving heart and soul of humanity.

"Right on," Timmy said. "That's exactly what we need."

"What better way to show them who we really are?" Lacey said.

Marshall was scratching his chin, deep in thought. After a moment he said, "We need more than a message—we need a movement. Each of those streams is coming from a different website." He edged closer to the phone and pointed to a hit-counter on the current video. "This one hasn't even collected half a million hits yet. We need something that will capture billions of hits in a few hours. The world's attention needs to be focused on these scenes." He pointed at the countdown monitor on the wall depicting man's violent history. "Instead of those!"

Timmy leaned forward, his palms on the table. "We'd need access to a massive base of web servers to handle the load."

"I've got a few friends who could help us with that," Kenny said.

"Me, too," Timmy added.

"Oh, yeah," Marshall said, a grin spreading on his face. "If we could get the hackers of the world united in a common cause, we could spread the message faster than wildfire in a windstorm."

As the significance of the news—and the plan—began to settle in, Francesca turned to see the sergeant major stride in. He'd led the hijack team and had apparently returned in the helicopter. He didn't stop until he stood in front of her. He clasped a small plastic baggie at his side. It held three bloody capsules that she recognized as RFID implants. She stiffened as she realized that they must have been carved from the skin of the three passengers on the cruiser.

The Aussie's uniform was wet. His lips were tight. He looked from Ahmed to Lacey to her, as if sizing each of them up. Finally, his gaze settled on Francesca.

He said, "So, I understand you come from a boating family."

Chapter 68

Grid Countdown: 1h:50m:30s

The Island
5:41 a.m.

THE WATER WAS COOL. IT FELT GOOD. JAKE SWAM ACROSS THE center of the pool toward the wall on the left edge of the falls. An undertow tugged at his legs. He pulled through it with strong strokes, grabbing a clump of dangling vines when he made the far wall. The roar of the falls was deafening. Mist and spray blurred his vision. The gap between the raging water and the sheer rock wall was less than eighteen inches wide. The rock glistened with algae, making it difficult to gain a handhold. A fingerhold here and there was the best he could manage as he edged his way behind the frothy curtain of water. He moved slowly, blinking constantly to clear his vision as he looked for signs of a tunnel or pathway. The falls tugged at his back, the plunging water pulling his feet outward like a rip current. His fingers trembled as he inched along the wall. Any slip and he'd be pummeled by thousands of tons of force. Bones would shatter.

He kept moving.

The strain he felt in his hands and forearms was severe, but it was also invigorating. He was alive. He was making a difference. He may have lost what others might have referred to as his superpowers, but he still had a few wild cards up his sleeve. For one, his brain and body worked in concert unlike ever before. It was more than simple eye-hand coordination. It felt as if his previously supercharged reflexes had left an imprint on his system. Like muscle memory. He wasn't superfast any longer, but he was still quick. And exacting. His body reacted to his environment instinctively.

The falls thinned, and he was out the other side.

There was no hidden passage.

His spirits fell.

He was halfway back to shore when the underwater current suddenly surged. It tugged him backward toward the center of the pool. He kicked hard and pulled toward the shore, but the current wouldn't let go. Jake fought back a wave of panic as it drew him backward with increasing speed. The agitated water spiraled in a widening whirlpool—as if someone had pulled a plug down below. When he realized the force was too strong to resist, he turned and swam with it, accelerating into the widening funnel. Centrifugal force was his only way out. So he lurched toward the center of the vortex, accelerated, and jackknifed up the other side.

But it wasn't enough—he wasn't going to make the outermost lip, and the widening funnel began to suck him backward. That's when he saw the rope unravel onto the water. He grabbed hold with a death grip, and his body twisted and spun like a lure on the end of a fishing line.

"Hang on!" Tony yelled, reeling him in hand over hand.

When Jake's knees scraped sand, Becker and one of his operators helped him up.

"You California boys are all the same," Becker said. "Always looking for that next wave."

Jake spit water. "I guess I found a way in."

"Yeah," Tony said. "Into a toilet, maybe."

"Either way," Jake said, "that's gotta be man-made. It's the first sign that there's more going on here than meets the eye. We're going to need scuba gear."

"Right," Becker said, motioning to the operator who'd helped pull Jake out of the water. "Jonesy, prep up for a look-see."

"Sir," the operator said. He was in his early twenties, leaner than the rest of the team, with sinewy features that hinted at a man built for speed. He unhitched his backpack and began removing gear.

Becker pressed the selector switch on his wrist display to issue a command to the drone. But his mouth froze half open. "Dammit," he grumbled, pulling out a waterproof placard from a cargo pocket. It was the cheat sheet Timmy had given him for controlling *Mother Ship*. He ran his finger down the list of commands, nodding when he found what he wanted. He spoke into his boom mike. "Record message."

"*Recording*," a sultry female responded.

Jake chuckled at Timmy's selection for the drone's voice.

"We've located an underwater entrance," Becker said into his headset. "Request immediate aerial drop of scuba gear for teams one and two. Launch backup teams three and four to our location. End recording."

"*End recording*."

Referring to the placard, Becker added, "Copy to *Homer One*."

"*Copied to* Homer One."

"Launch *Homer One*."

Jake followed Becker's gaze overhead. The sky shimmered, and the surveillance drone was suddenly visible. A wedge opened in the mesh umbrella above it, and an object flew out. The mesh closed, a quick shimmer, and *Mother Ship* vanished.

"Homer One *launched*."

The minidrone looked like an angry hornet. It moved just as fast, buzzing past Jake and disappearing over the jungle canopy. The image on his own wrist screen zoomed out as *Mother Ship* rose to an altitude that allowed it to take in the departing tracks of its offspring.

"It's headed for the ship," Becker explained. "As soon as it clears the energy field that's messing up our comm, it'll transmit the message."

Behind them, the whirlpool had vanished as quickly as it had formed. Jonesy had stripped to his T-shirt. One of the pockets of his cargo pants bulged. He wore fins and a face mask. Wires dangled from his headset to the waterproof cummerbund housing his battery pack and transmitter. He wouldn't be able to transmit while holding his breath. But he could still listen over the comm net. He carried a flashlight. A climbing rope was looped around his waist. Tony held the other end.

"Off you go, lad," Becker ordered.

The operator dove into the pool. Two kicks of his fins and he was out of sight. The minicam in his face mask allowed them to watch his progress on their wrist screens. He hugged the edge of the pool, diving to its depths. The flashlight panned left and right, the powerful beam reflecting off thousands of bits of agitated particulate matter twisting and swirling within an underwater tornado. The above-surface whirlpool had temporarily vanished, but the underlying current that had caused it was still flowing with full force. Jonesy's fins were suddenly visible on the video. He was sinking in a seated position, kicking steadily to prevent being pulled into the flow. Tony kept a steady tension on the rope wrapped around the operator's waist.

Visibility was limited to seven or eight feet. When Jonesy reached the bottom, it was apparent that the current was no longer tugging at him. The flashlight stopped panning. He'd spotted something. He moved toward it, and a metallic column came into view. It resembled a ship's smokestack, projecting seven or eight feet from the bottom of the pool. The funnel appeared wide enough to pass a car through. Jonesy hugged the bottom as he approached. He slid slowly up the stack. Handholds along the upper perimeter allowed him to keep from being sucked in. He peered over the top. The opening was covered with a mesh grate. Water rushed through it.

Jake ground his teeth. It figures, he thought. A tunnel. Filled with water. Pitch black. And his kids were somewhere at the other end. A claustrophobic's nightmare come true. He suppressed a shiver.

"Rig it," Becker ordered.

Jake watched as the operator opened his cargo pocket and pulled out the first C-4 demo-charge. He'd been under for fifty-seven seconds—Jake had kept track. He watched with admiration as Jonesy calmly placed a charge at each of four connecting points around the grate. Red warning lights illuminated on each as he armed them. When the last charge was set, he turned and made for the surface. Tony kept tension on the line. By the time Jonesy's head broke clear, the total elapsed time was two minutes and twenty-four seconds.

"The guy's a fish," Tony said.

No kidding, Jake thought. He remembered back to his days of holding his breath underwater longer than the other kids in the pool. He doubted that he'd ever gone longer than ninety seconds.

Jonesy removed his mask and fins and stepped out of the water. "All set, sir," he reported, pulling the remote detonator from his pack.

"Let her rip."

"Fire in the hole!" the operator said. He pressed the switch.

Jake heard a soft rumble. A moment later, a surge of bubbles disturbed the surface of the water.

"Back door's open," Tony said.

Cal's voice broke over the comm net. "Raider One, this is Rogue Two-Four. How do you read?"

"That was fast," Tony said.

Way to go, pal, Jake thought, grinning at Cal's choice for his call sign. It was a reflection of both his personality and his love for surfing the biggest rogue waves he could find.

"Loud and clear, Rogue," Becker said. "Welcome to the party."

"It ain't a party until the gifts arrive. And I've got a pile of 'em. I'm feet dry. Two clicks out."

Jake wondered at the clarity of Cal's transmission—and the fact that he couldn't hear the distinctive thrum of the helicopter's rotors. He said, "You're riding pretty quiet up there, Rogue."

"Our mutual pal calls it silk mode."

Jake knew he was speaking about Kenny. They never used names on the air. The stealth chopper was another one of Kenny's toys.

"Rogue Two-Four," Becker said, bringing the conversation to the business at hand. He pressed a designator on his wristband. "Sync to network Charlie Alpha Four."

"Roger, Charlie Alpha Four."

A flashing icon appeared on the perimeter of Jake's wrist screen. It was designated R24. Cal was now linked into their digital command network. His HUD—heads-up display—would provide him with the same images as those available on their wrist screens.

"Tallyho, Raider One," Cal said. "I'm ninety seconds out."

"There's not enough clearance to land, Rogue Two-Four," Becker said. "You'll have to winch it down."

"Copy, Raid—" Cal cut off and said, "Stand by, One. I've got activity." His voice was urgent.

"Movement on our flank!" one of the scouts reported over the comm net. "Ground force. Multiple targets. Danger close."

"Shit," Tony said, pulling his M4 to the ready position. He sprinted toward the trees. Jake and Becker were right behind him. Jonesy scooped up his SR-25 sniper rifle and made for higher ground.

"*Mother*," Becker ordered. "Scout rear. Two hundred meters."

"Where the hell did they all come from?" Tony said, looking at his wrist screen.

Two dozen hostile-designated icons fanned out behind their position.

"Gotta be a trap door in the jungle floor," Becker said. "We must have triggered a sensor."

"Standing off, Raider One," Becker said. "This bird's got no teeth."

"Get small," Becker ordered on the comm net. To Jake and Tony he added, "Problem is that the chopper is strictly recon. It isn't a gunship. Ground fire would eat him alive. And it's loaded with Aqua-Lungs, not reinforce—"

Gunfire erupted in the distance. All three men dove for cover.

"Weapons free!" Becker ordered, scrambling behind the base of a coconut tree. "Set claymores. Fall back to the secondary perimeter." Then he pressed the drone command switch and said, "Record message."

"*Recording.*"

"Emergency transmission. Under attack. Ground assault. Execute tactical plan Delta. End recording." He issued the launch commands.

More gunfire.

"Activate defensive systems," Becker added.

Mother Ship's voice remained sultry. "*Defensive systems activated. Twenty-one ground targets acquired.*"

The sharp crack of the first exploding claymore popped Jake's eardrums. A plume of white smoke broke the canopy less than one hundred meters ahead.

Gunfire resounded from within the trees. The buzz of a ricocheted bullet spun past the trio, and Jake ducked lower.

"*Thirty-eight ground targets acquired.*"

"Jesus," Tony said, kneeling behind the next tree. "They're popping out of the ground faster than rats from a flooding sewer."

Mother Ship switched to tactical support mode. It rose in altitude and superimposed an electronic grid on Jake's wrist display. Friend and foe were identified with glowing green and red icons. Jake's stomach tightened as he watched the scene unfold. The six outlying team members blitzed inward to form a defensive perimeter near the edge of the small clearing. Enemy icons closed in on them from three sides. Tactical plan Delta called for an orderly retreat that was dependent on backup support from teams three and four. But by the time they arrived, Jake and the rest of them would be overwhelmed. He'd never find his children. Victor would win.

No way.

Movement to his right caught his attention. The surface whirlpool was visible again.

A second claymore went off. More rounds buzzed overhead.

Jake ignored it all—including Tony's shout of dismay when Jake took off in a sprint toward the water.

He scooped up Jonesy's backpack, looped it over his shoulder, and dove into the pool.

Chapter 69

Grid Countdown: 1h:45m:30s

The Island
5:46 a.m.

THE LAST TWO TIMES SARAFINA HAD BEEN TAKEN HOSTAGE had been six years ago—first in the mountains of Afghanistan and then in the Venezuelan jungle. In both cases, she and her mom had been drugged and thrown into dirty cells without food, water, or dignity.

This time couldn't have been more different.

She and Alex—along with a hundred or so other kids and many of their parents—sat at long tables in a cafeteria. It was as big as the dining hall at Hogwarts. Unlike the fictional school for magic, however—where students wore drab uniforms—children on the island were encouraged to flaunt their personality and cultural diversity with their outfits. Every style and color imaginable was represented. She saw bright saris from India, lederhosen from Germany, and a group of daredevil Japanese teens dressed in a bizarre fusion of East-meets-West that belonged on the cover of a fashion magazine. Three African children wore neck, wrist, and arm adornments over richly colored wraps.

Sarafina couldn't have felt more underdressed. She and Alex still wore the jeans, T-shirts, and tennis shoes they'd purchased in Venice. They'd left their sweatshirts and backpacks in their room.

They focused on their food, avoiding the inquisitive looks of the families around them. Most of them were new arrivals as well. Quite a few had filtered into the room in the past few minutes. But they seemed different from the people she'd met when they had first arrived with Victor Brun. This group seemed out of place to Sarafina. It was as if they weren't part of the "in crowd." On the surface they seemed polite enough, but underneath she sensed a brooding well of apprehension. They may not have been dragged into this situation in the same way she and Alex had been, but they knew there was a lot more going on than met the eye.

It left a pall of tension over the room.

The food was good, but she still had to force herself to eat. The daylong flight and boat ride had taken them halfway around the world—a world that was on the brink of collapse. How could her mother and father possibly find them? And even if they could, what difference could they make? She'd never felt more alone. She pushed her plate away.

As if sensing her despair, Alex leaned his shoulder into her. His cheeks pulsated with the pasta he'd just stuffed into his mouth. He pulled her plate back in front of her.

He was right, of course. She needed her strength for whatever lay ahead. And she was anything but alone. Her little brother depended on her. Or was it the other way around? She drew strength from his calm demeanor. He'd grown so much in the last few days—in ways she couldn't fathom. Ever since that moment in San Michelle when he'd met Jake. It was as if some secret of the universe had passed between them, something that had convinced Alex that everything was going to be all right. It reminded her that miracles *do* happen. After all, her father had returned, hadn't he?—when they'd thought him dead for over six years? And with him back, *anything* was possible. One thing she knew for certain: he would stop at nothing to find them.

Suddenly, Alex took her hand and squeezed it. He stared up at her. His eyes were wide as saucers, and a strand of spaghetti dangled from his lip. A crooked grin brightened his face.

And suddenly she felt it, too.

In her mind.

Daddy's here!

Chapter 70

Grid Countdown: 1h:45m:30s

The Island
5:46 a.m.

WHAT ONE MAN CAN DO, ANOTHER CAN DO.

Jake repeated the mantra in his mind, recalling Anthony Hopkins's words from the movie *The Edge* as he had prepared to kill a 1,500-pound bear using nothing more than a sharpened stick—as Indians had done in the past.

Jake swam toward the widening vortex, drawing in a succession of ever-deepening breaths.

Houdini could hold his breath for three and a half minutes.

As he slipped over the lip of the deepening swirl, he purged his lungs of every bit of air. He allowed the current to sweep him in circles as he pulled on the mask from Jonesy's pack and grabbed the flashlight.

In 2008 Tom Sietas set the world record at over ten minutes.

Jake took one final breath, forcing air into every pocket of his lungs. Then he sealed his lips—and his fate—and jackknifed into the depths.

The force of the plunging funnel of water gripped him tighter than a straitjacket. He corkscrewed down at an alarming speed. It was all he could do to hold the flashlight in front of him in a double-handed grip. The intake stack was dead ahead. The rebar grate was gone. But the jagged edges of the four sheer points jutted inward like rusty daggers. He stiffened his body and cocked his extended forearms to one side, using them like a forward rudder to adjust his angle of entry. He torpedoed into the tube.

He was an underwater bullet train. The smooth walls of the man-made tube rushed past him. His speed accelerated, time ticked by, and his lungs burned.

What one man can do…

He spun and twisted through the water. After a long stretch, he had the vague sense that the tube had turned horizontal. But he wasn't sure. Up and down had no meaning. His world was reduced to the halo of light that stretched a few feet ahead of the flashlight. Jake didn't need to check his watch to note the elapsed time. His brain was way ahead of him.

One minute, fourteen seconds.

As his vision blurred at the edges, his lungs screamed for release, but he refused the order, allowing his mind to drift.

It could have been worse, he thought. At least in this circumstance he didn't have to suffer the agony of choice. There was only one thing he could do—keep his mouth sealed. The guy whose brainrush was ultimately responsible for the death of so many—if not the end of the world—ought to be able to do at least that. *Right?*

Two minutes, five seconds.

A dizzy part of his mind wondered if Jonesy had any duct tape in his pack. Too bad he hadn't checked before he dove in. He could've used it to seal his mouth and nose closed. That would've helped. Then, when his kids found his dead body, there wouldn't be any water inside it, and they'd know he'd done everything he could to survive.

Jake's chest began to heave involuntarily, expelling the CO_2 from his lips in fits and spurts. The organism demanded air. It wrestled for control, and the urge to suck in drove away all thought. He clasped his hands over his mouth and nose, refusing to give in, dimly realizing he'd dropped the flashlight. Darkness enveloped him.

Suddenly, the tube swerved to the left. His right elbow scraped against the wall, shredding uniform and skin. Then the flow straightened and he sensed that his speed had slowed. Shadows flickered on the curved walls surrounding him. He craned his neck to look forward, and that's when he realized he was floating upside down. He spun around. It took him half a beat to realize he was drifting in an open canal—surrounded by volumes of air. He jutted his head upward, removed the death grip from his mouth, and sucked in the sweet-tasting breath of life. His body reeled in relief as he drew in one breath after another. He ripped off his mask, floating through a well-lit space as vast as a jumbo-jet hangar. It looked like the inside of a power plant.

The lip of the concrete culvert was out of reach. It restricted his view, but he could still see the tops of three garbage truck–size cylindrical turbines. They dominated the space, each surrounded by a family of catwalks, piping, and ancillary equipment. Crane tracks and rows of metal halide lights dropped from the ceiling.

The water propelled him forward, and he passed beneath more catwalks and rows of high-pressure pipe. Up ahead, the water flowed beneath a low walking bridge. A loud sucking noise emanated from beyond it, and he realized that the water from the culvert was being drawn into another enclosed tube. He shuddered at the prospect.

Just before reaching the bridge, Jake dove down and springboarded off the bottom. He surged upward and clasped onto the rail supporting the walkway. Two more kicks, and he heaved himself out of the water. He ran in a crouch off the bridge. That's when he noticed there was a parallel culvert that flowed in the opposite direction. It exited the building at a different point than the entry flow. Steam drifted from its surface.

Cold water in. Hot water out.

His soggy boots squished with each step. He flattened himself behind a nearby pillar, water dripping from his clothing and backpack.

A constant thrum filled the space. The sound reminded Jake of a muffled jet engine. There was a gaseous taint to the air. He peeked around the pillar and saw three men in coveralls and yellow hard hats working on a raised catwalk beside the center turbine. Two armed guards walked casually at the other end of the main floor. Studying the layout, Jake identified manifolds, gas and steam turbines, condensers, and power generators. This was a fully automated geothermal power plant—drawing heat from magna conduits to power the turbines. Instead of a tower of air-cooled ventilators, the system used water for cooling purposes—fed by the pool at the base of the falls and discharged elsewhere.

Clever, Jake thought. Fully self-contained and hidden from the world. The system could output enough power to support a small city.

Or a new world order.

Chapter 71

Grid Countdown: 1h:32m:30s

The Island
5:59 a.m.

HE HAD A CLIPBOARD. THEY HAD PISTOLS.

Jake peered through the door's mesh window as the guards headed his way. They wore blue uniforms and baseball caps. From their casual demeanor, it appeared as if they hadn't been alerted to the firefight outside. Jake was in a locker room behind the first turbine. He'd exchanged his wet uniform for a set of coveralls and a hard hat. His boots were still soggy.

One of the guards hesitated beside the walking bridge. He swiped his boot back and forth in the puddle Jake had left when exiting the culvert. His gaze followed the trail of wet footprints…

Jake pushed through the door. He raised his clipboard overhead. "Be careful over there!" he said, waving them over. "It's slippery. Maintenance is on the way to mop it up. John had a little accident. The idiot fell in!"

The two guards approached. Neither of them went for his weapons. But Jake sensed their tension. "Oh, don't worry," he said with a chuckle. He glanced past them to confirm that they were beyond the sight line of the hard hats working on the second turbine. "He's okay," he added, motioning toward the locker room. "Toweling off inside. He feels pretty stupid." He shook his head. "I'm still going to have to write him up."

One of the men eased up. The other didn't. "I don't recognize you," he said, unfastening an electronic wand from his belt. He turned it on, stepped forward, and waved it over Jake's shoulder. The device beeped. One of four multicolored plastic nipples lit up. It was blue. The guard's eyes narrowed. He pressed a button, and a touch screen on the device flashed on.

Ignoring the man, Jake moved past him and pointed toward the culvert. "He slipped right over there." The second guard followed his gaze.

"Hey, wait a minute," the man behind him said.

Jake continued talking as his right hand slipped into his left pants pocket and grabbed the end of the pipe wrench he'd stored there. "If you ask me…" He twisted around and yanked the wrench out like a fencer would a foil, swinging it in an arc that connected with the man's temple. He went down in a heap, dropping the wand. The second guard spun around. He unholstered his weapon.

That was his mistake.

In the split second it took him to bring the pistol to bear, Jake swiveled around, hammering the heavy tool onto the crown of the man's skull. Bone gave way in a sickening crunch. He died instantly.

Grimacing against the brutality of the attack, Jake dragged the bodies into the locker room. Then he retrieved the fallen clipboard, pistol, and wand. When he was back in the relative safety of the room, he studied the scanning device. The face that was displayed on its four-inch screen didn't look anything like Jake. His job function was listed as BLUE TEAM–SECURITY OFFICER–LEVEL 3. Jake massaged the spot on his shoulder where the ship's doctor had implanted the RFID chip. It was the one Tony had taken from the body at the morgue in Geneva. Staring at the man's brutish face, Jake understood why Tony had referred to him as

Pit Bull. The man's real name was August Schmidt. Bringing the chip had been Timmy's idea. He had figured the identifiers would be incorporated into whatever systems the Order had in place for its new utopian community. It was a bit of a Hail Mary, but Jake had agreed it was worth a try. It had worked. That is, until the guard noticed that the blue designator light on the wand—which was apparently reserved for security types—didn't correspond to the coveralls and hard hat Jake was wearing.

He used the wand to scan the downed guards, memorizing their names and info. After trading his coveralls for one of their uniforms, he folded the bodies into lockers. Jonesy's pack was wet, but it no longer dripped. He slung it over his shoulder. Then he adjusted his holster, tipped the blue baseball cap low on his forehead, and marched into the facility as if he owned the joint.

The three hard hats were still working on the second-story catwalk surrounding the middle turbine. As Jake approached them, his eyes studied the freeways of pipes and valves leading to and from the machine, cataloging every detail, nurturing the seed of a plan in his mind. He cupped a hand beside his mouth and shouted louder than was necessary. "Hey!"

The three men turned as one.

"I'm looking for Cody and Molsen," Jake said, using the names of the guards he'd encountered. His voice was gruff. "You seen 'em?"

One of the men pointed toward the far exit. "They were headed toward the east exit a few minutes ago."

"No, I just came from there, dammit. They were supposed to meet me outside the control room. But they were a no-show."

At the mention of the control room, two of the men glanced unconsciously toward a doorway at the far end of the facility. That was the sign Jake needed. The third man shrugged. He said, "Maybe they—"

"Never mind," Jake grumbled, placing a finger beneath his earlobe as a pretext that he was receiving a message. He nodded his head, turned on his heels, and headed toward the control room.

A minute later, Jake pushed through the double doors. The space was the size of a three-car garage. Electronic control consoles spread corner to corner along three walls. Rows of switches, breakers, meters, and displays rose from the operators' desktops to the ceiling. The third wall featured a huge backlit display that depicted power flow across the entire island complex. It was divided into four sections. Three were dedicated to the vast underground levels. The fourth was an aboveground area the size of a university campus. Jake was taken aback by the immensity of it all. How had they kept this hidden? His eyes snapped like the shutter of a camera, signaling his brain to capture every detail.

There were two younger men seated at the consoles. A stout woman with graying hair stood behind them. She wore coveralls, a hard hat, and a stern expression. "Can I help you?" she asked in a thick German accent.

Jake elected to take a different approach than he'd used outside. He walked over and extended a hand, switching to German. "I just arrived," he said with a face that was filled with glee. "I'm waiting on…" He glanced at his clipboard. "Cody and Molsen." He paused before adding, "I—I just can't believe it's finally going to happen!"

The two techs glanced over and smiled. The woman was also disarmed by his charm. She took his hand and gave it a firm shake. "I am Frau Schultz. Welcome. But you really shouldn't be inside the control room. Would you mind waiting outside?"

"Of course not!" Jake said apologetically. But he needed one more bit of intel before leaving. He turned to go, stopping to give the wall schematic a wide-eyed stare. He focused on a section depicting the lowest level of the facility—where he was located now. There was a series of icons along the right side of the quadrant. He identified the one labeled MAGNA CONDUIT. If his plan was going to work, he needed to avoid it. He wanted to create a diversion, not bring down the mountain.

“This is brilliant. We’re somewhere around here, huh?” he asked, absently touching the screen. The display shifted to a schematic of the geothermal flow and control system. Jake blinked his eyes. “Oh, sorry!” he said, backing away.

Frau Schultz stepped forward and took his arm as a mother would a child’s in a china shop. She escorted him out the door. “I’m sure your associates will be here shortly,” she said stiffly. The door closed behind him, and he heard the lock engage. Jake’s smile vanished. It had been hard for him to keep his cool in there. They’d seemed so calm. So pleasant. Cocooned in their self-contained world—while the rest of the globe sat on the brink of extermination.

They called themselves the *Order*, Jake recalled. Well, welcome to *Chaos*, assholes.

He rifled through Jonesy’s pack and made his way to the turbines.

Chapter 72

Grid Countdown: 1h:45m:30s

The Island
5:46 a.m.

"Dammit!" Tony shouted. "Jake just dove into the whirlpool!" Tony ducked lower as more rounds ricocheted overhead.

"Bloody hell," Becker said, his back flattened against a tree. "All right, mate. Like it or not, he's on his own. If anybody can do it, he can. In the meantime, we need to hold the buggers off until help arrives."

"I hear ya," Tony said, but he wasn't happy about it.

"*Thirty-eight targets acquired*," updated *Mother Ship.*

"Andrew's been hit!" someone shouted over the comm.

"This way!" Becker said. He took off in a low crouch.

Tony followed. He heard the sharp crack of Jonesy's sniper rifle behind them. The kid had found his perch. There was so much return fire that it sounded like a string of Chinatown firecrackers. Hot lead shredded branches overhead.

Becker and Tony tore through the dense foliage. Ten paces later, they found Andrew. The young operator was on his butt behind a tree. His left arm hung loose at his side. The bullet had hit him square in the bicep. It must have shattered the bone.

Rivulets of blood dripped from his fingers. His face was white, his eyes glassy.

Becker slid to the boy's side.

Tony took up a cover position. He sighted down his red-dot scope and loosed short bursts. A man went down. Then another. Tony ducked behind a tree as a volley of return fire ripped past him. He felt the jackhammer blows of several rounds impacting the opposite side of the trunk. A green coconut dropped at his feet.

Becker yanked a tourniquet from his pack and cinched it above Andrew's wound. "Hang in there, kid," he said. "This one's no deal-breaker." He stabbed an autoinjector of morphine into his shoulder.

"*Thirty-four targets acquired,*" reported *Mother Ship.*

That's four less than a few seconds ago, Tony thought. But he was sure that Becker's team had brought down more than that, which meant enemy reinforcements were continuing to pour in.

Tony loaded an HE—high explosive—round into the M203 grenade launcher affixed to his rifle, checking his wrist screen to get a general idea of enemy positions. A cluster of six icons appeared to be attempting to flank them on the left. He switched to his weapon-mounted camera and edged the barrel around the tree. As soon as he targeted movement, he squeezed the trigger. The hollow thump of the launch was followed by a sharp explosion. Tony loaded and fired a second round in less than four seconds. When he switched back to overhead view, only two of the icons were moving. But they continued on a flanking track. Then another group of icons appeared out of nowhere and followed them. More of Victor's men were burrowing out of the ground.

"*Forty-one targets acquired.*"

That ain't good, Tony thought. He'd seen more than his share of action, and more often than not, he'd been in some tough situations. But none worse than this. An exchanged glance with Becker revealed that he felt it, too.

This battle was getting away from them.

"Teams three and four are feet dry," Cal reported from the chopper.

"It took us more than thirty minutes to get here," Tony said to Becker. "Even if they beat feet on the trail we blazed, they still can't get here in less than fifteen."

Becker knew the math. But his grimace was short-lived. He gave Tony a stiff nod and said, "Then I guess it's time to pull a roo out of the sack."

"What the hell are you talking about?"

Becker pulled out the placard Timmy had given him, studying it a moment. He kept his eyes on it while he spoke into his boom mike. "*Mother Ship*. Engage offensive systems."

"*Authenticate*."

"Becker. Five-seven-seven-two."

"*Offensive systems engaged*."

Gunfire intensified all around them. The team was fully engaged.

"Throwing frag grenade!" someone shouted. An explosion split the trees to Tony's right.

Becker continued to read from the card. "Target Designation Mode."

"*Target Designation Mode*."

"I'm hit!" Operator Phillips said over the comm .

Another operator responded. "I've got Philly!"

"Perimeter Assault Code Five," Becker commanded.

"*Identify proximity point*."

"My location," Becker replied.

"Last mag!" one of the operators shouted.

"*Proximity point accepted*."

"Designate targets one through twenty," Becker said.

"*Targets one through twenty designated*."

Tony checked his screen. The twenty enemy icons closest to their location began to blink.

Becker glanced at his own screen. Then he said, "Targets confirmed."

"*Targets one through twenty designated and confirmed.*"

The foliage on either side of them erupted from a blistering hail of bullets. More rounds bored into the trunk at Tony's back. He slipped his selector to full auto and sprayed blindly over his shoulder.

Becker hesitated a moment. His eyes narrowed on the placard as if to make sure he was reading it right. Then he blew out a breath and said, "*Mother Ship*, go native."

"*Confirm* go native *command.*"

"*Go native* confirmed!" Becker shouted.

Mother Ship hovered high behind them. Tony switched his screen to overhead camera view. He saw Becker, Andrew, and himself directly below. Then he caught glimpses of enemy movement among the dense vegetation in several locations ahead of them. The nearest was less than thirty meters away.

Suddenly, a swarm of shimmering hornets darted into view from behind the lens of *Mother Ship*'s camera. Each of the silvery objects had a bulbous torso and vibrating translucent wings. The swarm of robotic insects darted toward the canopy. They peeled off in scattered formations of two or three in a pack, vanishing into the jungle.

Going native, Tony thought.

"Weapons hold!" Becker ordered on the comm net. He didn't want their crossfire to interfere with *Mother*'s assault.

That's when Tony heard the first scream.

He grimaced. It reminded him of the shriek someone made when he'd been splattered with napalm. The worst kind of pain.

A chorus of death screams followed. Enemy gunfire faltered.

Becker zoomed *Mother*'s camera on one of several plumes of white smoke up ahead. Tony watched as a soldier writhed on his back. His palms were pressed to his eyes, and his mouth stretched wide in a silent scream. His shoulders, neck, and face were scorched. Licks of flame danced across bubbling skin.

White phosphorus, Tony thought with a shudder. The miniature dive bombs had detonated directly in front of each target's face. Death was certain. But not slow.

"*Targets one through twenty destroyed,*" *Mother Ship* stated matter-of-factly.

The screen zoomed back to a high-altitude tactical view. The icons representing the enemy's front line were motionless. The ones farther back were in full-scale retreat.

"Not a pretty sight," Becker said.

"Never is," Tony agreed. "But it may have given us the window we need."

Becker nodded. "Join up at the falls," he ordered the team.

Tony heaved Andrew over his shoulder. The soldier grunted, but he didn't cry out. Becker retrieved the man's weapon, and they trotted toward the water.

Jonesy was already there. He'd taken a knee. His rifle was trained on the tree line.

Tony set Andrew down with his back to a boulder. The kid grimaced. His eyes were dulled from the morphine. But he nodded and said, "Thanks, mate. I owe you one."

Two operators pushed through the brush and took up cover positions at the perimeter. Sergeant Fletcher and another operator were next. Philly hung between them. His arms draped over their shoulders. His head bounced loosely, and both of his legs dragged. A grim-faced shake of the head by the sergeant told them he hadn't made it.

Damn, Tony thought. One dead, one seriously wounded, and Jake probably drowned. Teams three and four were only halfway between the beach and their position. He hoped they got here soon.

The temporary lull wouldn't last long.

Chapter 73

Grid Countdown: 1h:40m:30s

The Island
5:51 a.m.

A single glance at Hans's expression was all it took for the Cristal champagne in Victor's mouth to transition from sweet to bitter. He set his stemmed glass down on a passing server's tray. It was his third. He was in the viewing room.

The sea of dignitaries parted as Hans stormed toward him, and a hush fell over the crowd. "They aren't pirates," Hans said, making no effort to lower his voice.

"Explain," Victor said calmly. He allowed his expression to show modest concern. But the alarm that churned in his gut threatened to burst out, bolstered by the effects of the champagne. He chided himself for the weakness.

"Australian commandos," Hans said. "Nine or ten of them."

Victor felt a jolt of fear. All eyes were on him, and he struggled to maintain his composure as he collected himself—drawing strength from the signature training session that had changed his life:

Victor was twelve years old. It was a Sunday evening. Mother was on a trip, and the staff had gone home. He and his father ate fruit and cheese at the kitchen table. He watched as his father bit into a third slice of the pear, burying his excitement beneath a practiced veil of indifference.

His father had taught him well.

Ever since that first lesson after his dog had died so many years ago, Victor had practiced in front of the mirror, training himself to appear calm and collected under the most extreme circumstances. He'd started by cutting himself with a knife, teaching his features to remain smooth during the pain. When that had brought unwanted attention from his mother, he'd progressed to mice and rats—drinking in their squeals. He'd been proud of his progress.

But his father hadn't been satisfied.

He'd watched his son like a breeder would a show dog. No sign of weakness went unnoticed. A twitch. A sniff. A brief narrowing of the eyes. Father had recorded them all in his mental notebook, to be revisited later during a private session.

The riding crop had always been within reach.

Over time, Victor's fear of his father had turned to shame. He'd wanted desperately to succeed, so he'd practiced at school, feigning emotions where none existed, ingratiating himself to those he cared nothing about, or picking fights with bigger kids and smiling through the pummeling.

But it hadn't been enough. His father had still found fault.

Eventually, Victor had moved on to domestic pets for his private sessions. Their mournful pleas had touched him deeply, helping him to hone his skills.

But Father kept on him...

And Victor's shame turned to hate.

It had all led to that special night, when father and son were seated at the kitchen table. Victor made casual conversation while his father downed the last slice of the drugged fruit. Fifteen minutes later, the lord of Castle Brun awoke to find himself gagged and tied to a chair in the tack room of the castle stables. Young Victor stood before him. He held a knife in one hand.

And a mirror in the other.

The next morning, the castle was crowded with people. Victor's mother had returned. Smoke lingered in the air from the accidental fire that had consumed the stables and killed Joseph Brun. His body had been burned to the bone in the intense flames. Family and friends had gathered to console the grieving widow—and the poor child who had witnessed the event.

The boy's touching expressions of sadness brought tears to their eyes.

"Four squads are engaged," Hans continued. He placed a hand to his ear. Another report was coming in through his earbud. "They're taking heavy fire. Several casualties. But we have them surrounded."

The jovial atmosphere in the room had vanished. Champagne glasses were abandoned. People gathered closer to listen to Hans's report. Their tension was palpable. Victor didn't like it. This was the Order elite. They were expected to maintain their composure, especially at this juncture.

Victor sensed an abrupt shift in Hans's comportment as he listened to another incoming message. The man's physical tells shouted that it was more bad news.

"Well done, Hans," Victor said before Hans relayed the message. He patted the man on his shoulder—something he rarely did. "I'm glad that your teams have it well in hand."

Hans understood. He kept his mouth shut.

Victor retrieved another glass of champagne and turned to the gathering. With a confident smile, he held up his glass and said, "To the culmination of a thousand years of planning." When they all found their glasses and raised them into the air, he added, "*Cæli Regere*!"

"*Cæli Regere*!" everyone chimed in. Several of them blew out sighs of relief.

Victor took a sip, placed his glass on a tray, and excused himself from those closest to him. He moved casually toward the far side of the room. Hans was at his side. For the benefit of those still eavesdropping, Victor said, “I’m sorry for the loss of your men, my friend. We will do something special for their families.”

When they were finally out of earshot, Victor positioned himself so that Hans’s back was to the crowd. Victor noticed a few people still scrutinizing the pair, so he offered Hans a consoling smile and waited.

Hans understood the cue. He lowered his voice. “Half of our team was just taken out by a drone of some sort.”

The news cut deep. First, Australian commandos, he thought. And now a drone? This was more than an exploratory mission. He felt his eye twitch. Anger battled with composure, and he forced himself to take two calculated breaths before speaking.

He lowered his voice. “Pull the squads inside. Then seal the hatches, collapse the tunnels, and deploy the remote guns. I don’t want anything left alive up there.” He nodded and smiled at a passing couple. Then he motioned toward the door. “Wait until you leave the room before issuing the order. The last thing we need right now is panic.”

Chapter 74

Grid Countdown: 1h:31m:30s

The Island
6:00 a.m.

"*Active defense system detected*," *Mother Ship* reported. The drone hovered over the jungle a hundred meters behind Tony and the Aussies.

Everyone checked their screens at once. The image zoomed on a compact machine-gun turret that had popped out of the jungle floor. A snare drum–size fixture rotated above it, bristling with lenses and sensors. The deadly box-fed weapon system sported an eighteen-inch barrel that swiveled from side to side.

As Tony's mind processed what he was seeing, the image shifted to a second turret rising into position.

"*Active defense system detected*," *Mother Ship* reported again.

"Son of a bitch," Tony said.

Another turret revealed itself. Then another. Two beats later, the drone rose to a higher altitude and announced, "*Multiple active defense systems detected.*"

"Drop to the ground!" Becker ordered. "No movement!"

Tony flattened himself against the moist earth.

"*Descending. Confirm landing command,*" *Mother Ship* said. It had construed Becker's order as a command entry. The ground rushed upward on the screen as the drone descended.

"No!" Becker shouted. "*Mother Ship.* Abort last command!"

"Aborting com—" A burst of heavy machine-gun fire silenced the transmission. Tony's wrist screen went blank. *Mother Ship* was destroyed.

"Nobody move!" Becker ordered. "There's no telling if there are any nearby."

Two chatters of more gunfire echoed from the distance.

The backup teams broke radio silence. "Raider Three under heavy fire. Taking casualties!"

"Three and Four, fall back immediately," Becker ordered. "Return to the ship. Repeat. Return to the ship. And stay low!"

There was another chatter of gunfire. The voice that responded on the comm net was laced with reluctance. "Acknowledged, Raider One. Raiders Three and Four returning to ship." A moment later he added, "Godspeed, sir."

"The turrets seem to be concentrated inside the tree line," Tony said. His cheek was plastered to the ground, the boom mike from his headset pressed into his skin. He knew that if one of the turrets was aimed this way, the sensor would detect the slightest movement. "If so, the closer we get to the pool, the safer we'll be."

Becker's face was turned away from Tony. He wasn't budging either. "Great theory," he said. "How we gonna test it?"

"Watch your heads, boys," Cal's voice suddenly said over the comm.

Overhead, Tony heard what sounded like the approaching motor of an old VW bug. The lush canopy twisted and swished as the stealth chopper streaked by. It was an eerie sight, Tony thought, without the familiar thrum of the rotors.

Tony's eyes went wide as the chopper dove toward the pool like a fighter on a strafe run. At the last possible moment, the tail rotor dipped, the nose pitched to the side, and the helicopter crabbed to a sideways stop like a hockey skater on ice. It banked so hard on its side that it seemed to Tony as if the primary rotor blades were about to lick the water. A huge bundle of equipment slid from its door and splashed into the pool. A ring of inflated bladders kept it on the surface. None of the remote turrets had opened fire. The chopper kept moving, righting itself and continuing sharply upward. It was so close to the falls that it disappeared in the mist.

"Eeeee-hah!" Cal shouted over the comm net as the chopper popped back into view. "Special delivery, boys. Lungs and ammo at your service."

Tony let out a held breath. "You crazy bastard!" he said over the comm.

"You kidding?" Cal said. He hovered the chopper a hundred meters overhead. "That was a blast. So now what?"

Becker belly-crawled toward the water. Tony was right behind him.

"Stay flat, lads," Becker said. "Snake toward the pool. No standing till you make water's edge. After that I reckon we're clear. If that screamin' brumby didn't draw fire, then I'm sure you brown-eyed mullets will pass unnoticed. First two to the water, retrieve that gear before the next whirlpool ruins our day."

Then he said, "Rogue Two-Four. We've got two to evac. There's not enough tree clearance for you to land on shore. So drop and hover for a water retrieval."

A few minutes later, Philly's body was aboard the helicopter. So was Andrew. He waved from the open doorway as it gained altitude and turned toward the trees. Tony and the rest of the team had donned their scuba gear. Sergeant Fletcher was the first to sink below the surface. Jonesy and one of other operators followed. Operator Hollister hung back to wait for Becker and Tony.

"You up for this?" Becker asked, donning his mask. He and Tony were knee-high in the water.

"Hell yes," Tony said. He spit into his mask and used his fingers to coat the lens. "It's time for some payback."

Becker wrapped his lips around his regulator and nodded. Tony was about to do the same when he noticed movement over Becker's shoulder.

A lone gunman staggered into the clearing, the soldier apparently shielded from the remote guns by his implanted RFID chip. Smoke drifted from the remnants of his uniform. His torso and head were scorched, and his eyelids had shriveled into his skull, exposing milky eyeballs that stared at nothing. But his hearing apparently still worked. The man turned his head to one side and aimed with his ear. The muzzle of his assault rifle rose, and he let loose on full auto. The first blast nearly cut Hollister in half. The operator was dead before he hit the water. An advancing line of pockmarks stitched their way toward Becker.

Tony lunged forward, shoving Becker so hard that the Aussie was swept off his feet and hurled across the water. Tony grunted in pain as a slug bit hotly into his thigh. His body twisted from the impact, and he splashed into the pool. More bullets zipped past him.

Strong hands pulled Tony under. A regulator was shoved into his mouth, and he was yanked deeper. He resisted at first, unsure what was happening. He blocked his body's instinctual urge to panic and forced his vision to focus. Stern eyes stared at him from behind a face mask. It was Becker, urging him to awareness.

Tony stopped struggling, allowing himself to sink with the Aussie. Becker used his buoyancy compensator to stabilize them ten feet or so below the surface. They were well clear of the underwater funnel. Becker held his palm in front of Tony's face mask. It was a signal to wait. Then he pointed to two dark shadows swimming upward toward the surface. It was Jonesy and Sergeant Fletcher. Going to take care of business.

Tony nodded. He used his fingers to make the okay sign. His leg was on fire, and a thick trail of blood swirled from the bullet wound. A minute later, Jonesy was at his side. He and Becker led Tony to the surface and helped him to shore. Sergeant Fletcher was on the radio with Cal. Hollister's body had been pulled to the water's edge. Operator Karch knelt beside him, his weapon panning the tree line.

Jonesy cinched a tourniquet above Tony's wound. He cut through the uniform at Tony's thigh and probed. Tony winced. It felt like a branding iron. "Hold still," Jonesy said, pulling out his knife. "The bullet's lodged right next to your femoral artery. I've got to remove it. It's gonna hurt."

Becker crouched beside him. He cocked his arm as if he were about to throw a dart. Tony saw it just in time, and his meaty hand caught the Aussie's wrist just before the morphine needle went into Tony's shoulder.

"None of that shit!" Tony snapped.

"Stop moving," Jonesy ordered.

"Just do it!" Tony said behind clenched teeth. He let out a steady growl as the knife went in. The pain blurred his vision.

But he didn't move his leg.

"Got it," Jonesy said, dropping the bullet into Tony's hand. "Looks like a five-six-two. Must've ricocheted off the water. Otherwise it would've gone clean through. You're lucky." He slowly released the pressure on the tourniquets. The wound bled but didn't spurt. He nodded and applied a thick pressure bandage. "You're going to limp for a while. But you'll live."

"Good," Tony said. "Then you can tell Cal we don't need him. I'm going with you."

Becker said, "Sorry, Tony. I can't allow it. Neither would you if you were in charge. And you know it. You'll endanger the rest of us. You've done your part, but you're gonna have to sit the rest of this one out."

"Bullshit!" Tony said. But the word came out slurred. And he suddenly felt dizzy.

"Yeah, I figured you'd say that," Becker said. "Which is why Jonesy dosed you when you grabbed my wrist. Sorry, but you're going for a chopper ride."

The last thing Tony remembered was Becker saying, "Thanks for saving my life, mate. I promise I'll put it to good use."

Chapter 75

Grid Countdown: 1h:20m:30s

The Island
6:11 a.m.

JAKE ESTIMATED THE SIZE OF THE FOUR-STORY UNDERground complex at 150,000 square feet, about half the size of a Forrestal-class aircraft carrier. It could easily house a couple thousand people. It had been carved out of the base of one of the island's twin peaks. He walked briskly down the underground corridor. Colored stripes on the floor coincided with directional wall placards. He used the memorized schematic to make his way toward the top-level exit, at one point ducking into the FIRE DEPARTMENT to avoid a group of guards. He followed a circuitous route, avoiding the DORM, SCHOOL, and MEDICAL areas, sticking to less-used corridors and utility stairwells.

He was halfway to the surface when he encountered a group of women and children walking in the opposite direction. They pulled suitcases behind them. The woman in the lead glared at him.

"You there!" she said. "Come here."

Jake hid his dismay at the sight of the young children. They stared at him with star-cast gazes. He sensed their trepidation. Of course it made sense that the Order had brought their children, he thought. He simply hadn't considered it before. Sure, every adult here knew what was going on. They were as guilty as sin, in Jake's book. But not the kids. Any more than Sarafina and Alex.

"How can I help you?" he asked.

"Take this," she said, rolling her suitcase toward him as if he were a bellboy. "We need an escort."

Jake ignored the suitcase. He'd met her type before. Better than everyone else, or so she thought. Jake held his anger in check. "You're looking for the dorms, right?"

"Isn't that obvious?" she said, motioning to her entourage. "But we're supposed to drop the children at the cafeteria first." She nudged the suitcase toward him. "We'll follow you."

"Sorry, but we don't provide escort service on the island," he said with a condescending tone of his own. He motioned over her shoulder. "Instead, we placed easy-to-read directional placards on the walls." He pointed to the floor. "And color-coded stripes on the floor. That way even a child can't get lost."

The scowl was still forming on her face when he pointed in the direction she'd just come from and said, "It's that way. Follow the yellow line. You can't miss it."

He tipped his hat, and as he started to walk off, he caught the eyes of the young girl standing beside the woman. From her features it was apparent she was the woman's daughter. She couldn't have been more than six or seven years old. She glanced nervously at her mother as if to ensure that she wasn't watching. Then she mouthed a silent *thank you* that melted Jake's heart. The subtle smile he offered her belied the twist he felt in his gut.

His mind raced through the implications as he left the group behind him. His children weren't the only innocents in this complex.

Jake picked up the pace. He passed storerooms, laboratories, and a vast underground farm with rows of vegetables. He skirted the kitchen and dining areas, though he was close enough to catch the aroma of cooked food and the din of voices and silverware.

It smelled like spaghetti. Two security guards stood outside the WEAPONS TRAINING room. They nodded as he walked past. There were a lot of new faces here in the past twenty-four hours, Jake thought. He was one of many. He kept moving, his mind reeling with the magnitude of the task before him. He passed the MUSEUM, GYMNASIUM, SWIMMING POOL, and RELIGIOUS CENTER.

All the comforts of home.

The lone exit was one floor up. He climbed the last set of stairs two at a time, stepping into a wide corridor that was busy with people. A dozen waited by a bank of elevators, most with suitcases. More gathered around an information kiosk just inside the gaping entrance. The opening to the outside world had been bored through solid rock. It was the width of a single-lane highway. The twenty-foot-long tunnel was framed in steel and concrete. At the exit point, massive blast doors were suspended on hinges to either side. The doors were at least thirty inches thick, with a network of hydraulic steel pins thicker than a man's thigh. Once those doors were sealed, he thought, nothing could get in.

Or out.

Jake exited the tunnel and stepped into a new world. The air was fresh and clean. The sun shone bright overhead. The sight before him took his breath away.

It was a deepwater lagoon surrounded by towering mountains. A latticework of Gothic structures rose and fell around three sides of the cove. Ornate spires and pinnacles peeked through lush trees and foliage. He saw homes, shops, and gathering places. In the background, waterfalls cascaded from one level to the next, joining to form twisting streams that flowed to the water's edge. The sprawling community was connected by graceful bridges and arched walkways that teemed with people in colorful garb. They all seemed to be headed his way.

Shangri-la, Jake thought. Or at least that's what the Order's designers had attempted to emulate. A peaceful enclave that spoke of a gentler time—*with an accompanying modern-day bomb shelter to protect them from an Armageddon that they prayed would come.*

Smoke and mirrors, Jake thought. Just like the man in charge.

Rows of boats and luxury yachts were moored at the far side of the lagoon. Which meant there had to be a hidden inlet somewhere, he thought, something the drones had overlooked. This end of the lagoon was lined by a long dock, where a hundred-foot yacht was disembarking a score of passengers. They were filing through a security checkpoint at the end of the pier. Wands were drawn. The new arrivals wound their way up the rising cobbled path leading to Jake's elevated position. He noticed a sense of urgency in their movements. Several of them glanced at their watches.

Jake shared their apprehension.

One hour and counting, he thought. Less than that for the little surprise he'd set downstairs. He was running out of time. And he still had no clue where his children were. One thing was for sure: he wasn't going to find them by standing here enjoying the view. He needed to speak to the man in charge.

Now.

There was an embedded camera over the blast doors. He removed his hat and turned to face it. Then he unholstered his sidearm, aimed at the sky, and opened fire.

Chapter 76

Grid Countdown: 1h:10m:30s

The Island
6:21 a.m.

VICTOR CHUCKLED OVER A JOKE VOICED BY THE MEMBER from Texas. Others joined him.

That's more like it, Victor thought, appreciating the return to normalcy. He'd calmed the room after the previous tension, and when Hans returned after issuing orders to his teams, Victor rested easy with the belief that the Australian incursion force would no longer be a threat. The remote machine guns would have ripped them to shreds by now. In any case, the tunnels had been sealed. The only remaining way into or out of the facility was the front blast door.

A startled shout from the other side of the room interrupted Victor's thoughts. A champagne glass crashed to the floor. A woman pointed at the streaming image on the wall screen.

A hatless security guard stood outside the blast doors. He was firing his weapon into the sky.

Why on earth…

The man stared at the camera, and someone zoomed the image.

Jake Bronson's defiant stare stole the oxygen from the room.

The sight jolted Victor like a live electric current.

"Curse that bastard!" he shouted.

The outburst shocked everyone in the room. No one more so than Victor.

"What are you waiting for?" he snarled, making no effort to ease the scowl from his face. He knew that if Bronson had made it inside, others would follow. "We've trained for this possibility countless times. Sound the alert. Security teams to their stations. All civilians need to be moved inside the facility. It's time to seal the complex."

The Order leaders responded swiftly. They knew what must be done. They advanced through either exit with military precision.

Victor was fuming. "Have the American brought to the chair room," he said to Hans. "And bring my tools!"

Chapter 77

Grid Countdown: 0h:050m:30s

The Island
6:41 a.m.

JAKE CRINGED AS VICTOR UNROLLED THE LEATHER TOOL pouch. The felt interior was filled with an assortment of long-stemmed hooks, clamps, snips, and knives. Victor's eyes went half-mast as he ran his fingers across their ancient bone handles. These were the tools of a master torturer, Jake thought. They appeared worn from use.

Victor slid a twelve-inch fillet knife from its sleeve. The blade glimmered under the overhead lights. The bone handle was deeply furrowed. He held it with the reverence of a priest with a chalice, and Jake imagined a lifetime of memories tracing across the man's mind.

After several long moments, Victor eased the leading edge of the blade across his own thumb. Blood dripped down either side of the neat slice—yet the man didn't flinch. Instead, Jake sensed that he embraced a perverse pleasure from the act. He placed the thumb in his mouth and—for the first time since he had entered the room—he looked at Jake.

"Sucking your thumb?" Jake asked. "Aren't you a little old for that?" He was strapped in the same chair as before. He was shirtless. The chair vibrated beneath him, and the fiber-optic lines leading from the chair into the ceiling were alive with activity. But his brain wasn't hooked into it. Instead, the skullcap hung loose overhead. A bundle of lead wires affixed to the underside of the cap led to a workstation with computer and comm equipment.

Victor chuckled at Jake's quip. The man's calm confidence was unnerving. He removed his thumb from his mouth. "You Americans are all the same. You imagine yourself as heroes. Making jokes in the face of death. It seems as if it's been embedded into your genetic codes by the movies you watch. I'll bet you're a Bruce Willis fan."

"You got that right," Jake said. He glanced at the computer display in front of the bank of equipment. It depicted streaming images of the island's population in prayer and the peaceful pursuit of art, science, and family. All of the scenes took place on the island. The rest of the world was conspicuously absent. So touching, Jake thought. Such a lie. This had to be the outgoing signal that Marshall and Timmy had used to isolate this island as their target. It was the Order's private appeal to the ultimate judge overhead. Victor would have assumed that the alien visitors would ultimately gain unlimited access to the historical evidence of man's violence, which made this transmission more critical than ever. It was like a defense attorney's closing argument, intended to sway opinion in favor of his particular client while throwing the other defendants—the remainder of humanity—under the bus. Although the sound was muted, Jake could imagine Victor's voice-over agreeing that mankind as a whole was not worthy, while proclaiming the Order's nonviolent pledge—*and blah, blah, blah*. The thought of it pissed him off.

Jake added, "And I guess it makes sense that you *wouldn't* be a Bruce Willis fan—seeing as how the megalomaniac bad guys he faces always get what's coming to them in the end. Just like you will."

He and Victor were alone. The room was sparse. Victor stood beside a rolling cart that held his tools. There were a couple chairs against one wall and a blacked-out observation window embedded in another. A suspended monitor in the corner streamed the images of violence that were being sent from the grid to devices across the planet. The countdown was at forty-five minutes.

Victor shook his head like a professor would to an ill-prepared student. He used a remote to switch off the monitor. Then he turned off the computer display. Apparently he didn't want any distractions.

"Poor Mr. Bronson," he said. "All tied up and nowhere to go. Did you really think you had even the slightest chance of standing in the way of plans that were centuries in the making? Some of the greatest minds in the world joined together to make this possible. Didn't you appreciate the level of detail that you encountered while wandering around our private world? Every contingency has been addressed."

"Is that so?" Jake said. He worried whether he'd done the right thing by allowing himself to be taken. At the time, it had seemed as if facing Victor was the only plausible shortcut. Now he wasn't so sure. They'd brought him to the chair, just like he had figured they would. But the energy surge he'd hoped for from the mini wasn't happening.

An announcement over the PA system proclaimed it was now 6:51 a.m. and that the blast doors were closing in fifteen minutes. He was running out of time.

"Keep talking," Victor said, stepping in front of Jake. "That will make the next few moments so much more satisfying." He moved the knife from side to side in front of Jake's face. The blade was inches from his skin, and he smelled the earthy aroma of the aged bone handle.

But he needed Victor closer yet.

"You think you're in charge," Jake said, returning Victor's stare. "But the truth is, you're not in control at all. You never were. Otherwise you and your lunatic buddies would have figured out a way to activate the pyramids long ago. No, it took an American action-film lover like me to start the countdown. You had nothing to do with it. In fact, I'll bet you shit your pants when the pyramid you brought here launched itself straight up out of the mountain, burning a hole in your electronic shield. Or was that part of your plans, too?"

Victor's face didn't flinch. But when the knife's smooth arc wavered for an instant, Jake knew he'd hit pay dirt. He pressed on.

"And you can bet that our buddies up in the sky aren't about to let you and your pals slide when the world's population is brought to judgment. In fact, I'm sure of it." It was Jake's turn to exude confidence. "And I should know, shouldn't I?" he added. "After all, I'm the only one who's ever had a two-way communication with them, right?"

Jake saw it. The man's tell. "Oooh, was that a little twitch in the eye?"

Victor drew back as if Jake had spit fire at his face. His nostrils flared, his face reddened, and the knuckles wrapped around the knife handle went white. The calm veneer vanished, replaced by a glare that was filled with hate.

This was the moment Jake had been waiting for. Either it would work or it wouldn't. He let loose a deep belly laugh—a mocking cackle like a bully would make to a kid who had just gotten pantsed on the playground.

Victor's eyes glared. He bared his teeth and pushed his face in front of Jake's. Spittle flew out of his mouth as he screamed, "You are a dead m—"

Jake bunched his shoulders and lunged forward. His forehead struck Victor's with the force of a battering ram. Victor reeled a step or two away, his eyes rolling into the back of his head. Jake arrested his fall by grabbing his trouser legs with the fingers of his strapped hands. The man teetered, Jake yanked, and the leader of the Order slumped unconscious onto Jake's chest. Jake held him fast, craning his neck as he looked for the knife. It had slid from Victor's grasp, but it hadn't fallen to the floor. It was wedged between Victor's thigh and Jake's lap—only an inch or two from his fingers. If he released his grip on the man's trousers, he should be able to…

Victor stirred. Jake reared his head and tried to butt him again. But the angle was wrong. The move served only to spark Victor back from his stupor. Jake released the man's pant leg and stretched his fingers toward the knife. His index finger was half hooked around the base of the handle when Victor pushed off.

The fillet knife clattered on the floor.

Victor staggered, shaking his head to clear it. A swollen lump had formed on his forehead. He glanced at the knife. Then back at Jake. His baleful glare was filled with vicious intent. He bent over and picked up the blade.

Jake was out of options.

There was a knock at the door.

Victor ignored it, taking a step forward. His eyes never left Jake's.

The knock became more insistent.

Victor held the knife like an ice pick. His hand trembled.

The knock transitioned to a pounding. "*Mein Herr!*" a voice shouted from the other side of the thick door.

Victor hesitated, battling within himself. Finally, he lowered the knife and unlocked the door.

Jake's shoulders sagged in relief. He let out a long, slow breath.

Hans stepped into the room. His callused hands were balled into fists.

"Something's happened," he said, moving to the equipment attached to the chair. He switched on the computer display. The streaming image had changed. Instead of the Order's peaceful scenes from the island, there was a series of short video clips. Some were grainy. Some were high-def. All of them jostled in a way that marked them as streams from handheld cameras. They showed live scenes of people from around the world. Praying, singing, and holding hands. Some of the videos were of small groups. Some depicted masses so large that the panning lens couldn't capture them entirely. All of them showed a world population committed to peace. Committed to one another.

"How is this possible?" Victor asked. His voice was unsteady.

"Someone hacked our signal."

"Well, shut it down!"

"We can't. Our lead programmer has tried. He said there's nothing he can do about it."

"Tell him to just unplug the damn thing!"

"It won't matter, *Mein Herr*." Hans made an entry on the keyboard and surfed to a Google site that displayed the same streaming images. "It's being broadcast via the Internet across the globe—on a massive scale. Our programmer explained that at this point our station is simply one of hundreds—if not thousands—of passive routing stations for the signal. So even shutting down the power won't help. Whoever hacked into our system knew what he was doing." He paused a moment before adding, "There's more. Reports indicate that violence in the streets has slowed. Instead, more and more people are joining in the global prayer for peace."

Jake couldn't have hidden his grin if he wanted to. *Way to go, Marsh!*

Victor swiveled toward Jake. The man's face was on fire. He rushed over to the back of the chair and switched it off. The vibration stopped.

"You did this!" Victor shrieked. He swung the knife in an outward arc that sliced across the left half of Jake's exposed chest.

Jake bared his teeth and grunted against the blinding pain. The sharp blade burned deep into his skin. Blood cascaded down his midsection.

Victor cocked his arm for another strike.

"Herr Brun!" Hans said, staying his hand. He'd used the remote to turn on the wall monitor. He pointed at it. The streaming images of man's violence—the ones coming from the alien grid—had paused.

So had the countdown to man's extermination. It had stopped at forty-two minutes.

Marshall's message of peace was working. The web of alien pyramids was reconsidering.

"*Nein*!" Victor yelled. His eyes went wild. His gaze bounced from the screen to Jake and back again. Then, as if a movie director had suddenly yelled "cut," Victor's demonic countenance vanished. Tension leaked from his shoulders. He smiled and turned to Hans.

"Bring the children," he said.

Chapter 78

Grid Countdown: 01h:01m:30s

The Island
6:30 a.m.

BECKER AND THE FOUR REMAINING OPERATORS SURFACED IN the underground culvert. The lip was just out of reach, limiting their view to the upper portion of the space. Becker saw catwalks, piping, and the top halves of three large turbines. The man-made cavern was vast. The team removed their masks and mouthpieces as the current pulled them along. Weapons panned left and right.

The waterway narrowed into another tunnel at the other end of the space. The sucking noise it made wasn't inviting. They needed to exit before then. A short catwalk spanned the water up ahead. A rope dangled beneath one side of it. *A gift from Jake?* Becker motioned toward it. The team stacked up behind him and shouldered their weapons. They'd need both hands for this.

The rope was knotted. Becker lunged upward and grabbed it halfway up, leaving the bottom two knots for the next man. Sergeant Fletcher grabbed hold. Jonesy was next. Before the current could pull him away, he latched a hand around Becker's combat harness. Then Sam and Karch hooked on to the sergeant.

The scuba tanks strapped to their backs made it cumbersome. But no one let go. They were stable.

And vulnerable.

"Give me eyes," Becker whispered to Jonesy.

Jonesy used his free hand to remove his under-barrel weapon cam. Then he pulled himself up to one of the metal struts. Becker had to twist his head to one side to avoid being hit by the kid's scuba tank. Jonesy positioned the camera on the mesh walkway and dropped back down. Becker checked his wrist screen. The space appeared to be vacant.

"Drop a line from that strut," Becker whispered, unhooking his scuba gear. "We'll bundle the gear and weight belts and tie it off below water level."

Two minutes later, they were ready.

"Go," Becker whispered to Jonesy.

Jonesy peeked over the lip of the culvert. He appeared as if he were about to pull himself up, when his attention was drawn to a fold of paper duct-taped to the adjacent strut. Something about it prompted Jonesy to pull it free and hand it to Becker.

That's when Becker saw the call sign RAIDER ONE handwritten on the outside of the paper. He unfolded it to find a hastily drawn facility map. He flipped it over and felt a surge of hope. A note from Jake. Short and to the point:

B, welcome to the party. This room unsafe 0655. Used all of J's toys. See you topside. JB

"Bloody hell," Becker whispered, checking the time on his wrist screen. He breathed a sigh of relief. It was 06:30. They had plenty of time. He shoved the paper in his pocket. "Move out."

Jonesy was halfway out when a Klaxon sounded in the cavernous space. He froze.

A voice sounded over the PA system: "Facility shutdown. Level three and four Blue teams to position Alpha."

Jonesy popped his head down faster than a startled jackrabbit. Becker looked on his screen and saw why. A stream of armed security personnel rushed through the swinging doors at the other end. There were dozens of them. The bulk of them double-timed toward the exit at this side of the facility. But several stopped to take up guard positions at each exit and beside each turbine. They carried assault rifles.

A procession of men and women wearing white lab coats and hard hats followed the soldiers. Becker was surprised to see that each of them wore a sidearm.

The Raider One team had floated into a hornets' nest.

"We wait," Becker whispered. He motioned everyone downward. They tucked under the bridge.

Becker counted the minutes.

Five. Ten. Fifteen.

Twenty...

A group of hard hats had gathered nearby. They seemed to be having a heated conversation.

Get moving already!

Guards remained positioned at the doors, and Becker's mind charged through their limited options. He wanted to wait for the space to thin out further before making their move, but they also needed to get the hell out of here before the gates of hell opened up.

Which was three minutes from now.

Jonesy had one hand around the strut, the other around his weapon. If Becker gave the word, the kid would be up and over in two seconds. The rest would follow. They awaited his orders.

Finally, Becker pulled a frag grenade from his vest. He motioned for Sergeant Fletcher, Sam, and Karch to do the same. He pointed to the guard positions at various locations on the screen. "That's yours, Sergeant," he whispered. "Sam, you take the ones here, and Karch the two on that side. Keep your tosses in the open areas. We don't want any coincident detonations with wherever Jake set his charges. Jonesy, you've got pin-pulling duty." The operator nodded. Since each man had only one hand free, it was a critical task.

Becker added, "Except for the sergeant's targets by the near exit, the rest are too far away for a direct hit. But if we can at least get 'em close, it'll shake up the bastards long enough for us to get feet dry." He pointed to the near exit. "I'm lobbing mine with the sergeant's. That's our exfil point. I figure the civilians will hightail it out the far exit as soon as the shooting begins. But stay frosty."

Becker held out his grenade. The others did the same. Jonesy yanked the pins, dropped them into the water, and readied his rifle.

"On three," Becker whispered, cocking his arm. On the third nod of his head, they launched four grenades over the lip. The sound of metal skittering along pavement was followed by four deafening explosions. Shrapnel spit into the catwalk overhead.

Jonesy waited a beat before heaving himself up and over. His suppressed assault rifle was spitting by the time Becker was beside him. The two guards by the near exit were dead. The double doors behind them had been blown from the hinges. Becker trained his sights on the guards at the opposite end of the cavern. They'd been the least affected by the blasts. One was on the radio. Becker took him out. The other two returned fire from cover positions. Three men and a woman wearing hard hats popped out from behind the second turbine. They opened fire with machine pistols, and Becker flattened himself against a pillar. Sergeant Fletcher slid beside him. Karch was half out of the culvert when a round took him in the forehead. He fell back out of sight. There was a splash.

"On the left!" Jonesy shouted. He let loose several short bursts. Becker's heart stopped when he saw why. A score of blue-clad soldiers and armed hard hats swarmed from beyond the gaping exit.

"Frag out!" Sergeant Fletcher shouted, lobbing a grenade in their direction. "That won't hold them long," he said. "We need a new exfil!"

But when Becker saw another platoon of soldiers spill through the far doorway, he realized that wasn't an option. Both exits were blocked. They weren't going anywhere. Bullets buzzed past him. Sam was halfway over the lip when Becker ordered, "Back in the water!" He pulled his last grenade, yanked the pin, and heaved it across the space. "Frag out!" he yelled as loud as he could. He wanted everyone to hear. Return fire stopped as the enemy took cover. Sergeant Fletcher and Becker charged for the culvert. Jonesy had already disappeared over the edge. Becker jumped over just as a fusillade of lead pummeled the low-slung walkway.

He and the sergeant tumbled into a tangle of grasping limbs. Sam and Jonesy had been ready for them. They'd slung their weapons and grabbed hold of the duo before the current could take them. They'd abandoned the knotted rope in favor of the line that held their equipment. They were neck deep in the water.

Sitting ducks.

Karch was nowhere to be seen.

Becker checked his wrist screen. The enemy advanced from either direction; they'd be on the team any moment. "We need to buy sixty seconds," he said breathlessly.

The men understood. They had only two grenades left between them. One flash and one frag. This time Becker was the pin-puller. "One at a time," he said. "Thirty-second interval. Flash first."

Sam lobbed the flash grenade. It would momentarily blind anyone looking this way. Becker watched on the screen. As soon as the grenade hit the pavement, the enemy contingent dove for cover. Several of them ducked behind the nearest turbine. The explosion was loud. A couple of them staggered, but the rest were quick to recover. Too quick. Only fifteen seconds had passed. They moved forward.

"Better go now," Becker said.

Jonesy nodded. He had the final frag. He glanced at Becker's screen and adjusted his aim. Then he heaved the grenade in a flat arc. The enemy soldiers saw it fly. Several of them dodged back to their hiding spot behind the turbine. The grenade slid toward them. Jonesy grinned in satisfaction.

But instead of continuing its slide beneath the elevated turbine, the grenade vanished into a floor grate. Two beats later, there was a hollow thump deep beneath them. A spout of flame burst from the grate. None of the enemy was wounded.

"Shit! Time to get small," Becker said. He took a breath and sank below the surface. The rest followed. They held on to the bundle of equipment to keep from being pulled downstream. Each of them grabbed the nearest regulator. The tanks still had plenty of air.

The water was eight feet deep. Becker hugged the bottom, rolling onto his back and staring at the surface, hoping like hell that Jake's watch had been properly synced with the team's.

Five seconds later, the world exploded. The cavern above the water went brilliant white. Becker's ears popped, the lights went out, and the camera view on his wrist screen went black.

Sergeant Fletcher was the first to flick on his flashlight. He made an okay sign with his thumb and index finger, receiving one back from each of the team. Becker surfaced, and the rest followed. The air was hot and smoky. It smelled like scorched electrical wires. Shadows flickered on the walls of the darkened cavern. Becker donned his night vision goggles and peered over the lip.

Intermittent licks of flame danced around the mangle of ruined equipment. Steam hissed, sparks jumped, and an orange glow emanated from the grate that had swallowed the grenade. There were bodies everywhere. Several of them still moved. None of them looked his way.

Yet.

Becker heaved himself over the edge. "On the double," he ordered into the mouthpiece of his headset. He crouched, bringing his M4 to the high ready position as he panned for threats.

Twenty seconds later, the rest of the team—except for Karch—was fanned out behind him.

"On me," Becker said, running in a crouch toward the door. "Watch your corners. And know this," he added, remembering the armed hard hats who had drilled Karch. "There's no such thing as a civilian down here."

Becker was as mad as a cut snake.

And darkness was his friend.

Chapter 79

Grid Countdown: 0h:42m:00s and Holding

Banda Sea
6:51 a.m.

Tony's vision cleared. He was on his back. He tried to sit up.

A hand on his chest held him down. "Don't move," the ship's doctor said. "I'm not done yet."

Tony lay back. He blinked several times to clear his foggy brain. He was onboard the yacht.

The doctor tied off a bandage around his thigh. "You need to stay off your feet for a while."

"Bullshit!" Tony said, sitting up. His head swam for a moment. His leg burned. He grunted, shook his head again, and slid off the exam table. "How long have I been out?"

"Not long," the doctor said. "They only gave you a short dose. But you lost a lot of blood."

"Yeah, but no worries," Cal said. He sat on the bed beside him. His left sleeve was rolled up. He had a bandage over the inside of his elbow. Tubes dangled from an IV stand between them. "We topped you off with top-grade surfer fuel."

Tony saw a similar bandage on his own elbow. He nodded to the pilot. The glance they exchanged said it all, but Tony added,

"Don't even think that means I'm going to be adding *dude* to my vocabulary."

"Maybe not," Cal said. "But you're gonna have to live with your new call sign."

"Huh?"

"Come on," Cal said, getting to his feet. "They're waiting on us in the control room."

Tony winced when he took his first step. His head was still fuzzy from the drug, but he was too angry about being pulled out of the action to let it slow him down. Cal offered him a hand. Tony waved it off. "Let's go," he said, limping out the door. Cal followed.

When they entered the converted boardroom, Marshall, Kenny, and Timmy greeted him with fist bumps and slugs on the shoulder. Sergeant Major Abercrombie stood to one side. He fidgeted like a benched linebacker anxious to get in the game.

"Welcome back to the fight, BK," Kenny said, sitting back down.

"BK?" Tony asked.

"Big Kahuna. Best dude on the beach."

Tony rolled his eyes. Cal shrugged.

"Check it out," Marshall said, swinging around his computer screen so Tony could see the streaming images of people praying. "We hijacked the island signal."

Timmy pointed to a wall monitor and said, "And it's having an impact."

The grid countdown was on hold. At least for now. Tony felt a swell of hope. His thoughts rushed to his wife and kids back home. He might see them again after all.

"On the other hand," Kenny interjected, "the tactical situation sucks."

Tony listened intently to Kenny's brief. He didn't like what he was hearing.

"So, to sum it all up," Tony said, "you're telling me that we're in the middle of the biggest fight of our lives, with nothing less than the fate of the world hanging in the balance. Jake, Sarafina, and Alex are still MIA, we've lost contact with Becker's team, and we've got two women and a kid undercover behind enemy lines."

"I tried to stop them," Marshall said defensively. "But Lacey wouldn't have it. Neither would Francesca."

"And if they went, Ahmed had to join them to complete the ruse," Timmy added. "Otherwise, why bother?"

Tony hated it. But he understood. The infiltration wouldn't have succeeded otherwise. The manifest called for two women and a child. He simply couldn't reconcile the idea of their being in harm's way without backup. He clenched and unclenched his fists, running through options in his head. But each one of them felt like a bull-in-a-china-shop approach that had zero chance of success. The remote turrets made the back door inaccessible. They knew about the hidden entrance to the inlet, but the defenses that were obviously there were invisible to them.

Maybe a small incursion force—

"Something's happening," Kenny announced, interrupting Tony's thoughts. "The drone signal—" He cut off. His eyes went wide. His mouth gaped. "Holy shit! The island shield just went down!"

Tony rushed to his screen. The rest of them gathered beside him. Kenny adjusted the image from the circling drone.

"Way to go, Jake!" Marshall said.

It was more likely Becker, Tony thought. But he let it slide. He hoped like hell it *was* Jake. That would mean he was still alive.

"We've got 'em!" Timmy added.

Hell, yeah, Tony thought, staring at the overhead view of a huge hidden cove. It was dotted with boats, surrounded by structures, and served by an inlet to the sea. He searched the eyes of the men in the room. Each of them appeared ready to follow his lead.

"Are any of you content to be sitting on the sidelines right now?" he asked.

"No way!" Marshall said. The rest of them were just as quick to respond.

"The men are anxious to get to work," the sergeant major added.

Tony blew out a breath. "Okay, here's what we're going to do."

Chapter 80

Grid Countdown: 0h:42m:00s and Holding

The Island
6:53 a.m.

An intermittent alarm sounded outside the room. The facility was going into lockdown mode.

"Your life will end in the next few minutes," Victor said. He was calm and composed.

The words barely registered in Jake's brain. He was still strapped in the chair. It was switched on. The computer leads running into the underside of the skullcap had been removed so it could once again be fitted over his head. Victor hadn't yet lowered it into position. He stood beside him. His kit of torture tools was unrolled next to him. The fillet knife was back in its sheath.

But Jake's focus was elsewhere.

Sarafina and Alex sat in the chairs across from him. Their mouths were gagged, their eyes were wide, and their hands were flex-cuffed on their laps. Alex's tablet was propped against his belly. Hans stood beside them. The pistol he held was pointed in their direction. Alex tilted his head and stared at Jake as if he were waiting for something. He twirled his index finger in the air in the same way he had when they'd first met.

Jake understood. He opened his mind and felt his presence immediately. Sarafina's, too. Each of them found strength from the bond.

"The Order has prepared for this day," Victor said. "We've been transmitting our proclamation of peace for months. Ever since the first two pyramids appeared. The minor interruption of the signal in the last few minutes cannot change that. However, I will admit that it is imperative that the grid countdown be restarted. We can do that with your help…or without it."

Jake didn't like where this conversation was headed. But with any luck, it wouldn't matter. He had his own countdown to worry about. So far, Victor had yapped for thirty seconds. Keeping the conversation going for the next ninety seconds was critical. "You expect me to help you?"

"That's up to you," Victor said. "You have two choices. Either link with the grid and find a way to restart the countdown, in which case your children shall be spared, or refuse, in which case they shall die in this room…"

As if to accent Victor's words, Hans pulled the slide back on his pistol to chamber a round. Jake tensed when he pointed it at Sarafina's head. She mewed.

Victor continued, "After which I will trigger the launch of nuclear missiles from six separate locations, including a US submarine. The targets have been carefully selected to ensure retaliation, especially in light of the current state of global panic. The result? World War III. The *real* war to end all wars. That should certainly be enough to restart the grid countdown, don't you think?"

Jake's shock must have registered on his face, because Victor smiled. "Don't be so surprised. It wasn't as difficult as you might imagine. After all, we've been embedding our people in all the requisite positions of authority for generations.

"So what's it going to be? Give your children a chance to live long and fruitful lives as part of our community—on a planet rife with life-supporting resources? Or trigger a nuclear winter that will poison the atmosphere and destroy most of the life on Earth, save those of us protected beneath the surface of our island?"

Victor paused before adding, "You have ten seconds to decide."

Ten seconds wasn't long enough, Jake thought. He needed twenty. "Okay, I'll do as you ask. But first I have one thing to say."

"And what is that?"

Jake focused his thoughts on the children, readying them for what was coming. Then he looked at Victor, counted down the last three seconds, and offered up his best Bruce Willis imitation. "Yippee-ki-yay, you sick bastard."

Suddenly, there was a deep rumble beneath them. The floor shook, the chair switched off, and the room was thrown into darkness.

The gunshot from Hans's pistol was deafening. The muzzle flash illuminated the scene like a flash camera. The still image froze on Jake's retina: Sarafina's determined expression. Her bound hands in contact with Hans's wrist. The pistol partially dislodged from his grip. The look of surprise on his face. Alex sliding from his chair…

The pistol clattered to the floor. There was a patter of footsteps across the linoleum, and Jake felt fingers slide down his forearm toward the wrist strap. His son was trying to free him.

"Kill them all!" Victor shouted. It sounded like he had moved toward the door. A shadow disturbed the faint glow of a numeric keypad beside the exit, and Jake heard the tones of a code being entered.

A struggle across the room. A loud slap. A gagged whimper from Sarafina. Alex's fingers fumbled at the buckle of Jake's wrist strap. Heavy footfalls coming toward them. The snick of a switchblade.

The door flew open. Emergency lighting from the hallway spilled into the room. Three forms stood silhouetted in the doorway. "Mr. Brun!" a woman's voice shouted. "This way!"

Victor bolted past them. "Help Hans," he ordered. "No one leaves alive!"

Jake's right hand came free, and Alex tumbled to one side just as Hans lunged forward with the switchblade. Jake snapped his free hand in a whip-fast knuckle strike to the nerve bundle on the inside of Hans's forearm. The German recoiled but held on to the knife. He maneuvered to Jake's opposite side and cocked his arm.

Chapter 81

Grid Countdown: 0h:42m:00s and Holding

The Island
6:51 a.m.

Francesca let out a long-held breath. They'd made it inside. Other than the two security guards who'd passed a wand over each of them when they had first stepped off the boat, no one had paid them particular attention. There were dozens of people around them. They seemed to be as relieved as she was to have made it past the massive blast doors. An intermittent alarm sounded over the public address system. A woman's voice announced that the door would be closing in fifteen minutes.

People hurried toward a bank of elevators down the corridor. Francesca, Lacey, and Ahmed followed. They wore the casual traveling outfits taken from the three Order members who'd been on the thirty-five-foot cruiser. Francesca cringed when she recalled the video of the Australian soldiers hijacking the boat. One of the occupants had made the mistake of firing at the operators. It was a woman. She'd been killed. According to her papers, she was a surgeon from Madrid.

Now Francesca wore clothes taken from the woman's suitcase. The RFID chip that had been embedded under the woman's *Cæli Regere* tattoo was taped to her shoulder. Lacey posed as her sister. The actress was unrecognizable. Her hair was bunned, her clothes were padded, and she wore thick glasses and creative makeup. She'd transformed herself into a plump and dowdy schoolteacher. Ahmed had replaced the doctor's fourteen-year-old son. The role was a stretch, especially in light of Ahmed's emotional growth in the past few days. But he'd embraced it. The real sister and son were trussed up onboard the yacht.

Francesca had been frightened to the bone at the prospect of attempting the infiltration. But she hadn't hesitated. Neither had Lacey. They were the only women available. So there was no other choice. And Ahmed had to accompany them if the ruse was to have any chance of success. The brave teen's only regret was that he hadn't been able to bring his new assault rifle along.

Pushing back a wave of nerves, Francesca steeled her resolve. The people in these corridors had assaulted her home, shot her father, killed her friends, and kidnapped her children. She would do whatever was necessary to find them and help Jake. She marched toward the elevators.

They were three paces past the information kiosk when Ahmed stopped them. He seemed to be eavesdropping on a conversation between a stern-looking couple and an attendant behind the counter.

Lacey took the abrupt halt in stride, straightening the collar on Ahmed's shirt like an attentive aunt preparing her nephew for his first day at prep school. "Oh, you'll be fine, darling. Sometimes it's fun being the new kid." Under her breath she added, "What are you doing?"

The woman was in her element, Francesca thought. Not only was she a consummate actress, she also had a calm confidence born from a lifetime of martial arts training from her sensei father.

"Too many ears to explain," Ahmed whispered. "Just follow my lead." He stepped up to the information counter.

“Excuse me, excuse me,” Ahmed said in an imitation of a distressed fourteen-year-old. His outburst interrupted the attendant.

“One moment, young man,” she said. “You’ll have to wait your turn.”

“Nooo!” Ahmed exclaimed. His face was beet red. He looked like he was about to cry. He’d reverted to mannerisms from his childhood. “I need to find my uncle!” His voice was choked.

Francesca was so taken aback by his instant transformation that she didn’t know what to do. Lacey was another matter. She placed a hand on Ahmed’s shoulder. “It’s okay, dear,” she said, wiping a tear from her eye with a trembling hand. “I’m sure he made it.”

“Pleeease!” Ahmed said. “They’re going to close the doors!”

The couple beside them was annoyed by the exchange. The woman placed her hands on her hips. She didn’t hide her disapproval. The man with her seemed to share her feelings.

Francesca stepped forward. “I’m so sorry,” she said to the couple. “He already lost his father.” Then she turned to Ahmed. “Please, son. We’re next—”

“He should know better,” the woman scolded.

“No, no, no!” Ahmed said, smacking his palms on the counter. “He promised he’d be here. But if you close the doors, he can’t get in. That’s not fair. Is he here or isn’t he? Why can’t you just—”

“Quiet down!” the man said.

“I won’t! I won’t, I—”

“Oh, just look it up and be done with it,” the woman said. She looked like she wanted to smack the kid.

The flustered attendant nodded. She placed her hands over her computer keyboard and gave Francesca an expectant stare. Francesca’s heart dropped. What was she supposed to say?

The attendant narrowed her eyes. “His name?”

“Uncle Augie,” Ahmed spit out. “Oh, I mean August Schmidt.” He crossed his arms on the counter and leaned forward like an anxious child waiting for a gelato.

The brilliance of Ahmed's plan enveloped Francesca like the sweet smell of jasmine in the courtyard of her home in Venice. He'd remembered the name of the man from whose body they'd dug out the original RFID chip. Tony had referred to him as Pit Bull.

Jake had taken the chip with him.

"Level three," the attendant said. "Room three seventeen." After a beat, her posture stiffened. "Oh, he's with Mr. Brun."

Francesca's insides cartwheeled.

"He's here!" Ahmed proclaimed, staying in character. He spun around and took both Francesca's and Lacey's hands. "Let's go!"

As he led them toward the elevators, Francesca collected herself enough to look over her shoulder and mouth her thank-you to the couple.

The woman huffed. The man shook his head in disgust.

Four minutes later, they were outside the room. There was an electronic keypad beside the door.

"Now what?" Francesca asked.

"Simple," Lacey said. "Let me do the talking." She cocked her fist to pound on the door. But a deep rumble beneath them stayed her hand.

It sounded as if there was a series of explosions deep in the mountain. The vibration under their feet felt like the aftershock of an earthquake. The lights went out, a gunshot sounded from the other side of the door, and a voice shouted, "Kill them all!"

Francesca trembled. A knot of fear tightened in her stomach.

A seesaw alarm sounded, and an emergency light opposite the doorway flashed on. The door swung open. Francesca and Ahmed lurched backward.

Lacey stood her ground. Light spilled past her into the room. Victor Brun stood before them. He squinted at the sudden brightness, and Francesca averted her face so he wouldn't recognize her.

"Mr. Brun!" Lacey shouted without skipping a beat. Her voice was filled with authority. Her backlit form would appear as no more than a plump silhouette to Brun. She motioned him forward. "This way!"

"Help Hans," Victor ordered as he rushed past them. "No one leaves alive!"

"*Jawohl, Mein Herr,*" Lacey growled. She charged into the room. Ahmed and Francesca were right behind.

The seconds that followed stretched into an eternity.

Light from the corridor emergency lamp spilled into the room. Jake was strapped to a chair. One hand was free. A man hulked in front of him. He held a knife. Lacey slid across the linoleum floor feet first, her heel striking the man at the ankle. He toppled, but he maintained his grip on the knife. Ahmed stomped on the man's stomach, but it didn't faze him. He swung the blade at the teen. As Ahmed jumped clear, the burly guard twisted around and kicked. The blow sent Ahmed flying into the shadows.

Jake was fumbling with the strap at his wrist as Alex watched wide-eyed from behind the chair. The German pushed to his feet and approached. But Lacey was already up. She surged forward with a vicious snap kick to the groin. But the brute only grunted. He advanced on her with the knife. By then Francesca was on her knees, working on Jake's ankle restraint. He was unbuckling his other foot. Sarafina screamed, and Francesca turned to see Lacey on her back, the German on top of her, the knife held in the air like an ice pick.

The three gunshots sounded like claps of thunder. The German twisted and lurched with the impact of each slug. The knife fell from his grasp. He folded to one side and lay still. Blood pooled from beneath him. Lacey grabbed the knife and scrambled to her feet. The tail of an elastic Ace bandage spilled from under her blouse. The gauze padding it had secured to plump her appearance was cockeyed.

Ahmed stepped from the shadows. He held the pistol in a two-handed grip. Smoke curled from the barrel. His hands were steady.

Francesca sensed no fear from him.

Jake helped her to her feet, and she rushed to pick up Alex. She peeled the tape from his mouth and squeezed her son to her chest, feeling the beat of his heart racing at double speed. "Are you okay?"

He nodded, then pointed to his tablet. It had fallen on the floor beside his chair. Lacey picked it up and tucked it into the holster clipped to Alex's belt. Then she used the knife to cut his wrist cuffs. She did the same for Sarafina, who'd already removed the duct tape from her own lips. She rushed to join her mother and brother.

Ahmed handed the pistol to Jake. They fist-bumped. "A-are you all right?" Ahmed asked, pointing to the ugly slash across Jake's bare chest.

"Thanks to you, I am," Jake said.

Lacey yanked the stuffing from around her midriff and pressed it against Jake's wound. He winced at the contact. He held the gauze in place while she wound the Ace bandage around his chest to secure it. When she was finished, he grabbed his shirt and put it on. Then he pulled Ahmed into a one-armed hug.

"You can fly on my wing anytime," Jake said.

"Mine, too," Lacey said, planting a huge kiss on Ahmed's cheek.

Jake crouched, and Sarafina charged over and threw her arms around his neck. "I knew you'd come," she said. "I just knew it."

"I always will, honey," Jake said. "But right now we gotta get out of here."

"I know," Sarafina said. "But first we have to gather the rest of the children."

Francesca felt Jake swell with pride at Sarafina's sense of duty. Francesca felt the same. When Alex added his nod to the conversation, she realized that this was the family she had always dreamed about.

“That’s exactly what we’re going to do,” Jake said. He held out his hands, and Francesca passed Alex to him. Jake used his free hand to pull Francesca into a quick kiss. It took her breath away. The glance that passed between them spoke volumes.

Everyone stacked up behind Jake at the door. But before he opened it, he looked into the eyes of his son and said, “Do you even have the slightest idea how awesome you are? You saved my life with your quick thinking. I’m so proud of you, I can barely stand it!”

Alex beamed. His lips parted in a crooked smile, and he spoke for the first time in his life. “Yippee-ki-yay, Daddy.”

Chapter 82

Grid Countdown: 0h:42m:00s and Holding

The Island
7:00 a.m.

ALEX'S WORDS BROUGHT A GRIN TO JAKE'S FACE. FRANCESCA gasped. So did Sarafina, Ahmed, and Lacey. It was the first time any of them had heard the boy's voice.

"You're just full of surprises, aren't you?" Jake said, positioning Alex so that he wasn't pressed against the wound on his chest. He didn't wait for an answer. They had to get moving. After confirming that the coast was clear, he moved out, leading with the pistol. The corridor seemed considerably warmer than earlier. Apparently, the power outage was having an impact.

The emergency lights were few and far between. Long shadows were separated by dim pools of light. Jake moved quickly. He still wore the blue security uniform. Francesca and the rest of them stuck close behind him.

Jake stretched his senses, scanning for threats. They were on level three. They needed to get to level two, where they hoped to find the rest of the children. He was headed for the utility staircase he'd used earlier. According to the floor plan he'd memorized, it was the only way up besides the elevators and the main stairwell.

He hesitated as he neared an intersecting hallway. There were voices coming from the right hall.

"In here!" Sarafina whispered, pointing to a door he'd just passed. "This is how that man brought us down."

The door was unmarked. Ahmed tried the handle. It was locked. There was a keypad beside it.

"We don't have the code," Francesca said.

The voices were getting louder. Lacey moved in front of Jake and peeked around the corner. "Better hurry," she said. "They're coming this way."

Jake tightened his grip around Alex. His son clung to his neck like a monkey. He was about to turn the group back the way they'd come when Alex said, "Seven-seven-four-six-two."

By the time Jake considered how his son could know the code, Sarafina had already entered it. The lock clicked. "Don't ask how," she said, swinging the door open. "Just trust him."

"She's right," Ahmed said, leading the way. "Alex is a rock star."

Francesca was next. Jake and Lacey rushed to follow, closing the door behind them.

The private staircase hadn't been indicated on the floor plan he'd memorized. Its use must have been limited to Victor and other VIPs. It appeared to extend from the sublevel all the way to the surface. Despite the current beehive of activity going on in the facility, no one else was using it.

"One floor up," Sarafina said, scurrying along the steps. "Then down the hallway to the right."

When they reached the landing, Jake handed Alex to Francesca. The boy didn't resist. "I need you to take the rock star," Jake said, winking at him. Alex tried to wink back, but all he managed was a blink.

Jake said, "Here's how we're going to do this." He pointed up the stairs, calculating their relative position in the facility. "If I'm not back in five minutes, that's your way out. It exits thirty paces from the main entrance. Once you're outside, grab a boat and hightail it out of here."

Lacey's pinched-brow expression seemed to say, *That's the entire plan? Uh…aren't you skipping a few steps?* Thankfully, she held her tongue.

"Ahmed's going with me to get the kids," Jake continued. "The rest of you stay—"

"No way," Sarafina said, ending the discussion by pushing through the door and stepping into the hallway. Lacey and Ahmed rushed after her.

Jake's shock didn't keep his feet from moving. He palmed the air in front of Francesca as he backed out to follow them. "Pleeease, stay here with Alex!" he whispered. "You'll be safe."

Francesca's mouth turned into a thin line. She tightened her grip around their son and stormed past him. "We're a family now. We stick together."

Jake rolled his eyes. He raced to catch up with Sarafina. She stood in front of a set of double doors. "I hope you know what you're doing," he said.

"The only thing I know for sure is that we can't leave without trying." She cracked open one of the doors. Children's voices spilled into the hallway. Jake maneuvered to get a peek inside. The interior space was dimly lit. He saw candles…

Suddenly, both doors were yanked open and Jake found himself staring down the barrels of several weapons. Someone raised a lantern to his face.

"Hand over the pistol," the stout, middle-aged woman standing in front of him said. She wore a khaki hunting vest over a button-down shirt, cargo pants, and tennis shoes. Her expression was all business. The chrome revolver she held was steady in her hands. It was aimed at his chest. Jake handed his pistol to the man standing beside her.

"Inside," she said, motioning with her gun. "All of you."

They were herded into the room. The doors closed behind them, and two men took up guard positions on either side. They were casually dressed. They seemed nervous; the grips they held on their submachine guns were awkward. These weren't professional soldiers, Jake thought. He took in the room. There were at least a hundred people gathered at the long dining tables: men, women—and a lot of children.

Their grim expressions were reflected in the dim candlelight. They seemed afraid, bunched together in family units. These were parents and teachers and their children. Not soldiers. They'd quieted to take in the scene.

"Check them," the woman said. Her stern expression reminded Jake of a middle-school principal. But he sensed her initial suspicion fading as she studied their group.

A silver-haired man with bifocals stepped forward. His plaid shirt, bow tie, and wrinkled vest reminded Jake of a college professor. He held one of the security wands, shrugging apologetically as he waved it across Jake's shoulder. The wand beeped, and he moved on to the rest of them. When he was finished he said, "They all check out except the child and the girl."

The woman sighed, lowering her gun. Tension eased from the room like air from an untied balloon. The murmur of voices from the tables was instantaneous.

"My name is Eloise," she said, extending her hand. "Sorry for our reaction. We were told there are intruders. Why aren't the children implanted?"

Sarafina stepped forward. "My name is Sarafina," she said. "And that's my brother, Alex." She placed her hands on her hips. "And the reason we're not tagged like some sort of pet is because we were being held hostage here by Mr. Brun."

The room quieted.

"What are you talking about?" the woman said. "Mr. Brun would never—"

"Please let me explain," Jake interrupted. "We don't have much time. You're not safe here. We can help you all escape."

The woman looked at him as if he were crazy. Jake had the sense that she was tempted to raise the revolver. He palmed the air. "Wait, just hear me out. That's all I ask. But trust me." He pointed toward the tables. "We came here for the children's sake."

After a brief hesitation, the woman nodded. "Okay, explain."

Jake lifted his voice so everyone could hear. "My daughter told the truth. She and Alex were kidnapped by Victor Brun."

There were a few utterances of disbelief from the adults at the tables. Jake ignored them.

"He took them in Geneva, right after he had orchestrated the deadly gas attack that killed world leaders at the Palace of Nations."

"Impossible," someone shouted.

"Lies," said another.

Jake continued, "Don't you see? He's behind it all. He wants the end to come. And he will do anything necessary to make it happen. When the grid countdown commenced, he was thrilled. And when it stopped a short while ago, he was devastated. I know. Because I was with him when it happened, strapped to a torture chair in a room down below." He pulled up his shirt to reveal the bandaged knife wound. It was blood-soaked. "And he wielded the knife!"

More angry shouts of denial from the crowd. Francesca edged closer to him. Alex jostled, and she set him down. He pressed up against Jake's leg. Lacey and Ahmed stepped forward to form a united front.

"It's not safe to stay here," Jake said. "The creators of the grid have intelligence beyond anything we know. Victor underestimates them. He thinks that his treachery will go unnoticed. But he's wrong. It will cost him his life. Yours, too, if you stay here. So come with us. Let's get the children out before it's too late."

There were murmurs, but no one moved to join him.

Jake said, "Listen to me! Right now Victor is holed up somewhere, setting the stage for the ultimate devastation. He's going to launch a barrage of nuclear missiles—"

"Enough!" Eloise shouted. "How dare you! Victor Brun is a man of peace. He has worked his entire life toward this end, helping us all in so many ways. To protect our children, our heritage, our lives—from a world torn apart by violence and terror. A world on the precipice of Armageddon, sparked by an inherent evil so rampant that it has finally drawn judgment from above. We are the last hope for mankind. We are the children of the arc. *Cæli Regere!*"

"*Cæli Regere!*" the crowd shouted. Several of the men rose and started toward Jake. They weren't happy.

Jake stood his ground.

Eloise couldn't contain herself. She yelled, "And you have the nerve to accuse him! And by association every one of us in this room! Of lighting the fire of man's destruction?" Her face was beet red. She raised the revolver. Her hand shook. Her voice squeaked. "How dare—"

She cut off when Alex stepped between them. He shouted, "Pleeease!" He was on his tiptoes. He held his small tablet over his head. The screen was pointed at her. The room stilled.

The woman's furious gaze shifted from Jake to the tablet and back to Jake again. Then she did an abrupt double take, her focus settling on the screen. Her eyes narrowed, and she lowered the revolver. "Rewind it," she said.

Alex lowered the tablet. He made an entry on the screen and handed it to her. Jake startled when he caught a glimpse of the paused video.

Brilliant!

Eloise held the tablet close to her chest. Only the professor was close enough to share her view. She tapped the screen to start the video. The volume was low. She titled her ear toward the screen. The professor leaned in.

Color drained from their faces. Their mouths gaped. Fifteen seconds later, she tapped the screen and handed the tablet to the professor. He was tight-lipped.

Her shoulders sagged. "Hook it up," she said, motioning to a large wall monitor.

The room was dead silent as the professor used a USB cable to connect the device. He turned on the monitor and tapped PLAY.

It was a video of Victor Brun, standing in front of Jake when he'd been strapped in the chair. The tablet had been on Alex's lap at the time.

"*You have two choices,*" Victor said on the screen. "*Either link with the grid and find a way to restart the countdown, in which case your children shall be spared, or refuse, in which case they shall die in this room...after which I will trigger the launch of nuclear missiles from six separate locations, including a US submarine.*"

Several people gasped, including Francesca. Jake noticed one man leave out the back door.

Victor continued, "*The targets have been carefully selected to ensure retaliation, especially in light of the current state of global panic. The result? World War III. The real war to end all wars. That should certainly be enough to restart the grid countdown. Don't you think?*"

"Dear God," Francesca said. "The world must see this."

Jake knew she was right. It would open eyes. Maybe even those looking down from above.

Alex nodded as if he'd heard Jake's thoughts. And in that moment Jake thought he saw the wisdom of the ages in his son's expression.

Most of the younger children in the room didn't understood what the video meant.

But everyone else did.

Especially Eloise. The color had returned to her face. Her fists were balled, her nostrils flared, and her voice was filled with authority. “Gather your things, everyone. We’re leaving immediately!”

She turned to Jake and motioned toward the door. “After you.”

Chapter 83

Grid Countdown: 0h:42m:00s and Holding

The Island
7:05 a.m.

VICTOR'S ANGER THREATENED TO SHRED HIS SELF-CONTROL. But he wouldn't allow it.

He had retreated deep into the facility, where a secondary blast door restricted access to what senior Order members referred to as the inner sanctum. The self-contained series of rooms had facilities and food stores to support one hundred people for up to twenty-four months. It was filled to capacity.

He paced back and forth at the front of the briefing room. His entourage of dignitaries fanned out around him. Several security guards stood nearby. The space was well lit. Its independent generators had kicked on as soon as the main power turbines went off-line. He listened intently as the uniformed officer completed his report.

"They entered through the waterway," he said with a thick German accent. He wore a headset that was plugged into a twelve-foot-wide control console behind him, where two lieutenants sat at workstations. The wall above them was embedded with a dozen video monitors. With the closed-circuit cameras down throughout the rest of the facility, only one of the screens worked. It displayed the hijacked message of world peace being transmitted to the grid. Victor ignored it.

"It was a small force," the officer continued. "Two of the turbines were destroyed. One was crippled. Electrical lines to the primary backup generators were severed. In the meantime, the island's camo shields are down, remote weaponry is off-line, and the exterior blast doors won't close."

There were several gasps in the crowd.

"However," the officer quickly added, "the engineering team has repaired most of the lines to the generators, and power will be restored shortly. In the meantime, we have deployed perimeter forces to the lagoon."

Victor had discounted the Australian commandos as a nonissue. Even if a few of them had avoided the gauntlet of remote guns, all of the back entrances to the facility had been sealed. Hundreds of meters of tunnels had been collapsed. There was no way in. Or so he'd been assured by his people. No one had considered the underground waterway. It had been a costly oversight.

But it wasn't fatal.

"Where are they now?" he asked.

"The last report has them—" He held a hand in the air. His eyes narrowed as he listened to an incoming communication.

"Sir," he said urgently. "The American has been sighted in the level-three cafeteria. His children are with him."

Victor's insides quaked. If Jake Bronson was alive, then Hans was not. The realization brought a rush of sadness. The man had been his only real friend.

"Dispatch the reserve teams to the cafeteria," Victor ordered angrily. "The Australian commandos will likely link up with him there. Shoot to kill."

"Yes, sir," the man said. He issued a series of orders into his headset.

Victor weighed the situation. The American was loose in the facility. He'd rescued his two children. But what else could he do?

Victor and his people were safe in this sector. It was impenetrable. So Bronson's recourse would be to escape. He and the commandos would die trying, Victor thought. Even if they somehow made it through the open blast doors, they'd be torn to shreds by the army of defenders that waited outside. One way or another, Jake Bronson would soon be dead. Victor only wished he could be there to savor the expression on the infuriating man's face when the end was upon him. It was a regret he suspected he would long carry.

"Sir!" one of the lieutenants at the console said, then reported, "An unidentified vessel has entered the inlet."

The knot in Victor's stomach tightened.

He glanced at the operational wall monitor. The grid countdown was still paused. He scanned the faces of the men and woman around him. They shared his concern. But, like him, they knew what must be done. The Russian general was the first to nod. The rest followed suit in short order.

Victor took pride in their resolve. He'd known each of them since childhood. Their fathers—and a long line of ancestors before them—had groomed them well. This was his family. This was the future of mankind.

Victor stepped up to the console. He reached down the collar of his shirt and pulled out a lanyard that was suspended around his neck. He unsnapped the key affixed to its end. The Russian general stood at the second console, his own key already in hand. Each of them flipped open a plastic cover, inserted their key, and twisted. Then, responding to computerized prompts, they confirmed their identities with iris scans and keypad entries.

"*Codes accepted*," the computer voice responded. "*Flash orders transmitted. Launch sequence will commence in eight minutes.*"

Victor felt a dark thrill rush up his spine.

Chapter 84

Grid Countdown: 0h:42m:00s and Holding

The Island
7:10 a.m.

One hundred forty men, women, and children were stacked behind Jake at the double doorway. A child sobbed. Others were hushed by parents. The air was thick with tension. Seven of the adults were armed. Four were posted at the back of the pack as a rear guard. The other three were beside Jake, including Eloise. Francesca and Ahmed were behind them. Alex had latched onto Ahmed's hand. A group of young teens had crowded around Sarafina.

"You ready?" Jake said to Lacey. She stood beside him.

"Oh, yeah," she said. She'd removed the rest of the padding from around her torso, knotting the leading edges of her button-down blouse snug around her slim waist. Her hair was loose, her glasses were gone, and her expression was fierce. She held Jake's pistol in a comfortable grip.

Jake had procured a submachine gun from one of the more nervous teachers. It was an MP7 personal defense weapon, with a forty-round mag and a reflex sight. He extended the telescoping buttstock, tucked it into his shoulder, and pried open the door.

The shadowed corridor was empty—and uncomfortably warm. He motioned the group forward, moving swiftly.

So far, so good.

The line of people behind Jake was so long that when he approached the door to the private stairwell, only half the group was out of the cafeteria. He reached for the keypad. That's when the screaming began. A man shouted, children cried out, and an exchange of gunfire echoed from within the cafeteria. Security teams must have entered from the back door.

Jake's adrenaline spiked. One of the armed men beside him ran toward the sounds. Jake swiveled to follow when angry shouts drew his attention toward the T-shaped intersection ahead. There was a heavy pounding of footsteps around the corner to his right. A lot of them.

"Get them into the stairwell!" he said to Eloise. "The code is seven-seven-four-six-two."

Jake raced past the door, sliding to his belly as he neared the intersection. A snap glance around the corner confirmed the worst. A squad of heavily armed guards trotted toward him. They were led by the teacher who had left the cafeteria during Victor's video. Jake flipped the MP7's selector switch to full auto. He stuck the barrel around the corner and sprayed the hallway with lead.

There were cries of pain and the heavy thuds of bodies toppling to the floor. "Cover!" someone ordered.

One of the armed teachers stood over Jake. He followed Jake's lead, firing blindly around the corner. Return fire sounded, and chunks of the corner wall exploded over Jake's head. There was a guttural moan, and the teacher's weapon clattered to the floor. He fell into the intersection, and his body danced and jiggled as more rounds impacted.

Jake cringed. He sent more lead downrange, and another man took the place of his dead associate. He held his weapon around the corner and opened fire. The weapon shook and kicked in the man's inexperienced grip. The rounds went wild. But damn, Jake thought, he sure as hell appreciated the courage of these men.

Behind him Jake heard Eloise shout, "Up the stairs. Hurry!" A corner of his mind prayed that Francesca and the children were among the first inside. Gunfire from the cafeteria still sounded. He wondered at the slaughter.

Around the corner, someone issued a series of sharp orders. Jake couldn't make out what was said, but he imagined the man was coordinating with other teams. They'd converge on Jake's group from all sides. Distant noises around the left corner seemed to confirm his suspicion. He glanced over his shoulder. Lacey knelt down beside him, backlit by the emergency light behind her. Families ducked into the stairwell as fast as they could, but there was still a thick line behind them. They'd be easy targets. "Shoot out those lights!" Jake said, motioning behind Lacey.

Lacey swiveled in her crouch, bringing the pistol around in a steady two-handed grip. Jake knew she drew on the lessons she'd learned as an action star on the big screen. But it wasn't just the moves that made her look like a pro. She could shoot. She fired three quick shots. Each one took out a light, and a blanket of darkness fell over the refugees.

The man above Jake stopped shooting. "I'm out!" he said, pulling back from the corner.

"Go help the others," Jake said. "Hurry 'em up!" The teacher ran off. That's when Jake noticed that the gunfire within the cafeteria had ceased. He didn't know if that was good news or bad. He hoped for the best, but he feared the worst. In any case, he had his hands full here.

Jake loosed another burst around the corner. His mag clicked empty after three rounds. "We can't hold 'em much longer," he said to Lacey, discarding the weapon and grabbing the MP7 that the first teacher had dropped. "See if you can get them moving faster back there."

"Bullshit," Lacey said. "I'm not leaving until you do." Light spilled from the two adjacent hallways, but with the lights out behind them, their position was shadowed.

"Count your rounds," Jake said.

"Did that when you first handed me the gun," she said. "Eight rounds then. Just used three. Five left."

"Make 'em count."

"No problem. Five bullets. Five assholes."

Jake checked the magazine on the teacher's weapon. He was down to eight rounds.

A hushed order from their right. Pounding footsteps. Jake readied himself, set to plunge his weapons around the corner at the last second. Lacey huddled beside him, the pistol ready.

Suddenly, there were several simultaneous spits from the left hallway. All of the emergency lights within the intersecting hallway seemed to go out at once. The charging footsteps faltered. Suppressed, controlled bursts from the left. Yelps of pain on the right. Heavy thuds. Weapons clattered to the floor. The gunfire ceased for a second. A moan. Twin spits. Then dead silence.

Jake braced himself. Lacey nudged against him. Padded steps approached from their left.

"Raider One, clear," someone whispered from around the corner.

Then Becker's voice said, "I sure as hell hope that's you, Jake."

Jesus!

"Beck?"

"Too right," Becker said, stepping around the corner. It was too dark to make out anything but a vague shadow. A flashlight flicked on, pointed toward the ceiling. "You're a tough bloke to follow!"

Becker flipped up the night vision goggles he was wearing. Jonesy did the same. "Enough lounging around on the floor," Becker said, extending a hand to help Jake to his feet. "We better keep this parade moving."

"We were flanked," Jake said.

"No worries—Sergeant Fletcher and Sam took care of them," Becker said. He pointed to a hand radio stuffed under his combat harness. A wire connected it to his comm pack. "One of Brun's men donated this. We've been listening in."

"Only four of you?" Jake asked, fearing the worst. There'd been nine of them when he'd dived into the pool.

Becker nodded, his expression grim. "Tony and Andrew were wounded. But they'll be okay. Philly, Hollister, and Karch didn't make it."

Two flashlights shone at the rear of the line of families. "That's the last of them," Sergeant Fletcher reported.

Becker's eyes went distant. He was listening to something on his headset.

"Move it!" he shouted, motioning toward the door. "Two large groups headed our way."

Sam brought up the rear, closing the door behind them. The stairwell was packed with people. Those who wouldn't fit on the single flight above were lined up on the lower staircases. Several of them were talking.

"Quiet!" Becker said in an urgent whisper. The space went silent.

Jake shouldered to the upper landing. Becker, Jonesy, and Lacey followed. They bunched at the top door. Ahmed, Francesca, and the children were already there.

"We have less than five minutes to get topside," Becker said. "The power outage prevented them from closing the blast doors automatically. But they've got a crew working on a manual override. In the meantime, they've deployed heavily armed fire teams outside to guard against incursion."

Jake gritted his teeth. Beads of sweat dripped down his cheeks. "It's like a sauna in here," he said absently. His mind was elsewhere, racing through options. None of them were good.

"Yeah," Becker said, wiping his brow. "That's because we broke something downstairs during our infil."

Jake ignored the comment. A plan was taking form. When he noticed Francesca and Alex both studying him, he closed off his mind. He couldn't allow them to know what he was contemplating. Sarafina crossed her arms as if she knew something was up.

Jake ignored them. This was on him. No time for a family conference. Step one, he needed eyes outside. He shouldered the MP7. Then he buttoned his shirt to the collar and tucked the tails into his trousers. "Don't move until I give you the signal," he said to Becker, avoiding Francesca's gaze. "Three raps on the door. Then get everybody moving out the front exit as fast as you can. Make for the nearest boat. There was a hundred-footer on the dock less than an hour ago. Load 'em up and get the hell out."

"Understood," Becker said, ushering the group away from the door.

Jake was reaching for the handle when the first explosions sounded from outside the facility.

Chapter 85

Grid Countdown: 0h:42m:00s and Holding

The Island
7:10 a.m.

"STAND BY," TONY SAID INTO HIS TACTICAL HEADSET. HE sat in a swivel chair on the megayacht's compass bridge. He flexed his injured leg out and back, preparing himself for what was to come. The ship's captain and first officer sat beside him. The navigation and control console stretched in front of them.

The ship was at maximum speed. Steep cliff walls rushed along either side of them—so close that Tony figured he could've spit on 'em. Three seconds later, the bow pushed through the inlet and into the lagoon. The towering mountains, the storybook village and structures, the expansive body of water with its rows of parked boats and yachts—it was all much grander than it had appeared from the overhead UAV images.

He couldn't care less.

"Jammers now!" he ordered, happy to be throwing in some of their own electronic interference for a change.

Marshall was in the control room down below with Kenny and Timmy. They were in charge of communications and the drones. "Jamming commenced," Marshall's voice reported over the intercom.

"*Mother Ship Two* away," Kenny added.

Tony wished Kenny had brought a dozen of the little *Mother*s along. The first one had saved his ass. *Mother Two* was the only one left. She would have to do.

Tony lifted the binoculars. The dock was one thousand meters ahead. A good-size bay cruiser and a hundred-foot yacht were tied off alongside. They were in the way. "That's where we gotta go," he said to the captain, pointing to the dock.

The uniformed officer narrowed his eyes on the scene. He knew what was at stake. There was a joystick in front of him. He ignored it. Instead, he used the padded steering wheel to change the ship's angle of approach. "It's going to be messy," he said, scratching his gray beard. "But I'll make it happen."

Tony turned his attention to the bow of the ship, where several operators crouched beneath the front rail. Each of them carried a Spike shoulder-launched missile system, equipped with heat-seeking and GPS fire-and-forget guidance. They were loaded with thermobaric "fuel-air" rounds—capable of creating a superheated inferno and blast wave that would bring down structures and incinerate anything within a ten-meter radius of impact. They were ideal for taking out gun positions.

Additional operators were hidden in sniper positions above deck. The remainder waited by the gangway.

"Hostile targets identified," Kenny reported.

The central monitor was linked to the imagery streaming from Kenny's drones. Tony saw at least a hundred individual targets moving within the trees and village. More streamed from the mouth of the blast doors. They all wore the blue uniforms that Tony had seen on the other side of the island. On the screen, each one was encased in a red square.

Ignoring them for the moment, he focused on the stationary targets along the ridgeline. Those were the fixed emplacements. And even though their sensors were being jammed by one of the drones, they still could shoot line of sight. They had to be dealt with first.

Kenny was all over it. "Stationary emplacements designated targets one through eight," he reported.

There was a rush of movement among the operators at the bow. Launchers were propped on the railing. A beat later, Sergeant Major Abercrombie reported, "Locked on targets one through eight."

"Open fire!" Tony ordered.

Hollow whoops sounded as each of the missiles left its tube, followed an instant later by the deep-throated roar of the ignition of solid fuel rockets. Eight trails of smoke arced into the sky, seeming to disappear at their apex. Two seconds later, a series of massive explosions thundered across the ridgelines.

"Launch boats!" Tony ordered. He glanced at the wall of video monitors embedded above the windscreen. The first of the two high-speed Special Operations Craft Riverines—SOC-Rs—slid down the yacht's aft launching ramp. The thirty-three-foot-long low-profile boat bristled with tripod-mounted armament, including two M134 Miniguns that could spew out 7.62mm bullets at a rate of six thousand rounds per minute. There were six operators onboard the first SOC-R, hungry for action. It splashed into the water and sped out of view. The second boat hit the water a moment later.

The two boats whipped past either side of the yacht like it was standing still. They raced toward the shoreline. The distinctive high-pitched buzz of their Miniguns battled with the rumble of their four-hundred-forty-horsepower diesel engines. Fire flashed from the barrels of their guns. Tracers arced across the water.

The initial volley must have stunned the island's forces.

But only for a moment.

All at once, return fire erupted from positions along the shoreline. Staccato cracks echoed across the water. RPG smoke trails burst from windows in the village. Spouts of water exploded around the Riverines. Heavy machine-gun fire spit from the trees, and white phosphorus tracers snaked wavy arcs in the air as shooters adjusted their aim at the dodging and weaving boats.

The ship's captain didn't waver. He motioned to the first officer. "Time to get below, Scott. I'll be right behind you."

"Aye, aye, sir," the first officer said. He disappeared down a spiral staircase at the back of the room.

The captain sat forward in his chair, maneuvering the ship so as to angle into the dock from behind the two parked boats. His plan was simple: keep his speed up and shove 'em out of the way. Tony appreciated the straightforward approach. But it sure looked to him like they were moving way too fast.

Most of the gunfire from the shore was directed at the fast movers. But as the megayacht neared the dock, Tony saw a string of tracers swerve in their direction.

"Down!" Tony shouted. He grabbed the captain's arm and yanked him to the deck. The windshield exploded above them. Heavy rounds slugged through the chairs and into the rear walls of the room.

"Time to steer this thing from below!" Tony said.

The wide-eyed captain didn't argue. He smacked Tony on the shoulder as a quick gesture of thanks. "Godspeed," he said, before scrambling on all fours to the spiral staircase. There was a duplicate control station in the watertight compartment beneath them. The first officer would've taken control by now. As long as the exterior cameras didn't get blown to shreds, they'd be able to park the ship from there.

Tony exited the bridge in a crouch. Waves of pain shot up his injured thigh as he hobbled down two flights of stairs to the main deck. Twin RPG explosions sounded overhead, and the compass bridge exploded in a ball of fire. Debris cascaded around him. He moved toward the gangway, where a score of operators already waited.

"Brace for impact," the captain's voice sounded over the comm net.

Tony slid next to the Aussie sergeant major. The soldier had a broad grin on his face. "Into the breach!" he said.

Both men placed their backs against the sidewall. Tony reached over his shoulder and grabbed hold of the rail.

"Five seconds!" the captain said.

The lurching impact threw Tony forward. His grip on the rail didn't give way, but he winced when his body twisted and his leg slapped the sidewall. The bow seemed to lift into the air in slow motion. There was an awful crunching sound, and Tony imagined the cruiser being crushed like a melon under an elephant's foot. The bow dropped, and then there was a second impact. This time, the nose of the ship jerked to the left toward the dock. Tony figured it must have wedged between the stern of the second ship and the pier. The yacht shuddered as its tonnage ripped through the dock's timber planks and pilings, causing an explosion of wood slivers that rained down on Tony and the operators.

After an extended, ear-piercing scraping sound, the yacht lurched to a stop.

The gangway was down faster than Tony could take his next breath. Operators charged onto the shredded pier, dodging around an upheaval of timber. Tony trotted after them, favoring his leg. He could almost feel Kenny's eyes on him through *Mother Ship*'s cameras. By now the kid would have identified the proximity targets and was probably itchin' to throw the switch.

"Clear us a path to the door, Kenny," Tony ordered.

"*Mother Ship*, go native," Kenny said over the comm net.

"*Confirm* go native *command*," the computer's sultry voice said.

"*Go native* confirmed!" Kenny said.

Tony skirted the last bit of rubble and hobble-skipped forward. Operators charged past either side of him. One of them went down, and a medic slid to his side.

"Incoming!" Tony shouted, going down to one knee and returning fire. The rest of the raiding party did the same. They knew the drill.

An instant later, the tree line on either side of the cobbled path lit up. Blinding flashes of white phosphorus were followed by shrieks of pain. As the last of *Mother*'s swarm delivered its deadly cargo, squads of operators peeled left and right. They disappeared into the trees to clean up any leftovers and establish a perimeter.

The blast doors were fifty meters ahead. They started to close.

Tony, the sergeant major, and a dozen more raced toward it.

Chapter 86

Grid Countdown: 0h:42m:00s and Holding

The Island
7:15 a.m.

The fighting outside had reached a crescendo. Jake pressed his ear to the door and tightened his grip on the MP7. Becker and his team were stacked up behind him—weapons ready, game faces on. They'd go first. This was familiar territory for the highly skilled operators. Jake held a hand in the air.

"There are still too many of them," he whispered, listening to the shouts and heavy footfalls beyond the door. Becker had relayed what he had learned by eavesdropping on the Order's radio chatter. There was a major battle taking place in the lagoon. Tony and the rest of them had waltzed through the inlet just as bold as you please. Spittin' fire.

Victor's defenders were taking heavy losses. They were trying to buy enough time for the engineers to rewire one of the backup generators in order to shut the blast doors.

The stairwell lights flashed on, and Jake felt a surge of adrenaline. They had to move. "Wait three seconds," he whispered urgently. "I'll draw their fire!"

He pushed through the door and bumped into a crowd of Victor's soldiers. His blue uniform bought him the precious seconds he needed to shoulder through them. He shouted with the angry authority of a general leading a charge, "There's a saboteur at the door!" He ran toward the exit tunnel. The soldiers followed.

Two seconds later, Jake heard the suppressed spits of the Aussies' weapons. Blood splattered, men yelped, and the solders around him flopped to the floor. One man rolled, coming to his knees with his submachine gun tucked to his shoulder. Twin holes blossomed in his forehead, and he was thrown back.

It was over in three heartbeats. Becker, Sergeant Fletcher, and Jonesy rushed forward in a choreographed pattern that covered all angles of the lobby. Two of the bodies moved, and they received extra spits from the operators' weapons. Sam watched their backs.

"Get 'em moving!" Becker said into his headset.

The stairwell door popped open, and Sam waved the group forward. Ahmed and Lacey were the first out the door.

"I've got comm with the ship!" Jonesy reported.

"Fill 'em in, lad," Becker said, switching frequencies so he could listen in.

Jake tuned out Jonesy's response when he heard a deep thrum from within the tunnel. He knew that it had to be the blast door mechanisms. He sprinted forward, and Becker and Sergeant Fletcher followed in his wake.

The inward-hinged blast doors swung slowly toward one another. Three men in jumpsuits and hard hats stood this side of it. They faced a wall-mounted control panel. One of them had his hand on a button. Two soldiers stood beside them.

"Wait!" Jake shouted, rushing to get to them before the door was sealed. The soldiers spun around at the sound of Jake's voice. But Jake's blue uniform didn't help him this time around, as one of the guards apparently recognized him. The man raised his assault rifle and squeezed the trigger.

Becker's linebacker shove drove Jake to one side, careening him into the wall. Bullets ricocheted off the floor. There was a series of spits behind him, and the three hard hats and soldiers went down. But the doors continued to close, narrowing the gap to the outside world. Jake dashed to the control panel, nearly slipping in the widening pool of blood around the bodies. He smashed his palm on the red EMERGENCY STOP button.

The mechanism responded, and the doors stopped moving. There was an eighteen-inch opening between them.

Jake flinched when Tony stuck his head into the gap. "Need a lift?" the big man asked, turning sideways to step inside. He clasped Jake's hand. "Seems like I'm always cleaning up your mess."

Several operators followed Tony inside. They ran down the tunnel.

Tony suddenly stiffened, and his hand went to his headset. His expression said he couldn't believe what he was hearing. "It's Marsh," Tony said. "It's all over the airways. An ICBM was just launched from mainland China. Target is Washington, DC. One of our subs launched in retaliation." A second later he added, "Shit! A launch from Pakistan." He hesitated a moment as Marshall told him the rest. Tony's face drained of color. "The grid countdown has restarted. Ten minutes and counting."

"Uncle Tony!" Sarafina cried out.

The two men turned to see her running toward them. Behind her, the tunnel was filled with families. Gunfire erupted behind them, and every bobbing head in the crowd seemed to flinch at the same time. An instant later, they stampeded toward the door.

"Get them out of here!" Jake shouted.

Tony nodded. "This way!" he roared, waving the crowd toward him. He stepped outside and began issuing orders over his radio.

Jake moved into the tunnel, encouraging people to speed up. He spotted Francesca on the opposite side of the crowd. She didn't see him. There were a number of children around her. She ushered them forward.

Jake saw Ahmed behind her. He locked eyes with the teen. "Keep them moving!" Jake shouted.

Ahmed nodded. Raw determination shone on his face.

Most of the crowd was past him when Jake saw Sergeant Fletcher lifting a body over his shoulder. It was Becker. His eyes were closed, and blood dripped from his dangling fingertips. Jake realized with a start that his friend must have taken a hit when he'd pushed Jake out of the way. Jonesy stood alongside. His hands were bloody. His face was a mask.

Jake watched as they followed the group down the tunnel. It was a long-practiced drill, Jake thought. *No man left behind.* Jake crouched down and retrieved Becker's pack.

His blood was on fire.

The gunfire had stopped. The Aussie rescuers had put down the latest surge of Order reinforcements. When the last of the civilians was outside, the remaining operators peeled back in cover formation. Jake waited by the blast door. He motioned for the final two operators to go through first, his mind tracking the grid countdown.

Seven minutes.

As soon as the soldiers stepped through, Jake moved to the control console and released the EMERGENCY STOP button.

The blast doors started to close. By the time the remaining hydraulic pins slid into place, Jake had already removed two of the four C-4 charges from Becker's pack. He set the timers for fifteen seconds. Then he placed them on the console and ran into the facility.

Ready or not, here I come…

Chapter 87

Grid Countdown: 0h:6m:30s

The Island
7:25 a.m.

THE BLAST WAVE FROM THE CONTAINED EXPLOSION KNOCKED Jake off his feet. The MP7 was thrown from his grasp. His ears popped, his vision blurred, and a hot wind blew past him. Rocks and smoke spewed from the mouth of the tunnel.

Jake scrambled on all fours to the private stairwell, yanking open the door and slamming it behind him. He bent over, hands propped on his thighs, breathing hard. The blast had carried more impact than he'd anticipated. He'd intended to destroy the console. Instead, the entire tunnel had collapsed. It brought an evil grin to his face. The only exit was sealed forever. Victor's utopian refuge had just become a prison.

He shook his head to clear it. Then he made his way down the stairs. A part of his mind relished the ruin he planned to rain down on the lord of Castle Brun. The master planner thought he'd covered all the bases. But he'd overlooked one of the most basic tenets of human conflict:

There's nothing more dangerous than a man willing to die for the people he loves.

But confronting Brun would have to wait.

First things first. The grid countdown was at five minutes. He had to try to stop it.

He raced down the staircase and into the level-three corridor. The air temperature was stifling. The power was restored, and the ventilation fans had kicked on, but the interior temp continued to rise. Whatever Becker had "broken" in the sublevel, he thought, it wasn't good.

He was five strides from the chair-room door when he felt the surge of energy. The sensation was unmistakable. The chair had been activated, and the mini had come to life, its power resonating with his brain. Jake tried the door. It was locked. He reached for the keypad, entering the master code Victor had used when he'd escaped the room. It didn't work. Someone had deactivated it from the inside. Jake bashed the door with his shoulder, but it didn't budge. Then he remembered the observation window.

He sped to the next doorway, entered the code, and burst inside. What he witnessed through the window collapsed his lungs.

The room was suffused in a bright glow. The chair's fiber-optic wires radiated with back-and-forth streams of pulsating light. The embedded mini shone like a brilliant star. And standing on top of the chair—with the skullcap lowered over his head—was Jake's son.

"Aaa-lex!" Jake cried out, pounding on the window.

Their eyes locked. And for the first time since father and son had met, Jake saw doubt on the child's face.

"Unlock the door, son!" Jake shouted.

Alex glanced at the door, but it was no use. He was trapped in the grid's embrace. The glow from the mini intensified, and Alex grimaced. Suddenly, he arched backward, his arms stiffened, and his eyes rolled into the back of his head.

Jake was frantic. He grabbed a nearby chair and swung it against the window. When it bounced off with a plastic thud, he realized it was polycarbonate. Even a sledgehammer wouldn't crack it.

The countdown was at ninety seconds.

Alex's body was shaking. Color leached from his face.

Jake pressed his hands against the window and mentally embraced his son. He outpoured every ounce of his being.

Their minds joined, and he felt Alex's fear. The grid sucked data from his son's brain, and Jake knew immediately it was too much for the young child. It was killing him. Jake remembered the sensation. He'd felt it himself in a cave six years ago in Afghanistan—when he'd triggered the devastating sequence of events that led to this moment. And again in Geneva, when it seemed as if the grid had gleaned everything available from Jake's brain…before discarding him like a corrupt hard drive.

Jake drew on his reserves. His focus was absolute. Only one thing mattered—his son must live. He reached out to Alex's consciousness, bonding their minds as they had when they'd first met.

In that singular moment, Jake Bronson bequeathed all that he had—and all that he was—to his son:

His love.

His strength.

His life force.

Thirty seconds.

Jake felt Alex's reaction as if it were his own. Jake's energy surged through his small frame. It fueled the boy's confidence. His consciousness seized control of the communication link with the grid. In the pause between heartbeats, he transmitted a kaleidoscope of images and emotions, drawn from all he had witnessed in his short life, including Victor's treachery. The underlying message was simple. It spoke of family. And loyalty. And accepting the differences in one another. Of embracing love and trust and second chances. Of the true character of mankind, capable of untold violence, but possessing the strength of will to control it.

It spoke of a belief in God.

It was his son's personal appeal to the grid's creators, his argument that mankind be spared, supported by the wisdom of inalienable truths, but laced with the innocence of a child.

And beneath it all was Alex's undeniable willingness to sacrifice his young life to make it happen.

The grid reacted.

Abruptly, Jake and Alex's perception shifted. They saw the planet as if viewing it from the stars. The geodesic matrix surrounding the earth brightened. It glowed with such intensity that night became day across the globe. Beams of light shot downward into the earth's atmosphere, destroying the nuclear missiles before they reached their targets.

Then, all at once, the light connecting the pyramids vanished. Then, one by one, each pyramid broke orbit and accelerated into space. It was over in moments.

Alex was filled with joy.

Jake was filled with pride.

Chapter 88

Grid Countdown: 0h:0m:30s

The Island
7:31 a.m.

THE BACKUP POWER IN THE MAIN FACILITY WAS ON, BUT Victor's engineers were having difficulty restoring the surveillance system. It was being rebooted for the third time.

The satisfied expression on Victor's face was not feigned. It would all be over soon, he thought. The missile launch had succeeded in restarting the grid countdown. The first of the missiles would impact in three minutes. It was of no consequence. Because the grid countdown was at thirty seconds. The incursions, the American's escape, the loss of Hans, and even the detonation of the nuclear warheads—in the final analysis, none of it mattered. His destiny had been fulfilled. The end was moments away.

A new world order would rise from the ashes.

The security system came back online, and one by one each of the surveillance videos flashed on. The power plant, the corridors, the lagoon—they were all there for him to see.

But Victor's focus was transfixed on a solitary scene that nearly stopped his heart. It was the American's son, standing on the chair, the skullcap draped over his head, the room aglow with light.

Victor's throat seized.

"There's activity from the grid!" shouted one of the men at the console.

"Lasers!" said another.

A beat later, the presiding officer gasped, "*Ach mein Gott*! The missiles have been destroyed. The grid has vanished!"

Victor's eyes got huge. His body trembled and he staggered backward.

On the screen, the boy stepped down from the chair. He swung open the door, and Jake Bronson rushed in and scooped him into his arms. Father and son twirled with delight.

The rage that overtook Victor was cold and distilled. Those around him edged away.

He clenched his jaws so tightly that a stab of pain blossomed behind one eye. It brought him back to full awareness.

He rolled his shoulders and wrapped himself in a mantle of calm serenity, extending a hand toward the nearest security officer. "Your weapon, please," he said flatly.

The man handed him his submachine gun.

Victor walked steadily toward the sanctum's exit.

Nobody followed him.

Chapter 89

THERE WAS NO OTHER WAY OUT, JAKE THOUGHT. HE HAD TO chance it. His son's life depended on it.

They were in the fire department on level four. Alex clung to his chest, his feet supported by the waist belt of the harness strapped to Jake's back. They both dripped with perspiration. The air temperature was at least 110 degrees. The insulated fire suit made it worse.

"You hangin' in there?" Jake asked as he zipped the torso of the oversize suit around them. The face mask and hood were in a bag slung from his elbow.

Alex nodded. He hadn't spoken a word since he had connected with the grid. It didn't matter. His son didn't have to speak for Jake to appreciate his courage. One of his small hands clung to Jake's shoulder harness. The other held a regulator and mouthpiece. It was a tandem connection to the tank slung on Jake's back.

"Show me one more time," Jake said.

Alex closed his mouth around the rubber, gripping it with his teeth. He allowed the pressurized air to fill his lungs. His eyes searched for Jake's approval.

"That's my boy," Jake said. He placed Becker's backpack inside an oversize gear bag. Slinging it over his shoulder, he said, "Off we go."

The silver reflective suit was bulky. It was designed for safety, not speed. Jake lumbered down the deserted corridor, wondering if his son could sense his apprehension. He tried to hide it behind a mask of confidence, using techniques he'd perfected long ago to keep Francesca from sensing his emotions. But he had a feeling that Alex saw through the charade.

Jake wasn't just nervous. He was scared out of his mind. The suit was designed to protect the wearer from high temps and noxious fumes.

But it wasn't a submarine.

The power plant was dead ahead. He pushed through the double doors and was immediately assaulted by the heat. A thick cloud of steam billowed from a grate beneath the first turbine. Moisture dripped from the tangle of catwalks overhead. The air smelled of sulfur. Jake climbed the short staircase to the walkway that spanned the twin culverts. Water continued to flow in both directions. The "once-through" cooling system was brilliant in its simplicity. It drew cool water from the pool beneath the falls, circulating it through the pipes to draw heat from the geothermal turbines, and then discharged the heated water elsewhere.

But where elsewhere?

Jake stared at the dark tunnel at the end of the discharge culvert. Doubt threatened his resolve. He'd expected the discharge flow to have cooled down somewhat—since the turbines were out of commission. Instead, steam rose from the fast-flowing canal. The water was hotter than ever. And if the heat wasn't coming from the turbines, then something worse was going on beneath their feet. It didn't take an enhanced brain to figure out what that was all about.

When they were over the canal, Jake removed the bundle of C-4 charges from Becker's pack. He'd already wrapped them together with duct tape. His hand hesitated over the timer. The underwater ride from the whirlpool into the facility had taken about three minutes. But the discharge tube shot off in a different direction. It was gravity-fed, just like the intake, which meant it didn't flow to the waterfall. It had to exit at a lower elevation from where he stood. They were surrounded by ocean on one side and lagoon on the other. It could spill into either of them.

The designers would have taken the shortest possible route, he thought.

He did a quick calculation, considering his current location in the facility, the distance to the ocean versus the lagoon, and the speed of the water. Part of him knew there were too many unknown variables to be sure. But it was better than taking a wild-ass guess and crossing his fingers. He set the timer for four minutes, zipping the charge within the gear bag, and tossed the bulky parcel into the hot culvert. It was swept away with the current, disappearing into the tunnel.

He crossed his fingers anyway.

The plan was simple. The bag would lodge against the grate at the end of the discharge tube, assuming there was one. The blast would clear the path. Jake didn't want to be anywhere close when it went off, so he wasn't going into the water until the full four minutes had elapsed.

"Okay, son," he said. "From here on out, use the regulator. I'm going to zip us up. But we've gotta wait four minutes before we jump. You down with that?"

Alex already had the regulator in his mouth when he nodded. His body trembled.

There was a loud spitting sound, and Jake turned to see that the plume of steam shooting from the grate had darkened. It seemed filled with soot. The base of the plume had an orange glow.

Jake donned his face mask, lowered the hood, and sealed up the suit. His mask included a built-in microphone and external speaker. "Can you hear me?" he asked. His voice sounded tinny.

He felt Alex's head bob up and down on his chest.

Jake unhooked the chain that acted as a guardrail, staring at the waterway six feet below. Surface steam licked at his legs. He counted down the seconds.

He had two minutes to go when he felt a sharp jab in his lower back.

"Excuse me," a voice said behind him.

Jake sucked in a breath. His muscles tightened. He turned around slowly.

Victor Brun stood before him. He held a submachine gun in a steady, two-handed grip. It was aimed at Jake's gut. Victor smiled broadly. "Oh, please don't leave just yet," he said, as if Jake were a guest at a party. "I'd hate for you two to miss the grand finale."

The surge of adrenaline in Jake's system was so intense that he couldn't speak.

"Nothing to say?" Victor asked. "No smart retorts?"

Jake's brain flashed through a dozen possible moves. But the constrictive suit eliminated every option. He considered jumping backward into the culvert. But he and Alex would be riddled with holes before they hit the water.

Victor's expression was smug. His words were laced with disgust. "You are a nuisance, Mr. Bronson. An insect. You think you've won here? Hah!" he snuffed. "You've done nothing but delay the inevitable. The world lies too close to the precipice for it to be prevented"—he raised the barrel of his weapon so that it was pointed at Alex—"by you *or* your son. Be it a thermonuclear war, global bio-attack, or simply the stupidity of man in not managing population growth, it will happen in time. And when the end is upon us, the Order will be there to rise from the chaos. Governments don't rule countries, Mr. Bronson. They never have. It is men like me that control the ruling puppets. That will never change. In another five years, perhaps ten, it will happen, and the Order will be ready." He tightened the grip on his weapon and added, "But you won't."

There was a maniacal glee in Victor's eyes. "Still no quips? Oh, come now," he said with an exaggerated pout. "Action-film fans would be so disappointed in you. You simply *must* say something!"

That's when the ground shook, the grate exploded, and lava spewed into the room with the ferocity of an uncapped oil well. The roar was deafening.

The molten inferno smacked into the ceiling and splattered in every direction. Fiery globs shot toward them.

The moment stretched.

In that brief instant of time, Victor's eyes narrowed and Jake knew that the man's brain gave his fingers the order to fire. It happened just as a molten missile hit him from behind, penetrating his torso. His back muscles contracted reflexively. His arms spread wide, his fingers squeezed, and the gun chattered on full auto, missing Jake and Alex. Victor's face peeled back in a rictus of pain. Smoke leaked from his gaping mouth. His wild eyes refocused for an instant, and he swung the barrel back around.

Alex shivered.

Hang on, son!

Jake lunged forward. He bear-hugged Victor and plowed him over the back rail. The gun flew into the air, and they somersaulted into the superheated water, plunging deep. The current grabbed them. Victor flailed, but Jake held on. They surfaced together, and Jake saw realization dawn on the man's blistering face. Death was upon him.

The last thing Victor Brun heard was Jake's rendition of Arnold Schwarzenegger's voice through the fire suit's speaker. "Hasta la vista, baby!"

Epilogue

Six Weeks Later

JAKE COULDN'T HAVE IMAGINED A MORE BEAUTIFUL SETTING. Marshall and Lacey stood beside him, ready to complete the ceremony they'd started six weeks ago. The priest stood in front of them, framed by a floral gazebo and backed by a sunny view of the Venice lagoon and the Isola di San Giorgio Maggiore.

They were on the terrace of the Hotel Danieli. Jake savored the familiar smells, the moist air, the distant calls of the gondoliers. The world had changed. He'd changed. But Venice remained the same. The ancient city had survived the worldwide panic, protected by the surrounding waters and bolstered by a heritage that knew more than its share of marauders. The Venetians had bounced back quickly, drawing on their love of the simple pleasures of life.

Other cities hadn't fared so well. Riots and looting had taken their toll. Fires had caused the worst of the physical damage, but it could be repaired, in time. Not so the psyche of every man, woman, and child on the planet—who now faced the indisputable fact that mankind wasn't alone in the universe. But just as fate had seen fit to grant Jake a second chance at life when it had defeated his terminal illness, so had the human race been given a second opportunity. He couldn't speak for mankind—at least not any longer—but, for his part, Jake planned to savor each and every day for all that it had to offer.

Being in Venice was like coming full circle. It had all started here six years ago, when he found purpose in the plight of two autistic children—and when he and Francesca had connected on the rooftop at the institute. He smiled at the memory.

As if sensing his thoughts, Francesca squeezed his hand. She stood beside him. He breathed her in. Ahmed, Sarafina, and Alex stood nearby.

My son, Jake thought. The miracle child who had saved the world. Of course, Alex didn't see it that way. By his way of thinking, he was simply "helping my dad." Or so he'd said. Even though Alex had started speaking, his words had been few and far between. And Jake had the keen sense that there was a lot more going on in his son's brain than he let on.

But Jake understood that.

He had a secret of his own—one that he refused to share.

One thing was certain, he thought. He and Alex were bonded for life—in a fashion that went beyond the link of father and son.

The terrace was packed with family and friends. Francesca's father, Mario, was in a wheelchair. The old man's constitution had pulled him through his injuries. He wouldn't be pushing a gondola anytime soon, but the doctor said he'd be up and around in a few months. Jake's mother and sister had become his constant companions since their arrival in Venice three days ago.

Becker was there, too. The bullet he'd taken for Jake had missed his heart by less than an inch. His military doctors had told him he couldn't travel; they'd said he needed two more weeks of bed rest. But he wouldn't have it. Nothing was going to keep him from this gathering. Jonesy had come with him. The operator hadn't found it too difficult to smuggle his boss out of the hospital.

Timmy and Doc had arrived the day before. In light of everything that he'd done, Timmy had been given a pass for stealing the mini and hiding Jake. Doc had been instrumental in making that happen.

Cal and Kenny were there, too. They'd saved Jake's life. Alex's, too. After the blast doors had closed, Kenny had reprogrammed the drones to search for Jake's RFID signal, concentrating on the shorelines. He and Cal had managed the search from the chopper. When Jake and Alex had popped up in the lagoon, his friends had been overhead in less than three minutes.

The lava flow had inundated the underground complex, and an estimated fourteen hundred Order members had perished. Those who had made it outside before the blast doors were closed—including the ones Jake had rescued—had been taken into custody by the Indonesian government. The idyllic village within the lagoon had been spared the mountain's wrath, and there was talk of it becoming a tourist destination. Jake wasn't planning on adding it to his vacation list.

He heard a whimper from Tony's four-month-old baby. The child and his mother and father were seated directly behind where Jake stood.

You always have my back, don't you, pal?

Tony's kids Andrea and Tyler had come, too. So had Sarafina's friend Josh, along with his guide dog Max.

Marshall shifted beside Jake. His buddy was as anxious as Lacey for this ceremony. Jake was proud to be standing next to them. Like Tony, the two of them had stood beside him through it all. Without their ingenuity, spirit, and courage, he wouldn't be alive.

The gang's all here.

Jake tapped the folded paper that was tucked at the bottom of his pants pocket. Tony had returned it to him when they'd reunited on the boat. He recalled the words:

Lives hinge on your ability to remain anonymous.

He blew out a soft breath, holding on to the faith that such was no longer the case.

The priest was wrapping up his introductory speech. His voice brought Jake back to the present. "You may remove the mask," the priest said.

"Ah, that's better," Marshall said, removing his blindfold. Then he nudged Jake with his elbow. "Your turn, pal."

Jake turned toward Francesca. He reached up and removed the red silk from around his own face. Francesca's gaze pierced him where he stood—the same eyes that had lived in his dreams when every other memory had forsaken him. Her beauty took his breath away.

Jake's lips curved up in a crooked smile.

The double wedding marked the happiest day of his life.

* * *

I hope you enjoyed reading *Beyond Judgment* as much as I did writing it. If so, it would be great if you left a comment on the Amazon Customer Reviews page. I'd love to hear from you!

Richard Bard

Acknowledgments

Of all the occupational challenges I've tackled in my life, from delivering newspapers to piloting aircraft to running companies, nothing has given me more satisfaction than becoming a novelist. Breathing life into Jake's stories is an immensely satisfying endeavor—so much so that I often find myself rereading scenes from the books for the pure thrill of the ride. I suspect that may sound silly to you. After all, it's not as though I don't know what's going to happen from chapter to chapter. But it's the truth. I'm Jake's biggest fan. For me a good story is like a good song. It evokes emotions that a listener—or reader—deserves to experience more than once. I'm the same way with movies. I have an extensive collection of films that have touched me in one way or another. I love dimming the lights and settling into my home theater with a bag of popcorn and one of my favorite movies. Wouldn't it be something if Brainrush was part of that collection some day? Fingers crossed...

But as much as I enjoy writing for the pure sake of imperiling Jake and his friends in order to test their mettle, the true icing on the cake for me as an author—the fuel that ignites my consuming passion for the craft—has been the thousands of positive reviews and e-mails I've received from Brainrush fans all over the world. To each and every one of you, please accept my heartfelt thanks. I'm humbled and inspired by your messages of support and enthusiasm. Please keep 'em coming!

I'd also like to thank all of the wonderful people on the Thomas & Mercer team: to the folks on the Author Relations and Marketing teams, especially Jacque and Danielle, to my developmental editor, Elyse Dinh-McCrillis, and the rest of the editing team, who helped keep Jake's story tight, accurate, and fast-paced. And especially to Senior Editor Alan Turkus, whose excitement for the Brainrush series brought me into the fold. I couldn't ask for a better advisor and cheerleader.

To my rock-star literary and film agents, Scott Miller of Trident Media Group and Jon Cassir of Creative Artists Agency, it's an honor to be working with both of you.

To my friends and family, your encouragement and understanding make it all possible.

And finally to my wonderful wife, Milan, who stands beside me through it all. Your unconditional love and support mean the world to me.

About the Author

Photograph © NewFacePhoto.com

Richard Bard was born in Munich, Germany, to American parents, and joined the United States Air Force like his father. But when he was diagnosed with cancer and learned he had only months to live, he left the service. He earned a management degree from the University of Notre Dame and ultimately ran three successful companies involving advanced security products used by US embassies and governments worldwide. Now a full-time writer, he lives in Redondo Beach, California, with his wife, and remains in excellent health.

Made in the USA
Charleston, SC
22 August 2013